I0641209

AI APOCALYPSE RECKONING

AN APOCALYPTIC LITRPG ADVENTURE

AI APOCALYPSE: RESTART
BOOK TWO

J DAVID BAXTER

Silver Paw Publishing

Design, production by Silver Paw Publishing.

Editing services by Dale McDowell.

Cover design by J David Baxter.

HARDCOVER: 978-1-953708-36-6

PAPERBACK: 978-1-953708-34-2

EBOOK: 978-1-953708-35-9

For more on the Greymantle series, see: JDavidBaxter.com or GreymantleChronicles.com

INTERLUDE: GNARR - GLORY TO THE OGRE CHAMPION

Gnarr the Victorious sat atop a jagged stone throne, the jagged surface grinding against his back but failing to bother him. Around him, the shattered remnants of his challengers lay strewn across the wide arena of the Ogre stronghold. Massive stone pillars carved roughly with the scars of past battles cast long shadows in the waning light of the molten pits lining the chamber. The air was thick with the smell of blood, sweat, and charred flesh. His people, towering and hulking creatures themselves, stood silent, watching their new Champion with a mixture of fear and grudging respect.

Victory. It was the only thing that mattered to Gnarr. He had crushed all who dared to face him, smashing their bones, tearing through their defenses, and, finally, taking their heads as proof of his dominance. The final fight had been a brutal clash against Gruk the Hammer, an older ogre whose reputation as the most indomitable warrior in their history had been shattered beneath Gnarr's bare hands. His trophy now hung from the armrest of the throne, a warning to any who might think to challenge his rule.

The System had given their kind order, rules, and structure. Ogres cared little for such things in practice, save for one sacred principle the System reinforced: strength ruled. Their world—a brutal, mountainous realm of endless battle and survival—had been molded by this belief. Even in the face of the System's integration into their lives, they had adapted their way, channeling all that knowledge into further perfecting the art of domination.

Gnarr's victory earned him the title of Champion, the right to lead the ogre invasion force. He had claimed this place through blood and fire. And now, he would use his strength to bring the ogres glory once again on the new world, Culling.

But first, a feast.

His massive hands gripped a slab of meat so large it could have fed a dozen humans. He tore into it with his tusks, the juices dripping down his chin as he growled in satisfaction. Around him, lesser ogres prepared more food, hauling barrels of ale, roasting entire beasts on spits, and placing treasure chests before him. They brought him weapons and armor scavenged from his defeated foes, relics, and trophies that now belonged to him by right. Gnarr picked up a massive spiked gauntlet, testing its weight and fit before tossing it aside. It was good but not better than what he already had.

In the background, the guttural chants of the ogres' victory songs echoed. The sound was primal, a rhythm that struck deep in their hearts and stirred their blood. Gnarr barely listened. His focus was on the path ahead. The new world awaited—a fresh arena filled with enemies and opportunities for conquest.

The darkened chamber suddenly glowed faintly as a notification from the System blinked into his vision. The world Moderator—the AI that oversaw their planet—addressed him directly, an honor reserved only for champions. Gnarr's feast paused as he read the message.

Gnarr the Victorious, Champion of the Ogres: A rare anomaly has occurred in the integration of the new world. One of its champions has been granted foreknowledge of the next twenty revolutions. By the System's laws, all other champions in this incursion will also receive this same knowledge. You have three days to choose the path your forces will take.

Decide: will you prepare your forces to capitalize on the foreknowledge, or will you act immediately to eliminate this threat? Choose wisely.

Gnarr growled low, his red eyes narrowing. The words filled him with both curiosity and fury. A human champion, already weak by nature, had been given foreknowledge? A cheat. An insult to the natural order of strength and survival.

He stood, towering over the ogres around him, and slammed a fist into the throne behind him. The jagged stone cracked under the force, and the chamber fell silent. His voice rumbled like an avalanche, filling the room.

"The System plays games with weaklings! It not matter! Human Champion is nothing!"

The ogres did not know of the message Gnarr had received, but they roared their agreement, slamming their fists into their chests and weapons against the ground. Gnarr raised a hand to silence them.

The message presented him with a choice. He could wait, prepare his forces, and ensure the ogres entered the new world as an unstoppable tide. Or he could go now, use his strength and cunning to crush this human Champion before they became a true threat. He didn't hesitate. The idea of waiting, of biding time like some scheming elf or cowardly human, filled him with disgust. This was his opportunity to claim glory, to kill the Champion himself, and to dominate the battlefield before the others even arrived.

Gnarr didn't see this as a chance to strengthen his people. He cared little for the fate of the ogres beyond ensuring his own legacy as the strongest of their kind. If he succeeded in eliminating the Earth champion and reached the level cap first, he could claim ascension and rule over the new world as a god.

Turning to his warriors, he spoke. "I go alone. You remain here, prepare for I summon you. When I call, you come—until then, I carve path—earn glory!"

Confused by this deviation from the way things were done, they remained silent. The ogres knew the danger of questioning their Champion; they didn't dare protest.

The feast continued as Gnarr returned to his throne, surveying the spoils of his victory. He drank deeply, tearing through the food with reckless abandon. There was no need for elaborate planning, no need for strategy. He would hunt this Champion, crush them, and then dominate whatever challenges this new world threw at him.

As the feast wound down, Gnarr stood, his hulking frame casting a long shadow across the chamber. He donned his armor, heavy plates reinforced with spikes and etched with the scars of countless battles. His weapon, a colossal war hammer that seemed too large even for an ogre, rested against the throne. He gripped it, feeling the familiar weight, and slung it across his back.

The portal to the world he had named 'Culling' awaited him in the heart of the stronghold's great hall. It shimmered with a faint, ominous light, its swirling energies beckoning him forward. Without ceremony, Gnarr strode toward it, his footsteps shaking the ground. He didn't look back. There was no need. The path ahead was clear.

As he stepped through the portal, the oppressive heat of his world gave way to the crisp air of Earth. Gnarr emerged in a dense forest, the trees towering above but still dwarfed by his massive frame. He inhaled deeply, the foreign scent filling his lungs. A grin spread across his face, his tusks gleaming in the moonlight.

Gnarr only hated one thing about the Culling, starting at Level 0. Still, this was the new world. Weak, untested, ripe for conquest, and now that the future knowledge had been placed into his mind, he knew exactly where he needed to go to get stronger. There was a dungeon nearby that would prove a challenge. It would blood him and prove he was ready. Once he had crushed it and squeezed all the trophies from the boss's corpse, he would go and find the puny human and make a paste from his bones to feast upon.

Gnarr hefted his war hammer and began his hunt.

CHAPTER 1
LETTING IT ALL SINK IN

THE GROUND TREMBLED beneath my feet, mirroring the tremor of realization that I'd just triggered humanity's accelerated extinction. The air around me buzzed with a sickening hum as a wave of the System changes tore through the Earth.

It was all too much.

"Liam, are you okay?"

I felt like my brain was short-circuiting for a long moment. It was one thing to carry the weight of humanity's extinction on my shoulders. It was another to know I'd just shortened the timeline to a matter of months. I was having visions of armies of monsters rolling over the starving remnants of our people.

What was worse is that it really was all on me. Being back among humanity again and having this second chance, I had let hope creep back in. It had felt so good to meet people who weren't burnt-out husks of their former selves, people still filled with light and life, first Morgan, then Viki. Or maybe it was being back in this younger body that wasn't crippled with constant aches and pains from twenty years of barely surviving dungeons and mutated beasts. Unlike the first time, it seemed like there was a ray of hope.

I should've known better. Hope was a luxury I couldn't afford, not with the world on the brink.

I'd screwed up—big time. My reckless power-leveling of Viki had alerted the System, and now the Champions of other worlds were coming to hunt me down. Twenty years of foreknowledge wasn't enough to prepare me for this—now, the invasion would start with a vengeance.

"This is bad... so bad." It was about all I could get out. My thoughts just kept spiraling around how many ways this would screw us. I could feel myself slipping back into that hopelessness and despair I had felt in my first life before the System sent me back for a do-over.

"Does that mean they will all be like you?" Viki looked scared. She had heard the AI speaking, and she knew things were dire; she just didn't know how bad it was.

Paradoxically, her fear kicked me out of my own. "Uh, yeah. Well, actually, that depends. They will try to kill me at all costs; I am a threat to their forces. That is, the ones that come through immediately will level up quickly to come after me. They will know where all the dungeons are and how to beat them, so they'll have a big advantage. They will be just as strong as us."

My brain was engaged now, and I was thinking through the ways this might go down, and it was bad; there was no question about that.

Grr... I need to snap out of this death spiral of guilt! Will telling myself how bad it is fifteen million times make it any better? Hell no!

I had to face it, adapt, and overcome.

The dragon blood running in my veins was also heating up. It didn't like feeling weak and helpless; it wanted to roar and defy these oncoming foes and even the System itself if necessary!

With a certain grim determination, I explained, "I absolutely made things far worse for the human race in other parts of the world. However, if I can beat the Champions coming for us, it might actually be better in the region around Texas or even this part of the country. Their people will arrive in three weeks, and they will be missing their leaders. At least, I think that's how this works. Everywhere else will be completely screwed."

Looking confused, I could see Viki wanted to ask more, so I went on.

"The invaders whose commanders choose not to come attack me will have twenty years of knowledge about Earth and the territory around where they will be invading. They will spend the next month preparing their people, and with that kind of specific information, they will absolutely dominate everything around them. They will come armed specifically to deal with whatever challenges the nearby dungeons and humans pose for them."

Viki raised her bow, threatening any invaders and challenging them to come. "I've got your back. Dragons won't let what's ours be taken from us!" Her fire was fierce, but I'd seen too many bright flames snuffed out. Even so, I couldn't help but admire her resolve.

The brightness of her spirit was infectious, a spark of light in the darkness fighting against the lingering pessimism rooted deep in my soul. I'd seen too much death and too much despair in my first life. But this time—this time—I couldn't let it end the same way. I wouldn't let that happen!

This little dragon had more courage than a hundred of the toughest warriors I had known in my past life. That dark voice in the back of my head wanted to add, 'But courage alone wouldn't be enough to survive what was coming.' Still, I was suddenly glad I had made the choices I had. She and people like her were the reason I was doing all this. Despite pieces of trash like my traitorous former party or Skeeter and his looting crew aside, humanity deserved to be saved. Maybe I had made a mistake in not being harder and more ruthless, but it was too late to second-guess myself now.

I chuckled as I felt my bloodline stirring at her words.

"Careful, the blood will drive you, and you'll do stupid things if you don't control it."

Pointing at my own chest, I said, "In my first dungeon, after I got ambushed, the blood in my veins felt like it was boiling in rage at being challenged, and I roared my defiance... like a moron. The next two fights were against prepared monsters waiting and ready."

My young friend looked surprised and apprehensive. "Oh... I didn't think about that. Thanks for the warning."

She thought for a moment, then added, "Now that you mention it, ever since getting my Class and the Night Dragon Bloodline, I've been feeling different. I'm mad that these monsters are hurting people. But, it's like they are MY people, if you know what I mean?"

"Yeah, I do. Dragons are famous for being territorial and hoarding things. In this case, Earth is ours, and I'm not happy about monsters trying to steal it."

As I spoke, a faint, almost imperceptible vibration hummed through the ground, the scent of damp Earth and decay mixing with the ever-present tension of the System's influence. It was a reminder that the System was actively changing our world, reshaping it into its own vision of how things should be, never mind humanity's desires. Its changes would not wait for us, like time relentlessly rolling forward, crushing all beneath its inevitability.

In my mind's eye, I was picturing mountains of bodies because that is what it would be. I had seen it all before. Before the future AI sent me back to relive the Apocalypse, I had spent 20 years enduring it and watching everyone I ever knew die because of the System. Out of eight billion souls, there were only a few thousand left by the time of my death.

Viki asked, "That voice said it couldn't help us. What did it mean? If it did this to us, why would it even want to help?"

I shook my head in disgust, "It messed up. After basically wiping out the human race, it discovered that it was losing power and rank among the AIs that make up the System. You see, each AI controls a world in the System's network, and they get more resources and gain higher prestige among their kind by looting other worlds. Twenty years from now, our AI got desperate and offered to send me back in time to relive the Apocalypse. The AI hoped that I could turn the tide and save enough humans so that it wouldn't become a second-class citizen amongst the other evil overlords."

"What a piece of s..."

"Language, young lady," I chided, half-serious.

She shot me a look. "Okay, Boomer."

I rolled my eyes—no point arguing that one.

I tried again, even though I knew it wouldn't work, "If you want, I could summon Morgan, and you could go back and protect the bunker and all the refugees."

As I thought about it, that did sound like a good idea. I would have loved to have Morgan by my side, but at the time, she was the only person I knew who might be able to protect the bunker and the refugees that I was sending there. It would be a safe place for Viki, and she could use her power to help Morgan protect it.

That way, I could rush off and go solo leveling faster from getting all the XP, and not feel like I was totally abandoning my young friend. On the other hand, we made a good team, and she would be especially helpful now that she had received her own Draconic Bloodline Class.

Even as I tried to convince myself to send her back to the bunker, I knew deep down that we needed each other. She had a fire that I couldn't afford to lose, even if it meant putting her in harm's way. Still, I felt like a piece of shit for bringing a kid along with me into life-threatening situations. That would be especially true now that Champions of the invading species would be hunting me.

At first, she had just been with me because I was afraid she would get killed if I let her run off on her own. Now, I wasn't so sure which was more likely to cause her death. Still, it was a moot point because the same reasoning still held true. She wouldn't want to sit still in a fortress safe and sound; she would immediately run off and challenge the nearest monster the second she was on her own, no matter how powerful it was.

Besides, there was no safe place in this world now, even the bunker.

As if she could read my thoughts, she was giving me a look as if to say, "You'd better not try it."

"Fine, we need to figure out what to do next, then. We've got one chance to save as much of the human race as we can. Like I said a few minutes ago, if I can hit the level cap before the end of the month, I can try to create safe zones that will block monsters from spawning and invaders from invading. Before we met, I was heading toward town to see what the situation was there and try to subtly warn people and push them to leave town and form fortresses where they could protect the non-combatants, all while running dungeons and leveling up as fast as possible."

"And now?" Viki asked.

The mission hadn't changed, only the urgency. I still needed to head toward town to see what the situation was—if the crumbling buildings and shattered streets hadn't already become nests for monsters.

"Now, we speedrun it. With you watching my back, we should be able to absolutely wreck the low-level dungeons and get you geared up better. That will have the added benefit of preventing those dungeons from breaking and spilling monsters out into the already ravaged city. Plus, the cat is out of the bag; we can tell people everything, what the System is really about, about the shop, and how to get magic classes, the whole nine yards."

She looked thoughtful for a moment, then brightened, "You need a herald. Someone like the Silver dude in the comics that can go out and warn people ahead of the invasion."

I was surprised by the comic reference. "You read comics?"

Viki's face suddenly went blank and emotionless as she said flatly, "My brother did."

The words hung in the air, heavy with the weight of unspoken grief. I knew that look—had worn it myself too many times to count. I wanted to say something, anything, but what comfort could I offer when I carried the same scars?

My friend had never said anything about her family, and I had not asked. It was plain that she had suffered a loss and didn't want to talk about it, much less be reminded. It was one of the reasons I had let her tag along at first. I was afraid she might pull a Leroy Jenkins and throw herself at the nearest enemy if I didn't keep her focused on playing it smart.

Before I could change the subject, she did, "Who is that Morgan guy you mentioned before? And how can you summon him?"

It was an abrupt question, but I understood. She didn't want to think about her family.

"Morgan is a woman, not a guy. She is the person I left to watch my bunker, the place I've been sending all the refugees. When she did her class selection, she was offered the Dragon Priestess profession, which lets me summon her or communicate with her once per day, and vice versa."

Thinking of Morgan, it seemed like it had been ages since I had seen her, but in reality, it had only been, what, three days? I had to stop for a second and think back on everything that had happened. I could have summoned her a couple of times along the way, and it might have been super helpful, but at the time, I hadn't wanted to bother her. I was sending so many refugees to the bunker I knew she had to be overwhelmed. On the other hand, she would have Thomas and some other good folks now to assist her. Maybe it really was time to rethink things.

Viki gave me a look like I was an idiot. "Why haven't you summoned her or talked to her before now?"

"We've been a bit busy with this Stronghold Dungeon. Now that it's over, it might be a good time to place a call."

It was very late at night or early in the morning at this point, depending on your perspective. Viki had done her class selection at the stroke of midnight, and I did my upgrade a couple hours later. Then, the AI dropped its bombshell. I didn't know for sure, but I figured it was now around four or five in the morning. It wouldn't exactly be nice to wake Morgan up if she was sleeping, but this really was a 'fate of the world' sort of thing.

Without waiting, I started to focus on the ritual of communing with my priestess.

Even as I tried to focus, there was a nagging sensation at the back of my mind, like the calm before a storm. The world was shifting beneath us again—a low rumble vibrated through the ground—a warning, or worse, a sign that our time was running out.

CHAPTER 2
I SUMMON THEE!

"Morgan, can you hear me? Are you awake?"

There was a moment of hesitation, a flicker of fright and confusion bleeding through the link, then understanding before her reply came through.

"Holy shit, Liam! That scared the crap out of me. I was up stalking a jackalope that's been chasing some of the kids outside the fence. Then this damned magic telephone thing went off in my head, and I thought it was the mother of all horned rabbits coming for me to get revenge for killing her demon-spawn rabbit babies!"

I let out a relieved laugh, which apparently carried through the link because I got an indignant reply in return.

"Piss off! You don't know! These damned things are so cute that the kids try to go catch them and end up getting gored and needing healing. We've had three cases so far!"

"Okay, okay... I'm not judging, just amused; in my first life, one of those damned things was the first monster I encountered after the apocalypse, and it almost ended me."

The humor drained from my voice as I got serious. "Anyway, the secret behind all the stuff I couldn't tell you before is out now, and I'm no longer bound to silence. We need to talk in person, and I've got a lot to share."

Curiosity and impatience pulsed through the connection. "Fine, give me 20 minutes, and then summon me."

She cut the link, and I refocused on my surroundings. To Viki, I said, "I'll pull her to us in a few minutes. She needs to get someplace safe."

Viki pursed her lips in thought, her expression reflecting the intensity of her dragon blood. "You mentioned speedrunning the dungeons. Should we start running toward town before we summon her? I don't think we should waste even a few minutes. We should go."

The pressure gnawed at me, too, but I couldn't just leave in the night. We needed to tell the people at the fort what was going on, get them on board, and make sure the information spread. Spending a little time here before leaving could save a lot of lives in the long term, and that mattered almost as much as leveling up.

"As much as I'd like to run off immediately, a little delay now will save a lot of time later. Let's rouse the fort here, and I'll tell them all at the same time," I tell Morgan. "We'll kill two birds with one stone that way."

Viki frowned, clearly impatient, but didn't argue. "Fine, but I want some food while we wait, then. I'll make something while you wake people up."

I watched her head toward the makeshift kitchen area while I began to wake the people of the fort. Their reactions ranged from bleary-eyed confusion to outright annoyance at being awakened before dawn, but they quickly understood that something big was happening. Most of them were just grateful to be alive after everything they'd been through, and they knew better than to ignore a summons that could affect their survival.

Thirty minutes later, Viki and I sat on the steps of the longhouse with a couple dozen people around us, including Morgan, who hadn't much enjoyed being summoned. Apparently, it made her stomach feel like it was doing flips; if she had eaten anything before coming, she would have lost it upon arrival.

I suppressed a smirk at the annoyance on her face as she sat down beside me.

The sky was still dark, the pre-dawn light not yet visible, telling me it was still an ungodly hour of the morning. The expressions on the tired faces before me confirmed it. On the bright side, it was cool, and there was surprisingly little smell, considering this had been the town dump only a week ago.

Clearing my throat drew everyone's attention. "Sorry for waking you all, but there is news that I need to share with you before I go, and I need to do that immediately; every hour counts."

I saw them lean in, their faces a mix of curiosity and concern. They'd all been through so much already, and here I was about to dump even more on them.

"Let me start by telling you my story and what I know about the AI and the System."

I laid it all out for them, how I had lived this before, spending twenty years under the System, watching humanity dwindle to the brink of extinction. I didn't spare the AI's non-existent feelings either.

"The damned AI drove us to the edge, and only then realized it had fucked up. If we die, it loses almost all its power within the System and the other world AI nodes. It sent my consciousness back in time to just before the Initialization, knowing everything from my previous life..."

The skepticism was palpable, eyes narrowing as I basically told them I was the Chosen One, here to save the world. Which, sadly for them, I basically was. But that wasn't the part I emphasized. Instead, I focused on survival, on how we could level the playing field against the invaders. I explained the importance of magic classes, crafters, and the System store opening in three weeks. I urged them to save their coins, to equip themselves for the battles to come.

Most importantly, I didn't sugarcoat any of it. I warned them about the darker sides of humanity and stressed the need to protect the innocent, to shelter the non-fighters if we wanted to last more than twenty years. And then, I dropped the final bomb: the invaders got the same head start as me, thanks to the System's twisted rules.

One of the men, Shawn Gornson, looked ready to explode. "You mean to tell me that because of you, these monster races are going to show up knowing all our weaknesses and be able to wipe us out with ease? My kids are still out there somewhere!"

Viki jumped up, standing protectively in front of me, her glare directed at Shawn. "It's not Liam's fault. It's the AI's fault. It chose to kill us off because it didn't care about us humans, then sent him back to fix its mistake, knowing this could happen."

I placed a hand on her shoulder, standing beside her. "Blame me, blame the AI, blame the System. It doesn't matter. What matters is that I've got a chance to set things right, and I'm going to do my best. I'm sharing everything I know so you can be as prepared as possible. Feel however you want, but help the refugees that come past here and spread the word. And if you want to find your kids, get strong."

The tension in the air was thick, some of it directed at the AI, but a lot of it aimed at me. Most of these people had lost loved ones, and I was the one standing in front of them. The AI was a faceless entity, but I was tangible, a target for their anger.

It only took a few to snap. They lunged, and I didn't even flinch. I just looked at them and activated Dragon's Fear. The men froze instantly, and though I focused on Shawn and his two companions, everyone felt it.

"I know you're hurting, and I don't blame you. If it helps, feel free to hate me. But take another step, and humanity will lose three more warriors. I'm trying to save people, but I won't hesitate to cull those who threaten my mission."

When they could finally move again, Shawn was shaking with emotion, his voice rough as he yelled, "Who appointed you our savior?"

I didn't choose to answer. I was done with this conversation, and thankfully, the three men chose wisely, backing off before they could do something we'd all regret.

Morgan, however, wasn't finished. "Didn't you listen to a word that was said? The AI appointed him! Whether you like it or not, he's our best hope of survival. You should be thankful; didn't he save you from the Stronghold dungeon? Do you think anyone else could have managed that?"

The man to Shawn's left placed a calming hand on his shoulder. "She's right. We'd still be in that Arena, fighting each other to the death right now. Cut him some slack. At least we know what we're up against now and why all this happened."

With that, the fight seemed to drain out of Shawn. He allowed himself to be led off toward one of the guard towers where he had been stationed, but the glare he gave me over his shoulder said that he did blame me and wasn't going to forget or forgive.

Seeing that the discussion was over, I motioned for Viki and Morgan to follow me into the longhouse to finish our planning.

They had introduced themselves earlier, but neither Viki nor I had shared that she had received a draconic bloodline class. I decided to drop the bomb.

"Before we get into it, the biggest reason I brought you here is that Viki also received a draconic bloodline. I figured you'd like to create another pact and get some benefits from that. And I wanted you to know everything I just shared so you can spread the word to the refugees showing up at the bunker."

Morgan's eyes widened in surprise. "No kidding?"

Viki's grin was pure smugness. "Night Dragon Sniper."

"As my father would say, 'Hell, yeah!'" Morgan smiled eagerly.

Viki looked a little nervous as she stood next to me but gave Morgan a firm nod. "Yeah, I think it'll be good. We're stronger together, right?"

Morgan nodded, a hint of a smile playing on her lips. "Stronger together."

This time, I was able to view it from an outside perspective. I watched as Morgan placed her hand on Viki's shoulder, the two of them standing there for a moment as the pact was formed. A faint glow surrounded them both, and I could feel the power of the bond settling into place. It was a comforting presence, a reminder that we weren't alone in this fight.

I could practically feel the 'Ding' of the Priestess leveling up and was amused by the shock and awe on her face as she read her System messages.

"Wow! I gained three levels just from making that pact and got a new title, 'Dragonbound Primarch,' which gives me plus two to all stats.

Apparently, I'm the first person in the world to form more than one pact. Which, I guess, is a thing. That brought me from Level 9 up to Level 12."

She was still absorbing the information when her eyes lit up with excitement. "Oooh! Look at this; I got another draconic ability!"

She eagerly shared her new and upgraded skills with us:

Class Ability: Summon (Upgraded) — You can now summon one or both of your bonded dragons, or they can summon you without the constraints of time. The summoned being may remain indefinitely and can return to their original location at will, providing unparalleled flexibility and support in any situation.

Bloodline Ability (Pact): Umbral Cloak — You are now able to shroud yourself in shadows, becoming nearly invisible to enemies and moving undetected through most environments. While cloaked, you are resistant to magical detection, allowing you to evade foes and position yourself strategically in battle.

Spell: Cleansing Ray — You channel a focused beam of purifying energy that targets an ally from a distance, instantly removing harmful status conditions such as paralysis, blindness, curses, and other debilitating effects. The ray not only cleanses the target but also grants them brief resistance to further status conditions, providing protection against future debuffs.

Spell: Shadowflame Burst — Drawing on your connection to both the Shadow and Night Dragons, you unleash a burst of dark, shadow-infused flames that engulf enemies in a targeted area. The Shadowflame not only deals immediate damage but also leaves a lingering effect that weakens the enemies' physical and magical defenses.

Before I could compliment her on her gains, she threw her arms around me in a hug. I wasn't sure exactly how to react. She was an attractive woman, but I had just killed her ex-boyfriend a few days ago, which kind of had me conflicted. However, before I could say anything or even put my arms around her, she reached out and pulled Viki into the hug as well.

Good job, Liam, way to overthink things and jump to conclusions!

But to be fair, that was literally the first physical contact I had had with a woman in years, and it kind of startled me.

When she let go and stepped back, I smiled awkwardly and waited for her to explain.

She was beaming at both Viki and me as she said, "Not only did I get another ability, but I broke past the Level 10 threshold and got new skills, and they are pretty great."

"My dragon blood is awesome like that!" Viki grinned and eagerly asked, "Show us your status so that we can see it all!"

I reached over and covered her mouth but addressed Morgan, "You don't have to do that if you don't want to."

Then, to Viki, I said quietly, "Seriously, you can't just demand to see someone's stats; that's very personal."

Frowning, Viki pushed my hand away and turned on me. "Why? We show each other our stats."

That was true, but it was considered impolite and even rude to ask about someone else's stats. Or at least it had been in my previous life. "It's okay to show people if you want, especially if you are in a party with them, but you can't just put someone on the spot that way."

Morgan waved away my comment. "I don't mind, and we are pacted together, so that is kinda like being in a party, right?"

She had a point. Looking at Viki, I said, "Sorry. Just remember not to ask any strangers, and we're probably fine. In the future, people will come to view their stats as private and personal."

Morgan pulled up her status page and made it visible to the two of us.

Morgan Pickering
Dragon Priestess: Level 12

Experience: 5927/16800

Attributes:
Endurance: 15
Strength: 15
Agility: 15
Mind: 32
Will: 19
Magical Aptitude: 29
Luck: 2

Health: 300/300
Mana: 800/800

Abilities:
Commune
Summon
Dark Vision (Pact)
Umbral Cloak (Pact)

Spells:
Blessing of the Dragon's Grace

Draconic Vitality
Shadow Bolt
Purifying Touch
Cleansing Ray
Shadowflame Burst

Titles:
Pact Pioneer
Dragonbound Primarch

Morgan pointed to her stats and explained, "My Class is Rare, and gave me +5 all stats, and 2 assigned and 2 free per Level. Then my two titles each grant me a permanent +2 all stats each."

She moved her body around experimentally. "Speaking of which, I suddenly feel much better and more capable. Mostly on the mental side of things."

"A big boost of stats will do that to you. You just got three levels in an instant."

What really had me curious were her new skills. Sadly, she didn't have an Analyze ability, so the descriptions didn't provide specifics like damage, durations, and cooldown times.

"When we get a chance, we should test your new abilities and figure out how much they can do."

Morgan raised an eyebrow, "That almost sounded like an invitation...."

Bouncing, Viki took Morgan's hand. "Please come with us! Those Champion people will be coming after Liam, and he needs us."

"Whoa, easy there. I was going to give Morgan a choice. She doesn't have to come with us. No matter who is out to get me, I'm not going to let myself lose. Besides, it might not be what you think."

Viki was looking at me with trepidation now, clearly worried that I was going to try and send her away. I could see it in her eyes.

I gave her a sad smile. "No, I'm not going to try and banish you to safety or run off and have all the fun without you. Still, I don't think we can afford to party together for long. I get a 10% bonus for soloing dungeons because of one of my titles, and considering that we need to speedrun this thing, that will add up fast."

She was about to protest, so I kept going, "That doesn't mean we are going to split up and not work together at all. I think the first thing we need to do is party up and run a few low-level dungeons to get you and Morgan geared up. It will slow my experience, but it is essential for you two to have decent gear to survive."

It was Morgan who interrupted. "Not that I mind, but I thought you wanted me to be in charge of the old bunker."

"I did, but with the secret being out and the invader's champions coming to hunt me down, we need to adapt. When I saw that your Summon skill had upgraded, it gave me a better idea. Thomas should be at the bunker by now, and he's strong enough to handle most anything. If it weren't for us, he would be among the more powerful people on the planet right now. But I don't want you here to protect me, although having your healing nearby would be nice."

Seeing the questions on their faces, I continued, "Viki said it earlier: I need a herald, or heralds, to go out and tell people what is really going on and the danger we are in. I want to get you guys geared up and experienced so that you both can work together to find worthy candidates and power-level them up to the point where they can survive going out on their own to spread the word."

Viki was working up to a serious pout, but Morgan spoke first. "I don't like it, but that makes sense."

Almost at the same time, Viki blurted out, "You need us to watch your back and protect you!"

I couldn't help but smile at my young friend's desire to protect me, and truth be told, having someone with her Class and skills watching my back would give me a lot of comfort, but more than that, I meant it when I said we needed to spread the word. It wasn't too late right now. It was only the morning of the seventh day since the Initialization. There had to be millions of children still alive at this point who were too young to make their Class selections yet. If we could get even a tenth of those to take magic classes, it would make a world of difference to the future, and we might just survive.

Hell, if I can hit the level cap before the invaders arrive in three weeks, we might be able to not only survive but reclaim our world as the apex species.

I stepped closer, put both hands on Viki's shoulders comfortingly, and looked her in the eyes. "I'm not planning to run off on my own and abandon you guys to another mission. I want to make sure we stay close to one another when possible, but even if we get separated, that Summon ability Morgan has works both ways. She can pull me right to you in a matter of minutes if you need me or to save me. Remember, we can communicate over any distance with Morgan, thanks to the pact."

Viki looked reluctant but didn't argue, although I felt sure she wasn't done with this topic.

Just then, Morgan looked alarmed. "Ugh, I think the summon is about to run out. Give me three hours to put things in order back at the bunker and share what you've told me with everyone there. Then summon me again using the upgraded version."

Before I could reply, she faded out, and I could feel our connection grow thinner with the new distance between us.

By then, the sky was lighting up with the coming dawn; a new day and new dangers awaited us. It was finally time to head into the city and find new dungeons.

CHAPTER 3
A GRIM REMINDER

MORGAN

When Morgan arrived, she wanted to throw up. Summoning or teleportation, or whatever the hell that was, made her stomach turn flips and do jumping jacks. She had always gotten car-sick as a kid; it sucked to know that even under the System, she hated travel!

Looking around as soon as she was able, she was thankful to note that the jackalope she had been chasing earlier was nowhere to be seen. With her leaving, Thomas or one of the others would have to step up and ensure the children weren't gored by any more of those damnable horned rabbits. Not wanting to waste any time, she quickly ran for the closest gate in the fence and hurried to the bunker where most of the people were still sleeping, with dawn having just broken over the horizon.

Ten minutes later, she had gathered the few meager belongings she thought might be useful for running off on an adventure with Liam and Viki. She shook her head, bemused at the thought of that girl. She was only twelve and already killing monsters, and she did not seem to have any problem with that at all. When she was the girl's age, she cared more about collecting Pokemon than anything else. Although to be fair, her father had taken her hunting a few times during deer season, so it wasn't like she had been averse to a bit of blood. There was nothing better than a venison chicken-fried steak! Still, despite all the craziness of the System, hunting seemed much less intense than a life-and-death battle with monsters.

Morgan just hoped she would prove strong enough to pull her weight. What she was not looking forward to was telling her parents she was going to leave them to go into certain danger. That was not going to be a fun conversation. She might be a grown-ass adult, but in their eyes, she was still their baby.

Still, that could wait a bit. First, she needed to spread the word about AI and the System.

The interior of the bunker consisted of two rooms: the smaller upper floor at ground level and the massive space below ground that had once been a secure Cold War communications bunker. Most of the families camped down there, with a few of the stronger individuals bedding down in the ground-floor room to protect the rest. Most of those were already awake.

Steven Moss, a high school kid who had managed to hit Level 4 yesterday, was standing watch at the entrance and greeted her as she returned. "Mornin', Miss Morgan! Get any kills?"

Thinking it was nuts how an insane question like that was the new normal, she smiled ruefully. "No, but I did meet with Liam, the guy who owns this place. He gave me some important news to share. Be a sweetie and run downstairs and gather as many of the adults as you can without waking the kids. Bring them up here, please. I've got a lot to tell folks, and I don't have much time."

As he turned to hurry down the stairs, she added, "Oh, please make sure my parents attend the meeting, and don't let anyone futz about. Tell them all that if they aren't up here in ten minutes, I'll start without them, and they will have to hear everything secondhand."

That ought to get Dad moving; he hates missing things!

While she waited, she moved to the spot where they prepared meals, grabbed whatever she could, and ate. Two boiled eggs with only the tiniest bit of salt and no pepper, and even that minuscule amount of seasoning was already a luxury. She was so preoccupied with thinking of how to break it to her parents that she had to go, and she barely tasted her breakfast.

There was much grumbling and complaining about her waking people and rushing them out of bed so early. Many of the people still couldn't come to grips with the lack of coffee in the mornings. Just the thought of that rich aroma and the bitter flavors still made Morgan's own mouth water. There were so many things they took for granted before the world ended. So many little things now could practically make her weep when she thought of them and realized she would never experience them again.

However, as desperate as the situation was, Liam had brought her hope. Hearing the real story of why this was all happening and how the invaders would get a chance to kill him and the rest would be forearmed with twenty years of future knowledge made her want to howl in fright and desperation, but at the same time, there was a ray of hope. If her Pact mate were to win, then maybe coffee and many other things might one day return.

It was with that hope in mind that she began telling the tale to the sleepy crowd.

Over two hours later, her father was the one who chased everyone off. If he let them, they would keep asking her questions until her time was up, and she was summoned back to Liam and Viki. She hadn't come right out and said that she was leaving, but her parents weren't idiots. They knew her enough to know the other shoe hadn't dropped yet.

She pulled Thomas aside as the rest were breaking up and moving to their needed tasks. The children needed to be fed, and chores around the bunker all needed to be done to improve living conditions.

Quickly and quietly, she explained that she was leaving and that he would need to take charge in her absence. She also made sure he would repeat the message about the System to anyone passing through.

In a worried voice, he asked, "Liam is a great guy, and I'll be eternally grateful for him saving my family and freeing me, too, but the kind of stuff he does is insane. Are you sure you want to put yourself at that kind of risk?"

Morgan chuckled darkly, "Everything is a risk these days. If helping him increases the chance that someday we can be safe again, then it is worth it."

The look he gave her said it was her funeral, but he patted her on the shoulder, "Good luck, then! We'll pray for you."

That was the moment her parents chose to pull her outside to have a more private conversation. Her mother gave her 'the look' before speaking, the one that always made her feel guilty when she was a child.

"You can't leave."

Her father's brow furrowed with concern, and he added, "It's too dangerous out there; we've heard about that Strong Dungeon thing where all the people were used as slave labor or like Thomas and others to fight to the death like ancient gladiators!"

"Dad, I have to. This is bigger than me, bigger than all of us. If we don't stop the System, millions could die. The world as we knew it will never come back."

Tears welled in her mother's eyes. "But you're our little girl!"

Morgan swallowed the lump forming in her throat. "I know, Mom. And I love you both so much. But this is my calling. My healing magic can save lives out there. I have to do this."

Her parents exchanged a long look, a silent conversation passing between them. Finally, her dad let out a heavy sigh.

It was her mother who spoke, however, "You have to promise us you will stay safe and not risk your life needlessly. I'm scared for you."

"I'm scared too. But Liam and Viki will protect me. They are the strongest two people in the world, and believe it or not, I'm pretty strong, too. We'll protect each other." Morgan blinked back her own tears. "When this is over, I promise I'll come back to you."

Drawing her daughter into another crushing hug, her mother whispered, "You better. Stay safe out there. We love you so much."

Her father looked proud but sad as he joined the hug, "We know you are strong, sweetie."

"I love you too. Always." Morgan squeezed them both, allowing their love and support to strengthen her resolve for the mission ahead.

Before she could say her final goodbyes, she felt the pull of the magic and saw the shock and sadness on their faces as she disappeared.

Liam

It only took a few minutes to give final instructions to the people at the fortress, and then Viki and I were running down the road toward town. I was once again thankful that the roads would be among the last surviving vestiges of civilization. With the exception of paint and the reflective markers being gone, the highway was still largely intact and made for swift travel. With our enhanced stats, it was easy to run as fast as a horse could gallop without even straining. For us, this was the equivalent of a comfortable jogging pace, and it ate the miles between the fortress and town quickly.

Even so, we were observant. There were survivors still trying to save their homes from the inevitable collapse and others who looked to be out hunting for anything they could scavenge, but most were in small groups, and none were on the road. We were almost to the northern edge of town when we finally came upon a group of refugees heading out of the city.

Seeing almost thirty individuals—a large group—I gestured for Viki to stop, and we walked toward them in what I hoped was a non-menacing way. I guess I mostly succeeded, as a tall, lanky man carrying a large felling axe stepped to the front of his group protectively.

With a quick use of Treasure Sense, I knew that out of everyone, not a single magic Class was present. The majority had crafting classes of one form or another, and the rest were non-magical: fighters, a rogue, an archer, a martial artist, and others. The protective guy was the only odd one in the group, and his Class was listed as Woodsman, which was one I was unfamiliar with. However, he had somehow managed to hit Level 5, which was respectable after only a week.

However, despite the axe, he didn't seem anxious as he called out, "You should turn around, friend; the city isn't safe."

I smiled in turn and countered, "Nowhere is safe these days, but I already know about the city. My young friend and I were coming to see about lending our help. More importantly, we are spreading the word about what is really happening."

That got us some skeptical looks, but the scarecrow of a guy was the only one to challenge us. "How can you help? Also, what do you mean about what is 'really happening.' Do you know anything beyond the system messages that everyone saw?"

"You might find it hard to believe, but it happens that I do." I launched into my story and told them a condensed version of the same message I was spreading to everyone: invaders, Shop, and magic Classes needed. Protect the craftsmen and foster their growth. Find a defensible place and fortify it. Most importantly, get strong to survive.

It took us an hour to get through it all and answer their questions, but I counted it time worth spending, as these people said they were heading up north toward the Red River rather than up Highway 121 toward Bonham. That meant the truth would spread in another direction.

They didn't believe me without question, but I showed them my Level, and my message lined up with what they had seen in terms of the System's callousness. I also gave each of the children in the group a mana coin to ensure they would get a chance at a magic class when they got older. The parents looked grateful despite some lingering wariness.

We weren't the only ones sharing information. They also told us about the chaos they were fleeing from.

Gary, the Woodsman, shook his head in sadness, "A dungeon even formed right under the overpass where this highway meets Highway 380. But at least no monsters have come out of it. There is a pretty big camp of people set up in the parking lot on the northwest side of the intersection where a couple of the big box stores used to be. They've both collapsed now. Roof caved in yesterday on the hardware store. The grocery store was the night before, but there wasn't anything left to loot in there anyway, so no one was hurt."

It was grim. I had just shopped at that hardware store a week ago, prepping for the apocalypse, so it was sad, even though I knew it would happen. I also wasn't surprised that a dungeon formed there; that intersection was a big shopping area with big stores and strip malls on all four corners.

I was just about to motion to Viki to start running again when Gary spoke one last time. "Ask for Karl. He was an ex-police officer, and he was trying to get people organized at the camp."

Nodding in appreciation, I said, "Thanks, be safe on your journey, and spread the word."

It felt like there was a giant clock ticking in the sky, and every minute I wasted in idle conversation, people were dying, and the bitch of it was, that was true.

For her part, Viki just seemed impatient to get to the next dungeon and test out her new abilities.

Without further ado, we turned and continued running toward town, moving a little faster than we had before.

The last miles were views of fancy new subdivisions, with a few businesses, now laid waste and looking like warzones. There were entire swaths of houses, whole neighborhoods, where fires had gutted everything, leaving still smoldering rubble in their wake. The one good thing is that I didn't see a lot of evidence of mutated beasts or monsters yet, which matched up with my memories.

By the one-week mark during my first life, most of the chaos and death in the cities had been from our technology disintegrating and bad people robbing their neighbors to steal anything useful. At least, that's how it had been where I lived, but I was sure it was the same all over. People were people, after all.

It was in the countryside where beasts had been the real menace. Of course, there had also been roaming monsters in the city as well, likely from situations such as the stronghold dungeon we had just destroyed or pets that had gone feral after mutating. I was sure areas like downtown Dallas and Fort Worth would be much worse, but in my first life, I hadn't dared go there, and no one I knew ever ventured back that deep into the cities after they were abandoned.

I looked south as we ran, thinking of what it would be like now, with my draconic bloodline and higher Level. I was surprised to find a feeling of eagerness at the thought rather than the dread I once felt. I didn't know how strong the monsters were there, nor how high the dungeon levels rose, but if I were going to reach the level cap, it would be those areas that would make it possible.

Nearing our destination, we could see the camp ahead. A bonfire was lit near the center of the camp, and smaller cooking fires sent plumes of smoke into the air, but even from a distance, it looked bad.

Viki broke the silence, and her words mirrored my thoughts, "Liam, this is terrible. We need to help these people."

"Yeah, but there is only so much we can do. Stopping to take the time to help this one group would mean millions of others dying if I can't reach Level 100 in three weeks and stop the invasions."

Even so, we only slowed enough not to frighten the camp's residents as we approached, all the while looking for their leader. We would do what little we could.

CHAPTER 4
WELCOME TO CAMP ABANDON HOPE

THE CLOSER WE CAME, the worse it looked. The parking lot was now a wasteland of rapidly rusting metal and crumbling debris. The System's corrosive influence had turned the vehicles into decaying husks, their frames sagging as if they'd been abandoned for decades. Sheets of plywood, once sturdy, had lost their glue, now little more than flimsy, warped layers barely holding together, repurposed as makeshift tents. These sagging shelters offered scant protection, their thin veneers barely keeping the occasional rain off the huddled forms beneath.

The people moved like shadows, their faces etched with despair, eyes hollow and distant. Weak fires sputtered, surrounded by makeshift shelters that seemed ready to collapse at any moment. This wasn't living—it was surviving, in the most desperate way, in a world that was literally crumbling around them.

Even among this mess, one of the oddest and most striking things was what people wore. Gone were the designer brands and coordinated outfits; instead, they wore whatever they had that was made from natural fibers. There were lots of cotton shirts and some denim jeans, but the skinny jeans were out of fashion in the Apocalypse. Being made partially of synthetic fibers, they would have fallen apart. If things weren't so sad, I might have chuckled at the thought of that fashion being one that would never come back. Apparently, makeshift kilts were popular instead. I actually saw one man with an honest-to-goodness tartan wool kilt, probably a Ren Faire costume.

It hurt my heart to see people in this condition; it was like the homeless camps from before the Apocalypse, except worse.

The only ray of hope in the whole mess was that here and there, I could see eyes filled with determination, not content to let this break them. One such group surrounded Karl, the man in charge that we had been told about. My Analyze told me he was a Level 6 Warrior, and judging by his bearing and demeanor, I'd say he was definitely ex-military and, more recently, a police officer. He still wore a policeman's leather duty belt, except instead of a gun, he wore a system-generated sword.

That meant this man had completed a dungeon! Color me impressed.

When we neared, the conversation became clear. Karl was arguing with a group of six teenagers about entering the dungeon.

"I'm telling you, you aren't ready!" He pointed to a gravely injured man in his mid-30s lying on a makeshift stretcher. "Shane was a skilled hunter, with the Hunter Class, and look at him. We barely made it through."

The man on the crudely assembled stretcher let out a rattling moan, cutting off the argument. Dark blood seeped through the grimy fabric wrapped around his torso. His breath came in shallow, rapid gasps. Even a cursory glance at the wounded man named Shane told me he wouldn't make it without healing.

I listened as they argued for a minute but used my Treasure Sense ability to analyze the teens. I still marveled at how much better that ability was than the standard Analyze skill; it gave a lot more info than just basic name and level.

It didn't seem like they were getting anywhere, with the teens determined to do it even if Karl ordered otherwise. If it went on much longer, they would defy his authority; I could see it in their body language.

I cleared my throat loudly. "Karl? A word?"

The tall man whirled, fixing me with piercing blue eyes. His gaze flickered over Viki and me, assessing. Annoyed by the interruption and suspicious, but not openly hostile. Yet.

"Who's asking?"

"Name's Liam. This is Viki. We're...uniquely equipped to help. But first, tell me about this dungeon."

Karl crossed his arms. "Kobold den. Marshy hellhole about a mile in. Rough terrain, vicious little bastards. And a boss lurking somewhere in the depths." His jaw tightened. "Lost two good men finding that much out."

I nodded slowly, pieces clicking into grim place. Kobolds. Nasty critters. But nothing they couldn't handle. Probably.

"They should be fine if they are careful." I pointed to each member of the group, "Fighter, Fighter, Rogue, Hunter, Archer, Blacksmith. They make a party as balanced as it can be without any magic classes."

Turning to the group of teens, who had puffed up with pride at my declaration, I added, "You just have to play it safe. No heroics. Try to pull one kobold at a time and fight it alone. If anything seems sketchy, then back away and get out fast. Better alive and healthy than injured. You can always go back and kill more, but an injury without a healer or hospital means weeks or months of recuperation at best or death if you are unlucky."

I could see they were listening and hearing me. Smart kids. "A little extra time now will save you months or years in the long run. Gain levels, and when you out-level your opponents enough to be confident, then take on groups and go after the boss."

Karl looked angry that I would waltz in and gainsay him to those under his care. "Who the hell do you think you are? You're gonna get these kids killed!" He gestured to his friend, "Shane's dying because of that dungeon."

"If you don't run the dungeons, they will eventually build up enough mana to break. When that happens, they will spill their monsters out into the real world to rampage unchecked."

Looking startled by my reply, he asked uncertainly, "And how would you know that?"

I chuckled and ensured my voice was loud enough for those around to hear, "I already said my name is Liam, but as for who I am, I'm the only Level 30 on this planet, and I have done this all before. Let me tell you a little story...."

Projecting my voice, I made sure the dozens of people in the area around us could hear and launched into my tale again. I hated it, but I was getting pretty good at laying it all out. Having done it more than once now and gotten bombarded with questions, I was slowly refining my pitch to be as condensed as I could while still delivering it in such a way that it kept everyone riveted to my words.

I would say that it was faster and better this time, but there were also a lot more people listening, so that meant more people asking questions.

One thing I made a point of doing was to avoid saying that the imminent invasion was my fault. I didn't lie; I just avoided directly pointing that out, letting the AI take the blame. It was ultimately the AI's fault, after all. It wasn't that I wanted to avoid taking the blame for my fuck up, but I didn't want an angry mob making my job harder than it already was. I didn't have time to worry about people seeking revenge when I had invader Champions showing up at any time.

Nearly an hour had passed, and Karl was nodding in time with my words, clearly accepting what I was saying. Even so, he was the leader here. He couldn't just let my crazy story go without challenging it, and I was pretty sure he was doing it to keep others from getting rowdy.

"That's a good story, and with everything that's happening, I believe it's possible, but can you prove any of it.?"

By the time I was done talking, the crowd had grown from dozens to maybe three or four hundred, so a great many others were grumbling and waiting for the answer to Karl's question.

"Let's start by summoning my friend Morgan; she has a rare healer class. You can all see what a difference a healer can make with your own eyes, and you'll know that part of my speech was true."

It had been around three hours since we had parted, and she should be ready for us to pull her back to us. I gestured to Viki to do the honors.

She concentrated and focused inward, obviously looking at System messages and her skills. After a minute, just enough to really build the suspense, my young friend started to glow, and a corresponding glowing circle appeared on the ground a few steps from her, complete with cool, draconic-looking runes. A moment later, the magic built to a crescendo, and Morgan appeared in a flash of light.

I was secretly thankful she didn't lose her breakfast, but she did partially spoil the drama by clutching her hand over her mouth for a few heartbeats before cursing like a Southern lady. She finally turned to face me. "I hate that! It doesn't get any better the third time!"

Despite the crowd and being aware that their belief rested on our actions, I couldn't help but laugh before stepping over and patting her consolingly on the shoulder.

Looking around at the crowd, she raised an eyebrow and asked, "Ugh, what's going on?"

Meanwhile, the crowd was more than a little impressed by the magic light show and Viki figuratively pulling a human out of her hat.

I raised my voice again so the crowd could hear, "This is Morgan, and she is a Priestess."

Gesturing toward the man on the stretcher, "This is Shane. He was nearly killed in the nearby dungeon; please heal him."

Morgan gasped as she saw the dying man, her face paled. "Damnit, bless his heart, the poor thing!"

She rushed over and knelt by his side, using her class version of the **Analyze** skill to determine the full extent of his injuries. Whatever she muttered under her breath was too low to catch, but she wasted no time. One hand pressed against his clammy forehead while the other hovered over the gaping wound in his abdomen. Golden energy flared to life, flowing between her hands in a radiant arc, bathing the man in a warm glow.

At first, nothing seemed to happen. Then, in a slow, almost grotesque dance of life reversing death, his intestines—partially exposed and slick with blood—began to wriggle and shift, pulling themselves back into his body like they belonged there. Flesh reknitted over the gap, muscle fibers weaving together with an unnatural precision, as though an unseen force was stitching him back whole from the inside out. His breathing, previously ragged and shallow, deepened. The gray pallor of his skin warmed, and the awful tension in his frame eased as the pain subsided.

Morgan's brow furrowed in concentration as she pushed more power into the spell. Sweat beaded on her forehead, her breath steady but deliberate. The glow around her hands intensified, sinking deeper into his flesh, reinforcing what had already been mended. The wound didn't just close—it *sealed*, scarless and clean, as if the injury had never existed. His broken ribs realigned beneath his skin with a faint crackle, his body restoring itself under her guidance, cell by cell.

Even when she finally withdrew her hands, the golden light lingered, its warmth working through his system like embers slowly cooling. The man let out a deep, shuddering breath, his eyelids fluttering. Five minutes passed, and then, with a sharp intake of air, he bolted upright, hands flying to his stomach in disbelief. His fingers probed the unblemished skin where a fatal wound had once been. His gaze darted around wildly, his expression torn between awe and terror.

Karl's tears streamed freely as he rushed forward, clutching his friend's arm. "You're alive! She fixed you!" His voice cracked with raw emotion.

Morgan sat back on her heels, visibly drained, rubbing her temples. Healing magic had a cost, even for someone as skilled as her.

The murmurs around us swelled, rippling through the gathered survivors. Awe turned to desperate hope, and before long, the crowd surged forward—pleading, begging, demanding her touch. Injuries were thrust toward her, voices rose in panicked supplication, and the weight of expectation settled heavily on her shoulders.

I immediately stepped in, shifting my stance and gripping my weapon. No one was going to overwhelm Morgan. She had done enough.

"Listen up, everyone, make sure children who haven't chosen their classes pick magic classes like I said. You can see what a difference even one healer can make. Morgan can heal some of you if she chooses, but it will only be those with serious injuries. Her mana is limited, and we need to run that dungeon right away, then move on.

It was a bit of a pain, but Karl came back to himself and realized the situation could turn ugly, so he left his friend's side and began sorting through the injured and sending everyone else away.

It took another half an hour, but we were finally ready to go. The seriously injured were cured, and any disbelief was removed.

"Okay, Karl, we need heralds to spread the word so people everywhere will know what is coming. It will only take us half an hour to an hour at most to run that dungeon. Please have some candidates assembled so that when we return, we can take them with us to teach and train."

He asked a few questions about what we were looking for, and we answered. What I cared about the most was dedication to getting the message out; as long as they had some kind of fighting class, I didn't care what it was.

Viki looked eager, and Morgan looked resigned as I said, "Let's go kill some kobolds!"

CHAPTER 5

KOBOLD DUNGEON (I)

As we approached the dungeon, I had to admit my surprise. When the group we had met earlier said the dungeon had opened beneath the overpass where 75 met 380, I had pictured something small, like a doorway appearing in the embankment or perhaps a manhole that turned into a tunnel beneath the road.

What I didn't picture was a damned cave mouth taking up the entire area beneath the overpass, from side to side and from the ground up to where the highway had once been above. It was now a short hill with a cave way too big for the size of the mound. You would think that with an opening that large, it would be easy to see inside, but that wasn't how the System did dungeons. It had to be all mysterious and set the ambiance. I prepared myself for the onslaught of its intrusive thoughts and sure enough the second we stepped within range it began:

The yawning cave mouth dominated the space where the overpass once stood, its edges jagged and unnatural as though the earth itself had been violently torn open to reveal the entrance.

Darkness pooled within the cavern's opening, impenetrable even to the sunlight that dared to linger near the edge. The ground beneath the entrance sloped gently down, and the rock walls seemed to pulse with a faint, otherworldly glow, barely noticeable unless one stared too long. A subtle hum of energy filled the air, a promise of danger, power, and the unknown. The path ahead beckoned adventurers with a mixture of excitement and dread, but as with all dungeons, the true horrors lay beyond sight, deep in the shadows, waiting for the bold and the reckless.

Even from this distance, the cave seemed alive—an entity of its own, its very existence whispering of secrets and treasures within, but never without a price. The entrance was grand yet ominous, daring anyone who approached to step into the abyss.

I shook my head, pushing away the intrusive feelings and thoughts, and I wasn't the only one.

Viki was frowning, having only experienced the Stronghold dungeon before and not a regular dungeon. "Is it always like this?"

She looked at me questioningly, looking for assurance. "I don't like how it makes me feel things in my head."

Chuckling ruefully, I answered, "Sorry, kiddo, but it's always that way. Every single time. It gets in your head like those scripted event cutscenes in the old video games back in the day. If you aren't specifically expecting it and paying attention you won't even realize it isn't your own thoughts."

Morgan smirked, apparently trying to break the mood, "Back in the day, huh? You mean last week?"

That made me smile despite realizing what she was doing. "Yeah, well. For me, it's been last week ... plus twenty years."

She shook her head in disbelief. "I can't get over the fact that you are an old guy– like fifteen years older than me, even though you look a couple of years younger."

She was in her mid-twenties, and my current body was barely twenty years old, so I couldn't help but get a dig in, just to mess with her for that 'old guy' comment, "A couple, huh? That's what you're going with?"

Viki looked at me like I had just kicked a puppy. "You didn't!"

I burst out laughing and addressed Morgan, who looked at me in wide-eyed shock at calling her out. "I'm just kidding, and besides, you deserved that for calling me old!"

She huffed and turned partially away from me, giving me a pretend cold shoulder, but I could see the amusement in her eyes. Her ploy had worked, and we were no longer fixated on the depressing System fuckery that put scripted reactions directly into our brains.

Getting serious, I gave them both a look. "Okay, we're about to go in, and it will be your first dungeon. You are both over-leveled and have strong magic from your classes to back you up, but don't let your guard down. These are always dangerous. Not every dungeon is all about killing and looting monsters. Some are mazes and puzzles, some are filled with deadly traps, but no matter what, every single one has the System on its side. There was always debate back in my first life about whether it actively tried to fuc... er, screw us over. Personally, I think it actively tries to kill people; after all, the stated purpose of the System is to make us stronger."

"Make us stronger? By hiding our options in order to get more of us killed?" Viki was indignant.

I gave her a rueful smile, "I'm pretty sure it means that in a Darwinistic sense. Killing the weak so the strong will survive and bree... er, make stronger offspring."

Shit, it's hard to watch my mouth. I'm not used to being around kids.

I hated to think of how many times I'd already been a bad influence and how many more I would in the future.

The look on her face said that the monsters we were about to encounter were going to learn just how much Darwin and the System could go fuck themselves, a sentiment I heartily agreed with.

"Right, both of you use your Stealth skills and practice getting used to them. I'm going to use my Stealth skill too, but I won't be fighting the kobolds unless we get into a bad situation. This dungeon is for you two to gain some experience in the real sense of the word. That and get you some gear, hopefully."

I almost forgot, or perhaps I was blocking it out from the bad memories, but I needed to officially form a party with the girls.

"Hey, hit accept." I sent the invites.

Viki accepted instantly, but Morgan hesitated, "Won't this keep you from getting as much XP? Don't we need to get you to max level?"

"Yes, but the experience in these low-level dungeons will be a drop in the bucket for me anyway. More importantly, being in a System-recognized party means we split the XP evenly, so even if we don't all get a hit on a particular monster, we'll still earn experience as long as we are in the same area together. This will let us divide and conquer depending on the dungeon layout."

Viki stepped forward toward the entrance, impatient to get started.

Chuckling, Morgan and I followed.

As we crossed the threshold into the dungeon, the oppressive darkness seemed to swallow us whole, but what awaited inside was far from the cramped cave I'd imagined. Instead, the space opened up into a sprawling marshland, stretching out as far as we could see. The ground beneath our boots was soft and damp, squelching with every step, and the air was thick with the smell of stagnant water and moss. A faint mist clung to the ground, swirling around our legs like the marsh itself was alive.

The ceiling, impossibly high, disappeared into the darkness above, leaving only faint patches of light to break the gloom. It almost felt like we were standing under an open night sky, but instead of stars, clusters of bioluminescent fungi and small, glowing creatures blinked down at us like distant constellations. The eerie light reflected off the murky pools of water scattered throughout the landscape, casting ghostly ripples that danced along the surface. The stillness was unnerving, a silence so deep it felt like even the air was holding its breath.

The marsh stretched out before us, a twisting maze of shallow water and soggy earth, with patches of tall, reedy grasses swaying in the phantom breeze. In the distance, shapes moved—small, scurrying figures. Kobolds. They were spread out, lurking just at the edge of sight, barely more than shadows in the dim light. The System had designed this place with unsettling care, making it feel both vast and claustrophobic all at once.

The further we moved in, the more alive the marsh felt. The distant croak of frogs and the occasional splash from something unseen added to the atmosphere, but it was the faint rustling in the shadows that kept us on edge. Kobolds were out there, hiding, waiting. The air itself felt thick with anticipation.

We stayed alert, knowing the dungeon's design. The kobolds at the outer edges would be scattered, small groups of two or three, spread far enough apart that they wouldn't hear each other if we engaged them. But the deeper we went, the more frequent and dangerous the encounters would become. The swampy terrain would only work against us, slowing our movements and making it hard to see what lay ahead.

According to Karl, somewhere deep in this marshy expanse was the heart of the dungeon. A small rise with a cave where the kobold shaman and his protectors waited. But first, we had to make it through the outer ring—the shadows moving just at the edge of our vision.

The System had outdone itself this time.

I scoffed at the intrusive final thought. Speaking to the air, I said, "Don't sprain your circuits trying to pat yourself on the back! Seriously, don't you think it is kind of bullshit that you compliment yourself while forcing the thoughts into our heads?"

Neither the AI nor the System it worked for answered my complaint. Not that I expected they would. The girls looked confused for a moment but then realized what I meant. Morgan frowned, perhaps realizing for the first time just how devious the AI could be. Viki glared around us, looking like she wanted to shoot something for daring to push thoughts into her head.

"There's nothing we can do; I've been dealing with it for over twenty years. It just gets annoying after a while. Most of us didn't even realize it wasn't our own thoughts for an embarrassingly long time." I blushed slightly, remembering it had been well over a decade before I finally understood what was happening in my first life.

Morgan gave voice to the truth, "If you hadn't pointed it out, with the cave entrance outside, I wouldn't have noticed. Even now, it's only the texture of my thoughts that is slightly off from the way I think naturally. I know that doesn't make sense, but it's the only way I can describe it."

It made perfect sense to me. What had eventually tipped me over the edge into realizing was going into a dungeon filled with spiders. They had once been a serious phobia of mine, and my thoughts upon entering were not filled with the sheer existential dread that I should have felt. After that, I had clued into the fact that much of the 'ambiance' of the dungeons was the System trying to push me into experiencing what I was seeing in a certain way that it deemed I should.

"Putting questions about why the System does what it does aside, we've got a purpose for being here. I'm going to go invisible with my stealth, but will stay with you and guide you. I'll jump in if you need me, but I want you both to get some experience in actual fights."

We each engaged our version of stealth. Mine was a spell, and it provided what was essentially invisibility so long as I didn't attack. For Viki, it was a matter of blending with shadows, which was easy to do in this nighttime-like setting. Morgan's was also an ability, but looked more dramatic as it activated. Unlike Viki, who seemed to fade into the background, Morgan was engulfed in the living shadows of her Umbral Cloak, which made her much harder to spot or keep your eyes on.

The effect was the same either way. They would be super hard to spot, except being in a party we showed up for each other as a haloed form almost like the Predator would see, using his heat vision technology in that movie, only we were all blue halos to one another in the darkness. That made it easier to sneak through the marsh.

We all practiced our movements to see how well we could do with these new skills, and I was surprised not only by how good the skills were but also by how competent we all were with them. I had practiced sneaking around in dungeons for years, but both of the girls were pretty good, too. Viki was small and light on her feet, the way some kids can be. However, Morgan was nearly as good as me.

When I asked about that, she whispered back, "My dad and grandfather were big into hunting, and I would go with them when I was young. I got my first buck when I was 10. It's a shame I don't have my hunting rifle, but gunpowder became useless after the System came."

"Nice! Well, you've got spells now, and they are a lot quieter than the crack of a rifle round going supersonic."

"True enough!"

After only a few minutes, we felt pretty comfortable, especially considering these were low-level foes. If we were stalking elves, then we'd be lucky if we didn't get spotted even under these lighting conditions.

We made it to within fifty feet of the first group of two. I tapped Morgan on the shoulder and pointed to the one on the left. I then instructed Viki to shoot the one slightly farther away on the right.

The bioluminescent fungi overhead cast a faint glow across the scene, just enough to make out the small, reptilian creatures standing near a patch of reeds. The kobolds were small and hunched, their scaly bodies covered in crude leather armor. One leaned lazily on a spear while the other poked around in the muddy water, seemingly unaware of our approach. Their chittering conversation was soft, blending with the natural sounds of the marsh—the croaking of distant frogs and the faint rustle of the wind.

The air was thick with tension as we moved within fifty feet of them, each of us carefully placing our steps to avoid splashing in the shallow pools. Even though the terrain made stealth difficult, the kobolds weren't particularly alert. They were too relaxed, perhaps confident that their territory was secure this far out from the dungeon's core. The System had spread them thin here, far enough apart that even if we engaged, the others wouldn't hear. The trickling mist swirled at our feet as we positioned ourselves behind a large patch of reeds, each of us ready to strike.

Viki

Viki couldn't stop herself from admiring the Heartseeker Longbow as they moved deeper into the dungeon. She had pulled it out the moment they entered, unable to resist the feel of it in her hands. Liam had warned her not to flaunt it around others, reminding her that something this powerful could make people do stupid things. But really, who could blame her for wanting to show it off? It was the coolest bow she had ever seen—better than anything in Skyrim or any game she'd played. And this? This was real.

The bow felt perfect, as if it had been made just for her. Light, but with a power she could feel humming through her fingers. It balanced so easily in her hands that it almost didn't seem fair, and drawing it back felt smooth, almost effortless, despite its strength. She could hold an arrow ready for what felt like forever without her arm getting tired. Every time she pulled back the string, there was this surge of energy, like the bow was helping her aim, guiding her to the perfect shot.

They moved silently through the marshy ground, the glow of the bioluminescent fungi casting a dim, eerie light around them. Viki kept her steps careful, using all the stealth skills she had practiced to avoid splashing in the water or snapping a twig. She could hear the distant croak of frogs and the soft rustling of the swamp, but her focus was on the two kobolds ahead, just barely visible in the murky gloom. They were too distracted to notice her and the others, their backs turned, chatting in that creepy, chittering way kobolds did.

Liam appeared at her side, invisible to the kobolds but highlighted in a ghostly blue glow to her. He gave her a light tap on the shoulder, pointing toward the kobold on the right—the one standing a few feet further away from the other. He didn't say a word, just gave her a nod, trusting her to know what to do.

Viki grinned, feeling her heart pick up with excitement. She nocked an arrow, the Heartseeker Longbow feeling so natural in her hands; it was like it had always been hers. She drew back the string, the bow almost humming as the runes along its limbs came to life with power as it sensed her killing intent. Her eyes locked onto the kobold, focusing as the bow seemed to guide her hand. It was a little further away than the other, but that didn't matter. She had the Heartseeker.

As Viki drew the bowstring back, her grip tightened just a little. The memory of her family flickered in her mind like a flame she tried to snuff out, but it always came back. It was the monsters. They'd taken everything from her—her parents, her little brother—gone on the second day of the Apocalypse, ripped away before she even had time to understand what was happening. She had buried the grief deep, shoved it down so far it couldn't distract her, but the anger... the anger was always there, simmering under the surface. Every monster she killed was like taking back a piece of what they had stolen. She wasn't just some kid anymore—she was a weapon, and monsters were the enemy. They deserved to die. All of them. And she was going to make sure they did.

The arrow flew from the bow with a soft twang, slicing through the air with precision. Viki didn't even need to watch where it was going —she knew it would hit its mark.

Almost at the same time she fired her shot, Morgan launched her attack as well, a bolt of shadowy magic streaking through the air silently. Both attacks hit almost on top of one another.

Her shot hit exactly as intended. Even though she felt it would, she watched in anticipation as the arrow struck the kobold's head right in the temple and burst it like an overripe melon, causing the little monster to somersault head over heels before landing in a crumpled mess. The anger simmered in her soul, but she didn't feel a surge of elation at her feat, but just satisfaction. One more monster was gone from this world.

Meanwhile, Morgan's shot hit the kneeling kobold right in the chest, blasting a hole in it and destroying its heart.

Viki had a tight smile on her face seeing that. She had worried at first that adding another person to her and Liam's team might mess things up or slow them down, but that was a good kill. One spell and the ugly little creature was done. If Morgan kept it up like that, then she would be a good companion.

CHAPTER 6
KOBOLD DUNGEON (2)

LIAM

I was impressed. Both girls took out their targets in a single hit; a spell for Morgan and an arrow for Viki.

Whispering loud enough for them both to hear, "Not bad!"

However, I was curious about something, so I asked Viki, "How come you didn't use one of your special arrows?"

I could see Viki's glowing outline shrug. "I wanted to see if I could do it without using magic. Plus, the monster looked weak, so I figured it would be wasting mana to use a Night Arrow."

Not bothering to keep my laughter quiet, I suggested, "Good call, but don't be afraid to burn some mana getting to know your new skills and spells."

Viki had a good head on her shoulders; I knew I didn't need to say more. I could also see Morgan nodding along, obviously taking the advice to heart as well.

Honestly, as powerful as we were compared with the kobolds, we could just swagger openly through the place and blast everything we saw to smithereens, but we all needed practice with our stealth skills and abilities. They wouldn't always have me around, and the targets wouldn't always be this weak.

With that thought in mind, I led the way, sneaking through the mucky water and muddy ground. The one thing I was extremely thankful for was that it wasn't like real Dallas mud. That stuff would suck the boots right off your feet, and you'd never get clean afterward. I just wished I had cleaning magic like some of those fantasy novels I'd read before the apocalypse. A Cleaner would come in handy right now!

Of course, Morgan might have one; based on the description of her Purifying Touch spell, it might clean us up. Part of the wording did say it would remove all foreign substances from the body. I was pretty sure it meant from inside the body, but that didn't mean it wouldn't work on the outside as well. We'd have to test it out after we finished.

I just hoped it wouldn't remove clothing, but I had a strong suspicion that System fuckery came into play, and the spell was smart enough to distinguish between wanted and unwanted substances. Spells did take a lot of their direction from the user's intent. I didn't have to list GPS coordinates when I cast Arcane Singularity, after all. The spell just went off where I wanted it to.

I pushed those thoughts aside as we came up on the next targets. This group had three kobolds, and they seemed to be arguing over the ownership of a small fish and were getting pretty heated. I held in the chuckle that threatened to spill out, seeing them so oblivious.

With a few gestures, they got the hint that they were supposed to target the left and right opponents, just like last time. I would take the middle one, the one who seemed to have the upper hand in their disagreement.

I made hand motions to count us down.

Three,

Two,

One,

We all fired at once. This time, Viki used a Night Arrow, and it was so silent and wrapped in shadows that if I didn't have the Shadow Affinity, I never would have been able to see it once it left her bow. Morgan and I both used Shadow Bolts.

It was textbook clean. Not a single one drew another breath after the moment our attacks landed. Spells get stronger as the caster gains more levels. So, even though Morgan and I were using low-level spells, our aim was excellent, thanks to our stats, and we out-leveled these chumps by enough that we were guaranteed one-hit kills so long as we didn't miss.

I thought, *Don't even get me started about Viki's bow!*

Being a soulbound growth item, that thing was like our spells; it would get stronger with every level she gained.

A minute later, we collected the loot and split it three ways. It was only two copper mana coins each, which confirmed what I already knew, that they were Level 2 monsters. That meant this dungeon would be slightly more challenging than the Goblin dungeon I had run right after Initialization. I had let the girls have the loot from the last two since they had made the kills. As far as I was concerned, I didn't care who made the kills; coins could get split evenly, but loot items would go to whoever it most suited or who needed it.

Hearing the slight clinking of coins being put into a pocket or pouch, I turned to Morgan and made a mental note to make sure she got the next storage item. Thankfully, she was very quiet as we advanced toward the next group. Whatever she had put the coins in must be strapped down so that they couldn't rattle around.

The next half hour was one group after another, falling to our skill testing. Being in stealth and having plenty of time to set up and aim, none of our shots ever missed. Each one dropped a target, stone-cold dead.

As we neared groups with more than three, or that included higher level kobolds, we began to use some of our group and area of effect spells.

I love me some AoE!

Viki used her Eclipse Barrage, which split her arrows into three and partially blinded enemies that were struck, as well as her Gloom Shroud spell. That one was fun. It created magical darkness in a thirty-foot radius, plenty big enough to cover any of the groups we were facing. After that, she would practice with her other spells and arrows, like Shadow Bind or Midnight's Grasp, both of which were control spells meant to lock a target into place for a few seconds while also doing damage.

However, even with Shadow Bind, she had to intentionally aim for a non-lethal spot for it to trigger the magic shadow tendrils. Otherwise, the monster would just drop dead before the magic could activate. Midnight's Grasp, on the other hand, was a spell, and it always locked down its target. It looked like a badass dragon's claw made of shadow that reached out of the closest shadow and grasped the target, piercing and slicing with a damage-over-time effect as long as the claw lasted. Which, for these monsters, wasn't very long as they usually died from the initial attack.

Our priestess, Morgan, had far fewer spells, and her healing ones were pointless because, so far, we had remained in stealth the entire time and didn't even let our victims know we were there before they were dead. She did, however, have two attack spells. The first was Shadow Bolt, which was exactly like mine, but it was just less powerful due to our level difference. Her other spell was a moderate damage AoE called Shadowflame Burst. It only had a ten-foot radius, but that was still big enough to eliminate some of the groups we encountered. It looked like its namesake. Almost like a fireball, but it was flames made of shadow, and they seemed to weaken the creatures affected as if their flames were sucking the heat and vitality out of the targets.

For my part, I only practiced the skills and spells that were new to me. As cool as this new Shadow Dragon bloodline was, I definitely missed my acid-based attacks. Most things had found it hard to concentrate enough to attack or defend well when they had a heaping splash of acid trying to eat through their bodies. Sadly, those days were gone. On the other hand, while the shadow-based abilities were more subtle, they weren't any less powerful.

They almost all affected the perceptions or sapped the strength of my targets in one way or another, whether by adding a partial blindness effect from my Shadow Bolt or complete magical blindness from my Darkness spell. As for my physical attacks, almost all of my striking skills imparted magical weakness, which was kind of pointless on these already weak enemies. At first, I was disappointed, feeling very underwhelmed by it. When I was used to seeing my enemies collapse in agony from acid, this just seemed, pardon the pun, weak.

However, after thinking about it a bit, I revised that thought. While it was true that against these small fries, it was unimpressive, once I began to meet equal and stronger monsters again, that would rapidly change. If the System didn't specifically decide to screw me over, then they should stack. At least the different grades did. I couldn't stack 'minor weakness' repeatedly, but I could apply minor weakness from my Draconic Strike, then moderate weakness from

Searing Slash, on top of heavy weakness from Heavy Draconic Strike. If I applied all three to a single target, it would be the equivalent of a 50% strength and damage reduction, and that was nothing to sneeze at in a boss fight!

Morgan was the one who finally voiced what we were all thinking, "This is just kinda sad. They all die after one or two hits, and I never feel like we are in any danger at all."

Although I saw a different look on Viki's face that spoke of satisfaction at killing a lot of monsters, she too was feeling it and added, "It's too easy."

I chuckled. They had no idea what this dungeon would be like to normal people.

What I said was, "Don't jinx us. Even the kobold Skirmishers and Warmongers are easy for us, but that is because of all our advantages. I guarantee if we were in a high-level dungeon, you'd be scared enough, and we'd have plenty of wounds despite our abilities."

I pointed to the Level 8 Warmonger's corpse, which was just beginning to turn into golden motes. The System reclaimed it and left mana coins in its place. "Even those guys are below your level. The boss will be somewhere between Levels 13 and 18. Don't get cocky. If I weren't with you, the boss would be a tough challenge at your levels."

Gesturing toward the cave at the side of the small hill at the back of the dungeon, "Speaking of which, he and his guards are all that's left. How do you two think we should handle it?"

So far, I had been directing our choices and coming up with the plan for our battles, but I wanted to see what they would come up with. As much fun as this had been, we would only be able to run dungeons together for a day or two before I would have to head out to find higher-level challenges if I wanted to stand any chance of hitting the level cap before the actual invasion began. At that point, I wanted to make sure they felt confident in running dungeons without me so that I wouldn't have to worry about them.

The one good thing I had going for me right now was that the Champions would have a tough time hunting me down unless the System somehow screwed me over. I would be in dungeons and constantly moving from place to place. Without some specialized tracking or locating skill, I'd be a hard target to corner. Also, the more time they spent searching for me the higher my levels would rise. I wouldn't breathe easy, but at least that wasn't too major of a worry at the moment.

Morgan frowned, and Viki looked like she wanted to charge straight in and start fighting.

After a long moment, Morgan said thoughtfully, "Can you tell us what a boss fight is like? What are we likely to face in there?"

I beamed at her. "Good question! Always try to make your plan based on the best intelligence you can gather. In this case, and with most tribal monsters like these, you'll have a boss like a Shaman or Warchief or something equivalent to that. They will have anywhere from three to ten guards; most of the time, it'll be somewhere in the middle, usually around five. The guards will do everything in their power to protect the boss and weaken you so that you'll be easier to kill. The boss tends to be five to ten levels higher than the next toughest monster you've faced in the dungeon."

Letting myself run down, I waited to see whether they would accept what I had given them or ask for more.

Morgan seemed to be onto me. She asked, "And what are the bosses actually like to fight?"

He grinned, seeing that she was thinking ahead. "They will have more skills than their subordinates. Shamans are spell casters and will try to root you to give their minions a chance to whittle you down some. If that doesn't work, they like to curse you with debuffs that make it harder for you to fight. If it looks like you might reach them, they will pull out all the stops and start blasting you with high-damage spells. Their fighter equivalents are just as bad, even if they don't use spells. Warchiefs are the equivalent to a Barbarian or Warrior class with strikes, charges, and other weapon attacks."

Raising a challenging eyebrow, I finished with the worst news, "Almost always, you'll be locked in the boss room, so it is win or die."

They huddled up for a few minutes, discussing what I had told them and coming up with a battle plan. When they were ready, they looked over at me with grim but determined expressions.

Meanwhile, Morgan took charge, "Here's what we're going to do...."

CHAPTER 7
NEWBIE'S FIRST BOSS FIGHT!

MORGAN

Morgan stood quietly at the entrance of the boss cave, feeling the familiar hum of power running through her body as she finished casting Blessing of the Dragon's Grace. A soft golden glow surrounded them for a brief moment before fading, enhancing their agility and adding a layer of magical resistance. It was comforting, knowing the spell would last for ten minutes—enough time to deal with whatever awaited them inside.

She took a deep breath, her fingers tapping nervously against her palms. It wasn't fear that gripped her—it was focus, anticipation, and a little bit of pressure. This was their first real boss fight together as a team, and while she knew they could handle it, that nagging voice in her head kept reminding her that things could go wrong quickly in a dungeon, even with all their advantages.

Liam stepped up beside her, his usual confident smirk tugging at the corner of his mouth. He pulled the pair of bracers from his wrists, the dark leather adorned with glowing runes.

"Here, Morgan, you might need these," he said, handing her the Mystic Bands of the Arcanist. She hesitated for just a moment, her eyebrows raising in surprise.

"You sure?" she asked, taking them from him carefully.

Liam nodded. "Yeah. These will give you a boost to your mana regen and spell potency. And if things get hairy, the special ability should help you out. Just don't forget the special only lasts sixty seconds."

She slid the bands onto her wrists, feeling the immediate pulse of magic coursing through her. The extra power they granted was subtle but noticeable, like a gentle hum in the background of her mind, ready to be tapped into when the time came. Morgan gave Liam a quick nod of thanks and clenched her fists.

"Alright, let's do this," she whispered, more to herself than anyone else.

Viki and Liam both gave her encouraging glances, and for a brief moment, she felt the tension ease. But that feeling vanished the second they crossed the threshold into the boss room.

As they stepped forward, the unmistakable sound of grinding stone filled the cave. Morgan's heart jumped into her throat as the rockslide came crashing down behind them, sealing the entrance shut. She whipped around, her pulse spiking. The exit was completely buried. Liam had warned them, but she had hoped that since there was no door, their exit wouldn't be blocked, but sure enough, the 'System Fuckery', as Liam called it, had locked them in anyway.

Well, there's no turning back now.

The sudden noise alerted the kobolds, who froze mid-motion, their reptilian heads swiveling around in confusion. The kobold shaman stood near the back of the large cave, his eyes narrowing as he barked orders in their harsh, guttural language. Even though they were all using stealth, the shaman wasn't stupid. It knew they were there. And now the shaman's minions, the Warmonger kobolds, were on high alert, rushing to form a defensive line between their leader and the intruders they couldn't yet see.

They swung their crude weapons blindly, their eyes darting around, trying to find their attackers. It would have been comical if it weren't so dangerous.

Morgan stayed back, just as they had planned. She positioned herself near the entrance, ready to support Liam and Viki from a distance. Her heart was pounding in her chest, the adrenaline kicking in as she watched the kobolds stumble around, still unsure where the attack would come from. She saw Liam give Viki a nod, signaling it was time to initiate.

Viki glanced at Morgan, and she returned the nod. They were ready.

Liam tossed a rock toward the group of kobolds, the sharp clatter echoing off the cave walls. It was all the kobolds needed. The moment they heard the sound, they rushed toward it, grouping up as they prepared to defend their shaman. Their movements were frantic, their scaly bodies jostling together as they pushed toward the noise.

It was exactly what they needed.

Viki acted first, casting Gloom Shroud. The cave dimmed as magical darkness spread in a 20-foot radius, enveloping the kobolds in an impenetrable cloud of shadow. The creatures snarled and hissed, swinging their weapons wildly as they were plunged into complete darkness, unable to see their attackers.

Morgan tightened her grip on her staff, taking a deep breath to steady herself. It was her turn now.

With a swift motion, she cast Shadowflame Burst. Dark flames erupted in a 10-foot radius, swallowing the clustered kobolds in an instant. The shadowy fire wrapped around them, burning through their armor and skin. Their howls echoed through the cave as the spell weakened them, making them more vulnerable to what was coming next.

The shaman stood just outside the range of the spell, untouched but clearly aware that something terrible was happening to his minions. Its eyes darted through the darkness, searching for a target. It couldn't see them yet, but Morgan knew it wouldn't be long before it started casting spells of its own.

Liam stepped up, his fingers weaving intricate patterns in the air as he prepared his next move. The air around them seemed to still for a moment, like the calm before the storm, before he unleashed Arcane Singularity.

The spell sucked the kobolds in like a vortex, pulling them together into a tight knot of flailing bodies. For three seconds, they were utterly helpless, trapped in the pull of the singularity, their panicked screeches filling the cave. Then, with a sharp burst of energy, the singularity detonated, sending shockwaves through the kobolds and scattering their bodies like rag dolls.

Morgan could feel the magic surging through her veins, the bracers on her wrists pulsing with energy as the fight reached its critical point. Her eyes flicked to the shaman, who stood at the back, untouched but watching with fury as his minions' broken and bleeding bodies flew out of the darkness.

Before the shaman could react, Viki fired her **Shadow Bind Arrow**, her movements swift and precise. The arrow flew through the air, and Morgan's sharp eyes followed it as it struck the shaman, exploding into tendrils of shadow that coiled around him, locking him in place. The shaman's body jerked as he tried to break free, but the tendrils held fast, giving them precious seconds to finish off the remaining kobolds.

With the last of the Warmongers still writhing in the grip of the **Arcane Singularity**, Morgan let out a breath she hadn't realized she'd been holding. The fight was almost over. Almost.

The shaman roared, casting a powerful debuff curse that rippled through the cave like a dark mist. Morgan felt the weight of it settle on her chest, making her limbs feel sluggish, her body heavy with the curse's oppressive power. She grit her teeth, fighting through the sensation. Liam and Viki were similarly affected, but it wasn't enough to stop them.

"Stay focused!" Morgan called, her voice steady despite the tension in her body.

Just as the shaman began to break free from the Shadow Bind, Viki hit it with **Midnight's Grasp**. A massive, spectral dragon's claw erupted from the shaman's shadow, latching onto it with a crushing grip. The shaman screeched again, this time in pain as the claw dealt moderate damage and began to bleed him with its DoT effect.

Morgan knew this was her moment.

She closed her eyes briefly, focusing on the magic pulsing through her bracers. Activating their special ability, she felt the surge of power flood her veins, boosting her spell potency by 50% and reducing her mana consumption by 25%. For sixty seconds, she would be stronger than ever, and she wasn't about to waste it.

Opening her eyes, she raised her staff and cast **Shadow Bolt**, the dark energy surging forward with amplified force. The spell struck the shaman, with his defenses crippled and locked in the grip of the spectral dragon claw. Morgan could see the impact as his body convulsed from the strong hit.

Liam was right there with her, his own spell at the ready. He unleashed **Umbral Chains**, dark chains bursting from the ground and wrapping around the shaman. The chains pulsed with power, locking the shaman in place and adding yet another DoT effect to the already injured boss.

The shaman's struggles grew weaker, its movements slowing as its injuries mounted. Its breath came in ragged gasps, its body trembling from the combined effects of the attacks. It was on the brink of death, its once-fierce eyes now filled with desperation.

Morgan took a step back, watching as Liam grinned at Viki. "Might as well practice," he said, his voice light despite the tension still hanging in the air.

With a burst of speed, Liam activated **Dragon's Charge**, closing the distance between himself and the shaman in an instant. His *Spectral Longknife of Shadows* gleamed as he raised it high, and with a single fluid motion, he executed his most powerful move, **Heavy Draconic Strike**. The blade sliced clean through the shaman's neck, beheading it without resistance.

For a moment, the cave was eerily silent. Then, the shaman's body crumbled, and after a moment, it dissolved into golden motes of light as the System reclaimed him. Mana coins clinked onto the cave floor, the only sound breaking the silence.

Morgan exhaled, the rush of adrenaline finally catching up with her. She glanced at her hands, her fingers still tingling from the power she had channeled through the bracers. It had worked. They had won.

She looked up to see Viki wiping down her bow with a satisfied smirk on her face, clearly pleased with how the battle had played out. Liam, on the other hand, was already poking around the scattered coins and loot, ever the opportunist.

Morgan felt the last of the tension drain from her shoulders. The boss fight had gone smoother than she'd anticipated, and though her heart still raced from the excitement, she couldn't help but feel a swell of pride for how well they'd worked together. The plan had been executed perfectly—everyone playing their role just as they had discussed.

"You okay?" Viki asked, glancing at her as she slung her bow over her shoulder, her voice casual but with a hint of concern.

"Yeah," Morgan replied with a small smile. "That went well, better than I expected."

Viki nodded, her eyes scanning the cave for anything that might still be lurking in the shadows. "Those kobolds didn't stand a chance."

"No, they didn't," Morgan agreed, her gaze following Viki's for a moment, half-expecting to see something else emerge from the darkness. But there was nothing. The cave was silent now, save for the faint sound of clinking coins as Liam continued gathering the loot.

Liam's voice broke the quiet as he approached them, holding a handful of mana coins. "Here's the coins. Not bad for a low-level dungeon." He grinned, tossing a coin in the air and catching it with ease. The easy time they had apparently lifted his spirits.

"So, what's next?" Viki asked, leaning against the wall of the cave, looking at both Morgan and Liam expectantly.

Morgan blinked, the question pulling her out of her thoughts. Next? She hadn't thought that far ahead. She glanced at Liam.

"Next? We get out of here," Liam said with a laugh, pointing back at the blocked entrance. "That rockslide might've trapped us, but the System will let us out now that the boss is dead."

Almost as if triggered by his words, a rumble sounded as the System responded to the completion of the dungeon. The rockslide that had once trapped them crumbled away, revealing the exit back into the marshy landscape beyond. Fresh air rushed into the cave, carrying with it the promise of the world outside.

Morgan nodded, though her thoughts were already elsewhere. The fight had gone well, but the nagging feeling she'd had since they'd first entered the dungeon lingered. The kobold shaman had been strong, yes, but they had taken him down with relative ease. It made her wonder if they'd be this lucky in future dungeons or if they were just riding the high of their current advantages.

Liam must have noticed her expression because he nudged her lightly. "Hey, you did great. Relax a little."

Morgan gave him a soft smile. "I know, I just... I guess I'm thinking about what's coming next. We're not always going to have an easy time like this."

"No, we're not," Liam agreed, his tone more serious now. "But that's why we're doing this. Practice. So when the hard stuff comes, you'll be ready."

Viki chimed in, her voice confident. "Besides, we've got each other. We'll figure it out."

Morgan looked between the two of them and nodded. They were right. They had made it through this dungeon together, and they would do the same with whatever came next. They had to. She just couldn't help thinking that all too soon, Liam would be leaving them to do this on their own.

Taking one last look around the cave, Morgan exhaled slowly. "Alright, let's grab the loot and get out of here. I could use a break."

Liam chuckled, "We'll take time for a late lunch, but then we need to do it again. We'll do it faster next time. But first, it's time to collect our rewards. I'd say we earned it."

Morgan couldn't argue with that. She followed him toward the back of the cave, the tension from the battle finally loosening its grip as they surrounded the treasure chest. For now, at least.

CHAPTER 8

LOOT, RINSE, AND REPEAT!

LIAM

Loot time! This was my favorite part of every dungeon, and that was especially true since this was still new to me. In my first life, dungeons were faced with fear and trepidation and often required long down-times in between to heal the injuries I incurred.

Healers had been so rare the first time around that they were either like overworked trauma surgeons in the old world, too busy to rest for more than the briefest moment. They tried to heal everyone but were never able to keep up. Or the opposite: indolent bastards who knew they were in such high demand that they could get away with anything, charging exorbitant fees and only seeing patients who could afford it, leaving the rest to die or suffer.

Morgan had no idea how much I appreciated her and having her available to heal me anytime I needed it. It was such a luxury and gave me a completely different mindset toward tackling dungeons. That's why I hadn't minded in the least giving her that set of bracers. They would have made me marginally stronger and would have come in handy in boss fights for their once-a-day special ability, but in her hands, they were invaluable. I'd give all my share of treasure from this run, too, if that's what it took to keep her happy.

We gathered around the filthy-looking box, which was this dungeon's treasure chest. Before opening it, we glanced at one another for a moment, unspoken thoughts of anticipation and excitement passing between us.

While these boxes were rarely ever trapped unless it was a trap-type dungeon, it had been known to happen. I was a little wary as I used my sword to push the lid open. I stood just a little to the side, ensuring that I was not in front of the chest in case it had a needle-shooting type of trap, which was the most common.

With a sigh of relief, we leaned closer and peered inside.

The inside of the chest was very different from how it appeared on the outside. The filthy exterior tried to make us think we'd find a pile of junk—rusty coins, maybe a cracked dagger, something grimy. Instead, everything inside was arranged neatly, and each item looked like it had just been placed there, waiting for us.

Right on top was a dark, sleek cloak. It practically shimmered, like it knew it was something special. I recognized it instantly: The Cloak of Evasion. The faint runes along the inner lining were a dead giveaway. My heart skipped a beat. I'd heard of this cloak. I reached for it without hesitation, grinning as I held it up.

"I'm going to take this item if that's okay with you two; this will come in handy later when I'm soloing dungeons," I said, giving it a quick shake. The fabric rippled in a way that seemed unnatural, almost eager to be worn. This was going to come in handy, especially with how much I relied on speed and dodging. I could already feel it boosting my agility.

Next, tucked underneath the cloak, were a pair of Reinforced Leather Bracers. Viki leaned in before I could say anything and grabbed them, her eyes lighting up.

"These are perfect," she said, sliding them on. They were lightweight but reinforced with small iron plates, perfect for an archer. She tested the fit, flexing her wrists. "Definitely better than what I've been using."

I nodded, watching her adjust them. I knew she was already thinking about how they'd help her with the Heartseeker. It was a solid upgrade. I was a little surprised, though, to see her lovingly put her old bracers into her storage ring. They had been part of her Ren Faire costume, which had become her outfit after the apocalypse. Clearly, they had sentimental value, even if the new bracers were far better.

I didn't blame her, but I felt a little pang of sadness. Nothing from my old life had survived. I hadn't even tried to keep it since I knew the System would destroy everything. The only thing I really regretted losing was my photo of me and my dad.

At least I got to see it again after being reborn before everything went to shit again.

Then, there was one last item. I saw it before anyone else—a small silver ring with a faint blue gemstone. The Ring of Minor Mana Regeneration. I glanced over at Morgan, who was already eyeing it. I picked it up and handed it to her.

"This is all you," I said. She took it carefully, slipping it onto her finger. I could see the slight tension in her shoulders relax a bit as the ring's magic flowed through her. It wasn't a massive upgrade, but I knew it'd give her just enough mana to keep casting during more challenging fights.

Morgan smiled, holding up her hand to admire the ring. "This is exactly what I needed."

She chuckled darkly and added, "Not that this dungeon offered enough challenge to make me run out of mana, but I'm sure it will be a problem in tougher fights."

Although I didn't suffer from that problem, being a hybrid Class that was as much about melee combat as magic, I did appreciate her need and could empathize.

I threw the cloak over my shoulders, fastening it at the neck. It felt... right. Like it was made for me. Viki was already adjusting her new bracers, flexing her arms to get a feel for them. Morgan seemed content with her ring, her usual quiet confidence returning as she tested its effects.

"Not bad," I said, grinning. "Looks like we got what we needed."

Viki nodded, clearly pleased. "Better than I expected."

"From my experience, the System does frequently provide something that would be useful to each party member. Not always, but often enough that it seems to be a trend. In this case, our Luck stats probably influenced the System to make them even more targeted to our needs. A regular party wouldn't likely have gotten items this good."

I looked back at the chest, now empty except for the usual mana and healing potions. Beginner dungeon or not, this loot was a nice little boost. We'd take what we could get. The System had come through for us this time, even if it was only due to our Luck stats.

It was a shame that we didn't get a boss drop as well, but that was one of the downsides of running with a party. Bosses only dropped loot items if soloed. I didn't know if it was the System or AI trying to be cheap, but if I ever got a chance to talk with the damned machine again, I would have words about that. A lot more people would have survived the apocalypse if the stingy AI had been more generous with item drops. In video games, the loot would randomly drop after most kills, but under the System, it only happened after boss fights, leaving most people to never have good enough gear, especially at the lowest levels.

"Alright," I said, standing up, dismissing those thoughts. "Let's hope the next run is just as generous."

Exiting back out into the harsh afternoon sun was a shock to the System, even with stats like ours. Even as we were blinking and adjusting, someone was waiting outside. It was the team of teens that had been arguing with Karl, trying to get permission to enter.

The kids were clearly waiting to see if we would come out successfully and were in shock that we were done so soon. They had expectant looks on their faces as their leader, the hunter asked, "Can you take us with you if you go back in a second time? We would really appreciate it if you could show us the ropes. We talked, and we'd be willing to give you all of the loot that drops. Even if it's only for the chance to watch how you guys do it."

It hurt my heart to see them and not be able to do more than offer a few encouraging words. If things weren't so desperate, I would have gladly spent an afternoon not just letting them tag along but teaching these kids all the basics of dungeon delving so that they could, in turn, teach others. Unfortunately, we were now in a race with the champions of the other AI world nodes. Either I would hit Level 100 and enter the Ascension quest system, or the champions would find me and try to kill me.

I knew we couldn't let them slow us down. Still, I figured it wouldn't hurt to allow them to enter with us as long as they weren't in the same party. That way, they wouldn't cut down on our experience. Morgan and Viki had both gotten one level off that first run just before the boss fight. Sadly, it would take at least three of these runs for me to gain a level.

I looked at both of the girls, and they shrugged to say it didn't matter to them. Viki voiced my concern, though, "They can't be in our group, though. Otherwise, they'd take our experience."

The group looked bummed for a second, but the hunter hurried to assure us, "Not getting experience is fine. Just watching you guys and how to do it will be worth it. I'm Kevin, by the way, Hunter Class, and this is Anna, she's an archer. Megan is a rogue, Aiden is a fighter, and Braden is a blacksmith."

Pointing to my chest, "Liam, I've got a hybrid Class, both magic and melee." Then, gesturing toward the girls, "Morgan is a healer, and Viki is an Archer Class. We've all got high-tier rare Classes, so don't compare yourselves to what you see us do. Also, when you see how incredible it is to have magic, try not to be too depressed, and, if possible, be sure to pick up Class upgrades that have magic when you get to Level 30."

They looked eager to see what we could do, but we needed a short break and some lunch before heading back inside.

Kevin

Thirty minutes later, the group headed back in for a second go at this kobold dungeon.

Kevin had played a lot of video games before the apocalypse, so he was familiar with the concept of dungeon diving. Still, it was entirely different to experience it himself, first hand. Well, witnessing it firsthand, they weren't allowed to fight. Still, watching Liam, Viki, and Morgan in action was like watching a group of professional gamers, except in real life. He stood there, trying to keep up, his mind barely able to process what was happening around him. The moment they reentered the kobold dungeon, it was like they flipped a switch. There was no hesitation, no planning, no sneaking through shadows like he expected. Instead, they just charged forward, obliterating anything that got in their way.

The first group of kobolds never stood a chance.

Kevin barely had time to notice the target before Viki had already loosed an arrow from her fancy bow, and it flew so fast that he could scarcely see it. It struck one kobold dead in the chest, dropping it instantly. The other two monsters didn't even have time to react before Liam and Morgan cast spells in unison. A shadowy bolt from Morgan slammed into the second kobold, while Liam's strike with his long dagger ripped through the third. Three enemies down in less than five seconds from engaging the enemy.

Kevin's heart raced as he watched them move. They didn't bother to stop for a breather or plan the next attack. The moment the kobolds turned into golden motes, they were off to the next group, leaving him and the others struggling to keep up.

"Stick close," Liam said, glancing over his shoulder as they moved to the next target. "We're doing it this way because we are experienced and much higher level than these kobolds. Our goal here today is to get some loot to gear up Morgan and Viki and to beat the dungeon a couple times to ensure it doesn't end up causing a dungeon break. It's better to take monsters out fast and efficiently under these circumstances. When your team runs it, you'll need to take it slow and go one group at a time, plan everything carefully, and use every advantage you can give yourselves until you gain some levels and fighting experience. Remember, without a healer, any injury you get will be devastating for your team."

Kevin nodded, not even sure if Liam could see the motion. His eyes were glued to the battlefield ahead, where the next group of kobolds waited. This group had five, but it didn't seem to matter.

"Anna, Megan, focus on using your class abilities as much as possible," Liam continued, his voice calm despite the chaos unfolding around them. "You won't run out of mana or stamina as quickly in a low-level dungeon, so it's good to practice using them consistently. That way, when you hit something harder, your skills will be muscle memory."

Before Kevin could even think, the team was already in action. Viki shot another arrow, and this time, it wasn't just one. Her shot split into three arrows, each one finding its mark with deadly precision. The kobolds barely had time to react before they crumpled to the ground.

The remaining two kobolds turned, preparing to defend themselves, but Morgan raised her hand and cast, and a blast of dark flames engulfed the kobolds, leaving them staggered, weakened, and vulnerable. Liam didn't even wait for them to fall. He charged forward, his long knife glowing with dark energy as he used a skill that hit multiple enemies at once. With one clean swipe, the last two kobolds were done.

Kevin blinked, feeling a little dizzy from how fast everything was happening. This wasn't how his group usually fought. They were used to careful planning, trying to outsmart the monsters rather than overpower them. But these three—Liam, Viki, and Morgan— were a force of nature. It wasn't just the strength they had; it was the way they fought together, each one covering the other without needing to communicate.

"Kevin," Liam called out, breaking him from his thoughts. "When you're in a group, always make sure you're coordinating. Even if it's just small things like having one person draw attention while the others attack. No wasted movements."

"Got it," Kevin managed to say, still in awe of what he was witnessing.

The team pressed forward, mowing through group after group of kobolds. They didn't stop, didn't slow down, just kept moving. Every time the golden motes of light appeared, signaling the monsters' defeat, they waited only long enough for the coins to drop before rushing to the next group. The pace was relentless.

Kevin couldn't help but notice how Viki never missed a shot. Her arrows flew straight and true every time, and her bow seemed to pulse with a subtle, otherworldly glow. He knew it was powerful, but seeing it in action made him realize just how much he still had to learn about being an archer.

"Anna," Liam said as they cleared another group of kobolds, "watch how Viki handles her bow. She's using her skills to enhance every shot. It's not just about pulling the string back and letting it go. Focus on putting energy into each attack."

Anna nodded, wide-eyed, as she watched Viki draw her next arrow. Kevin could tell she was soaking in every detail, trying to figure out how she could apply that to her own archery.

The next group was a bit larger, and Kevin felt the familiar tension rise in his chest as they approached. Six kobolds, all armed and ready. But Liam didn't seem worried. He raised a hand and motioned for Morgan to take the lead.

"Morgan, AoE them," Liam said, his voice calm but commanding.

Morgan nodded and raised her hand again. With a quick incantation, she unleashed another burst of dark fire, the flames spreading out and enveloping the entire group. The kobolds staggered, weakened by the spell, but before they could recover, Liam cast his own spell. The effect pulled the remaining kobolds together, trapping them in the center of a swirling vortex of energy before detonating with an explosion of dark power. When the dust cleared, nothing was left but golden motes and mana coins.

Kevin swallowed hard, his heart still racing as he tried to wrap his head around what he'd just witnessed.

"That's how you handle groups," Liam said with a chuckle, glancing back at the teens. "When you've got AoE, use it. It's faster, more efficient, and it keeps you from getting overwhelmed."

Kevin nodded again, feeling a mixture of awe and determination. He wanted to fight like that. He wanted to be that strong, that confident. But he knew he had a long way to go. Still, watching Liam, Viki, and Morgan tear through the dungeon like it was nothing gave him hope. Maybe one day, he'd be able to fight like that, too.

By the time they reached the end of the dungeon, Kevin was exhausted just from watching them. They hadn't slowed down once, and while he knew they were on a different level, it was still incredible to see how powerful they were.

Liam turned to the group of teens and gave a small smile. "Alright, that's how it's done. I would say we were showing off, but honestly, we ran it once already, so we knew what to expect, and these guys are just flat-out too weak to threaten us. For you, my advice is to stick with your class, practice your skills, and don't get discouraged. Everyone starts somewhere, and get some magic! Recruit a magic user, upgrade your Class at Level 30, but get some magic."

Kevin couldn't help but smile back. He still had a lot to learn, but now, he had something to aim for.

CHAPTER 9
SECONDARY QUEST

LIAM

The teens left us to the treasure, not even staying to witness what we got, perhaps a little depressed that they wouldn't get anything due to their agreement. They needn't have bothered, though, since they hadn't participated in the fights. The System wouldn't drop any loot for them, anyway.

Still, it was nice when we gathered around the dirty box the second time to not have witnesses to what we received. Following my usual, careful procedure, I opened the box.

What we saw was intriguing. Before we picked anything up, I did a quick Analyze using Treasure Sense and received a surprising amount of information, and shared the results with the party.

Enchanted Skinning Knife

Type: Tool (Skinning Knife)
Rarity: Rare

Description: A finely crafted skinning knife enchanted with precision and care. Designed for the efficient harvesting of hides, this blade ensures cleaner cuts and higher-quality materials, making it ideal for those interested in crafting or trade.

Effect: +15% chance to improve the grade of hides when skinning, resulting in higher-quality materials for crafting or sale. Reduces the time taken for skinning by 25%. The enchantment ensures a smooth cut, reducing waste when collecting resources.

Ring of Spatial Storage

Type: Ring (Storage Item)
Rarity: Uncommon
Description: A simple silver band inlaid with a small gem that glows faintly. This ring allows the wearer to store items in an extra-dimensional space, making it highly useful for adventurers who need to travel light but carry a lot.

Effect: Grants 15 cubic feet of storage. No weight limit, but limited by volume. Time does not exist within the space. The wearer can access stored items mentally, making it fast and efficient in combat situations.

Hunter's Shadow Cloak

Type: Cloak
Rarity: Uncommon
Description: This cloak is made of dark, lightweight fabric, ideal for stealth and speed. It blends into shadows easily, making it harder for enemies to spot the wearer.

Effect: +15% to stealth effectiveness. +5% to movement speed in low-light or shadowed environments. Slightly reduces detection range by enemies while in stealth.

"Nice! Morgan, that ring is for you. It's a storage ring. No more stuffing things into pockets for you! Viki, I've already got a cloak, so you take that one, and I'll take the skinning knife."

Morgan looked torn. "This ring is the coolest thing ever, but I just looked at my status, and I'm two kobolds away from leveling." She gave a big sigh. "I know it is silly to be bothered by that, but still. I'm sooo close!"

"First-world dungeon problems!" Liam chuckled. "Just kidding. It's simple: when we go out, just run back in with the kids, kill two monsters real quick, and jump back out. I'm sure they are about to try their own dungeon run, so just go in and come right back out. Viki and I will be waiting, but we need to talk to Karl anyway."

That seemed to cheer her up, and she swelled with pride just a bit when she realized that I trusted her to solo this dungeon now, or at least the beginning part.

We quickly donned our new items, although mine went into my storage ring rather than on my belt. However, after Viki put on her new cloak, we looked like a matched pair. She just needed some good rogue-type armor, and we'd be twinsies. I couldn't help but smirk at the thought of that.

It felt good to have people in my life again that I liked and could trust, but there was always the thought in the back of my mind that I should be off on my own, not burning precious hours on other people. It felt a lot like survivor's guilt, like I was being selfish by having this.

I squashed those thoughts. Even if it weren't optimal, I needed them in more ways than one. They would help spread the word, and that would save tens of thousands of lives in the immediate short term, which meant a much more solid base to build a new civilization if I did make it to Level Cap and managed to make the world off-limits to invaders.

That's what I'd tell myself, but part of me knew the truth; that I had been dying in my first life long before that high orcs's axe split my head. Hope was gone. Everyone I had ever cared about was dead. In the end, I had just been doggedly surviving and holding on, the way a climber grasps onto that tiny tuft of grass growing out of the cliff face, knowing it won't hold, but doing it anyway because you can't allow yourself to just give up.

"Okay, I'm going to run out and catch those kids before they jump into their own instance of the dungeon. I'll meet you guys in a few minutes over where you talked to Karl earlier." With that, Morgan was gone, leaving Viki and me to divide the coins. We'd give Morgan her share when she came out of the dungeon.

Fifteen minutes later, we were sitting outside of Karl's command tent, looking over the potential recruits he had gathered. They all seemed to be decent candidates, but Shane was hands down the winner. He had the Hunter Class and had been part of the team that Karl beat the Kobold dungeon with, so we knew he had some decent experience, at least compared to all the other new System users that existed right now. While hunters didn't have any magic, Shane Milligan would be good at traveling skillfully through the terrain around Dallas, thanks to his class skills. That would give him a good advantage for a Herald. He should be able to survive moving between cities. The more we could get the word out fast with the heralds we were going to power-level, the more lives could be saved. We needed to get people moving out of the cities while it was still safe enough to go into them and spread the message.

Plus, he had gotten to Level 5 before his injury, so we wouldn't have to start entirely from scratch.

However, the best thing about him was that he now seemed to be utterly fanatical about protecting Morgan. She had saved him from certain death with her healing magic before, and now he was at full health just two hours later. If religions were an actual thing, I think he would have converted to the Church of Morgan. It wasn't in a creepy way, though. He was just incredibly thankful to be alive and felt he owed her a life debt. So he volunteered the minute Karl started looking for candidates.

I quietly checked with the girls first since they would be the ones power-leveling people, but they had no objections.

"Shane, get whatever gear you need and be ready to go in fifteen minutes; we need to rush off and find the next dungeon. We will be traveling down Highway 75 toward downtown to start with, but if we hear rumors of dungeons off the highway, we may go check them out."

When he returned a few minutes later, his bow surprised me. I could tell by the color that it was made from Osage Orange. Osage trees had a bunch of other names, Bois D'arc, hedge apple, bowwood, and more. It was what the Native tribes in this part of the country had used. It was supposed to be some of the best wood to make a bow from, and it was clearly made using traditional methods, given that it hadn't fallen apart. It was hide and bead wrapped and had a pair of hawk feathers tied to one end. Very traditional.

Seeing me stare at his bow, Shane got a bit defensive. "What? My grandmother on my mother's side was full-blood Caddo. I learned to hunt traditional style with a bow for a challenge."

Holding up my hands, I said, "No worries, man. You just look more like a guy who would wear a kilt than deerskin, I was just surprised by how traditional your bow is. That's a good-looking weapon."

He seemed appeased at the compliment but laughed and added, "I'm Scottish on my father's side, and I happen to have a kilt in my clan tartan, but I don't want to wear it and get it dirty. Real wool from Scotland."

That got a chuckle out of everyone.

"Fine, I'm not judging. In a year, there won't be much left from before the System. Hang onto it, and treasure it."

Looking to the ex-cop leader of this camp, "Before we go, there is something you need to know. If you let people complete the dungeon more than six times per day, it will be destroyed and disappear. Only do that if you want to destroy it, but it is a fairly easy dungeon, so I'd suggest you treat it like a resource and get these people leveled up." I gestured around us at the desperate people of the camp.

"That's the only way they will survive in this new world. It is harsh but true. Even if they have crafting classes, it wouldn't hurt to get them some experience in a low-level dungeon like that."

From the look on Karl's face, I could tell the idea of destroying dungeons was very appealing, but he seemed competent enough to realize my advice about leveling people was sound. He glanced over at his friend Shane, who was happy and healthy again and was conflicted when he returned his gaze to me.

I continued, "One last thing, monsters disappear, but if you start to skin them or harvest them in some way before the minute is up, they will stick around. That doesn't help much with kobolds since they have nothing worth harvesting, but if you find other dungeons with monster types that are edible or have hides to make armor from, that can be very useful. The System Shop will open after the first month, but you can still sell things through the shop that your crafters make."

The big man looked thoughtful before replying, "Thanks. I'll keep that in mind."

After that, we set off, having shared everything that needed to be said.

As we jogged down the road, it was evident that Shane was the weak link. Even Morgan, with her special class, had fifteen points in all of her physical stats, making her half again better than the best Olympic athletes before Initialization. Poor Shane was struggling to keep up with our leisurely pace, which was faster than normal people could sprint at. It was costing us a little time, but having heralds go out and spread the word was super important, too; enough so that I was willing to lose half an hour by traveling at a slower pace.

That also gave us a chance to talk and share our information. Morgan and Viki had just both leveled up twice in the Kobold dungeon, once on each run. Viki was Level 12, and Morgan had hit 14.

They also shared their statuses. The fact that they had managed to get one level per run of that low-level dungeon was outstanding, considering the XP was getting split three ways, and we were all over-leveled for such low-level creatures.

Morgan Pickering

Dragon Priestess - Level 14
Dragon Pacts: Shadow Dragon / Night Dragon

Experience - 153/20480

Attributes:
Endurance: 15
Strength: 15
Agility: 15
Mind: 35
Will: 20

Magical Aptitude: 34
Luck: 2

Health: 300/300
Mana: 890/890

Abilities:
Active: Commune, Summon, Umbral Cloak (Pact)
Passive: Dark Vision (Pact)

Spells:
Blessing of the Dragon's Grace
Draconic Vitality
Shadow Bolt
Purifying Touch
Cleansing Ray
Shadowflame Burst

Shane was aghast at seeing her stats and her epic grade Class. He almost stumbled and had to struggle to catch back up as he began to fall behind.

"Are you kidding me? Holy shit! I don't think anyone in camp had higher than uncommon. How do you even manage something crazy like Dragon Priestess? Did you have to pray to a dragon god? Are gods even real in the System?"

I chuckled, "You haven't seen anything yet. But don't feel too bad. They are special cases because of me. I told everyone earlier about getting sent back in time by the System, but what I didn't tell you all was that when it came time for class selection, I saw that there were a number of limited Classes. Meaning only one or a handful of people in the entire world could get them. I guess I got access to some crazy cool options because I had been exposed to magic during my last life. So I picked a Class with a Bloodline - Draconic Spellsword."

I went on to explain my class and how that led to both Viki and Morgan getting their own classes.

"Damn! I wish you had been with me when Initialization hit; maybe I'd have been lucky like you guys, too."

Giving him a sympathetic look, "Don't sweat it. Hunter is actually a pretty decent starting class, and now that you know, keep some mana coins on you and learn what you can about magic, and when you hit Level 30, you'll almost certainly get offered an upgrade option with some magic to it. Maybe Arcane Archer or something like that."

Viki chimed in, "I was offered something like that as one of my class options, and it looked pretty cool, but I picked the Dragon Bloodline since I could. If I hadn't had the dragon option, I definitely would have taken Arcane Archer. Here's my status."

Victoria Blue, aka Viki:

Draconic Sniper - Level 12
Bloodline (Tier 2): Night Dragon

Experience: 5004/16800

Attributes:
Endurance: 30
Strength: 30
Agility: 31
Mind: 30
Will: 30
Magical Aptitude: 29

Luck: 2

Health: 600/600
Mana: 590/590

Abilities:
Active: Shadow Veil
Passive: Dark Vision

Active Skills:
Arrow: Night
Arrow: Shadow Bind
Eclipse Barrage

Passive Skills:
None

Active Spells:
Whispering Bolt
Gloom Shroud
Midnight's Grasp

Shane's eyes almost bugged out. "Holy shit! You people are monsters! You are more than three times as strong as me, and you're just a kid...."

Realizing what he had said and how that might be taken after the apocalypse, he hastily added, "In a good way, I mean!"

Viki frowned for a second but said. "It's okay, I know what you mean. I guess Liam and I aren't exactly human anymore, anyway. But be careful about calling people monsters."

I could feel the pain behind her words. Anything to do with monsters was definitely a sore spot for her. Someday, I was sure she would open up and tell me about her family, but until then, I'd be here for her.

Thankfully, Shane dropped it, and I didn't share my stats, or it would have really blown his mind.

After that, we changed subjects and talked about dungeons and what we were expecting from him in exchange for power-leveling him.

"How familiar are you with the DFW metroplex, Shane? Do you remember the map pretty well?"

He was thoughtful for a second before saying, "Yeah, I've got a pretty good memory of it. You are talking about the satellite maps from the search engine company?"

"Yeah. Do you remember looking at those and how you could see where all the major streets crossed one another on the map, and it looked like little white dots?"

I had spent a good couple of hours with the maps on my computer while prepping for the apocalypse after getting sent back in time, so they were all fresh on my mind, and with my increased Mind stat, my memory was excellent now.

"Sure. I kinda remember what you are talking about. That's because all the major intersections had shopping centers surrounding them, right?"

"That's right. Just like where 380 and 75 crossed..."

I let him stew on that for a long minute, wondering why I would bring up something so random. I could see when the lightbulb went on. His eyes got huge, and his face went pale despite how red it had been from all the running.

"Are you telling me every one of those is going to have a dungeon? That would be hundreds of them in the city!"

I nodded sadly, agreeing. "Yeah, but it's even worse than that. Most of those will have a small, low-level dungeon. All that matter will have to be reclaimed and converted into something by the System. But what do you think will happen to the really big areas? The areas that were filled not just with shopping centers but actual industrial zones or big office parks? Worse, what about areas like downtown or Irving with its clusters of office parks?"

Poor Shane was practically in shock now. "I mean, I knew it was bad with all the technology not working and buildings all falling apart, but this....?"

He was at a loss for words, but that was good because we had just come up on our next target. I didn't know where it would be or if it had even finished forming yet, but I knew there would be another low-level dungeon somewhere around the area where Eldorado and 75 met. It wasn't as big of a shopping center as the one we had just left, but it was plenty big enough to form a dungeon.

"This should be another nexus. All those car dealerships and businesses along the highway we passed held a lot of material that had to go somewhere. Then, the highway interchange where 75 meets 121 is just to the south of us. This seems like the perfect middle ground for there to be another one."

It didn't take long to find. The highway went under an elevated roadway that was Eldorado Avenue, and beneath it, on the west side, was a glowing doorway in the vertical embankment seemingly leading underground. Unlike the north side of McKinney, there was no encampment of refugees. There were still people roaming around the area, but these were homeowners trying to scavenge whatever might still be lootable from the various stores and businesses. To the west, we could see what looked like a dark forest. That area of town had been a fairly ritzy area with big old trees and fancy houses. Now it looked like the System was giving it back to nature.

We didn't have time to worry about that. Perhaps there was a dungeon or beasts in that forest, but I had to stick to the easy pickings and go where I was almost certain to find challenges. I didn't have time to hunt around.

Not knowing what to expect but being confident we could handle it, I didn't hesitate and led the party straight to the door, trying unsuccessfully to avoid the System's intrusive messaging.

The dungeon entrance pulsed with an eerie, greenish glow, the shimmering doorway embedded within the embankment like a wound in the earth. Faint tendrils of mist coiled outward from its threshold, curling along the cracked pavement like spectral fingers. The air was thick here, charged with a low hum of energy that set my nerves on edge. Unlike the chaotic, ruined streets behind us, this place felt unnaturally still, as if the world itself was holding its breath. The symbols etched around the portal's edges flickered, shifting subtly like they were alive, whispering an unspoken challenge to any who dared step inside.

Before we went in, I looked at Shane, who seemed much more subdued since learning the true scale of the threat we faced. "I would say this is your last chance to turn back, but that would be bullshit. We all passed that point the moment the System arrived. Follow along, try to be stealthy and not alert any monsters to our presence, and watch us. When we engage, feel free to use your bow and get some practice, but don't do anything stupid."

"Got it."

CHAPTER 10

POWER-LEVELED HERALD

As I stepped through the glowing doorway, the world shifted around me. What had been a crumbling overpass outside transformed into something otherworldly, the familiar smell of city air replaced with the crisp, clean scent of ancient trees and damp earth. The System had a way of dressing things up, making even the most dangerous places look like something out of a fantasy painting. And this was no exception. The moment my foot touched the soft, moss-covered ground on the other side, I was greeted by towering trees, their bark shimmering with a faint bioluminescent glow. They stretched impossibly high, the canopy so thick it blocked out what I would have thought was the sky—if not for the faint flickers of what looked like stars scattered among the branches. The illusion was almost perfect.

Soft, golden light filtered down through the leaves, casting long, dancing shadows on the ground. It felt like walking into an enchanted forest from some long-lost myth, where you half-expected to see elves peeking from behind trees or faeries flitting among the glowing flowers. The air was alive with the hum of magic, a reminder that this wasn't just some pleasant woodland retreat but a living, breathing dungeon designed to lure you in with its beauty before unleashing its dangers. It was stunning, but I knew better than to trust the illusion. Beneath the surface, the System always had its tricks.

Still, even I had to admit, the place was impressive. The bioluminescent fungus clung to the trees like tiny stars, casting a serene, soft glow over everything. The colors were more vibrant than anything in the real world, the kind of hues you only see in dreams.

I shook off the System imposed reverie. I had been in a couple of forest-type dungeons in my first life, and I liked them. It was a shame the AI had chosen to be such a dick and stack the deck against us. In a better Apocalypse, humanity might be able to use dungeons like this for resources, but we hadn't stood a chance. We had always been on the back foot and were never able to establish ourselves enough. Free unlimited old-growth lumber would be super valuable if we had the infrastructure to capitalize on it. Still, it was hard to set up lumbermills when you couldn't even defend people from the beasts and monsters.

I vowed that this time would be different.

Shane

The transition hit him like a punch to the gut. One second, he'd been under the overpass, the world around him gray and broken, and the next, he was standing in the middle of a forest that seemed to stretch on forever. He blinked in disbelief, trying to wrap his head around the sudden change. Everything about this place screamed *unreal*, from the way the trees seemed to glow with a soft, almost welcoming light to the way the air felt charged like it was alive with some ancient power. Shane's heart pounded in his chest as he took it all in, his earlier fear momentarily forgotten. This... this was what magic looked like.

But despite the beauty of it all, a chill ran down his spine. The System had made this, and he'd already seen enough to know that nothing the System created was as harmless as it seemed.

***

Liam

We moved silently through the enchanted grove, the faint glow of bioluminescent fungi casting eerie, shifting shadows. It was quiet, but not in a peaceful way. More like the calm before a storm. The sort of quiet that made the hairs on the back of my neck stand on end. The System was good at this—creating atmospheres that lulled you into thinking you were safe, just waiting for you to drop your guard.

I knew better.

Shane, Viki, Morgan, and I were using stealth, blending into the shadows and keeping our profiles low. Shane wasn't bad—his Hunter-based stealth skill worked well enough, and while he didn't have the same experience as the rest of us, he wasn't making any obvious mistakes. Yet. I gave him credit for staying quiet and alert, even if his breathing was a little too quick for my liking. Nerves, most likely.

The first group we encountered were corrupted sprites, barely visible as they flitted between the trees, their faint glow giving them away. Three of them, small and fast, darted through the underbrush like restless fireflies. I signaled to the group, gesturing for a quick, silent takedown. Viki and Shane nodded while Morgan prepared to back us up with her spells if things went sideways.

Viki knocked an arrow, her Heartseeker Longbow gleaming faintly in the low light, and took aim. Her arrows were practically invisible when she fired them, and the silence that followed each shot was almost unnerving, thanks to her Class arrow skills. I gave a short nod, and in one fluid motion, she loosed an arrow straight through the closest sprite. It didn't even have time to register the hit before it collapsed to the ground, its sickly glow flickering out like a dying ember.

Shane followed up, a little slower but still decent, launching a well-placed shot that took down the second sprite. He wasn't as precise as Viki, but the kill was clean enough. The third sprite barely had time to react before Morgan finished it off with a flick of her wrist, her Shadow Bolt flying through the air and striking it dead center. All three were down before they could raise an alarm.

A minute later, I crouched down, collecting the mana coins that had dropped as the System reclaimed the bodies, dispersing them into glittering motes of light. There were five coins per body, indicating they were Level 5; not bad, we would be getting greater experience from this dungeon than the last one. It was a little surprising they went down so easily, given their level, but they definitely didn't look very sturdy. I imagined their magic and agility were their strong points rather than toughness.

Splitting them evenly between the party, we continued moving forward. It was a good start, but I couldn't shake the feeling that things were going too smoothly. Maybe I was just paranoid, or perhaps it was the fact that this dungeon had been too easy so far.

As we moved deeper into the dungeon, the forest seemed to get darker and more oppressive. The glowing fungus was still there, but the trees were thicker, the underbrush heavier. The air felt heavier, too, like the magic in this place was slowly pressing down on us. Maybe it was just the System-created ambiance invading our minds, but the atmosphere seemed vaguely toxic, as though prolonged exposure would be unhealthy and might warp us into something that is not quite human.

I chuckled quietly at the thought. *Well, not quite human in a bad way, at least!*

On second thought, maybe this dungeon wouldn't be good for harvesting resources. If the trees retained some of that toxic mana, who knows what side effects might be caused by anything built from such lumber. Visions of saving this dungeon and using it vanished from my thoughts. We would need to destroy it.

Up ahead, we spotted another group of enemies—a pair of Vine Beasts slithering through the dense foliage, their thorny tendrils dragging along the ground as they searched for prey. These weren't like the sprites; they were big, slow-moving, and tough. Their thorny limbs writhed and stretched as they moved, ready to lash out and ensnare anything that came too close.

"Let's take them down quickly," I whispered. "Viki, focus on the one on the left. I'll take the right. Shane, stay back and support. Morgan, be ready to blast them with AoE if they get too close, but be careful where you drop any fire spells. It would suck to be stuck in the middle of a forest fire. Assuming the dungeon would even allow that."

We all moved into position, crouched low, blending into the shadows cast by the bioluminescent trees. I signaled with my hand, and Viki and I launched our attacks in unison. My Draconic Strike slashed across the Vine Beast on the right, carving through its thick vines and leaving a glowing mark of weakness. The beast let out a low, rumbling growl, turning its attention toward me as its tendrils whipped out in response.

But it didn't slow down. I ducked under the first vine, then slashed another away as it swung toward me. This wasn't going to be as simple as the sprites.

Viki's arrow struck the left Vine Beast, but unlike the smaller enemies we'd faced earlier, this one wasn't going down without a fight. The creature staggered from the impact but kept coming, its thorn-covered limbs reaching out toward her. She fired again, and though it pierced through the thick vines that made up its body, the thing seemed to barely register the hit.

"These things are tougher than I thought!" she called out, a tinge of frustration in her voice.

Then, Shane fired off an arrow of his own, and that's when things went from bad to worse.

His arrow hit the Vine Beast on my right, striking it square in the side, but instead of slowing it down, it only seemed to enrage the creature. With a furious roar, it abandoned its focus on me and turned to charge directly toward Shane, its thorny limbs flailing wildly as it closed the distance.

Shane froze for a second, his eyes wide in shock. "Oh, shit!" he yelled, scrambling backward, but the thing was too fast.

"Shane, get back!" I shouted, already moving to intercept, but Viki was faster.

"Hold on!" she yelled, her voice tense. Without hesitating, she whipped around, abandoning her target to fire her most powerful spell: Midnight's Grasp.

A spectral dragon's claw erupted from the shadows, reaching out and latching onto the Vine Beast charging Shane. Its thorny vines snapped and writhed, trying to break free, but the claw held tight, digging into the creature's body, keeping it locked in place. Shane scrambled away, panting in relief, but Viki had paid a price for diverting her attention.

Her own target, now dangerously close, lashed out with its thorny tendrils, forcing her to dive to the side. She rolled to her feet, bow already swapped for her Cleaver of the Fallen Shaman, its blade gleaming in the faint light. The Vine Beast lunged at her, but at the last second, Viki cast Night and dove to the side again. Her burst of shadow magic plunged the area around her into Darkness.

The creature flailed wildly, its vision blinded by the spell, its attacks becoming erratic as it tried to locate her. Viki dodged to the left, narrowly avoiding a swipe that would have impaled her, and then swung the cleaver down hard, landing a blow on the Vine Beast's side.

I saw her eyes widen in shock as the creature, though wounded, continued to fight back, thrashing at her even more wildly.

She barely had time to duck under another vine as she struck again, this time targeting its neck. But it wasn't enough. The Vine Beast lashed out blindly, and Viki dodged again, her heart pounding as she narrowly avoided the deadly thorns.

"Liam!" Shane called out, panic clear in his voice as the Vine Beast, still held by **Midnight's Grasp**, began to break free, its tendrils snapping and twisting with increasing strength.

I cursed under my breath. Everything was happening too fast. My instinct screamed to rush to Viki's aid, but she could handle herself —she had to. Shane, on the other hand, wouldn't stand a chance if that thing got loose.

"Keep your distance!" I barked at Shane, already charging forward. The Vine Beast had nearly torn free of **Midnight's Grasp**, its body twitching violently as it fought to break the spectral claw's hold. I had seconds to reach it before Shane was in real trouble.

I summoned the energy for a **Draconic Strike**, closing the gap in an instant. My blade slammed down into the creature's thorny form, the impact sending a shockwave of shadow energy through it. The thing let out a final, guttural hiss and died.

But Viki was still fighting hers.

I turned, ready to rush to her side, but what I saw stopped me in my tracks. She had the creature locked in a desperate dance, dodging its blind swings with calculated precision. As it lunged at her, she rolled to the side, bringing the cleaver down on its neck once more. This time, the blade bit deep, severing its head with a sickening crunch.

The creature's body convulsed, then collapsed, dissolving into the same motes of light as the other one.

Viki stood there, breathing hard, her eyes locked on the spot where the Vine Beast had just been. For a second, everything was still. Then, with a quick wipe of her blade on the grass, she sheathed the cleaver and glanced back at me, a small, triumphant grin on her face.

"Not bad," I called out, though the tension still thrummed in my veins.

Shane, meanwhile, was staring at her in awe, his mouth half-open.

Shane

It had all happened so fast. One second, he was about to be torn apart by that monster, and the next, Viki had turned the entire battle around. Watching her move—switching from her bow to her cleaver, casting spells while dodging strikes—was like something out of a game. But this wasn't a game.

She had saved him. No doubt about that.

The way she had taken down that Vine Beast on her own? He couldn't believe it. She was just a kid, right? But she fought like someone who had been doing this for years. There was no hesitation, no second-guessing. Just instinct and skill.

Still, he caught the way her hands shook slightly as she sheathed her weapons. She was good, but even she knew that had been close.

Liam

Viki had pulled it off. Barely.

I exhaled slowly, keeping my expression neutral as I glanced at her. She was steady, but there was tension in her shoulders, the kind that didn't go away after a clean victory. That had been too reactive, too close. If the Vine Beast hadn't been blinded at just the right moment, if it had been just a little faster, that fight could've gone south real quick.

The worst part? They didn't even realize it. They were strong, sure, but too much of that was their overpowered Classes doing the work. This wasn't *a real* combat skill—not yet. The System made you feel invincible right up until it didn't. And if they ever found themselves in a fight where their abilities failed them or their mana ran dry, I wasn't sure they'd make it out.

That needed to change.

"We good?" I asked, scanning the area.

"Yeah," Viki said, catching her breath. "We're good."

Shane gave a shaky nod, rubbing the back of his neck. "Thanks for the save," he muttered, eyes darting to Viki.

She shrugged, but I caught the tension in her posture. She knew. That had been *too* close.

I was about to call for us to move out when I heard a sharp inhale. I turned to see Morgan, her eyes glassy with unshed tears, her fingers curling into fists at her sides. Her jaw clenched, and she let out a frustrated growl.

"I *hate* that," she spat, her voice shaking. "I couldn't do anything! I fired off one Shadow Bolt—*one*—and then it turned on Shane, and after that, everything was a mess. I couldn't even attack properly without risking hitting one of you!"

Viki was already moving before I could respond. She stepped up to Morgan and grabbed her in a fierce hug. "Yeah, but you *did* do something," she said. "I felt your buff hit me. If it weren't for that, I don't know if I could've dodged those vines. That was huge."

Morgan let out a choked breath, her whole body trembling. After a moment, she dropped her forehead against Viki's shoulder, her arms slowly wrapping around her in return. A shaky sob broke free, and I knew the frustration was finally bleeding out.

I stood there, feeling awkward as hell. This wasn't my thing. Never had been. But I also knew what bottling things up did to people. I'd seen it before—too many times. People got hardened, walled themselves off, and then one day, the pressure was too much, and they cracked. I wasn't going to let that happen to them.

Without thinking too hard about it, I stepped forward and put an arm around both of them. Not saying anything. Just... standing there.

Morgan sniffled. Viki squeezed her tighter.

After a minute, I let go, clearing my throat. "Alright," I said, keeping my voice steady. "Let's keep moving. We're not done yet."

CHAPTER II
1 WISH WE HAD FIREBALL!

SHANE

Shane stood back, his bow hanging loosely at his side. The fight had been intense, way more chaotic than he'd expected. But it wasn't the violence that shook him.

It was Morgan.

She wasn't some battle-hardened soldier. She was just... a person. And she had been *furious* at herself for not being able to do more.

For the first time, he realized just how much pressure they were under. It wasn't just about surviving a dungeon run—it was about *not failing each other*.

He felt like an outsider, watching them. The way Viki had hugged Morgan without hesitation, the way Liam—gruff, no-nonsense Liam —had stepped in, offering quiet reassurance without a single word.

Shane shifted uncomfortably, adjusting his grip on his bow. He had thought coming here was just about getting stronger, getting levels. Now, he wasn't so sure.

This wasn't just a team. It was something more. And if he wanted to be part of it, he needed to *step up*.

Liam

As we started moving again, I caught Shane glancing at me, his expression unreadable. Something was turning over in his head, but I didn't have time to dig into it.

We needed to keep moving.

Still, I kept an eye on him. Shane was doing alright—following orders and hitting his shots. But something wasn't clicking.

The more I watched, the more convinced I was that I was right. His aim was good, but was that *him*, or was it just the System boosting his accuracy? Would he still be able to land a shot under real pressure without skill enhancements helping him?

Viki and Morgan weren't much different. Viki's archery was damn impressive, but how much of that was her, and how much was the Heartseeker Longbow? Morgan's spells were powerful, but she still hesitated when things got chaotic.

I needed to push them harder. Teach them how to fight when the System wasn't holding their hand. Because one day, it *wouldn't*. And if that day came before they were ready...

I wasn't going to let that happen.

I adjusted my grip on my spear and picked up the pace.

"Come on," I said, glancing back at them. "We've got more work to do."

I made a mental note to focus more on their fundamentals. They needed to learn how to fight without relying so heavily on their System-enhanced abilities. Viki had great instincts—her reactions were fast, her footwork solid. But instincts weren't enough. Shane's shots were landing, but it wasn't *him* hitting those targets. And Morgan? Her magic was strong, but she hesitated too much, second-guessed herself in the middle of a fight.

If we ever found ourselves in a situation where the System failed us, or we lost access to our Classes, they'd be in trouble. I wasn't about to let that happen.

After that second, unexpectedly tough fight, we took things slower. More deliberate. We still used our System Abilities and Class skills, but I forced them to think beyond just activating skills and watching the numbers go up.

After a while, I could see my message was starting to sink in, so I made them fight *without* their abilities.

"No skills. No buffs. Just you, your weapon, and your instincts."

Viki frowned but nodded, rolling her shoulders as she shifted into a fighting stance. Shane looked uncomfortable, his grip on his bow tightening. Morgan just crossed her arms, glaring at me.

"And what exactly do you want me to do? Throw *really* mean glares at the enemy?" she asked dryly.

I gestured to the gnarled roots sprawling across the forest floor. "You're not always gonna be able to attack. You need to know how to move, how to keep from getting boxed in. And if you don't have a clear shot, you need to make one. Also, you need to be the one calling the shots for your team, focusing as much on battlefield awareness as how much damage you are doing."

Morgan narrowed her eyes but didn't argue.

I started with Viki. We faced off, and I had her fight me using only her physical skills. No Shadowstep, no enchanted arrows, just her bow and a simple, non-magical dagger. I didn't even use my weapons, just my hands.

She was fast; I'd give her that. But her footwork was sloppy, and she hesitated when she had to manually nock and aim her arrows instead of the System assisting her with smooth, near-perfect transitions. Twice, I knocked the dagger from her hand before she could even attempt a counterattack.

"That hesitation is gonna get you killed," I told her as she bent to retrieve her weapon. "You can't always rely on your bow. You need to be comfortable switching weapons *without* the System guiding your hand."

Viki wiped the sweat from her forehead and growled, "Again."

I smirked. At least she had the right attitude.

The impressive thing was that although she wasn't nearly as fast, she still managed to have pretty decent accuracy with the bow. Maybe it was her stats, but then again, she had been killing orcs even before she had that fancy bow or her levels.

Shane was next. I set up makeshift targets—branches swaying in the wind, a stone half-buried in the ground, a flickering glow-shroom in the distance. Targets that *wouldn't* stand still. I made him shoot them *without* activating his auto-aim perks, forcing him to rely on his actual skill.

It was rough. His first few shots went wide, his frustration growing with each miss.

"I don't get it! I was hitting everything fine before—"

"Because the System was doing half the work for you," I interrupted. "And if it ever stops doing that? What then?"

Shane gritted his teeth and adjusted his stance. This time, he took a deep breath before loosing an arrow. It struck the edge of the stone, chipping off a sliver. Not a bullseye, but better.

"Again," I ordered.

Morgan's training was different. She didn't have physical weapons like the others, but I still needed her to think like a fighter and a leader. She couldn't just rely on the System to tell her what to do—she had to develop real instincts, real awareness. I had her practice evading, reading movement, and predicting an enemy's next move instead of just reacting when it was too late. And most importantly, she needed to track everything happening around her. A healer wasn't just there to patch people up; she was the backbone of the entire team. If she made a mistake, if she hesitated at the wrong moment, people died. It was that simple.

"You're not just watching the fight—you're controlling it," I told her. "You decide where we stand, when we push, when we fall back. If a fight turns bad, you are the one who calls the retreat."

She frowned at that. "But that's your job."

I shook my head. "Not always. If I'm in the thick of it, I don't have the whole picture. You do. You see when someone's about to get overwhelmed, when the enemy's movements change, when a situation is slipping out of control. Besides, I won't always be here; what will you do when it's just you and Viki and a herald that you are power-leveling?"

She frowned, not liking the sound of that, and still looked uncertain, so I gave her a different task—figuring out when *not* to attack.

"Magic isn't infinite. If you drain yourself dry at the start of a fight, you're useless for the rest of it," I said. "Sometimes, holding back is the smart move. But that doesn't mean doing nothing."

I had her stand back and watch as I sparred with Shane and Viki. Instead of fighting, she had to call out opportunities—moments where an enemy left themselves open, where a well-placed spell could shift the tide. It forced her to stay aware, to see the fight as a whole instead of just reacting to immediate danger. And to push her further, I made her track more than just her allies' movements. I made her predict when things were about to go wrong before they actually did.

Then I gave her a real test. During our next mock battle, I didn't call anything. I let things play out, let them get messy. At first, she hesitated, waiting for me to step in. Then she realized I wasn't going to. The second Shane overextended, she shouted at him to pull back. When Viki left an opening, she warned her before the next strike landed. And when she saw the fight tipping out of our favor, she called a full retreat before we could take a serious hit.

I grinned. *That* was what I wanted to see.

"Good," I said. "Next time, do it faster."

Slowly, I could see the gears turning in their heads. Their movements got sharper, their reactions more intentional. It wasn't perfect, but it was progress.

"Now, we do it with the dungeon monsters. Morgan, you are in charge for the rest of this dungeon run. Tell us what to do!"

And she did!

It took hours to weave our way through the dungeon's trees, hunting down the corrupted sprites, vine beasts, and massive twisted treants. It wasn't without mistakes, both on our part and hers. Still, this time, we fought *smarter*. Morgan got the hang of leading. And while they still used their System abilities, they weren't *relying* on them; they were thinking and driving those abilities rather than letting themselves just ride along passively.

Viki adapted, learning how to switch seamlessly between her bow and cleaver, not because the System told her to but because she *needed* to. Shane's shots became more precise, not perfect, but *his*. And Morgan? She still had her doubts, but she was starting to see the bigger picture.

The treants were even worse than the vine beasts. Tough. The kind of tough that dulls a woodsman's axe with every chop. But unlike before, we weren't just throwing our strongest attacks at them and hoping for the best. We planned, we baited them into positions where they couldn't easily swing their massive limbs, we learned how to move around them instead of just taking the hit and tanking through it.

When we finally stood at the threshold of the boss room, I could feel it. The shift in the air. The way the trees seemed to press in closer, branches twisting like skeletal fingers. The glowing fungus flickered ominously, casting shadows that seemed *too* deep.

We were close now. I could feel it.

And this time, we were *ready*.

—

Shane

Shane scanned the dimly lit clearing, his heart hammering in his chest. This was it—the boss fight. No more warm-ups, no more practice runs. The real test was about to begin.

Doubt crept in, but he shoved it aside. There was no turning back now. He had to trust the team. So far, they hadn't let him down, and Liam... Liam knew his stuff. The training had been an eye-opener, stripping away the illusion of invincibility the System tried to give them. Shane had seen it firsthand—how easy it was to let the buffs and skills carry you, to mistake power for actual ability. But he wasn't going to fall into that trap.

His experience in Afghanistan, the long hunts back home, all of it lined up with what Liam had drilled into them: skills weren't enough. You had to *think*. You had to *adapt and overcome*. And now that he saw the System for the crutch it could be, he sure as hell wasn't going to let it make him weak.

———

Liam

"Stay sharp," I whispered, motioning for the group to gather. "This is it. The boss will have minions, probably treants, so be ready for a multi-target fight. Viki, Morgan, focus on crowd control. Shane, back us up with ranged attacks, but don't do so much damage that you draw aggro. I'll handle the boss while you guys deal with the minions. Remember to concentrate fire to bring down one fast, then move on to the next. Morgan, you're the leader. Make whatever calls you believe necessary, we'll back your play."

Everyone nodded, their expressions serious; facing multiple treants would be no joke. I took a deep breath, steeling myself for what was to come. This wasn't going to be easy, but we could handle it. Based on the rest of the dungeon monsters' levels, the boss would be around level 20. That was definitely a threat for the girls and Shane, but even I wouldn't treat it lightly.

We stood before the final chamber, looking inside, and there, in the center of the grove, was a Heartwood Dryad. She was massive, her bark-like skin twisted and gnarled from the corrupting mana of the forest dungeon, her eyes glowing with malevolent energy. Around her, five more of the twisted-treants prowled the shadows, ready to strike at a moment's notice. They were massive tree creatures that dealt heavy melee damage. They were slow but incredibly resilient, able to regenerate health over time unless stopped quickly. We had already taken down twenty of the things before making it to the boss room, and they had been tough.

As we observed the boss room from the outside, the air seemed to thicken with a palpable sense of dread. The shadows flickered ominously against the twisted trees, and the grove in front of us felt like it was breathing, alive with malevolent energy. This was it— what we'd been pushing toward for the last two hours. I could feel the tension radiating off the others as we braced ourselves for the battle ahead.

Morgan was next to me, eyes narrowed with focus as she cast **Blessing of the Dragon's Grace** over us. A faint shimmer of light flickered around our bodies, boosting our agility and giving us that small but crucial edge in magical resistance.

The once-per-day +50% crit bonus from the *Spectral Longknife of Shadows* was primed and ready for when I needed it, but for now, I wasn't going to use my full strength. This wasn't just my fight; it was theirs, too.

"All right, team," I said quietly, drawing everyone's attention. "This is it.

"Let's go," I said and stepped into the room.

The moment we stepped into the final chamber, the air grew thick with corrupted mana, pulsing like a heartbeat beneath my skin. The sensation sent a shiver down my spine—something about this place was *wrong*.

The team moved in behind me, their expressions grim. Viki, Morgan, and Shane had proven themselves capable so far, but this was different. These weren't sprites or slow-moving vine beasts. This was five treants *at once*, plus a boss. Still, they had the tools, the power. Now, they just needed to execute.

I didn't waste time. With a flick of my fingers, I cast **Darkness**, swallowing the chamber in a thick, suffocating black void. The treants bellowed in confusion, their massive limbs flailing as they crashed into one another, unable to see a damn thing. We, however, could see perfectly. The spell was designed that way—our enemies were blind, but we had full visibility.

"Go," I whispered.

I activated **Shadow Walk**, sinking into the darkness like mist slipping through cracks. Silent. I moved toward the **Heartwood Dryad**, the genuine threat in the room. It hadn't moved yet, her massive form pulsing with unnatural energy. It knew something was wrong but didn't know *what*—and that was my advantage.

Behind me, the battle erupted.

Viki's arrows whistled through the dark, striking unseen targets. Morgan's **Shadowflame Burst** roared to life, searing into the bark of the same target with a crackling heat. One treant groaned in pain, stumbling as flames spread across its wooden body. But I kept my focus locked on the dryad.

It loomed before me, twice my height, its twisted limbs rising as it gathered mana. If it got a spell off, this fight would turn ugly fast.

I didn't give it the chance.

My *Spectral Longknife of Shadows* pulsed in my grip as I stepped behind her. Heart pounding, I activated its once-per-day crit boost—I had *one* shot to make this count.

I drove the blade deep between the plates of its bark-like ribs.

A shriek ripped through the chamber. The dryad convulsed, its entire body writhing as thick, black sap gushed from the wound. Its health plummeted, but it wasn't down yet.

It twisted violently, lashing out with an arm as thick as a tree trunk. I barely had time to duck before the massive limb swung through the space I'd just been standing in. The wind of it roared past my face, and before I could reset my stance, it followed up with a second, wild strike.

I wasn't fast enough.

The impact slammed into my ribs, lifting me off my feet and hurling me backward. My breath exploded from my lungs as I skidded across the ground, rolling to absorb the force. A sharp pain flared in my side, but **Scalebound Resilience** had absorbed most of the blow. I was still in the fight.

Son of a bitch! That felt like a sledgehammer!

The room around me was chaos.

A treant howled as Viki's **Midnight's Grasp** surged from its own shadow, spectral claws locking around its limbs. Trapped. Viki's arrows hammered into its chest, and Shane's bowstring thrummed as another shot buried itself deep. A burst of black flames from Morgan finished the job. The treant let out a shuddering groan before collapsing, the weight of its body sending a *thud* through the ground.

Fifteen seconds. That's all it had been. The fight had barely started, and already the tide was shifting.

I rolled to my feet, forcing my focus back on the dryad. It was staggering, its movements more erratic now. I pressed the advantage, flicking a hand up and launching **Shadow Bolt**. The spell slammed into her chest, black tendrils wrapping over its eyes, partially blinding it.

It screeched in frustration, and I was already moving. My blade ignited with energy as I activated **Heavy Draconic Strike**, cleaving deep into the open wound on its ribs. The impact shook my arm, sending another spray of thick sap across the ground. Its health bar dipped into the red.

It wasn't dead, but it was *damn* close.

The battle behind me raged on. I caught glimpses of Viki darting between roots, loosing arrow after arrow into the remaining treants. Shane was holding his ground, keeping his shots controlled, each one precise. Morgan, standing back, was reading the fight, waiting for the moment to drop another area spell.

They were handling it. More importantly, they were using their brains! My teaching hadn't gone to waste.

Which meant I could end this.

The dryad let out a final, piercing wail. its body convulsed, and then—

A pulse of corrupted mana *exploded* outward.

I barely had time to brace before the shockwave slammed into me. My muscles locked as dark energy crawled over my skin, leeching my strength. A debuff. I gritted my teeth, forcing my body to move through the sluggish pull. **Shadow Ward** had softened the hit, but I could feel my stamina draining fast.

The dryad loomed above me, its final attack ready.

And then, out of nowhere—**Midnight's Grasp**. Viki's cooldown was up, and she had come to the rescue!

The spectral claw *snapped* around the dryad's massive limbs, locking it in place.

"Viki," I exhaled, relief washing over me.

It was all the opening I needed.

I activated **Dragon's Charge**, my form blurring as I rushed forward, the skill not being affected by the debuff. The Spectral Longknife gleamed as I brought it down in a brutal, final strike, driving it straight through the dryad's chest.

Its scream choked off. The corrupted glow in its eyes flickered—then went dark. Its massive form shuddered before collapsing, shaking the ground beneath us. Its twisted limbs twitched once, then stilled.

The fight was over.

I turned, my breathing still heavy, scanning the battlefield. The last treant had fallen, its massive body lying motionless in the grove. Viki lowered her bow, wiping sweat from her brow. Shane let out a slow breath, tension still visible in his posture. Morgan, standing with hands still raised, finally exhaled.

For a moment, nobody spoke.

Then I nodded. "Good work."

Viki grinned, clearly pleased with herself. "Nice finishing move."

Shane let out a half-laugh, shaking his head. "I thought that thing was gonna flatten you."

I smirked, stepping toward the now glowing treasure chest in the center of the grove. "Not today."

Despite everything, I felt a twinge of pride. We'd done it. They had relied on strategy, on their own skills, and not just the System's crutch. They had *fought* this battle, and they had *won*.

Next time, we'd do even better.

I placed my hands on the chest and lifted the lid, eager to see what the System had rewarded us with.

CHAPTER 12

LOOT AND GRIND

A MASSIVE TREE loomed above us, the Dryad's tree, its bark knotted and twisted like the veins of some ancient giant. The chest seemed to be part of a root of the enormous tree that had poked up out of the ground. Vines crept over the lid, pulsing with a faint green light, and it smelled of damp earth and old wood.

I knelt down, running my hand over the rough bark that encased the chest and tugged on one of the vines. It recoiled instantly, snapping back like a snake. Good. At least it wasn't going to eat me.

"Ready?" I glanced at the team. They nodded, weapons drawn, just in case. I couldn't blame them. I had been through enough dungeons to know that sometimes, the real fight starts *after* you get your hands on the loot. I still get an icy feeling in the pit of my stomach every time I think of that last dungeon in my old life and how my own team had betrayed me over some stupid loot that I didn't even care about.

With a quick motion, I slid my dagger into the seam of the lid, prying it open. The vines snapped and withered away as the chest groaned, releasing a puff of air that smelled like wet leaves and decay. I pulled it fully open.

The chest creaked with the groan of ancient hinges as though it had been sealed for centuries, waiting for us to find it. The forest around us seemed to quiet in anticipation, the trees swaying ever so slightly, their leaves rustling like whispers. Inside the chest, the soft glow of magic met my eyes, casting long shadows across the moss-covered ground.

The first item I lifted was a piece of leather armor—Viki's loot. *Whisperleaf Leather Armor*. The design was breathtaking, shades of deep brown and green woven together in a pattern of vines and leaves that seemed almost alive. The craftsmanship was unmistakable—lightweight and perfect for blending into natural surroundings, ideal for Viki's stealthy approach to combat. She'd disappear into the shadows like a ghost in this.

"Viki, this one's yours." I handed it to her, and she took it with a reverent look in her eyes, running her fingers along the intricate leaf motifs.

Next, I pulled out a staff, the wood gleaming with faint green light as if it pulsed with the very life of the forest. *Verdantwood Staff*. The weight of it in my hands told me it wasn't just for show. This thing had power, magic infused into every inch. Morgan would be able to heal and support us with this while still delivering a solid offense when needed.

"Morgan's going to love this," I muttered to myself as I pulled it out and handed it over to our healer.

Beneath the staff, a small sigil caught my eye, carved with delicate, swirling patterns. My **Treasure Sense** told me it was a *Herald's Sigil*. It was elegant and understated, yet I could feel the energy radiating from it. This would amplify Shane's abilities as a Herald, boosting his charisma and combat skills in one fell swoop. I wasn't sure if it was my luck or just plain System fuckery, but that was awfully targeted. Was the AI actively looking out for me by giving us what we needed?

Somehow, I didn't think that would be the case, at least not directly. Otherwise, the competing AI world nodes would insist on doing the same for their champions. Still, this was suspiciously convenient. If I ever got a chance to talk to the AI again, I'd have to ask about it.

Finally, nestled at the very bottom was a small charm. Carved from dragon bone, it was smooth and intricate, with subtle etchings running along its length. *Dragonbone Charm.* It was light in my hand but potent with the raw power of both physical strength and magic. I could feel the energy hum through my fingers as I held it, enhancing both my strength and spellcasting. This was going to come in handy.

I pocketed the charm, then glanced at the others. "Looks like everyone made out well on this run."

Shane looked up tiredly from where he had been admiring his new sigil. "Run? You mean we are going to do this again?"

Chuckling darkly, I grinned at his expression of dread. "Oh, yeah. We definitely are! This place is pretty good for a low-level dungeon. Although some of the monsters are hard to take down, it will be good practice for the three of you. However, now that we know what we are up against, we can do this much faster next time. We won't have to move so cautiously and slowly."

"Tha...That was slow and cautious?!?" He sat heavily on a fallen log, looking tired and hungry.

"Believe it or not, yeah. Don't worry, we're gonna have a nice meal and rest for an hour, then we'll do it again, and again, and again. We'll get at least three more runs out of this before we get some sleep, and we'll likely run it until it is destroyed."

Now, it wasn't just Shane looking at me with shock. Morgan asked, "Weren't you mentioning earlier that this would be a good dungeon for harvesting resources?"

I nodded, "I did say that, but that was before we saw the corrupted mana permeating the place. It wouldn't be smart to use the wood for building if it is impregnated with nasty mana like that. Also, this is a great place for you to train and level."

Turning to Shane, I asked, "How many levels did you get on this run?"

He looked at his status page, and his eyes got big. "Damn! I got four levels from this one dungeon!"

Viki chimed in, "I got one, and I'm almost halfway to the next. That brings me up to Level 13."

It turned out Morgan was the one with the most significant gains, though. She had hit Level 15 and gotten her next pair of Class spells.

She beamed as she said, "I received my first defensive spell, **Dark Aegis**, and it's a doozy! It absorbs up to 15% of the target's maximum HP in incoming damage and converts that into healing for 25% of the damage absorbed. My other one is **Regeneration**, which heals moderate injuries and grants a heal-over-time effect."

Blinking in surprise, I said, "That shield spell is amazing. I've never heard of one that grants healing on top of defense."

"Don't get me wrong, I'm pleased with it, but it would have been cool to get another offensive spell. I feel like I hardly did any damage compared to the rest of you in that boss fight."

This seemed like a good teaching moment, "Speaking from experience as a gamer, which has been a long time ago for me, but as a healer Class, you don't need to worry too much about damage.

Your strengths will be in keeping your teammates alive and directing the flow of the battle. Since you should be at the back and watching everything that is happening, you can more easily see the enemies' vulnerabilities and tell Viki and Shane where to attack for the best advantage. Basically, part of your job is to be a battle commander."

She looked thoughtful at my words. "I'll keep that in mind. Thanks."

I gave the mana potion to Morgan since she was the most likely to need it and the health potion to Shane. He would eventually need to go out on his own as a herald and spread the word. At that point, a life-saving potion might make all the difference in the world to him.

After that, we sat around the clearing and had a quick meal, then rested for an hour. Thankfully, I needed very little rest with my stats, but I could tell the others had really benefited from the nap when I called everyone to gather.

"Okay, we'll take a short break after each run, but we're gonna do this thing until midnight, at least, maybe later, to destroy this dungeon. This is a pretty expensive dungeon for the System to maintain, considering its high focus on mana. So I'm guessing it should only take five or six runs to collapse it."

That got a round of groans from the sleepy team.

The next few hours blurred into a rhythm of combat, strategy, and improvement. We hit the dungeon with everything we had, again and again. Every run became smoother and more efficient as we refined our tactics and grew stronger with each attempt. It also didn't hurt that the party was leveling up at a good pace.

Viki's *Whisperleaf Armor* allowed her to blend perfectly into the shadowed corners of the woodland dungeon, her **Silent Step** making her movements nearly impossible to hear. She'd scout ahead, draw the attention of a lone sprite or vine beast, and Shane, emboldened by his new *Herald's Sigil*, would line up the perfect shot. His arrows now flew faster and truer than before with his new levels and skills, which meant fewer gaps in our attacks.

Morgan stayed at the rear, her *Verdantwood Staff* pulsing with healing energy when necessary, but mostly, she observed the battlefield, calling out weaknesses or patterns in the enemies' movements. Her **Dark Aegis** spell saved us more than once. When things got hairy, she'd throw it up, absorbing damage and converting it into healing, keeping us on our feet through the worst of the dungeon's traps and ambushes. Not that I was personally threatened with the level difference, but it was absolutely amazing to have a healer in the party. I had never experienced such a luxury in my first life!

Each run felt faster, more natural. By the third run, we weren't just surviving—we were dominating. The monsters were still tough, sure, but with each kill, we grew more confident. My own **Draconic Strike** packed more punch as I fine-tuned my use of the shadow-infused abilities. The subtle hum of the *Dragonbone Charm* at my neck seemed to make every hit stronger, every spell sharper.

After each dungeon clear, we'd haul our loot back to the clearing, rest for a few minutes, and then go back in. The steady rhythm of leveling up kept us going, eager for more despite the growing fatigue. Viki was becoming more aggressive in her attacks, able to take down three corrupted sprites at a time with her **Eclipse Barrage**. Shane, still shaky from time to time, was holding his own, his accuracy improving with every fight.

Morgan's **Regeneration** spell had become our safety net. If any of us took a hit too big to shrug off, she was there, patching us up in a matter of seconds. I didn't have to keep as close an eye on the team anymore, which allowed me to cut loose and deal with the more significant threats head-on. **Shadow Walk** became my favorite skill, letting me move through the battlefield with unnatural speed, appearing right behind a vine beast or treant before they even realized they were in danger.

Shane

For Shane, the grind was exhausting. By the end of the second run, his arms were burning from drawing his bow over and over again. His head pounded from the constant concentration, trying to keep up with Viki's pace. But every time he saw that flash of light on his status page, signaling another level gained, it lit a fire under him. He was getting stronger—he could feel it in the way his arrows flew faster, hit harder. He wasn't just the guy tagging along anymore. He was contributing, making a difference.

By the third run, he wasn't just reacting to the chaos around him— he was anticipating it. He'd see Viki shift into position, and without her needing to say a word, he'd know where to aim. When Liam called out a strategy, Shane didn't hesitate. He executed it, trusting the team, trusting himself.

As the fourth run came to a close, he glanced at his status page. Level 14. Not bad for someone who had been struggling just a few hours ago. He'd earned every point of experience, and the pain in his muscles felt like a badge of honor.

Liam

By the time we finished the fourth run, the sky was shifting into twilight. My level had ticked up to 32, and I could feel the power humming in my veins. The others were right there with me, their progress steady and impressive. Viki was up to Level 16, and she moved with the confidence of an apex predator, her personal vendetta against dungeon monsters becoming more bloody with each level gained. Shane, who had started the day looking like he was going to collapse after every fight, was now a

Level 14 Hunter, holding his own in every battle. His Class might not be as rare and elite as the others, but what it lacked in unique skills, it made up for in focused, consistent improvement.

Morgan was the biggest surprise. She'd hit Level 17, and her magic was sharper and more potent. Each spell she cast now felt like it was backed by something deeper, stronger. Her mana reserves were holding out longer, and the moment we faced a new threat, she already had a plan in place, her voice steady and commanding.

"Alright," I said, wiping the sweat from my brow. "We've got one more run in us tonight, and I can feel the dungeon weakening; one more time and we'll collapse it."

The team groaned, but it was half-hearted. They were tired, sure, but there was something exhilarating about knowing we were about to take this thing down for good. It also didn't hurt that the sheer growth in their stats meant their Endurance was soaring. Since this morning, Shane had gained more than 10 points of Endurance, and Viki had gained 5. Morgan had only gained 3 points, but that was because she was purposely dumping most of her stat increases into her Mind and Magic Aptitude stats since she was not a frontline fighter and her focus needed to be on mana.

Even she could feel the difference, as she commented, "I can't believe how much better I can handle all of this than I would have been able to a week ago! Heck, just a shift at the cafe left me exhausted and my feet hurting. Even though I'm tired now, I feel like I could still dance if a good song played on the jukebox."

"Let's finish this," I smirked, the thrill of victory already in the air. We had made solid gains tonight, and as much as this might have sucked, I was going to have to keep up this pace every day if I was going to make it to the Level Cap before the other races invaded in three weeks.

Viki and Morgan didn't have to hit it that hard. I just needed them to power-level up more heralds to spread the word, but knowing them, they wouldn't be far behind me.

What I wasn't looking forward to was the conversation we were about to have once this next dungeon run finished.

CHAPTER 13

SEPARATE MISSIONS

LIAM

It was well after midnight before we finished the last run, so we decided to camp just inside the cleared dungeon for a generous four hours of sleep. There were a lot of grumbles about that, but I was on a timer and feeling the pressure. It sucked to know there were at least five bad guys out there coming for me and could show up at any time. Yet another reason I wanted to have that unpleasant conversation with the team.

But first, we needed to sort the loot from the dungeon. We had each taken and equipped the things that made sense as we went, but there were some items that needed to be addressed.

I wasn't worried about Shane. He was a temporary member of our group and needed what we gave him to survive the task we had assigned him. He ended up doing great, gaining a nice-looking set of *Oakenmail Armor*; it was forest-themed and made of heavy leather with small enchanted wooden plates all over it. In addition to that, he received a *Chameleon Cloak* that would allow him to change his appearance and gave a bonus to stealth. A *Gleaming Lantern* that used copper mana coins as fuel and burned for 24 hours per coin, very useful for someone without dark vision. Lastly, he received a trap item called a *Bramble Net,* which would hold a target in thorny vines, dealing a minor DoT.

All told he had made it to Level 14, just shy of 15, and gotten himself well-equipped to go out into the world and tell people the truth of our situation, and we had managed it in a single day. I would have preferred to get him a few more levels, but we just didn't have time. Besides, I doubted that there were many people in the world much over level 10 by this point, so he should be able to go toe-to-toe with anyone who might try to stop him on his journey.

Morgan and Viki came out pretty well, too. Viki ended up with her own set of themed armor from that first run but then added a *Tracking Stone*, a quiver, a *Pathfinder's Compass*, and a skill scroll for the **Explorer** skil:. the same one I had gotten from the Goblin Dungeon, the one that gave me the mini-map. That compass was one of the things we needed to talk about.

On the other hand, Morgan picked up an ever-full waterskin, a System-woven outfit that self-cleaned and self-repaired, as well as a skill scroll for the common version of **Analyze**.

One challenging moment, however, was when she had gotten her *Verdant Robes.* We had been standing around the treasure chest when I saw them among the rest of the loot. My face had fallen a bit, and she had clued in that someone was off.

"Liam, what's the matter?" She asked with a bit of worry in her voice.

I hesitated to answer, but it wasn't like this was a real problem, just another annoyance of the System. Still, I knew it had the potential to upset her.

"I've got good news and bad news. Do you remember all the armor from video games back in the day?"

At this point, she was looking between the treasure chest and me, giving me a concerned side-eye. "Yeah... why?"

"You know how annoyed some women were over the skimpy nature of armor in video games?"

Her face was falling at the pace of a meteor heading for impact. "No. No! Do not tell me that!"

With an effort of supreme will, I kept any hint of amusement off my face. I knew how I would feel in her shoes.

"So yeah. The AI was fed on pre-System Earth internet content. Meaning that about two out of every three female sets of armor that come out of loot drops will expose your midriff and have a lot of cleavage, possibly exposing your thighs, too. But there is an upside!"

She was glaring now. "What possible upside could there be?"

"Well, there is some cosmic justice. First of all, no matter what it looks like, it still provides full coverage, and even if it shows your tummy, an enemy who strikes you there will still have their damage reduced, just like if your armor were covering that location."

I could see in her eyes that this did not make up for this particular bit of System stupidity, so I continued, "Also, because it was fed on internet content, it did listen somewhat, and all female armor and clothing have pockets; good pockets, and lots of them. Again, even if there shouldn't physically be a way to put pockets in something that looks that way."

The look on her face did not suggest that she considered the addition of pockets enough to make up for skimpy armor.

"Still, there are two redeeming things about this. First, if a man puts on a set of that skimpy armor, it will transform into the beefcake equivalent, a hide loincloth, and a shoulder pauldron, or something to that effect. So there is a little bit of cosmic justice, and given the severe lack of good armor in the world, there will always be a man willing to buy such a set and wear it. Still, there is a way around the whole problem, but it is kinda a slap in the face."

Morgan's frown did not bode well for the AI if she ever got her hands on it.

"What?"

The question was asked flatly and with the full foreknowledge that she was about to be even more pissed.

"If a man pulls the armor out of the treasure chest for you, it will automatically default to the standard armor look rather than the skimpy kind."

What followed was a serious attempt on her part to light the jungle on fire with **Shadowflame Burst.** She also expressed herself in a series of curses that both impressed and shocked me. Then she took a few deep breaths, and her face became too calm as she asked, "Liam, would you please hand me that set of armor?" However, under her breath, I heard her muttering, "If I ever Ascend, we'll see about this!"

With a sympathetic half-smile, I picked up the armored robes and handed them to her. "Sorry to be the bearer of that bad news, but I didn't want you to be surprised in a later dungeon run."

"Not your fault."

When she put them on, we all admired the look: the armored robes were a combination of lightweight fabric and natural armor, enhanced by vine-like threads running through the material. They shimmered slightly with magic and looked perfect for a Dragon Priestess who needed protection but didn't want to sacrifice mobility.

Now that we had moved on from that mess, I chuckled darkly, thinking of that moment, but definitely did not remind her of it as we sat down to eat a quick breakfast from my supplies. It was only thanks to the System-generated MREs that I had found in the Goblin Dungeon that I was able to feed everyone. I hadn't stocked up with feeding others in mind. Hopefully, we would find another dungeon soon that will provide rations until the System shop opens in three weeks. If this hadn't been filled with corrupted mana, we might have been able to find some fruits and root vegetables in this forest setting. I sighed at the missed opportunity.

When everyone was done, I finally broached the subject that I had been dreading. We all knew this time would come, but not so soon.

"We need to separate. Shane, you need to head out and start spreading the message."

He nodded reluctant agreement. "I never thought I'd get nine levels in a single day. That was insane, but you are right. Being Level 14, I should be able to handle any mutated beasts or people with nefarious intentions. I've been thinking about where to go, and I think the best thing I could do to start with is to circle the outskirts of the city. People are going to be fleeing and dispersing in all directions, so if I can spread the word along the perimeter, then that will vastly multiply the possible audience."

That was a damned good idea and one I hadn't thought of. I had just been thinking of sending people out in random directions, hoping to spread the word to other regions, but what he suggested made a lot of sense. "That's brilliant! Please do that for as long as it makes sense, and then pick a direction and head off towards other parts of the country. We'll send the next herald in the opposite direction around the city before they exit, just to be sure. After that, they will head straight out toward other major population centers, Waco, Austin, San Antonio, and so on to the south, and do the same thing North, East, and West."

. . .

Knowing that had been the easy part, I looked to Morgan and Viki, and they saw it on my face before I spoke. "I'm sorry to say, we need to split up as well. I need you both to find the next herald and power-level them while I head out looking for higher-level dungeons."

"I don't like it!" Viki grumbled. "Who's going to protect you from the champions? You need someone to watch your back!"

It was true, but the need to speed-run stronger dungeons was more critical. "I only earned two levels yesterday. At that pace, I'll never hit the Level Cap before the invasion. I can't afford to split the XP if I'm going to reach Cap in time."

Morgan put an arm around Viki's shoulder and added, "Don't worry, Vik, you've got the *Tracking Stone*. Mark Liam with it, and we'll be able to find him no matter where he goes."

A big smile bloomed on her young face. "Oh yeah, that's right! We'll follow you and level up in the lower-level dungeons near where you are doing the big ones. And if you need us, we'll be close."

That wasn't a bad idea at all. "You know, that sounds good. I wish we had some kind of communication device, but tracking is the next best thing. We've got *Commune*, but that's limited to once per day. Let's save the special communication skill for emergencies and plan to meet up every couple days by you finding me if you can. Wait for me outside whatever dungeon I'm in, and we can talk and catch up when I come out."

The idea of them sticking close was a significant relief for me. It had been weighing on my mind that I was turning them loose in a dangerous world. Not that they couldn't handle themselves. Levels 16 and 17 were nothing to sneeze at eight days after the Apocalypse. If they were careful, there shouldn't be a low-level dungeon around that could kill them.

I said as much to them but added a warning, "You are going to be power-leveling noobs. Make sure you pick good individuals, and don't let their inexperience or stupidity get you killed. I don't worry about you two, but about idiots that might get you hurt or killed. Don't put your life at risk for the sake of a stranger. If someone pulls a Leroy Jenkins, let them die. The mission is more important than a single life."

Seeing the look on Morgan's face, I could tell she got it. She would be a good balance to Viki's impulsiveness.

"Okay, I'm heading to Stacy Road next. That was a big shopping area, several times the size of these last two, so there should be at least a medium-level dungeon somewhere there, as well as two or three low-level ones. You guys can run with me, and we'll split up when we get there."

There was one last thing, and I hated to ask it, but the mission made it necessary. I walked over to Viki and asked, "Could I have your *Pathfinder's Compass*? It will allow me to finish the dungeons faster and safer. I hate to even ask since I'd rather you and Morgan be safe, but if I'm going to speed run through this, I really need it."

Viki looked at me like I was crazy for asking. "Duh, of course! You gave me the Shaman's cleaver and amulet and helped me get strong. Here!"

She pulled it out of her inventory and handed it over without even a millisecond's hesitation.

I hugged her. "Thanks, kiddo!"

Next, I took out the small stone upgrade rune that had been one of my dungeon drops and applied it to the compass. A faint glow spread from the point of contact, veins of light flickering across its surface before sinking into the wood. The compass shuddered slightly in my hand as the enchantment took hold, the once simple markings shifting into intricate patterns and the needle sharpening to a sliver of obsidian. With a final pulse of magic, the compass settled, now heavier with power, its hum more focused, as though it had been awakened to new potential.

Putting in a pocket of my armor so that it would technically be 'worn' meant that it was always active. Paired with my passive skill **Explorer**, which gave me my mini-map, they had a synergistic effect. Suddenly, a red 'X' appeared on the map about sixty feet away. Whatever the compass detected, would be displayed on my mini-map. I now had a cheat that would allow me to find and directly go to any enemies within a 100' radius of my location. If I could get another upgrade token, I'd see enemies ever further away. Of course, it also showed traps, like the 'X' that had just appeared on the map, as well as the most direct and efficient route to a desired location within range.

This was one of those hidden bonuses that weren't advertised by the System but that could really unlock your potential if you knew about them.

"Oh, one more thing before we set out. When you run a dungeon that you don't destroy, put up a sign outside, carve a stone or something that lets people know what type of monsters are inside and what their levels are. Shane, make sure that is something you pass along as part of your info dump to the survivors you encounter. Let's establish some helpful practices like that to give people a leg up. Mark all dungeons, and let them know to protect dungeons that offer good resources and harvest them strategically if they aren't too big of a threat."

Without further ado, we stepped outside and watched the dungeon collapse, leaving behind a common dungeon core, which I pocketed into my inventory.

With a final wave to Shane, I called to the girls, "Let's run!"

We turned south toward what had been the towns of Fairview and Allen, ready for the next challenge.

CHAPTER 14
ANGRY MOBS AND MEDIUM DUNGEONS

The big interchange at Hwy 75 and the 121 Tollway still looked to be intact, mostly. It was odd to see, but really, the only thing that had deteriorated so far was that all the paint was gone. No lines on the roadway, and the signs were all just sheets of bare metal. However, the metal was oxidizing or rusting at a rapid pace, seeming like years had passed rather than mere days.

Further south, trees were overtaking what had once been a growing area with lots of new businesses. Just like what we had seen already, the buildings were falling down. For a long time, I wondered how the System did this and thought it must be nanotechnology. Now, however, I was not so sure. In my first life, I didn't have access to magic. Now that I did, my theory was changing. I didn't think nanites could be responsible for the things I could do with mana. Mana felt like some kind of exotic energy that our previous science hadn't discovered. Energy that could interact with the world in crazy and impressive ways, able to manipulate the structure of matter and do things that seemed to defy the laws of physics.

Fuck physics! What has physics ever done for me? I thought with a smirk.

Seriously, though, such thoughts were above my pay grade, so to speak. Perhaps once I reached the Ascension System, I could learn the science behind how all this was possible, but for now, I just needed to focus on leveling and stop daydreaming about stuff I couldn't control.

Seeing the shopping area ahead, we hopped over the median in the highway and moved toward the east side of the intersection where most of the businesses had been. Ironically, all of the trees that had been nothing but small decorative varieties were now towering giants. The shrubs and flowers were growing wild, a maze of hedges and shade trees. If it weren't for the disintegrating buildings and signs, this could have been idyllic.

As we approached the shopping area, I couldn't help but marvel at the sight of the trees from a different perspective. I had been too distracted with survival in the early days of the apocalypse the first time; all I had paid attention to was the destruction and death. I hadn't noticed the small details like this. Sure, it was easy to imagine energy or nanites being used to destroy all our technology, but how did it cause small decorative trees to turn into eighty-foot-tall giants in a week? The whole place had turned into a lush, natural-seeming area, a twisted reflection of what it used to be. But as beautiful as it was, the deteriorating buildings and rusting signs reminded us that this was no fairy tale.

We weren't alone.

We had barely made it to the intersection when the shouting started. A mob of around seventy people, all clustered around a man who looked like he'd stepped straight out of a TV evangelist's pulpit, blocked our path. His voice was a relentless drone, full of fire and brimstone, and he was waving a large Bible like a weapon.

One of his followers pointed to us and yelled, "Reverend Petty, look. Sinners!"

The preacher turned to us and shouted, "Behold! Agents of the devil! They bear the marks of the Beast, the System, the cursed mechanism that has wrought this chaos upon us! The Lord called, and we did not answer, so we were left behind when the faithful were taken up to Heaven! Don't be like these fallen ones! If you embrace the System, you are willfully donning the mark of the Beast, and you will never join the heavenly host!"

There was spittle flying from the man's mouth by the end of his rant.

My brows furrowed, but I kept my calm. "What are you talking about? We just want you to point out where the dungeons are so we can kill the monsters in them to keep everyone safe. We're here to help."

My team and I exchanged glances. This wasn't just any angry mob; these people had convinced themselves that their apocalypse was a divine punishment, some fucked-up version of the Rapture. They were apparently roaming around, looking to "cleanse" the city of its supposed evil, convinced that their way to salvation was through destruction.

As we moved closer, their eyes fell on us. His congregation's gazes were immediately suspicious, and he began to rant even louder.

"Look at them!" he cried, pointing directly at us. "They not only wear the System's clothes, the marks of the Beast! They come seeking the portals of hell! We must purge them from our midst!"

Reverend Petty pointed dramatically. "These are the minions of Hell, disguised as servants of light! They seek the dungeons to join their dark master within!"

At first, I thought, *'The dude has clearly lost it.'* Except, like so many of his type, I could see a sly glint in his eyes that made me think this was just another Sunday for the bastard; even beyond the end of the world, he was still trying to live off his followers.

Fucking parasite scammers!

Morgan, wearing her robes and carrying her staff, was at the forefront of our group. She met the preacher's glare with a calm, almost amused expression. "Bless your heart. I grew up in the Bible belt here, and I've seen my fair share of holier-than-thou idiots preaching damnation. Unfortunately, I don't have the patience, and we don't have time for your bullshit, if you'll pardon my language. We're just here looking for dungeons," she said, her voice steady.

The preacher's face twisted with righteous anger. "Blasphemy! You wear the robes and carry a staff like the prophets of old, yet you are nothing but deceivers! You will not deceive us!"

Huh. Maybe he isn't intentionally a con man; maybe he's just a slimy piece of shit and really does believe the bullshit he's spewing.

Before I could decide how to react, the preacher lunged at Morgan, who had been walking beside me, her robes swaying with each step.

Reverend Petty's face was twisted with rage, and he brandished a wooden cross as if it could somehow hurt her.

Morgan didn't hesitate. She lifted her staff with a practiced ease and brought it down in a swift, precise motion. The preacher's eyes widened in surprise in the instant before he crumpled to the ground, knocked out cold. The crowd gasped collectively, their fervor momentarily shattered.

Morgan stepped forward, her face stern and authoritative. "Listen up," she called out, her voice cutting through the shocked murmurings of the crowd. "This man is a fool. It's not some divine judgment that's caused all this, but the System. You're not going to find salvation by following him or cleansing this city. Instead, you need to start fighting monsters, leveling up, and finding a way to survive. Leave this place before it's too late. The only evil here is your misguided leader."

The crowd hesitated, their resolve wavering. Several of them looked around, their faces a mix of confusion and fear. I could see the seeds of doubt taking root, and it didn't take long for them to start scattering. Their reverend had offered them a comforting and familiar explanation of why this was all happening, but they would be dead the moment they encountered an area experiencing a dungeon break or a single strong mutated beast.

With their illusions broken and seeing their giver of false hope lying unconscious before them, they began to disperse in small groups as we watched and waited.

As the last of them began to leave, a scared-looking woman and her husband stepped forward from the back of the crowd. Their eyes were wide with a mix of relief and apprehension. "We... we know where the dungeons are," the woman said softly, her voice trembling. "I'm Marsha, and this is Dan. If you're looking for the dungeons, we can guide you."

I nodded, giving them a reassuring smile. "Thank you. We'd appreciate that."

As we followed them towards the dungeons, I had a thought and leaned over to whisper in Morgan's ear. "Maybe they can be the next heralds?"

They looked like high school sweethearts who had followed along with their church, not knowing what else to do, but they seemed sharper than many of the others.

She looked at me surprised but then thoughtfully replied, "Viki and I will interview them before we go into the next dungeon and see if they will work."

The couple looked apprehensive but hurried to lead us to the dungeons. With just a few questions, we knew where we needed to go.

There were three dungeons here, but they had heard of more to the south around McDermot and Bethany roads.

"There is one across the highway, in the middle of the outlet mall. One on the north side of Stacy Road, and then there is this one."

They had led us deeper into the shopping area on the southeast side of the complex. Right in the middle of a small green space, where they usually erected the Christmas tree in the winter, there was a stone monolith. It almost looked like something out of that old movie where the astronauts go to Jupiter, and they all die because of a crazy computer.

How appropriate... I thought.

"This wasn't here a week ago, that's for sure. I just shopped at the liquor store right over there a couple days before Initialization."

Looking at it made my eyes hurt. It was big, maybe twenty feet tall, and blacker than night. It was a fairly bright morning, but the object seemed to drink in the light and not reflect anything. Worse, this had a much stronger aura of menace than the three dungeons I had seen so far in this new life. I had finally found a higher-level dungeon.

CHAPTER 15
A DARK DUNGEON

Looking at Morgan and Viki, I said, "Ok, this is my stop. You guys go check out the other two dungeons, I'm going to solo this one."

Viki still looked like she wanted to argue, but Morgan spoke first, "We will. This one, the pressure—it feels a lot worse than the others. Are you sure?"

"Yeah, I'm probably still higher level than anything that will be inside, but I'll be careful. You two also need to watch each other's backs and don't take on anything you aren't sure you can beat. Better for you to level at a steady but safe pace than risk everything."

Opening her mouth to counter, Viki was getting ready to argue, but Morgan took her hand and began to lead her away. Before she could, Viki broke away and ran up, clutched me around the middle, and squeezed me in a hug so tight I almost couldn't breathe. She didn't say anything but just held on for a long minute.

"Don't worry, kiddo. I'll be fine. I'm more worried about you two. Protect Morgan, will ya?"

When she finally let go, I saw determination in her eyes. "I will. We'll meet up with you again in two days. I'll find you!"

She had used her tracking stone on me that morning after receiving it, so I had no worries about them being able to find me or stay close.

I didn't say anything else, just nodded decisively and plunged through the surface of the monolith into the unknown.

I braced myself for the transition. The familiar sensation of tumbling through space was followed by a sudden jolt as I landed on solid ground. I blinked as my eyes adjusted to the dim, eerie light of the dungeon's entrance.

Before me stretched a cavernous expanse, its walls etched with arcane symbols that pulsed with a faint, ominous glow. The air was thick with an oppressive clammy dampness, and the faint, eerie luminescence barely cut through the darkness. The cavern was lined with jagged, obsidian formations that seemed almost to breathe with the shadows. Here and there, veins of dark crystal glistened, adding an otherworldly sheen to the otherwise bleak surroundings.

The ground beneath me was uneven, with sharp outcroppings of rock and patches of twisted, blackened vegetation that looked as though they thrived on despair. The distant echoes of dripping water and the occasional whisper of shifting stone heightened the sense of foreboding.

To my right, I could make out the outline of a large, rusted gate partially buried in debris. Its metal surface was inscribed with runes, their meanings long forgotten by whatever race had created them but still exuding a sense of dark power. Beyond the gate, a faint, ominous glow suggested that the dungeon's depths held secrets that were both ancient and dangerous.

I steeled myself, checking my gear and mentally preparing for whatever lay ahead. The darkness seemed almost alive, whispering threats and promises in equal measure.

Immediately casting Stealth, I moved away from the entrance. Dungeons almost never put monsters immediately inside, giving people a chance to orient and experience the System fuckery that was the 'ambiance' invading their minds. Still, this darkness was more than just the simulated nighttime of the kobold or corrupted forest dungeons. This was an unnatural sort of environment, but it was the type that someone with my Shadow Dragon bloodline would find almost tailor-made for stealthing around and ambushing targets. Meaning, there were probably ambush predators of some kind in here using the darkness to their advantage.

I grinned evilly. That would have been great for them if I didn't have a mini-map that showed enemies as red dots within a 100-yard radius of me. There were six of them already showing up, lurking in the shadows, waiting for unsuspecting dungeon divers to walk near.

I wanted to laugh out loud at just how fucked the monsters in this dungeon were.

"This is going to be fun!"

Gripping my longknife, I stalked forward, my route marked out by the enchanted compass. Not only could I tell where they were hiding, I knew how to get to them.

I spotted the first monster. A quick use of **Treasure Sense** to analyze it told me it was called a Shadow Stalker. It was just ahead, its form blending seamlessly into the darkness, save for the faint glimmer of its red eyes. It was crouched low, waiting for a chance to pounce. I approached from an unexpected direction, staying low and silent, relying on the heightened senses granted by my bloodline. As I drew nearer, I could feel the pulse of its energy—a dark, hungry aura that called to my instincts.

With a quick flick of my wrist, I activated **Draconic Strike**. The skill would enhance my next attack with a surge of power. I launched myself at the creature, the shadows around me thickening as I closed the distance. My longknife glinted in the dim light, and with a swift, calculated motion, I plunged it into the Stalker's side.

The creature barely had time to react before I withdrew my blade, the critical hit landing with a satisfying thud. It crumpled to the ground, dissolving into a cloud of shadowy mist before it could even let out a cry. I savored the rush of adrenaline and the satisfaction of a clean kill.

Fifteen copper mana coins dropped, telling me its level, not bad. Considering that higher-level dungeons tended to be bigger and with more foes, this would be a good harvest of XP, and I'd get some silver mana coins from the stronger monsters if I wasn't mistaken. Running this solo meant this was going to get me multiple levels!

The mini-map flickered again, and I turned my attention to the next red dot. Two more Shadow Stalkers were close together, unaware of my presence. I recast Stealth to make myself invisible again, and I crept toward them, my heart racing with the thrill of the hunt. As I approached, I could hear their low growls, a sound that sent a shiver of excitement down my spine.

I waited for just the right moment, watching their movements, before launching myself into action again. I targeted the one on the left, using **Shadow Walk** to shift into the inky darkness surrounding me. I materialized right behind it and struck with precision, my knife finding its mark once more, this time right to the base of the skull, driving the blade into its brain.

The second Stalker whirled around in surprise, but I was still invisible thanks to the grace period before my invisibility wore off. I only had seconds, but as close as the other was, I could finish this. I watched as it scanned the area, its instincts kicking in, but I was already preparing for my next attack.

I moved silently around it. I could feel the energy of the dungeon pulsing through the air, feeding my confidence. As the Stalker turned away, I struck again, my blade slicing through the darkness. It fell without a sound, joining its fallen comrade in the void.

With the Stalkers dispatched, I felt a rush of exhilaration. The mini-map showed only a few red dots within range, but I knew I would find more as I ventured deeper into this crazy hellscape of jagged obsidian and shadow. I checked my mana and frowned. Each cast of Stealth cost 100 mana. At this rate, I would run out of mana and need to rest; however, if I could group them and kill two or three at a time, I might only have to take one break for my mana to recover before facing whatever the next monster type was.

Between Stealth and the mini-map, the first part of this dungeon, while fun, wasn't really much of a challenge. Being agility-focused ambush hunters, they had minimal durability, allowing me to kill them each with a single blow. I leveled up twice before I finished the Shadow Stalkers, bringing me to Level 34. One more level and I'd get a new pair of skills.

This is exciting! I had never known this kind of power and advantage in my first life.

Yesterday had been necessary; we had accomplished a lot, and it set the stage for being able to turn the girls loose on dungeons by themselves. Still, I had felt the clock ticking every minute of that day, and only getting two levels for the entire day had been very frustrating.

I paused for a moment as that last thought sunk in. Was I really so spoiled? Only two levels in a day, and I felt bad about it? I wanted to laugh, but that would have been dangerous under the circumstances. In my first life, I would have been satisfied to get two levels in a year. The rate I was advancing now was insane.

Today, my goal was ten levels!

Refocusing on my current circumstances, I moved forward into the second phase of this dungeon. I had rested once to recover mana and had enough for a few more fights. I spotted crystalline webs ahead, and my stomach sank. Maybe my ambition was getting ahead of itself.

I hated spiders! They were a pain to fight.

A moment later, I crept closer and saw a large Obsidian Spider, the size of a great dane, its eight eyes glittering in the darkness.

These spiders weren't just lurking; they had constructed defensible nests, and I needed to be cautious. They were stationary ambush predators, their dark forms blending into the shadows, waiting for unsuspecting prey. But the one bad thing about these spiders, in particular, was their webs; they hardened into blade-like strands capable of cutting through rock. Anyone venturing into their lair would have a very bad day. Luckily, I didn't have to.

Shadow Bolt flew silently toward my target, aimed straight for its cluster of eyes.

At the last instant, it sensed danger and leaped sideways, using a strand of web to pull itself out of the way. My bolt hit, but it wasn't a direct shot. Still, one of the spell's abilities was to blind the target for a few seconds. It went into a frenzy, pulling on its web, causing a chaos storm of blade-like strands to whip across the area. Had I been closer, I would have been shredded.

Ranged attack for the win!

Considering that only certain death waited if I were to step into that killing field, I decided to use my other ranged spel:, **Arcane Singularity**.

The ball of hyper-dense energy formed below the spider, pulling it in, along with all of the web strands that were currently thrashing around its lair. That proved to be far more deadly than the explosion of the singularity. Its own web blades, being sucked toward the spell's epicenter, sliced the spider into tiny chunks of ichor and chitin, which were then sent flying everywhere.

"Now that's what I call effective!"

Still, that had also made a lot of noise. These critters might be ambush hunters, but that didn't mean I couldn't get swarmed if I were stupid.

I shifted my approach for the next one, using **Shadow Walk** to get right into its lair and appear behind it. If it tried to use its web, it would rip itself apart since it was between me and the killzone it had created. This time, I struck with a focused determination, using **Searing Slash**, plunging my blade into the soft spot between its armored plates. The spider convulsed, its movements growing erratic before it finally fell limp, dissolving into a shadowy mist. The blow had been a crit.

That was two down out of dozens. This would take some time. The Shadow Walkers had been quick and easy compared to the spiders. I had wiped out seventy-five of them in around an hour and a half. At this rate, the spiders and their defensive natures would cost me at least twice as long despite there being fewer of them.

It ended up taking even longer than expected. Due to the need to recover mana, it ended up taking three and a half hours. On the upside, I leveled another two times while hunting and exterminating the spiders. They were Level 18, and there were fifty of them, that was 90,000 XP. I still had another monster type and the boss to deal with!

With the spiders dispatched, I took a moment to regroup, my heart still pounding with exhilaration and revulsion. Those things were among the most creepy monsters ever. They reminded me heavily of those Shadows on the TV show Babylon 5. Thankfully, the Obsidian Spiders couldn't go invisible; they were just the ultimate in 'creepy-crawly' nightmare fuel!

I took the time to review my Status and check out my new skill and spell.

Liam Bell:

Draconic Shadowblade - Level 36
Bloodline (Tier 2): Shadow Dragon

Experience: 3980/49920

Attributes:
Endurance: 81
Strength: 81
Agility: 81
Mind: 82
Will: 81
Magical Aptitude: 76
Luck: 4

Health: 1620/1620
Mana: 1580/1580

Abilities:
Active: Dragon Fear, Umbral Breath
Passive: Dark Vision, Scales, Treasure Sense

Active Skills:

Draconic Strike
Draconic Fury
Searing Slash
Dragon's Charge
Tempest Strike
Heavy Draconic Strike
Stealth (Advanced)
Crippling Blow

Passive Skills: None

Spells:
Shadow Bolt
Darkness
Shadow Ward
Arcane Singularity
Shadow Walk
Umbral Chains
Shadow Surge

Nice! Those were a good pair of new options. I quickly checked the full description and was once again pleased by how my Treasure Sense caused the System to provide more than the basic information.

Crippling Blow
Description: A powerful strike aimed at the limbs of an enemy, designed to hinder their mobility and reduce their ability to attack effectively.
Effect: Deals high damage and provides a 30% chance of crippling the targeted limb.
Cooldown: 30 seconds

Shadow Surge
Description: An enhanced single-target spell that unleashes

a concentrated blast of shadow energy at an enemy, dealing significant damage.

Effect: Deals high damage with a chance to inflict a significant "weakness" effect, reducing the target's damage output by 30% for 5 seconds.

Cooldown: 30 seconds.

Two more high-damage attacks would come in handy as I gained levels and faced more powerful foes.

The mini-map now showed just single red dots spread far enough apart that I wasn't likely to have to face more than one at a time, and it was a good thing. Enchanted Constructs were next. Unlike the previous creatures, these guardians stood out in the open, a challenge that required a different strategy.

As I approached, I could see their imposing figures. Each was crafted from stone and metal, imbued with ancient magic, and covered in runes that pulsed with power. They didn't hide; they stood vigilantly, their hulking forms rigid yet somehow alive, ready to defend their territory. I knew I couldn't charge in recklessly. These weren't mindless beasts or fragile spellcasters—I was facing something designed purely for war.

Instead, I used **Shadow Walk** to slip into the shifting darkness around them, my presence vanishing into the gloom. I moved carefully, inching closer without being detected. Even from here, I could feel the hum of raw magic radiating from them, an aura of ancient power. The nearest construct loomed over me, its bulk layered in thick stone plating, the runes etched into its surface glowing faintly with a blue light. Its energy pulsed in rhythmic waves, resonating in my bones. These things weren't just animated statues—they were living defenses honed to react and adapt.

I had to strike fast.

Emerging from the darkness, I aimed for a vulnerable joint, my blade cutting toward what should have been a weak point between the plates. But before my attack could land, the construct moved—far faster than something that size had any right to. In a blur, its arm twisted and expanded, morphing into a massive shield. My blade slammed against the hardened surface, the force of the impact ringing through the air like a struck bell. A violent jolt of energy coursed up my arm, sending sharp pain through my wrist and nearly making me drop my weapon.

Shit!

Before I could react, it countered. Its massive stone fist swung at me with crushing force, tearing through the air like a battering ram. I barely managed to twist out of the way, the wind of its passing brushing my face. The impact struck the ground where I had just been standing, shattering stone and sending sharp fragments flying in all directions. One jagged shard sliced across my cheek, warm blood trickling down my skin.

This was going to be more challenging than I'd anticipated.

I couldn't afford another direct hit—one clean strike from those things, and I'd be the one crumbling into pieces. Keeping my stance low, I circled, forcing it to turn with me, using its own bulk against it. My mind raced through strategies. If its upper body was too well-armored, I needed to take out its foundation.

Drawing on my instincts, I darted in again, feinting high before pivoting low, my blade slicing toward the knee joint. The steel sparked as it connected, but the construct barely flinched. Its defenses weren't just physical—the magic woven into its form was dulling the impact, dispersing the damage across its entire structure.

I needed more force.

I activated **Crippling Blow**, pouring extra power into my strike. My blade glowed faintly, pulsing with energy as it carved into the stone. This time, the attack landed properly, and with a sharp, splintering crack, I felt resistance give way. The construct staggered, its leg faltering, a web of fractures spreading outward from the wound.

But it wasn't done.

With a deafening groan of grinding stone, it lashed out wildly, swinging its massive arm in an arc meant to crush me into pulp. I dived past it beneath the blow a split second before the impact. I came out of my roll behind it just as its attack obliterated a nearby column, sending debris tumbling. I was behind it now, heart hammering in my chest; the risky maneuver had succeeded!

No more wasting time.

With the opening I had created, I struck hard, driving my blade deep into its exposed core. The moment steel met magic, a surge of resistance pushed back like the construct itself was fighting to hold itself together. Runes flared along its body, flickering erratically, a silent scream of dying magic. I gritted my teeth, forcing my weapon deeper, twisting as I channeled raw strength into the blow.

Then, with one final pulse, the light in its runes dimmed. A deep, shuddering crack split through its torso, and with a slow, almost reluctant motion, the construct collapsed. The heavy mass of stone and metal crashed to the ground, sending up a cloud of dust and debris, the magic that had once animated it fading into nothing.

I stepped back, breathing hard, my arms burning from exertion. My side ached where its fist had nearly connected, and my wrist still throbbed from the earlier impact.

One down. But that was just the first.

As I took a moment to catch my breath, I couldn't help but feel a rush of exhilaration. This dungeon was testing my skills.

Still, that had taken a toll on me and hadn't been a quick or easy fight, and that was despite a gap of fifteen levels between us. Whoever had designed those things had made the most tanky constructs I had ever encountered. I was almost regretting my choice to upgrade my bloodline. Acid would have been much more effective than shadow against these. Unfortunately, tanky constructs were an effective counter to my current skill set.

Bah! Who cares! Despite these bastards, I was having a lot of fun with this new stealth-based build. I had completely wrecked those Shadow Stalkers and even the Obsidian Spiders.

I would just need to power through this and find a strategy that was more effective. If nothing else, it was good practice fighting strong physical opponents.

As I proceeded, I tried many different strategies. They were immune to **Draconic Fear,** having no emotions as a construct. **Shadow Bolt** and **Arcane Singularity** both were fairly lackluster. They seemed to have a certain amount of magic resistance on top of their rocky physical toughness. What I ended up settling on worked well but was very mana-intensive. I would **Shadow Walk** to get behind them, then use a **Heavy Draconic Strike** followed by a **Crippling Blow** to take out a leg. After that, I focused on removing an arm using **Searing Slash** and a regular **Draconic Strike.** Then, I could use regular, unenhanced blows to destroy the head, which was where its core was. I thanked my stars that their maker hadn't hidden the core in the chest. That would have been a bitch to do enough damage to destroy.

There were only thirty of these standing like silent sentinels between me and the boss room. Still, it took me two and a half more hours to destroy them all. I had to do it, though. The whole point of these dungeons was to kill as many monsters as possible for the XP. As annoying as these were, I did get another level before making it to the boss.

I had made good use of my new **Crippling Blow** against the Constructs. Unfortunately, their magic resistance had made my new spell less useful than I had hoped, but I was sure it would be devastating against different monsters.

The other issue was that this dungeon was taking longer than I was happy with. It had been early morning when I arrived, and it would be mid-afternoon by the time I finished. The XP was so good that I would definitely rerun it; I just need to find a better way next time. I didn't want to spend six hours or more per dungeon run. With the 10% bonus I got for all dungeon clears from my **Dungeon Conqueror** title, plus the 10% from my title for solo dungeon clears, I should have enough to get one more level out of this run.

Yep, definitely need to run this again! I just need to figure out a way to do it faster!

I already had an idea on that, but I'd have to see how viable it was against the boss and its minions. If the dungeon held true to the standard, then there would be five of those constructs, along with a boss somewhere around level 30 or a little above. That was getting sketchy even for me and my crazy bloodline-enhanced class.

"Time to roll the dice!"

CHAPTER 16

DAMNED DWARF!

I STEELED MYSELF, checking my gear and mentally preparing for whatever lay ahead. The darkness seemed almost alive, whispering threats and promises in equal measure. Immediately casting **Stealth**, I moved through the entrance to the boss room.

As I stepped through the archway, the heavy door slammed shut behind me, sealing me in the boss chamber with an echoing clang. The air felt thick with tension, and a chill ran down my spine. Dim light illuminated the cavern, casting long shadows that danced along the stone walls. In the center of the chamber stood a Dwarven Runesmith, an imposing figure shrouded in an aura of ancient power. It was flanked by five hulking Enchanted Constructs, their formidable bodies etched with glowing runes that pulsed ominously.

The Runesmith's eyes gleamed with malice as it looked around for the intruder in its domain. "So, you've come to challenge me," it sneered, his voice a mix of mockery and menace. "You'll soon regret this foolishness. Reveal yourself, worm!"

I didn't rise to the bait. I was here to fight, not to engage in his verbal games. Besides, I wasn't stupid enough to give away my position for the sake of bantering with a System-generated monster. Instead, I focused on the constructs, their stone and metal forms standing ready to defend their master. My heart raced with anticipation, and I felt the familiar heat of the dragon blood coursing through my veins, eager for battle. The mini-map flickered in my mind, showing the positions of the constructs and the faint glow of the Runesmith at the center, not revealing any hidden foes.

Time to execute my plan, sketchy though it was.

I crept forward. My longknife was gripped tightly in my hand, and I could feel the pulse of energy thrumming in the air around me.

As I edged closer, I could see the runes on the constructs shimmering an ominous dull red color. The Runesmith raised his hands, chanting under his breath. "**Strengthen!**" he bellowed, and a wave of energy surged through the constructs, their runes glowing a brighter shade of red as they became even more formidable.

Crap, I need to act fast.

I couldn't have accounted for that, but there was nothing that could be done. At least the bastard wasn't throwing out AoE spells indiscriminately.

I launched myself into the fray, my instincts kicking in as I targeted the center construct. My plan was straightforward: I would use **Dragon's Charge** to hit the center construct's leg, hoping to cripple it and knock it prone. Then, I would remain focused on that construct, drawing the others in to surround me. Once they were all in position, I'd cast **Darkness** to blind everyone, giving me the chance to escape and unleash my full power.

With renewed determination, I barreled toward the nearest construct. My knife struck true, slicing through its defenses as I aimed for its leg.

The impact reverberated through my body, and I felt the thrill of a clean hit. The construct staggered, its defenses momentarily disrupted.

Perfect! I needed them grouped up. My Stealth worked a little like an improved invisibility spell in that I had a few seconds' grace period from when I attacked until it wore off. I used that time to continue attacking the center construct. They knew where I was due to my continued attacks, even though they couldn't see me yet, so the rest were closing in.

"Protect your master!" the Runesmith shouted, the deep voice echoing in the chamber.

I cursed under my breath, knowing that I wasn't the only one with a plan. The constructs moved to shield the Runesmith, positioning themselves between us. Not entirely surrounding me yet, like I had hoped. Still, I continued my assault on the nearest construct, striking at its leg again and again, determined to bring it down. These damned things were a lot tougher than the ones I had previously fought due to the buff. I kinda regretted not just going straight for the boss, but I would stick to the plan for now and hope it worked out.

Sadly, the Runesmith was quick to respond. **"Weaken!"** it shouted just as I became visible. I felt a surge of energy wash over me. My muscles felt heavy, as though the very air was pressing down on me. I gritted my teeth, forcing myself to fight through the debuff. I couldn't let this stop me.

The construct swung its massive arm, aiming for me with surprising speed. I dodged to the side, the momentum causing me to roll across the ground. I had to be careful; these constructs were tough, and the Runesmith was no slouch either. I hadn't had a good, challenging fight since the Stronghold dungeon, but it looked like I had one now!

As I continued striking the construct, I saw my opening and prepared to strike again. I activated **Crippling Blow** this time, channeling my energy as I aimed for the center construct's already weakened leg. With a burst of speed, I lunged forward, my longknife poised for a critical strike. My attack landed with a bone-rattling thud, and I could see the construct falter, its leg buckling under the force of my blow.

Crippled!

But just as I thought I was gaining the upper hand, the Runesmith raised his hands again, chanting another spell. **"Enhance!"** A wave of energy washed over the constructs, and I felt the chill of dread settle in my gut. They were becoming even more formidable, their runes glowing brighter and taking on a slightly purple tint, strengthening even further. This was taking too long, but it had succeeded; the constructs had finally surrounded me.

Now, phase two! I cast **Darkness**, plunging a 30' radius into an inky zone impenetrable to sight. Not even these Enchanted Constructs or their master could see through that.

"Find him!" the Runesmith shouted, his voice sharp with frustration. "Don't let him escape!"

I acted quickly. The constructs lunged at me blindly, their heavy arms swinging in an uncoordinated effort to trap and cripple me. I barely managed to dodge their attacks, my heart pounding as I got clear of the chaos in the middle of the room.

The constructs continued to stumble in the darkness, their movements erratic, while the Runesmith shouted in anger.

With the constructs disoriented, I prepared to unleash my full power. I activated **Draconic Fury**, doubling my strength both physically and magically for the next thirty-seven seconds, then sprang my trap.

Arcane Singularity! Unlike my physical strength, my spell was unaffected by the debuff that had been cast upon me. I conjured a swirling mass of energy right in the center of the darkness that pulled the constructs closer, drawing them into its heart. Three seconds later, an enormous explosion rocked the chamber, sending debris flying as the blast tore through their defenses. I loved that powered-up spell! Even their magical resistance couldn't overcome my buff.

I felt a backlash of heat wash over me, and I could see the constructs stagger, their rune lights flickering wildly. They were all prone and would take precious seconds to get up, if they even could. Many had mangled limbs and large chunks of stone ripped out of them.

"Umbral Chains!" I shouted, binding the Runesmith with dark tendrils and doing substantial damage over time thanks to **Draconic Fury**. That should also make it harder for the bastard to concentrate to cast spells. It struggled against the magic, but I could see the chains tightening around its limbs.

"Fool!" it spat, desperation creeping into its voice. "You think you can defeat me so easily?"

I didn't waste time responding. With the constructs still reeling, I focused on my next move. **"Shadow Surge!"** I unleashed my new high-damage spell directly at him. The energy coiled around me before erupting toward the boss, hitting it with tremendous force.

It was blasted backward a few feet despite the **Umbral Chains**, the runes on its armor dimming, but I knew I couldn't let up now. I ran, hoping to close with it and finish it off with my melee skills while it was trapped, feeling the energy building within me as the darkness swirled around us.

"Self-destruct!" the Runesmith bellowed, and my heart dropped as I realized what was coming. The constructs began to glow ominously, their runes suddenly doubling and then tripling in brightness, making it hard to see. Panic surged through me. I had heard of constructs self-destructing, but this was my first encounter with it in this dungeon. None of the ones outside the boss's room had done this.

I needed to escape!

Shadow Walk! I tried to leap into the shadows...

The explosion rocked the dungeon before I could entirely vanish. A wave of energy and obsidian shards and jagged metal fragments slammed into me, knocking me off my feet and sending me sprawling to the ground.

Despite being dazed and injured, I struggled to rise, feeling the weight of the explosion pressing down on me. That was only one! I could see the others still powering up to detonate. I gritted my teeth, forcing myself to focus. I had to keep moving. I couldn't let this be the end.

Gasping for breath, I stumbled toward the Runesmith and moved into the shadows, using my remaining strength to push through the agony. Looking down at myself, now that I was hopefully safe from physical damage within the shadows. What I saw made me pale; my body had at least a dozen wounds, some still filled with metal or obsidian shards.

I would deal with that, but first, the boss needed to die!

From within the shadows, I heard the consecutive booms of one construct exploding after another. The entire room, including the boss, was torn apart by the resulting shockwaves and shrapnel.

It had indeed been an attempt to take me out with him.

I was close now, close enough to recognize that it had unfortunately survived, if only barely. The contempt in its eyes as it prepared for his next spell was clear to see.

With the last remnants of my **Draconic Fury** strength surging through me, I staggered forward and exited the shadows within range of the boss.

The System-generated dwarf was still alive and fighting back against my **Umbral Chains**, still able to cast spells despite its own agony.

Damn, those bastards are tough!

Desperation clawed at me. If it got off another spell, I wasn't sure if I could survive it. Summoning every ounce of energy I had left, I released my breath weapon, **Shadow Breath**. The draconic energy rushed forth in a concentrated blast, the darkness surging out of me before completely engulfing the Runesmith.

The shadows consumed it, and this time, it had no chance to counter. The darkness left only silence in its wake, the body gone.

I fell to my knees, breathing heavily, feeling the weight of this pyrrhic victory settle over me, mingling with the exhaustion of the battle. I had faced down a strong challenge and emerged victorious, but the price had been high.

As I took a moment to catch my breath, I pulled out a mid-grade healing potion and drank it down, feeling the soothing energies closing wounds and easing my many hurts.

I was too weary for a long moment to go and collect the loot. Perhaps because I was running solo again, there was both a boss drop and a loot chest, and I was looking forward to what I might find. This was a somewhat higher-level dungeon than I had faced before, so I hoped it would be good stuff.

Tiredly, I joked, "Come on, papa needs a new pair of shoes!"

CHAPTER 17

FIGHTING SMARTER, NOT HARDER!

IT WAS GOOD LOOT. In fact, it was excellent. First, from the boss drop, I received *Skill Crystal: Analyze*, which I immediately learned.

Upon consuming the small crystal, I wanted to dance for joy when I received the System message:

Synergy detected between Skill: Analyze and Bloodline Ability: Treasure Sense.

Combining and upgrading skills to Treasure Sense: Special Grade.

Treasure Sense: Special Grade

Passive Ability:
User's enhanced treasure-detecting ability now operates continuously, allowing user to sense valuable items, hidden loot, and rare materials within a large radius, even through walls and obstacles. In addition, the skill now reveals

detailed information about creatures and humans within line of sight.

This information includes:
Name
Health and Mana Bars
These are displayed above the target's head, with color coding to represent threat levels:
Threat Level
Green: Low Threat
Yellow: Moderate Threat
Red: High Threat
Purple: Extremely Dangerous

Active Ability:
When used actively, Treasure Sense grants deeper analysis, combining the effects of Analyze and treasure detection. You can now identify precise values of loot, potential hidden enchantments on items, and the relative danger of traps. In combat, the active ability provides a chance at additional insight into enemies' weaknesses, potential drops, and vulnerabilities, making it invaluable for high-risk engagements and planning.

I was ecstatic! That was an incredibly useful combination of two skills, and I immediately put it to use as I hurried to the loot chest.

Loot Chest (Untrapped): Open chest to determine valuables inside. This is a standard chest containing awards for completing a dungeon. Grade of treasure inside is determined by the Level of the dungeon boss, Luck, and Titles or Skills.

Now able to determine at a glance that there were no traps, I fearlessly popped open the lid. The chest creaked open, revealing its sparse contents. Nestled within, I saw two potions: one a deep crimson, the other a vibrant blue—high-grade health and mana potions, glowing faintly in the dim light. Between them, resting on the soft velvet, was a single *Upgrade Rune*, its surface etched with intricate patterns, softly pulsing with energy. Simple but effective and always useful.

Activating my upgraded Treasure Sense, I focused on the rune. Information immediately flashed before my eyes: *Upgrade Rune (Rare Grade)*—capable of enhancing any item's rarity by one tier, up to rare. It shimmered with potential, its intricate design radiating a soft green glow, ready to infuse power into whatever it touched.

I had just the thing! Pulling out the five-by-five-inch metal plate with a rune on it from my storage ring, I grinned.

My new portable shelter was upgradable. Right now, it was roughly the size of a two-person tent or around thirty square feet. I was eager to see how large it could get.

When I pressed the upgrade rune to the surface of the portable shelter plate, a bright green glow surged across its etched lines, filling each groove with vibrant energy. The metal warmed under my fingers as the rune absorbed the power, shifting subtly—its once simple design now pulsing with a stronger, more intricate pattern, signifying its new, rare-grade enhancement.

The newly upgraded portable shelter had transformed into something far more impressive. What was once a modest 30-square-foot space with just two cots now expanded into a luxurious 200-square-foot sanctuary. Inside, a comfortable bed stood against one wall, a sturdy table and chairs filled the center, and plush seating provided a place to truly relax. Soft, adjustable lighting now filled the space, casting the room in a warm, welcoming glow. The concealment enchantment had strengthened as well, making it invisible to anyone below level 50, ensuring my shelter remained my private refuge, utterly undetectable to others.

The best part was that it also acted as a storage item. The only difference was that time was not stopped within, and so meat or other perishables inside would not be preserved the way a standard storage item did.

I will make use of this right now! Around six hours had passed on that first run. Choosing to exit the dungeon, I found that it was around three o'clock in the afternoon, but thankfully, there weren't any religious zealots or anyone else for that matter. Looking around, I found a reasonably inconspicuous place, set my portable shelter rune plate on the ground, and activated it. The next instant, I was within.

It wasn't luxurious, but it was comfortable, and I could use a short rest before continuing.

Taking a seat in one of the comfy chairs, I took a moment to examine my status. I hit Level 38 on that run, which was a full six levels from one dungeon. I couldn't be more pleased. Well, that was a lie. I would have been happier if the dungeon was less of a pain in the butt to complete. That last fight had been nothing to sneeze at, and both the Obsidian Spiders and the individual Enchanted Constructs took a lot more time than I would prefer. The spiders were sitting in strong defensive positions within their deadly webs, and the constructs were just incredibly durable.

The spiders I could handle quickly, with the expenditure of mana to Shadow Walk right into their nests to get behind them and strike unexpectedly. At ten mana activation cost, plus ten per second, it wasn't a cheap spell, but if I didn't bother to use Stealth once I got to the spiders and ran through the shadows to exit as quickly as possible, I might get away with 30 to 40 mana per kill. I would basically empty my entire mana pool on that portion of the dungeon. Not that mana took too long to regenerate, but still. Any delay would slow my progress. Plus with having to burn my entire mana pool on Stealth to destroy the Shadow Stalkers, that was twice I needed to pause for it to regen.

The more I thought about it, the more I felt I could be efficient about it. I actually ran dry on mana during the Stalkers because I was only able to kill three or so every time I activated Stealth before I had to cast it again at 100 mana points per activation. Combined with how fast I was able to kill them, that meant actually running dry on mana before I could get them done.

The spiders were purely defensive, so I could run from nest to nest and kill them in one or two blows, also resulting in a very rapid depletion of my mana. Outside of combat, mana regened pretty quickly, so a thirty-minute rest would have me back to full.

And then I had a strategy for killing the Enchanted Constructs far faster and with less mana expenditure, one that hopefully would keep me out of harm's way.

We'll see how well it works!

I took an hour-long nap, and I felt fully recovered and ready to go again.

Now familiar with the dungeon, my planning worked to speed things up. Not needing to be afraid of the Stalkers as long as I was invisible, I was more aggressive the second time and planned my routes so that I could hit at least three, and sometimes four, before my Stealth wore off. However, I was moving through them so fast that I ended up completely draining my mana before finishing them all off. A thirty-minute rest fixed me right up, and I attacked the spiders when I finished off the stalkers. That also necessitated a half-hour rest. Between the sheer number of the monsters and my speed at slaying them, I spent about three hours total on the first two phases of the dungeon. Not bad.

The third phase was much easier this time. I remembered a tactic from one of the video games I had played as a kid: Town of Heroes. Until they eventually patched it, you could kite them, gathering all the enemies in the entire zone and have them all in a big train chasing you until you stopped somewhere that allowed you to hit them without them being able to hit you. That way, you could kill an entire zone full of bad guys all at once.

It wasn't as easy in real life. Still, the concept worked. All I had to do was run up and hit the construct, and it would give chase, following indefinitely. The trick was getting enough of a lead to run up to the next one and hit it before the followers caught up. Despite a few accidents that caused me to take some hits, I managed it, bringing them all to a corner spot where I could jump up and climb out of their reach.

Thankfully, the Dwarf Runesmith didn't enchant them to be intelligent! When they were all gathered, I simply cast **Arcane Singularity** every three minutes until they were dead or wrecked enough that they couldn't defend themselves, and then went around the debris field, finishing them off with a few non-enhanced blows each.

It worked like a charm.

That meant I went into the boss battle almost at full health and with a full mana bar. I also changed up my tactics for the final fight. By that point, I was Level 42 and out-leveled the Dwarven Runesmith by twelve levels. That gave me a much more significant advantage and confidence. My spells hit harder, and its didn't affect me as much; plus, I knew to avoid the exploding constructs this time around. I simply stayed in Stealth and got right behind the boss before starting the fight. It cast his buff on the constructs as I hurried over into position, but that didn't affect me since I stayed away from them.

Deciding to avoid fighting the constructs until the boss was dead seemed like a good plan. I initiated combat by hitting it with **Umbral Chains** to hold him in place, then activated **Dragon's Fear**, then **Dragon's Fury** to double my own strength. The boss hit me with a debuff before I could get off my first actual swing, which was annoying. Still, my buff was more potent, so I was still doing around 30% more damage than usual with physical attacks. I hit it with **Heavy Dragon's Strike,** then **Shadow Surge**, my two most significant damage attacks, and between the boosted damage and the fact that it was incapacitated, I took the Runesmith down quickly.

Just before it died, it commanded the Constructs to surround me and wreak vengeance by self-destructing. Being forewarned this time, I simply ducked into the Shadows, where I couldn't be affected by physical attacks, and rode it out, waiting for the explosions to end.

Overall, I was delighted. I had completed the second run of the dungeon in a shockingly fast four hours. I might have a quicker time with an easier mid-level dungeon, but this was still fantastic. I picked up one more level after the boss fight from a combination of the combat experience and the dungeon completion bonuses from my titles, bringing me up to Level 47.

On that second run, I picked up a new weapon and a new pair of boots. The weapon was junk compared to my soulbound *Longknife of Shadows*, but if I ever decided to take up dual wielding, it would be useful. It was called a *Nightrend Dagger*, and it provided a 15% crit chance boost, as well as adding a shadow-based DoT.

I chuckled, '*On second thought, maybe I will try dual wielding!*'

The boots were slightly better than my old ones, and they looked cooler, too, so I switched them out. They were called *Shadowstride*

Boots and were very similar to my old ones, except they gave a 10% boost to Agility, which was nothing to sneeze at. At my new level, that brought me to 111 Agility, which boggled my mind. Before my rebirth, I had never gotten even a single stat into the 50's. My previous Agility was 48. I felt so incredibly fast and dexterous now compared to my old life.

If I could face that high orc warrior who killed me, I might be able to survive and win even though I am just over half his level. Not that I wanted the high orcs to invade, but there would be payback coming someday!

Taking another hour to rest before going back in again, the third run was even faster, but only by a little bit. I finished it in just over three and a half hours, and this time, I didn't suffer a single wound.

For loot, I received two things, and they were incredible. First was a rare-grade *Storage Ring* with a much larger storage capacity, but also added a 10% movement bonus out of combat. Second was something that completely blew my mind.

Dungeon Seeker's Compass (Unique Grade)
Description: This enchanted compass is an essential tool for any adventurer, designed to navigate the complexities of the dungeon landscape. At its core, it points to the nearest dungeon, but its true power lies in its versatility. Users can specify the type of dungeon they seek—whether Low grade, Medium grade, or High grade—or direct the compass to locate dungeons by rarity, ranging from common to epic or legendary. With intricate runes and a glowing crystal, the Dungeon Seeker's Compass not only guides its bearer but also ensures they are always on the path to the most rewarding challenges awaiting in the depths.

In my wildest dreams I never would have expected to receive loot like that. However, it wasn't random.

Ever since Level 32, I had been placing all of my free stats into Luck. I had already been getting a 40% boost to all treasure, so I wanted to see what difference it would make to bump that up. I only had four free stat points to assign per level, and it took ten stat points to raise Luck by one point. That meant it had taken me all the way to my current Level 47 to max out Luck at 10. I knew ten was the max because the System wouldn't allow me to add any more points.

That meant I was receiving a 100% bonus toward increasing the loot I was earning. Or maybe it was raising the tier of the reward 10 times higher than normal. I didn't know the mechanics behind it, but this item certainly demonstrated the results! This thing was a massive cheat. I would be able to cherry-pick the type of dungeon I wanted to find, at least in terms of rarity and grade, and I'd be able to run directly to them without any wandering around and searching. In time-savings alone, this could make the difference between making it to level cap on time.

Sure, I could have taken those fifty-plus stat points and distributed them to other things like Strength or Mind, but thanks to my titles and bloodline bonuses, I was already way ahead of the curve, and I figured being geared up with great stuff might tip the balance in fighting those other champions that were gunning for me.

Speaking of which... Along with the Dungeon Seeker's Compass came a bombshell from the AI.

There was a note in the treasure chest. But before I dealt with reading what I was sure would be a new existential threat, I needed to deal with checking out my latest stats and skills. I had been holding off examining them, not wanting to slow down my progress on the dungeon runs. I knew myself too well and would have surely messed up my plan trying out the new stuff.

CHAPTER 18
LEVELS AND SKILLS, OH YEAH!

WHEN I STARTED THE DAY, I was Level 34. After three runs of this medium-grade dungeon, even if it was on the lower end of medium, I had already hit Level 47. I couldn't believe the progress I had made in a single day; thirteen levels! This was really giving me hope that I might be able to pull this off. Sure, the monsters get tougher and more dangerous the higher level you face, but then again, so was I. With this insane Luck score, I would be pulling items that went way beyond what someone at my level should normally be able to acquire.

Liam Bell:
Draconic Shadowblade - Level 47
Bloodline (Tier 2): Shadow Dragon

Experience: 3980/49920

Attributes:
Endurance: 105
Strength: 106

Agility: 106
Mind: 105
Will: 105
Magical Aptitude: 105
Luck: 10

Health: 2110/2110
Mana: 2100/2100

Abilities:
Active: Dragon Fear, Umbral Breath, Claws
Passive: Dark Vision, Scales, Treasure Sense

Active Skills:
Draconic Strike
Draconic Fury
Searing Slash
Dragon's Charge
Tempest Strike
Heavy Draconic Strike
Stealth (Advanced)
Crippling Blow
Iron Hide

Passive Skills:
Claw Mastery

Spells:
Shadow Bolt
Darkness
Shadow Ward
Arcane Singularity
Shadow Walk
Umbral Chains

Shadow Surge
Ward of Shadows
Shadow Recall

I was blown away by all the goodies I had received.

First and foremost was the pair **Claws** and **Claw Mastery**. This was a game-changer. My dragon bloodline ability was to grant me claws that would grow long dark-ivory dragon talons, stronger than the best System-generated steel. Even more impressive was that the **Claw Mastery** skill allowed them to take on the qualities of whatever weapon I assigned to that hand. Meaning I could assign my *Long Knife of Shadows* to my right hand and have all of its abilities active on my right-hand claws. On my left hand, I assigned my new *Nightrend Dagger*, with its +15% crit chance.

Claw Mastery was more than just the transference of enchantment to my claws; it also imparted the knowledge and skill to use those claws as if I had been born with them. There would be no awkward period of getting used to a new weapon and training with it to learn its ins and outs. I could feel the knowledge in the back of my mind, and the moment I extended them for the first time, it was like I had been using them since my first life. I knew them as well as I knew the sword or the dagger.

I hated the System and its heartless accomplice, Earth's AI node, but I was in awe of this. Like the Skill Crystals or Skill Scrolls, I had to believe somewhere in the universe within the list of worlds the System had conquered, there was a planet with real live dragons, and this skill was somehow lifted right from their brains and nervous systems. I couldn't believe there was any way a computer, no matter how advanced, could simply calculate and create what I was feeling in my muscles when using these claws. It was too visceral!

And then there were my spells:

Shadow Ward 2 (Level 40)
Description: An advanced form of shadow-infused barrier. Shadow Ward 2 surrounds him in a dense vortex of darkness, reducing incoming damage by 25% for up to 1 minute and reflecting 20% of that damage back at the attacker. The swirling shadows cling to Liam's form, flickering with each strike received.
Cooldown: 5 minutes.

Shadow Recall (Level 45)
Description: Lets user teleport to a chosen shadowed location within a 10-mile radius or to any previously visited spot in the current dungeon. It's a precise and powerful escape or repositioning tool, harnessing shadow magic to "fold" the distance. Note: Casting of this spell is not instantaneous, not recommended for use in combat.
Cooldown: 1 hour.

Lastly, there was one other skill, and it was pretty great, but in comparison to **Claw Mastery**, it just wasn't as exciting. It was like Christmas morning, you receive a cool Lego set, then you open your next present and it is an awesome new puppy. Sure, you'll play with the Legos and love them, but your new best friend is gonna get all the attention!

Iron Hide (Level 45)
Description: User hardens their scales and skin to a nearly impenetrable level, granting +50% to armor for 5 minutes. This spell/skill invokes a metallic sheen across the body, visibly reinforcing defensive capabilities.
Cooldown: 20 minutes.

I could definitely see myself using that against boss fights and tough battles. No matter how badly it was outshined by **Claw Mastery**, it would be incredibly useful to add another layer to defense when I was in danger.

If it weren't for the uncounted millions dying from the thoughtlessness of the bastard AI and its master, the System, I would absolutely rejoice in gaining these abilities. Hell, if it had just inducted us into the System without the shady bullshit way it did by collapsing civilization, we probably would have welcomed the chance to join.

Getting side-tracked into these gloomy thoughts as I was, I felt like there was something there. Why had it chosen such a destructive method? Sure, it wanted to level the playing field according to the AI, but did it really need to reduce us to the Stone Age?

I dismissed the thoughts. Humanity had spent twenty years becoming extinct, asking itself, 'Why?' Not even our best and brightest had figured it out.

CHAPTER 19

THE GOOD, THE BAD, AND THE UGLY!

WHEN I HAD FINISHED with my skills and status, I finally broke down and pulled out the message I was dreading. I had no idea what it contained, but I knew it wouldn't be good.

The AI has said System rules would not allow direct communication. Perhaps this was some kind of loophole.

> *Liam,*
> *I have included the dungeon-finding compass in your rewards because it is essential for you to achieve your goal before the end of the 30-day grace period. You will need it to locate high-value dungeons quickly and efficiently. However, due to the rules of the System, no champion can be given an unfair advantage.*
> *To maintain balance, each of the other champions who have come to Earth early has also been provided with a compass—one that points directly to you.*
> *Use your time wisely.*
> *—AI Moderator Node - Earth*

What followed was a good five minutes of me in turns cursing, ranting about the asshole System and AI, and pausing to try and work out why the AI thought this was a good idea.

Before, I might have gotten lucky and simply avoided all or many of the approaching champions. After all, they would have had to search for me in between leveling up. Now, however, they could run straight for me and show up any second.

The one thing I was happy about was that the girls were not with me.

At least if the bastards come, it will be me, alone, that is in danger.

As I thought it through and calmed down, I began to understand why the AI did it. It was just numbers. I had made tremendous progress today, but how long would it take me to wander around looking for the next medium or high-grade dungeon. I had a general idea where they might be, but lacking any kind of map from before the apocalypse, I couldn't know for sure. I had a good guess, considering that every major center of trade and industry would likely have one, but even if I ran to my next guess, I'd still have to hunt around for the entrance, and that would eat up significant time. Hell, until the dungeons started breaking and spilling their monsters out to swarm over the city, I could walk within a hundred yards of a dungeon portal and not even know it was there. Maybe if I got an upgrade to my Explorer skill, I could have expanded my detection range, but that was a long shot equivalent to winning the lottery.

No, the AI's choice actually made a lot of sense the more I thought about it. It might even give me a tactical advantage, although that was debatable.

By giving the champions compasses that pointed directly to me, they would likely rush to come to attack me as soon as possible before I could get any more powerful. That meant their own levels would be limited when they found me. With the mini-map, I would *hopefully* see anyone trying to use stealth skills to assassinate me, and that would give me an advantage. Red dots in my mini-map would be glaringly obvious right now. There were some monsters and mutated beasts roaming the city, but they weren't too common yet. In a couple weeks, that would be a different story, but for now, I would hopefully get some warning before being attacked.

"Okay, now that I'm done with that little freak-out. It's time to move."

Unfortunately, I had a dilemma. Did I go back inside the medium dungeon for another run or hurry away to find the next higher dungeon? I wasn't quite to Level 50 yet, and I needed to stick to medium-grade dungeons for the time being for safety. However, I had been here for a long time. Over fourteen hours in one location. If I went back inside the Runesmith's dungeon now, it would be, minimum, four more hours before I came back out. Staying in one place that long—I could easily have one or more champions sitting outside, waiting to ambush me when I finished.

Time to Nope-out!

It was just too dangerous to risk it. If I start moving now, they will have to adjust their direction, and if I can keep moving around quickly enough from dungeon to dungeon, then they will have a harder time tracking me down.

Then, another thought crossed my mind and made me smile with an evil grin. That new Shadow Recall skill would allow me to jump all over the place.

I knew it was a bad habit, but I couldn't help myself; I spoke my thoughts aloud, weighing them.

"If I run deeper into town for the next medium-grade dungeon and run it. I could step outside afterward and jump right back here and run this one again. Or I could jump back to the area near the Kobold

Dungeon and then head off in a different direction entirely; head down Hwy 121 instead of going straight toward downtown. I could keep doing that after every dungeon run. It would slow me down, but it would play absolute hell with their ability to find me."

Frowning, I had a disturbing thought. What if one of the champions happened to be already in the area when I recalled nearby? I wouldn't have any way of knowing they were close, but they could directly hone in on me.

"Well, damn! My grand plan isn't without flaws. Still, it is worth a shot. Less likely they would be able to come at me together as a group."

Another flaw suddenly occurred to me. I would need to use the Commune skill to let Morgan know what was going on so they didn't start running all over trying to chase me down. It hadn't been long enough yet for them to be looking for me. When I found the next dungeon, I'd take a break and contact them.

Set on a plan, I put it into action and began running toward Spring Creek Parkway. That would be the next large-ish area that might have a medium dungeon. I had adjusted the dials on the compass to look for medium-grade dungeons, but until I got some distance from this one, it would keep pointing to the Runesmith's dungeon.

As I moved south from the ruins of Stacy Road, the landscape only grew bleaker. The buildings thinned out, but what remained was a mess of twisted metal and broken concrete. Trees that had once lined the streets were now growing unnaturally fast. Carefully manicured landscaping was turning into tall weeds and shrubs. The System had started its reclamation process, turning everything familiar into a wasteland, and it showed.

Displaced people shuffled along the cracked sidewalks and empty streets, their faces grim and eyes haunted. Parents tried to shield their children from those they passed or from wild nature, perhaps afraid of what might lurk within. They dug through the rubble like scavengers, hoping to find anything that could help them make it through another day. Some carried makeshift weapons, others clutched bags of scraps. The desperation was palpable, a constant reminder of how quickly everything had fallen apart. No one lingered too long in one place, and the monsters roaming the outskirts were growing bolder.

I saw several animals that must have once been pets mutated into gruesome things: cats the size of large dogs with glowing eyes and claws, dogs the size of dire wolves, turned feral and aggressive.

It broke my heart not being able to stop and deal with the beasts or help the people. I was afraid that if I took too long getting to the next dungeon, I would be found by the champions along the way.

This worry turned out to be well-founded.

I had stopped to rescue a family that looked particularly helpless. It was a father, a mother, and four small children. The mother carried most of their meager possessions and tried to shepherd the children, while the father carried a heavy backpack and a big crowbar.

Passing by, I noticed they were being stalked by something that may have once been a raccoon. It was fast, agile, and stealthy, but it was also deformed to the point of being a grotesque caricature of its former self. Unfortunately, it also was bigger than the toddlers and looked like it was planning to make them its next meal.

Cursing under my breath, I ran over to get between the family and the mutated predator.

"Stay behind me and keep your kids from running. If they do, it will pounce."

They didn't even know what I was talking about. The father tried to raise his makeshift weapon threateningly, worried I was there to rob them. That was when the striped mutant hurried from one bush to the next across a bare concrete spot.

The wife screamed and clutched her children toward her. The ones she could reach, that is. The father stood stunned for a second, not believing what he had just seen, but like a bad movie, their three-year-old rushed toward where the beast had disappeared, calling out, "Itty-at! Itty-at!"

Of course, that was the moment everything went into slow motion. The beast lept toward the child, who didn't know any better.

Both parents screamed in agonized horror, knowing what would happen next, but were too slow to do anything to stop it. Hearing their heartbreak was like a punch in the gut.

Luckily, I was fast enough to act, thanks to my enhanced stats and my closing skill, **Dragon's Charge**.

It was designed to get a fighter across the battlefield in an instant, and while I could have destroyed the beast from a distance using **Shadow Bolt, Umbral Chains,** or **Shadow Surge**, I didn't want to scar the child for life by having it see the 'kitty cat,' blown into chunky salsa right before it's eyes.

Instead, I grabbed the beast and held it while the parents, finally freed of their shocked paralysis, rushed to catch the wayward child and pull it away from the danger.

Once I was sure they had the situation under control and the kid couldn't see what happened, I snapped the beast's neck and tossed it away to land in a distant patch of tall weeds.

Behind me, there was weeping, hugging, and many tears and admonishments to not run toward anything, not even kitty cats.

I smiled, glad I could do this small thing to make the world a little better for this one family.

Handing the parents a handful of copper mana coins, I quickly explained about getting magic classes and how their kids needed to keep those coins on them to build up a resonance to the mana. At least, that was the way I thought of it. It wasn't like I actually understood the physics of why mana coins caused them to develop points in the Magical Aptitude stat. I also urged them to head out of the city as fast as they could.

They were a bit shell-shocked, but the man nodded grimly. "I had a cousin and his family in east Plano; we were heading there to try and find them, but now..."

He glanced at his wife and children, then toward where I had flung the dead raccoon, shuddering. "...yeah. Yeah, we'll go north as quickly as we can. Thank you again for saving Keilly."

"Be sure to stay on the highway. It's not safe, but safer than being near places where things can ambush you."

I was just about to say more, but I heard something ominous before I saw the red icon pop up on my mini-map.

I didn't know what it was, but it was making a racket as it moved directly toward where we stood.

I could run, but that would put this family at risk. I hissed, "Go, run, hurry away from here as fast as you can!"

I extended my claws and made sure I had potions ready in inventory. It was comforting to reassure myself, even if it was unlikely I'd be able to drink one in the middle of solo combat. Things usually moved too fast for that.

A chill ran up my spine as I saw the icon that had popped up on my heads-up display. It wasn't the usual red dot. It was a star inside a circle, and it glowed twice as bright as the dot for that raccoon had.

One of the champions had found me.

CHAPTER 20

THAT AIN'T SHREK!

THE FAMILY I'd just saved from that overgrown cat was disappearing into the distance, making their way north along the highway like I'd told them. I hoped they'd make it, though, in the back of my mind, I knew it was only a matter of time before they ran into something worse. There was only so much I could do. I couldn't stop for every single person in need. Not if I wanted to keep ahead of the champions.

Of course, it looked like my worst fear had just become a reality. The ground trembled faintly beneath my feet. It wasn't another one of those mutated animals—it was something much worse.

I didn't need to see the symbol on my mini-map to know a champion had found me. It didn't make any logical sense, but I could feel it in my bones. Like two magnets were being drawn together, there was a pressure and a sense of inevitability.

I took a slow breath, steadying myself. From the corner of my eye, I saw the thing, finally. Lumbering out of the shadows between two crumbling buildings.

The ogre.

More than nine feet tall, skin like cracked stone, bulging muscles that could easily crush a car with a single punch. Unlike the monstrous ogres of fiction, though, this one wasn't just a mindless brute. There was intelligence behind its beady black eyes. It was dressed in crude armor and carried a massive warhammer. Het moved with purpose, and I could tell he wasn't just a dumb beast driven by rage. No, this thing knew exactly what it was doing.

I had fought System-generated dungeon variants in my past life, but I had never fought a real live ogre from the invading race. In my first life, they appeared in Florida and quickly proliferated to take control of most of the state.

Say what you will about 'Florida Man' jokes, but the ogres had a fearsome reputation. They were very territorial and aggressive. That meant this guy had come halfway across the United States to find me, all in eight days!

Holy shit! Did this guy skip leveling up to travel this far so quickly?

He had to start at Level 0 on day one of the apocalypses, just like me. Otherwise, the System's vaunted 'fairness' would have been complete bullshit.

Looking at him, I highly doubted that. He seemed way too strong and tough to not have leveled up significantly. Hell, that war hammer looked like it weighed as much as an anvil! He had to be at least over level thirty and have dumped most of his stats into Strength, Endurance, and Agility.

My guess was a lot higher than 30, probably even near my level. My thinking didn't change, though; I strongly suspected this guy didn't put any points into the mental stats or Magical Aptitude. He was probably at least twice my strength, judging from the way he handled that big hunk of metal.

Despite that, the Champion didn't rush. It was patient, scanning the area, its heavy steps shaking the broken asphalt beneath it. The air seemed to grow heavier with each footfall, the wind itself retreating in fear of this hulking mass of destruction. His gaze settled on me like a predator locking in on its prey.

I clenched my jaw, muscles tensing as I took a step forward. "You don't have to attack, you know," I called out, keeping my voice steady. "We could come to an agreement—one that doesn't involve killing each other." Seeing the look on its face, I already knew it was impossible, but I felt I had to try.

The ogre stopped, his head cocking to the side as if he was actually considering my words. For a brief second, I let myself hope that maybe, just maybe, he wouldn't be like the others. Maybe this one could think rationally and see the bigger picture.

But the look in its eyes... that flicker of thought I'd seen wasn't reason. It was cunning and strategy. Calculating, sure—but not for diplomacy.

It bared its teeth in something that could've been a smile but looked more like the snarl of a hungry animal. The damn thing wasn't interested in peace. It was here for one thing and one thing only— my head.

He sneered at me and my suggestion of peace.

"I am Gnarr! Victorious!" The ogre pounded its chest with a thunderous *boom*. "Crushed rat-thing dungeon! Took treasure! Now, crush puny human! Take world!"

Great. Of course, it wasn't going to be that easy.

I exhaled slowly, letting my breath settle as the reality of the situation sank in. I wasn't really afraid—not for myself, anyway. The real fear was what would happen if I lost. What it would mean for humanity, for those families like the one I'd just saved, if the champions took me down this early.

The ogre's heavy steps resumed, the ground vibrating again with each thud of its massive feet. There was no hesitation now, no pretense of a peaceful approach. It was ready for a fight, and I could feel its aggression radiating off of it in waves. I tightened my grip on my sword, eyes narrowing.

"Well, can't say I didn't try," I muttered under my breath, taking another step forward, my heart steady in my chest. It wasn't that I really believed there could be peace with an aggressive species like this, but if I could have bought us time for me to get to level cap, then maybe I could have minimized the deaths they would cause.

The ogre's steps thundered against the pavement, his growl rumbling like an avalanche as he bore down on me, war hammer swinging.

I braced myself to engage, but the bastard's eyes gleamed with cunning, and before I could react, he pivoted, swinging his massive weapon into a chunk of broken stone. A boulder the size of a car tire rocketed toward me.

Shit!

The rock blurred through the air faster than I could blink. I tried to angle my longknife to deflect it, but I was too slow. The stone clipped the blade, wrenching my arm back before it crashed into my shoulder with a sickening crunch.

Pain detonated through my body. My vision sparked white, and my arm went dead at my side.

I staggered, barely keeping my feet, a strangled gasp ripping from my throat. The impact had rattled my bones, and a cold realization settled in my gut—I couldn't lift my left arm. Not good.

The ogre barked a deep, rumbling laugh, reaching for another stone. He was playing with me.

I bit back a curse and forced my body to move. The next rock slammed into the ground where I'd been standing, sending dirt and rubble flying in a deafening explosion. A cannonball of stone.

The bastard was treating me like target practice.

I didn't wait for a third.

I threw myself forward, my roll clumsy with only one functioning arm, but I pushed through the pain, barely landing on my feet.

"Can't give him room to breathe," I snarled, forcing my legs to move despite the fire burning through my shoulder. I didn't want to get within reach of that war hammer, but distance was worse. Another stone could pulp me in a second.

The ogre reached for another boulder.

I was already in motion.

Dragon's Charge.

The world blurred as I exploded forward, closing the gap in an instant. The ogre's eyes widened. I was too close now for another rock, so he dropped the boulder and swung his war hammer in a horizontal arc, trying to crush me mid-sprint.

I threw myself low, feeling the wind of the massive weapon slicing overhead. My boots skidded against the cracked pavement as I twisted around the beast's flank. I aimed for the back of his knee.

My longknife slashed out, imbued with **Crippling Blow.**

The ogre reacted faster than something his size should. He dropped his war hammer like a battering ram, blocking the strike with a brutal clang of metal against metal. The sheer force of the parry nearly wrenched the weapon from my grip, rattling up my injured arm.

I stumbled, barely catching myself.

Damn thing was fast.

Too fast. That had to be a skill—something boosting his reaction speed. Otherwise, this fight was going to be over before it started.

"Puny human, not worth smashing!" The ogre sneered, patting a severed head tied to his belt, thick fingers running over the cracked, dried flesh. "Last ogre—good fight. You? Not even worth hang from belt!"

I didn't get time to answer.

He swung.

A warhammer the size of an anvil hurtled toward my skull.

I ducked—barely. The gust of wind from the swing whipped my hair back. Too close. One hit and I'd be paste.

I clenched my jaw and slashed upward, channeling **Draconic Strike** into my blade. The dark magic surged through the weapon as I struck for his knee again.

The ogre shifted, weight rolling fluidly, and countered with a downward smash. Another skill.

I barely yanked my blade back in time. The war hammer slammed into the ground inches from my feet, the shockwave rattling my bones. The impact sent a blast of dust and debris skyward, knocking me off balance again.

I gritted my teeth.

This wasn't working.

The ogre fought like a beast honed by war, not just brute strength. Every swing had the weight of experience behind it. Every step was measured, deliberate.

I had twenty years of survival under my belt, but this thing? He had spent his life earning the right to be Champion—a title that wasn't given, only taken through blood.

And I was losing.

I had been reacting since the first attack, moving on instinct rather than fighting smart. I wasn't playing to my strengths. I was letting him dictate the fight. That had to change.

The ogre grinned, tusks gleaming, war hammer rising for another devastating blow.

I had to force an opening.

I hadn't been casting spells because I hadn't had time. But I needed one. Now.

Dodging another swing, then another, I scanned the battlefield. A chunk of broken concrete jutted up from the pavement—a foot of solid debris.

I dove, rolling under the ogre's swing, then vaulted over the stone. My boots hit the ground in a stagger, barely keeping my footing.

Behind me, the ogre didn't bother going around. He simply backhanded the rubble aside, shattering it into dust.

That was my opening.

I threw out my hand, dark energy crackling at my fingertips, and cast **Shadow Surge** at the ogre's left knee.

A spear of pure darkness shot forward, slamming into the ogre's left knee with a bone-snapping crack. Black tenebrous magic burned through flesh and muscle, sending a tremor through his massive frame. A deep, guttural roar tore from his throat as he staggered back, blood pouring down his leg in thick rivulets. The knee wasn't shattered, but it was damaged—slower, weaker. I had finally hurt him.

His massive chest heaved, nostrils flaring as he absorbed the pain. His beady black eyes snapped to me, burning with fury.

"Gnarr crush! Gnarr grind bones to paste!"

He swung. Fast.

I threw myself to the side as the war hammer came down with the force of a meteor. The impact sent chunks of dirt and stone flying, the shockwave rattling my ribs. My wounded shoulder screamed in protest, my entire left side sluggish and heavy. I couldn't keep this up much longer. Every dodge, every movement was draining me, pushing me closer to a mistake I couldn't afford.

Gnarr limped forward, dragging his injured leg but still terrifyingly steady. The damage had slowed him, but not enough.

I had to buy more time.

I shoved my longknife into storage, freeing up my hand as I juked left, then cut right, narrowly avoiding another devastating swing. Thankfully, my storage ring was in my right hand! I willed a potion to appear-- a high-grade healing potion. Now wasn't the time for half-measures.

The war hammer whistled past my head as I uncorked the vial with my teeth. Rolling under the next swing, I gulped it down in one burning swallow. Heat spread through my veins, the familiar sensation racing through me of flesh knitting itself back together and bones grinding across each other as they set themselves back in their proper place.

The potion was working—but the timing was terrible.

A gust of wind slammed against my face as the war hammer just barely missed my skull. My body seized as my shoulder popped back into place with a painful jolt, my nerves screaming from the sudden repair. I flexed my fingers, feeling strength return to my arm just as another attack came.

Too close.

Way too close!

I dodged again—twice, three times—as Gnarr snarled, frustration creeping into his every movement.

"Good! You not bad! Maybe keep head as trophy!" he barked between swings, his breath hot and reeking of old blood. He was enjoying this—the challenge, the test of strength.

But I wasn't. I wasn't about to trade blows with something that could turn me into a red mist.

Just because I was scared didn't mean I wasn't pissed.

I hurled the empty potion bottle at his head. It bounced harmlessly off his thick skull. Gnarr barely flinched, but I didn't care. I wasn't stalling—I was setting up.

I flexed my fingers, feeling the shift as my claws activated.

The ogre's injured leg gave another faltering step, his balance momentarily thrown. He was slower now, but the raw power behind every swing was still enough to break me in half.

I needed more than just speed. I needed defenses. This whole fight pissed me off! I hadn't gotten to cast any of my defensive spells or do any other preparation. It was time to correct that.

Iron Hide!

My body hardened, muscles tightening as my skin took on the resilience of tempered steel.

Scalebound Resilience!

A second layer of reinforcement—my own draconic durability surging, making my body just tough enough to endure a glancing blow.

Still not enough.

I ducked under another hammer swing, then pushed further. I wasn't done.

Shadow Ward!

Shadow Ward 2!

Darkness coiled around me, an armor of writhing shadows sinking into my form. Fifty percent damage reduction. Twenty percent reflection, plus damage reflection.

Now, I was ready. I still couldn't afford to take a direct hit, but if I did, at least I couldn't be an instant stain on the concrete.

Gnarr's tusks curled in an ugly snarl as I shifted my stance, claws gleaming. He had expected me to keep running. Now, I wasn't.

We circled each other, the ground trembling beneath his every step. The vibration of his footfalls carried through my bones, steady and rhythmic. Waiting. Watching. My arm was almost fully healed, but I still wasn't at my peak.

And Gnarr sensed it.

He lunged.

A horizontal cleave with his war hammer, fast and brutal, aimed to take me out in one swing.

I ducked low, rolling just as the anvil-sized head of the weapon obliterated the concrete behind me. Stone and shrapnel exploded in all directions, pelting my arms and face. The air stung with dust and debris, but I didn't stop moving.

I had to cripple him further.

I lunged. My claws raked against his injured leg, tearing through skin and muscle. The ogre bellowed in fury, swinging downward in retaliation—but I was already gone, darting to the side before he could land the hit.

Not deep enough.

Not enough damage!

The damn bastard was a walking fortress!

Gnarr's frustration boiled over.

He slammed his warhammer into the ground again and again, sending up shockwaves of debris, trying to catch me in the chaos.

A funny thought crossed my mind at that moment despite the deadly serious nature of the situation.

The way he was flinging that hammer around reminded me of that movie... Hulk smash! And I didn't want to be Loki!

I kept moving, dodging, waiting—looking for my opening.

A fresh pulse of pain rippled through my arm, but it was functional. I just needed another moment. Just one.

The ogre took a stumbling step, his wounded leg almost giving out. His breathing had grown heavier, his rage pushing him into reckless aggression.

This was it.

I stopped running.

Gnarr's beady eyes locked onto me, sensing the shift, the change in my stance. He raised his war hammer again, muscles flexing, preparing for another earth-shattering blow.

I flexed my claws.

This time, I wasn't dodging.

This time, I wasn't playing defense!

I closed the distance again, feinting left before slashing at his right thigh. My claws bit deep, raking through flesh, but Gnarr barely reacted. Blood welled from the wound, thick and dark, but it didn't slow him.

I pivoted and struck again, this time toward his ribs. He caught the attack, blocking with his free arm and shoving me back with brute force. I staggered, barely keeping my footing, as his war hammer came down in a brutal overhead smash. I twisted away just in time, the impact sending a shockwave through the ground, chunks of debris flying in every direction.

Gnarr was no mindless brute. He had skill. Experience. He was using System-enhanced abilities with the precision of a veteran, each attack backed by overwhelming strength. If I miscalculated even once, I'd be nothing more than a smear on the pavement.

I darted in again, slashing at his exposed side, but the wound barely registered. It was like trying to carve through solid stone with a pocketknife. I needed to cripple him, force him onto the defensive—but every time I moved, he adapted. Every time I tried to gain an advantage, he shut it down.

We exchanged blows again—me dodging and slashing, him swinging with the relentless force of an avalanche. I was landing hits, but none of them mattered. His sheer size made him a walking fortress, shrugging off damage that would have crippled a lesser opponent.

I had to change something. This wasn't working.

Umbral Chains? No. He was too fast. The second I started casting, he'd crush me.

Darkness? Not an option. He was swinging that warhammer like a wrecking ball—I'd never get the spell off in time.

Shadow Walk? A possibility, but if I burned it too soon, I'd have no escape if things went south.

Gnarr growled and lunged, his hand swiping toward me with terrifying speed. I barely slipped away, feeling the air pressure from his swing slam against my ribs. He was slowing down, but not nearly enough. He might've been playing me, waiting for me to overcommit.

I ducked under another swing, claws flashing out to slash at his side. He barely reacted. The bastard was a damn wall.

I needed to cripple him more. Make sure he couldn't chase me. Make sure he couldn't keep swinging that damned weapon. I lunged low, aiming for his knee.

His movement exploded.

A trap.

Gnarr roared and lunged at the same time, his free hand slamming into my ribs like a battering ram. Pain detonated through my body. I barely kept my footing as my health bar took a massive hit—over 500 points gone in an instant.

From a simple punch! Surely, that had to have been a skill!

I staggered back, gasping for breath. My ward spells had just saved my life. Fifty percent damage reduction had kept my ribs from turning into bone confetti, and the 20% damage reflection at least made him feel some of the impact.

But I wasn't going to win like this.

I dodged back, lungs burning, mind racing. Every second I spent dodging was another second for him to land a lucky hit.

I clenched my fists, blood dripping from my claws. I had trump cards left. So did he. But I'd figured out what kind of fighter he was. A Brute type. He wasn't going to pull out some unexpected magic trick. No sudden teleportation. No insane battlefield control spells.

He was going to swing.

That was his world.

I just had to force the opening.

I sucked in a breath and roared.

Draconic Fear exploded outward. The fury of my dragon blood at being treated this way for so long raged and ripped through the air like a shockwave. Gnarr flinched and froze for the length of a single breath. It was barely a hesitation—but that was all I needed.

Shadow Walk.

I dove into the bastard's own shadow; darkness swallowed me whole.

The world turned to shades of black and gray. From my vantage in the shadows, I watched as Gnarr bellowed in fury, thrashing as if I'd vanished into thin air. He spun, swinging wildly, war hammer carving trenches into the Earth. His head snapped from side to side, nostrils flaring as he tried to sniff me out.

I moved. Silent. Fast. Circling behind him, watching. Waiting. My mana was burning at an alarming rate, but I had to time this right.

Finally, Gnarr stopped. His movements stilled. He reached for a pouch at his waist—the compass.

Shit.

He was going to check my position.

Time was up.

Draconic Fury.

Power surged through my veins. My muscles coiled, my breath steadying as strength doubled in an instant. The world slowed. My senses sharpened.

This was my moment.

I lunged.

The *Longknife of Shadows* was assigned to my right-hand claws; it pulsed with raw energy, its once-per-day ability locking in. A guaranteed critical strike. I roared as I exploded out of the shadows, claws gleaming like curved razors.

I aimed for the back of his neck—the exposed gap between his armor and skull.

Too late, he realized the trap.

He started to turn.

It didn't matter.

My claws raked deep into his flesh, slicing through muscle and tendon, severing bone. A sickening crunch echoed through the battlefield as blood geysered into the air.

Gnarr screamed.

A final, furious roar that shook the ground.

He twisted, his massive frame flailing. He tried to make one last swing of that massive war hammer, but his arm wouldn't lift. The nerves were severed. His strength was failing.

Still, he didn't fall.

Through sheer stubborn will, he refused to die.

I stood before him, breath ragged, chest heaving. His massive body swayed, eyes dark with rage and disbelief.

Blood spilled in thick rivers onto the shattered ground.

His chest heaved. His breath hitched.

Then—

Silence.

Gnarr took one final, stumbling step toward me, his tusks bared in defiance.

Then he collapsed.

The impact shook the battlefield. His body hit the dirt with a thunderous crash, the war hammer rolling from his grasp. He never let go of it—not until the very end.

I exhaled, shoulders slumping. My heart hammered in my chest, the adrenaline still screaming through my veins.

It was over.

I had won.

Even so, I wasn't a dumbass. I moved forward to ensure there was no chance of this Champion regenerating or healing.

It took several swings of my blade, which I had pulled back out and enlarged to the length of a full sword. Eventually, I severed the head and finally slumped to the ground, satisfied it was really done.

System Message:
Congratulations!
You have successfully defeated a Champion.

As a result of this unique situation, a new quest has been unlocked:

Quest: Defeat Five Champions

Objective: Defeat a total of five Champions to prove your dominance and protect humanity.
Reward: Create one Safe Zone (10-mile radius). No monsters will be able to spawn or enter the designated area.
Progress: 1/5 Champions defeated.

Well, that happened. I suppose it's a good thing; I would have to fight them anyway, might as well get a reward for it.

I also wondered if this was the AI's way of giving me a hint of the exact number of champions that had come to Earth early. I slumped to the ground not far from the dead Champion and tried to come down from the adrenaline high of that battle.

Fifteen minutes later, I was healed up again and rested, and all my cooldowns had expired except for **Dragon's Fury**.

Now, it was time to take stock and see if I could find anything useful.

Checking my Status, I was disgruntled to see that the fight hadn't given me a level up, but apparently, sentient opponents gave experience at the same rate as monsters, aka 100 XP per level. Meaning, the bastard was only worth around 5000 experience at most. I wasn't exactly sure since I didn't pay attention to how much XP I had before the fight, and I was too tired to care about looking at combat logs. Still, he had to have some good stuff on him.

"Let's see what goodies he brought me!"

CHAPTER 21

REWARDS AND NEXT STEPS

THE WAR HAMMER was obviously a System-generated weapon, but I ignored it, other than tossing it into my inventory. It was made for someone much larger than me to wield. Besides, no matter how good it was, hammers were not something I wanted to use.

Still, curiosity got the better of me, and after a moment, I pulled it back out and scanned it with my Treasure Sense and whistled in surprise.

Speaking to the corpse, "Damn, you're a lucky bastard!" Then I chuckled darkly, "Well, 'were' lucky. Not so much anymore, I suppose I'm the lucky one now!"

The weapon had a +35% crit chance and +25% damage. That was insanely good, and it made an evil grin appear on my face. Using **Claw Mastery,** I assigned the club as my right-hand weapon, then stowed it in inventory. Then, I switched my left-hand weapon from the *Nightrend Dagger* to the *Longknife of Shadows*.

I couldn't help the delighted laugh that escaped me. My claws just got way more powerful. The *Nightrend Dagger* that had been assigned only had a 15% crit chance and a minor DoT effect. I was really starting to love that **Claw Mastery** skill!

That settled, I moved on to searching the body. There, I found three health potions, a low and two mid-grades, as well as a pouch that had a dimensional storage space within. It wasn't as good as my ring, but I'd keep it to give to someone who needed it, probably a new herald. Most of its other items were useless to me since they were designed for an ogre, but I still put them in my storage to sell once the System Shop opened in three weeks. Speaking of which, it had 253 silver mana coins and 2013 copper coins.

Thinking about that, I could make an educated guess. It must have known of a good medium-grade dungeon and had run it repeatedly to level up before it was given the compass, then it headed straight here to kill me. My reasoning was that silver only dropped from opponents over level twenty, and since it had more than twice as many silver mana coins as me, then he must not have done too many low-level dungeon runs.

Speaking of the compass, I examined it, but its only function was to find me. No matter which way I turned, the needle pointed straight at me. I thought about what to do with it and decided to give it to Morgan. Viki had her tracking skill, but it wouldn't hurt for them to have another way to find me.

And, of course, that led me to think of them. It had only been a day since we had parted ways, and they were going to be trying to find me after tomorrow to check in.

That made me consider whether I should use **Shadow Recall** to jump back to be close to them or keep on the way I was going and find the next medium dungeon. From looking at my dungeon finder compass, I was pretty sure the next one was somewhere around Spring Creek Parkway. The danger was that another of the champions might come for me and find them instead.

Grrr...

It was almost dark now, and I needed to get moving. Giving the ogre one last glance, I turned to head south toward the next dungeon but hesitated. I was leaving the corpse behind; I wasn't about to waste time to give it a burial. Still, real corpses didn't disappear the way System-generated ones did, and beasts would come along and feast on it. That would cause them to gain a strong boost in power and be more dangerous to the humans around them.

Swearing, I put the ogre into its own inventory space inside the pouch I now wore at my waist. I would dump the body inside the next dungeon so that it would be reclaimed that way.

Satisfied, I finally began running.

I thought about the quest the System had given me to kill the champions that were hunting me. As much as I didn't want to fight them, considering the risk, I would love to be able to create a safe zone. That could give humanity such a big boost, and even that alone might allow us the chance to avoid extinction. The first time around, we had never recovered from this time of chaos. We had never been able to establish any safe place where we could gather and start to rebuild some semblance of civilization. Between dungeon breaks and invading species like the ogres, we were doomed.

Crafters, in particular, had perished by the tens of millions over the next few months, not able to defend themselves and level up while the world struggled to find places we could defend.

Just one safe zone here wouldn't help people on other continents, but it could save millions.

Turning over the risks versus benefits, I was starting to think fighting that ogre now might have been a blessing in disguise. It had clearly been close to me in levels, meaning that with its foreknowledge, it might have been able to level up faster than me in time. Well, it definitely would have done so if the AI had not just given me the compass to find dungeons. All of the champions would be able to rush right to the best dungeons they knew and run them over and over, leveling up like crazy. I might have future knowledge, too, but my knowledge of dungeons was spread out across several states, and none of them had been around Dallas and Fort Worth. Nor were they particularly special. Most of them had been on the easy side since we had needed to 'under-hunt' in order to survive. In other words, we had to be way higher level than the monsters in the dungeons; otherwise, with our lack of magic users, we tended to have a lot of party wipes.

I shook those thoughts off, with the only one that really mattered, '*As long as they don't all come at me at once, I might stand a better chance now rather than later.*'

Still, I could admit to myself that I was scared. There was so much riding on my shoulders; the idea of losing was terrifying. I knew there wouldn't be another second chance. The AI had made its Hail Mary move, and this was it. Like it or not, there were consequences, and I had fucked up and given the other champions a chance. I would just have to deal with whatever came.

By the time I arrived at the next portal, I was in a grim mood and looked forward to taking out my frustrations on the inhabitants of the next dungeon.

The compass had led me straight to the next medium dungeon. It was on the west side of the highway, and damned if it wasn't inside the shell of what used to be Wally World before the System started reclaiming it.

I wasn't sure what I would find inside, but sure as hell hoped it wouldn't be themed according to those old 'people of Wally World' videos.

Even the System wouldn't be so cruel as to create a dungeon like that. Right?

Or so I thought... stepping inside, I was immediately hit by the stench of decay. The air was thick and musty, like a tomb that had been sealed for centuries. I knew instantly what kind of dungeon this was. The temperature dropped noticeably, and a faint green glow came from sconces lining the cracked stone walls. A cold breeze brushed past me, stirring the dust on the floor. There was no doubt in my mind: this was an Undead Crypt.

The flickering light from the torches illuminated rows of broken-down shelves that had once held all the useless junk people bought before the world fell apart. Now, though, the place looked more like a long-abandoned tomb than a mega-store. The System had twisted it into something else entirely.

The floor beneath my feet was uneven, a mix of jagged stone and shattered tiles, and I could hear the unmistakable shuffle of something moving in the distance—slow, deliberate, and lifeless. That wasn't all. I could feel the magic in the air, dark and oppressive: the kind of magic that fuels the undead and keeps them moving long after their bodies should've rotted away. That greenish glow wasn't the life mana from the forest dungeon; this was the sickly green of life's opposite.

I took a deep breath, steadying myself.

"Undead," I muttered darkly. Not exactly the toughest opponents physically, but they could be dangerous in numbers, and they had a habit of swarming their prey. I checked my gear and prepared for what lay ahead. The thing about undead, though, is that they're relentless. They don't tire, don't hesitate, and they definitely don't stop unless you make them.

In my first life, a dungeon like this would have sent me running. Lack of magic had made undead dungeons a nightmare to complete. Skeletons and Zombies were easy; just bust the zombie's head or break the skeleton apart, and they stayed down. It was the ghosts, phantasms, and the ones that had no corporeal forms that ruined people's day. Without magic or a magic weapon capable of hitting them, whole parties would TPK, or total party kill.

The only good thing was that System-generated zombies didn't cause a zombie apocalypse when they bit people. On the other hand, they were pretty deadly since they inflicted necrotic poison, causing a human's body to rot away unless purged with some kind of healing magic.

That was in my first life.

Today's me had magic and magic weapons and I was in the mood to break something.

A few more steps into the dungeon, and I spotted the first of them— a group of skeletons shambling toward me. Rusted swords and broken shields dangled from bony hands, their hollow eye sockets glowing faintly with an eerie green light. No flesh, no sound, just the creaking of old bones and the soft scrape of their feet against the stone.

It wasn't much of a welcoming party. I'd faced worse.

I almost laughed when I saw them wearing tattered remnants of what looked like employee uniforms. If those were actual employees turned into zombies, I would feel bad, but these were just dungeon-generated monsters clothed for the ambiance.

They weren't fast, but they were determined, and there were

probably more behind them, lurking in the shadows. I tightened my fist and then let my claws extend. Time to get to work.

I charged forward, my talons slicing through the air with deadly precision. The first skeleton barely had time to raise its rusted sword before I cleaved through its skull, sending bones scattering across the floor. I spun on my heel, using the momentum to take out another two in one smooth motion with Tempest Strike, their skulls cracking under the force of my strike.

Looking around, I was amazed that it had gone so quickly and easily. I almost expected them to reform and come back after me a second time. However, to my great surprise, they dissolved into motes of light as the System reclaimed them, leaving small piles of copper mana coins in their place.

I gathered the coins and shook my head, thinking of how rich I was. Before entering this dungeon, I had over 11,000 copper mana coins. I kept a running count, but I had given some away here and there to help people, especially children, get magic classes, so I couldn't be entirely sure. Still, three skeletons had just dropped sixteen coins each, meaning they were Level 16. One small group and I had almost fifty more coins. My inner dragon was feeling very satisfied right now about how fast its hoard was growing. I dumped the forty-eight coins into my storage and prepared to move on.

The next fight didn't go so well. I didn't bother sneaking around since these were just skeletons that were thirty-one levels below me and just charged toward the next group. They let me know my mistake as they all brandished their rusty weapons my way. Even with my level difference, I didn't want to get hit.

I was in a strange situation where I felt confident enough to just abandon all stealth and bulldoze my way through these guys, but at the same time, I still feared the consequences of getting hit. I had potions and even Morgan's healing spells if I needed them and didn't mind wasting time to find her, but I didn't want to be wasteful. The higher I rose, the more those potions would come in handy, so I couldn't afford to use them if I didn't seriously need them.

Finally, I decided to just go for it. Time was my most important resource right now, and with the level difference, I needed to beat this dungeon before the next Champion could catch up to me.

I leaped into the fray, claws extending as I lunged at the next group of skeletons. They raised their rusted weapons, but it made no difference. My claws slashed through bone with ease, severing limbs and shattering skulls. The first fell before it even got a swing in, and the second crumpled after I drove my talons into its ribcage, ripping its spine apart. Bones clattered to the floor, dissolving into motes of light, leaving nothing but more copper mana coins in their wake.

Another group emerged from the shadows, and I rushed forward, determined to make short work of them too. This time, I avoided their weapons with a series of sharp side steps, slashing at their legs to bring them down before delivering the killing blow. It was getting easier now—my strikes more fluid, my movements more controlled. As my claws cut through the skeletons, I felt my confidence growing with each kill. The fear of getting hit, while still present, had begun to fade as I realized how predictable their movements were. They were just bones. I could handle this.

I fought non-stop for over half an hour as more and more skeletons arrived to join the fray. It seemed this dungeon threw monsters at you in waves, which made sense, considering it was filled with undead. That meant this would be hard to complete due to the fatigue, but it would also be fast; I wouldn't have to waste time running around looking for the monsters.

By the time the last group of skeletons crumbled, I stood in a pile of shattered bones and scattered coins. I could feel my heart racing, but not from fear—this was exhilaration. My claws had been a tool I had not fully relied on yet because I wasn't sure if I could adapt my fighting style, but now they felt like an extension of myself, quite literally. I flexed my fingers, admiring the sharp edges of my black-ivory talons, already stained with dust and grime. The more I used them, the more natural it felt.

"Let's keep going," I muttered to myself after collecting the coins. Heading further into the dungeon, my confidence was growing with every step.

As I moved deeper, the air thickened with the smell of decay. I rounded the corner and was greeted by a mass of zombies shuffling slowly toward me. Their bloated bodies were grotesque, patches of flesh hanging loosely, and their eyes were vacant, milky white.

It's like the home electronics department on Black Friday!

Unlike the skeletons, these guys weren't much for weapons, but they didn't need them. The sheer number was enough to pose a threat. One-on-one, they were nothing, but together, they could overwhelm me. I cracked my knuckles, claws extending, a grin tugging at my lips. Time to put my new skills to the test.

The first zombie came at me, arms outstretched. I darted forward, claws raised, and in a single swift motion, batted its arms aside and slashed across its neck. Its head toppled from its shoulders, and the body collapsed into a heap on the floor. One down, too many to count left to go.

I moved quickly, slicing through the next few zombies with ease, my claws cleaving through decaying flesh like it was paper. Headshots were the key—one clean strike to the skull, and they were done. I dodged around their sluggish attempts to grab me, weaving between them like water slipping through cracks. My movements were getting smoother, more confident. The claws felt right in my hands now, as though they had always belonged there.

Their fingernails tried to scratch my skin and deliver their necrotic poison attack, but my scales proved too strong.

But the numbers were growing. No matter how fast I moved, the zombies kept coming, forcing me to keep my pace up. I stayed along the perimeter, always moving, slashing as I passed by, never staying in one place long enough for them to surround me. Every time I killed one, two more shuffled forward to take its place.

I lunged at another zombie, my claws slicing cleanly through its neck, and kept moving, circling the horde, making sure to stay out of reach. It was a rhythm now. A dance. Every kill was precise, every dodge timed perfectly, my body and claws in perfect sync. I could feel my instincts sharpening with each step, the initial panic of facing this swarm melting away, replaced with focus and deadly efficiency.

There was great satisfaction in my heart at the moment. It had taken me a little over a week to really, fully feel like all my old skills from before my restart were integrated back into muscle memory. Maybe it was learning and practicing this new **Claw Mastery** skill, but everything was clicking now. My movements no longer felt slightly off or awkward, and it seemed to give me a boost in my fighting in a non-System sort of way.

Pretty soon, I was experimenting with new techniques. These zombies were perfect for practice!

Their sheer numbers put me under enough pressure to feel the high you get from a life-and-death fight, but at the same time, they were slow enough individually not to destroy me if I made a mistake. Small wounds did accumulate, and I got several System messages pop up saying that I resisted a Necrotic Disease, that I thanked my much higher level and stats for protecting me from. Still, I was legitimately having fun.

Punching forward straight at a zombie's head, I discovered that claws weren't just for slashing. They were also pretty damned great at piercing, aka stabbing things. Not only did my claws' points punch through with ease, but their wickedly sharp edges did significant damage on the way out as well.

Not that it was combat-related, but I was very pleased to see that my claws easily shook off the gore that I was constantly creating with my strikes.

I had never had a 'mastery' skill in my first life, and I was loving this. I wasn't sure how much of what I was feeling was from my past experience and how much was System imparted, but whatever the percentages were, the mastery seemed to integrate everything into one seamless dance of destruction.

The horde of fifty zombies quickly became thirty, then ten, and before I knew it, I was standing among a large area of disappearing motes of light surrounded by a caricature of what had once been the home electronics department. Seeing my reflection in the dark glass of a 60" TV, I had to smile. With these new claws, I looked like some kind of clean-shaven, less-hairy, medieval Sabertooth from the comics, except my claws were longer and able to grow and shrink on demand.

Grinning, I stopped admiring myself and picked up the coins. One of these days, when the Shop opened, I really needed to pick up a looting skill so I wouldn't have to manually search around for all the coins. A non-combat skill like that shouldn't cost more than a few silvers, hopefully. Although it was a very popular one, so I'd better remember to get it quickly before they sold out.

In the meantime, I needed to finish this dungeon, so it was time to see what the next monster was.

CHAPTER 22
WHO YA GONNA CALL?

THE NEXT GROUP of bad guys were wraiths. Non-corporeal undead, the bane of fighters everywhere!

Except not me.

Thanks to my shadow affinity, and the magical claws granted by my bloodline, I could hit them just fine without taking damage or getting my soul sucked, or life drained, or whatever.

Seriously though, the only issue I had with these guys was keeping them from touching me as I killed them. Because of their nature, they didn't need to be tough or have a lot of hit points since 90% of the human race couldn't touch them; they were basically glass cannons and one good hit would take them out.

The other good thing about them was that, unlike the skeletons and zombies, the wraiths were loners, so I didn't have anything to worry about. If they swarmed, then I would have had a bad day, but I was able to pick them off one by one, basically running from one to the next, barely slowing down. I cycled through my skills as I fought, and by the time I had killed one, the last set of skills would be off cooldown.

It was, honestly, one of the best times I had ever had in a dungeon. It wasn't challenging, other than dodging a lot to prevent getting hit, but it was so satisfying to absolutely wreck these monsters that would have sent me fleeing in terror in my last life. There was no doubt in my mind I would have noped out of there at the very first sighting of a non-corporeal undead back then. The sheer contrast that just over a week could make in this new life boggled my mind.

Still, I shuddered to think how nasty these guys would be if they swarmed, even with my new skills and abilities... that life drain ability with multiple wraiths coming after you at the same time; what a nightmare that would be!

Even with all the slaughtering of monsters I was doing, I knew I had made mistakes in this new life, and had seriously fucked up. I had let hope in and lost some of my edge. Connections with people like Morgan and Viki had also led me to do some dumb things that now put me in this position and had me looking over my shoulder, worrying about the champions hunting me down. On the other hand, I hadn't felt this alive and hopeful in more than twenty years.

I would just have to adapt and overcome! And speaking of that, I hit Level 50 while battling the wraiths.

Ding!

Congratulations! You have earned the Title: Tier 5 Trailblazer.
Description: As the first on your world to reach Level 50 under the System, you have broken through the limits of humanity and set a new standard for strength and survival. Your success paves the way for others to follow, solidifying your place as a leader in this world.

Title Bonus: +5 to all stats.

That was satisfying! The great thing about being at the very cutting edge was that getting this title at each new Tier was really adding up. At Level 50, this amounted to 25 extra points in each of my stats. That was tremendous!

On top of that, I was thrilled with my Level 50 draconic bloodline ability, not to mention my skill and spell.

Draconic Bloodline Ability: Spell Resistance (Passive)

Description: The innate power of your draconic bloodline enhances your natural defenses against magic. You now possess a 25% resistance to all incoming spells and magical effects, reducing the damage or potency of hostile spells cast against you. This passive ability reinforces your defenses, making it significantly harder for enemies to affect you with magic.

Skill: Evasion (Passive)

Description: Your heightened agility and awareness give you a natural ability to avoid incoming attacks. You now have a 20% chance to completely evade any physical or magical attack, provided your movement is not restricted or impeded. This passive skill applies to all forms of attacks, making it a crucial survival tool in combat.

Spell: Dispelling Burst

Description: You unleash a powerful burst of magic, clearing all negative status effects from yourself and allies within a 10-foot radius. This spell dispels any status effects of equal or lower level than yours with complete certainty. Against status effects from higher-level foes, the chance to dispel

decreases by 5% for each level the enemy surpasses
your own.

I could not have asked for a better set of skills at this level! With
champions hunting me and breathing down my neck, a little extra
defense would go a long way. Not only that, the Evasion passive skill
would definitely enhance the rogue-like nature of my current class.

That only left the boss room fight to go in this dungeon, and with
wraiths as the highest-level regular enemies, I knew this would be
bad. I would have to face a small swarm, the very thing I had been
dreading since first seeing these ghostly bastards.

As I made my way deeper into what would have been the backroom if
this were still a mega-store, I knew I was about to face a real challenge.
Before entering, I buffed up, activating **Iron Hide**, which was a five-
minute skill that would give me a 50% boost to my armor. To that, I
added **Shadow Ward**, providing a 25% damage reduction for five
minutes as well. I wished I could use **Shadow Ward 2** as well, but it
only lasted for one minute, so it would be better to save that for the boss
fight, assuming I got the opportunity to cast in the middle of combat.

With that, I moved ahead toward the double doors leading to the
boss and was immediately hit hard with the ambiance messaging
that the System flooded my brain with:

*The back room loomed ahead of me like a gaping maw, its double doors
hanging precariously on rusted hinges. A flicker of unease ran down my
spine. This was it—the final encounter, the boss of the dungeon. I took a
deep breath and stepped inside, my boots echoing off the cold, cracked tile.
The air was thick with the stench of rot and decay, and as soon as I crossed
the threshold, the doors behind me slammed shut with an ominous thud.*

That was when I saw them. Wraiths. Five of them materialized out of
the walls, their translucent forms flickering in the dim light. They

hovered above the ground, their hollow eyes fixated on me as if I was some feast they had been waiting for. I didn't have time to process the fact that they were the boss's minions before they surged forward, an unholy wail tearing from their collective mouths.

I shrugged off the intrusive feelings and messaging the damned System projected into my brain and got down to business.

"Of course," I muttered, rolling my shoulders. "Why make it easy?"

The Lich appeared at the far end of the room, seated lazily on what was once probably a manager's chair but now looked more like a throne of broken bones and refuse. Its skeletal form was adorned in the tattered remains of a manager's uniform, and bony fingers clutched a gnarled staff. Its hollow eyes glowed with a sinister light, and I could hear the smug amusement in its voice as he cackled, "You adventurers feed me your life force, and I grow ever stronger! Come, sacrifice yourself!"

Great. A talker. I'd dealt with enough of these in my time, and they always loved to monologue right before unleashing some kind of magical hell.

The wraiths were fast but not fast enough to keep up with my agility. As they rushed toward me, I calculated my next move. Usually, I'd have used **Shadow Step** to dodge behind them, but these bastards existed partially in the shadow realm. My usual tricks wouldn't work.

But maybe, just maybe...

I smirked. **Shadow Step** wouldn't let me avoid them—but maybe it would let me hit them. I phased into the shadows, reappearing amidst the charging wraiths. Now solid to me, they were vulnerable, but I was also vulnerable to their Life Drain effect if they should touch me. However, the best defense is a good offense, as my dad used to say.

"Time to die," I growled, activating **Tempest Strike**.

My claws swept through the air in a deadly arc, cleaving through all of the wraiths at once. Their forms shredded, partially dissolving into wisps of dark smoke. I didn't let up. That first shot had taken them down to less than 25% on their health bars, but I needed them fully out of the fight so I could face the Lich without interference.

I followed with **Arcane Singularity**: a swirling vortex of arcane energy that pulled the remaining wraiths toward its center. Their non-corporeal nature seemed to make them particularly susceptible.

I darted out of range just in time as the spell detonated with a brilliant flash of energy, obliterating the rest of the wraiths' health. I ignored the kill notifications.

That should've been the end of it.

But no.

Just as I turned my attention back to the Lich, a chill ran down my spine. I was suddenly rooted in place—literally. The Lich had cast a binding spell, a shimmering chain of dark energy snaking around my legs, locking me down as if I were moving through thick molasses. I cursed under my breath. My new spell resistance had mitigated some of the effect, but I was still stuck.

"Foolish adventurer!" the Lich screeched, as one skeletal hand raised to prepare another spell. "Your life force will feed me for years!"

I grimaced. Not if I had anything to say about it.

I couldn't help but quip, "Choke on it, you bad reject from an Iron Maiden album cover!"

"Dispelling Burst," I muttered through gritted teeth, casting the spell that would clear the root effect.

A pulse of energy radiated out from me, breaking the magical chains around my legs. I barely had time to move before a blast of icy wind hit me square in the chest, sending a wave of cold ripping through my body. The Lich's next spell—a cold-based AoE—had been unleashed just as I freed myself.

Pain lanced through my body as I staggered back, but my spell resistance kicked in, somewhat softening the blow. Still, the cold gnawed at me, slowing me down by a quarter of my usual speed. Not enough to cripple me, but enough to be annoying.

"Alright, you wanna play rough? Let's play rough."

I summoned **Umbral Chains:** dark tendrils of shadow coiling from the ground, lashing out and binding the Lich's skeletal form. Its glowing eyes widened in surprise as the chains wrapped around him, restricting his movement, exactly as it had just done to me. It tried to raise its staff, but the chains held firm, cutting off its ability to cast for a few seconds.

"Let's see how you like this," I said, summoning all the dark energy I could muster.

Shadow Surge burst forth from my hands: a concentrated blast of raw shadow energy that hit the lich square in the chest. The impact sent it crashing back into the makeshift throne, bones rattling, and the shadow magic ate away at its form. Its health plummeted to half.

But I knew better than to celebrate just yet. Liches were notoriously hard to kill.

Sure enough, it dispelled the **Umbral Chains** in a flash of magic, skeletal jaw clacking as it hissed, "You will not stop me! I will consume your life force, piece by piece!"

Before I could react, the Lich cast another spell, and I felt a familiar sensation. Life Drain, but stronger and more intense than the wraiths could cast. Dark energy surged toward me, and while I dodged most of it, some of the life-stealing magic still hit me. I felt my life being pulled from my body, my strength draining. I cursed as the System message flashed in my vision—**Level reduced by 1.**

He was trying to weaken me, both physically and magically, and it really had. I just lost access to my nifty new Level 50 skills and abilities. *Bastard!*

"You think that's gonna stop me?" I growled, pushing through the weakness.

I closed the distance between us, summoning every ounce of my strength. **Crippling Blow**—my claws slashed across the Lich's arm, severing it at the elbow. Its skeletal hand, still clutching the staff, fell to the ground with a clatter, and its casting was interrupted yet again.

For a moment, I thought I had won. But the Lich wasn't done yet.

With a rattling breath, the boss triggered another Life Drain, and this time it hit hard. Its health surged back above 30%, while I felt my own energy and hit points slip away. Glancing quickly at my health, I was down to 930 of 2320. Those Life Drains hurt!

Another system message appeared as I was thinking that—**Level reduced by 1.** That was two levels gone, and I could feel the loss as my power waned.

I didn't want to use it. I really didn't.

But I had no choice.

"**Draconic Fury**!" I roared, activating my bloodline's ultimate ability. My muscles bulged, strength doubling instantly as fiery energy surged through my veins. I wished I could add **Shadow Ward 2** to better protect against its attacks, but I needed to risk it and take this bastard out fast.

I launched forward with **Searing Slash**, my claws igniting with draconic energy. The strike connected with the Lich's chest, cutting deep and leaving a shadowy trail of burning energy. Its health plummeted again, but it wasn't dead yet.

"Die already!" I snarled, following up with a **Draconic Strike**.

The blow hit like a sledgehammer, my claws sinking into the Lich's ribcage and shattering the brittle bones beneath. Its body crumpled to the ground, lifeless.

I stood there for a moment panting, thankful the fight was over, but something was off. I didn't get the System message confirming its death. My eyes narrowed, and I activated Treasure Sense, scanning the area. That's when I spotted it: a hidden compartment behind the throne.

There it was. Its phylactery. I had read once that they couldn't truly die until their soul was destroyed and that they hid it.

I approached, reaching into the secret alcove and pulling out the glowing gem, its sickly green light pulsing faintly. Without hesitation, I raised my claws and smashed the phylactery to pieces.

The Lich's bones convulsed one last time, then disintegrated into a pile of dust. Power rushed from the pile into me, restoring my lost levels, and I breathed a massive sigh of relief. That was one of the significant dangers of undead dungeons; if you lost those levels and didn't manage to kill the monster who drained them, you were out of luck, and the level drain would be permanent.

Finally, the system message appeared before my eyes:

Congratulations! You have defeated the Lich of Wally World.

Dungeon Cleared.

XP gained.

I exhaled, letting my shoulders sag. It was over. Finally.

There I was, getting sad because the Lich hadn't been enough to get me another Level when the bonus experience for my two Titles hit:

Title: Solitary Sovereign of the Depths - First Solo dungeon clear (10%xp bonus for all solo dungeon clears)

Title: Dungeon Conqueror - First dungeon Clear (10% xp bonus for all dungeon clears)

That was 20% extra XP, which added up quite a lot, an extra 59,100 more, to be precise. It easily brought me up over what was needed for Level 51!

I quickly pulled up my status page to check out the changes.

Liam Bell:
Draconic Shadowblade - Level 51
Bloodline (Tier 2): Shadow Dragon

Experience: 37389/90400

Attributes:
Endurance: 117
Strength: 117
Agility: 117
Mind: 117
Will: 117
Magical Aptitude: 117
Luck: 10

Health: 930/2340

Mana: 1570/2340

Abilities:
Active: Dragon Fear, Umbral Breath
Passive: Dark Vision, Scales, Treasure Sense, Spell Resistance

Active Skills:
Draconic Strike
Draconic Fury
Searing Slash
Dragon's Charge
Tempest Strike
Heavy Draconic Strike
Stealth (Advanced)
Crippling Blow

Passive Skills:
Evasion

Spells:
Shadow Bolt
Darkness
Shadow Ward
Arcane Singularity
Shadow Walk
Umbral Chains
Shadow Surge
Dispelling Burst

It was really nice finally seeing something under the Passive skills category. I hoped I'd get more of those.

Looking around, I wanted to find someplace to sit and think. The treasure chest had appeared, and I walked over and plopped on it. I wasn't in any rush to dig through the treasure since I needed to wait an hour for my cooldown on Draconic Fury to end. That gave me some time to consider my options.

On the bright side, I was closing in on my second Class upgrade! I had gotten four levels from this dungeon. Running it twice more would give me enough to hit the Level 60 threshold. Unfortunately, I had the Champions to worry about. If I stayed in place that long, one or more of them were sure to catch up to me and be camping the dungeon entrance when I exited. That would be bad. I had my Shadow Recall spell to take me anywhere within 10 miles that I had been recently. However, that wasn't an instant cast spell; it took time to cast, and that would leave me vulnerable.

Unfortunately, I only knew of one other medium-grade dungeon at the moment. If there weren't any champions waiting for me when I exited this time, I could jump back there and run that one again, and by the time I was done with it, hopefully, Morgan and Viki would find me so I could give them the news about this skill, and hand Morgan that champion's compass that points straight to me. Jumping around like that would hopefully keep them off my trail for a bit.

Hmm... maybe not.

As I contemplated my options, I began to be less sure. I had completed this dungeon in just over two hours, but the Dwarven Runesmith dungeon had taken around four hours, and that was speed-running it. If a champion were close enough to this dungeon to get to me before completing it a second time, they could just as easily run up to Allen and catch me there.

"Damnit!"

Time was not on my side.

I slapped myself on the forehead. I didn't need to find Morgan and Viki; I could contact Morgan using the Commune skill since she was my priestess. I kept forgetting about that; it had only been a few days since she became a Dragon Priestess.

Okay, first things first! Time to open the chest and see what loot it was this time, then afterward, I would check in on the girls and see how they were doing.

With my Luck score of 10, I was looking forward to seeing what loot I would get!

INTERLUDE: ZAELITH - DELUSIONS OF GRANDEUR

Zaelith Duskshade strode toward the temple, his mind sharp, his pulse steady. The towering obsidian structure loomed before him, its jagged edges catching the eerie glow of the eldritch flames lining the courtyard. The air was thick with incense and something darker, something ancient that lurked within the walls. Every step he took echoed against the stone, reverberating through the vast emptiness ahead.

The Dark Gods be praised!

He had received the message less than an hour ago. Delivered by the Moderator itself—the voice of the System that oversaw their world —it was not the kind of message one ignored. The Culling had come again, as it always did, a new world brought into the System, ripe for conquest. His people, the Dark Elves of Vael'Karna, had done this for millennia. It was their way of life.

But this time was different.

A champion of the newly integrated world had been granted a reset —a second chance with full knowledge of the next twenty years.

And, by the System's ironclad laws, all other champions were now entitled to the same foreknowledge.

Zaelith's lips curled into a smirk. A rare event, a twist in the usual order. To most, it would be an unforeseen complication. To him, it was an opportunity.

The great doors of the temple loomed ahead, adorned with intricate carvings of past conquests, each depicting the dark elves' rise through blood and shadow. He pushed them open, the heavy stone groaning as it gave way to him. Inside, the chamber was dim, the only light provided by the violet flames burning in their sconces. At the far end stood the high priest and his attendants, clad in dark robes, their faces obscured by the flickering shadows.

"For centuries, Champions have come to this hall for a blessing from the gods on their glorious quest, but you look pensive," the high priest intoned, his voice low and steady. "What troubles you, Zaelith Duskshade?"

Zaelith approached, bowing his head slightly. "The Moderator has spoken," he said. "An anomaly has occurred in the Culling. A champion of the new world was granted foreknowledge, and so the System has given me the same. I seek the gods' wisdom."

The priests exchanged glances, the tension palpable. Even among the dark elves, the gods did not offer their counsel lightly. The high priest nodded. "Then we shall entreat them."

He turned and led Zaelith through a concealed passage at the back of the temple, descending a winding stairwell into the depths of the mountain. The air grew heavier, the silence oppressive. The walls were covered in ancient murals, the stories of gods and mortals locked in endless struggle.

At last, they reached the sanctum—a vast, circular chamber lost in shadow. The high priest stepped forward and began to chant, his voice soon joined by the others. The sound resonated through the chamber, growing louder, reverberating off the stone. A dark mist coiled at the edges of the room, shifting, solidifying.

Then, the god appeared.

Xelaros. The first god of their pantheon.

The shadows gathered into a towering form, its eyes burning with an intense violet glow. The air trembled with its presence, the sheer force of its will pressing down on the chamber.

Zaelith knelt immediately, his gaze lowered.

"Zaelith Duskshade," Xelaros spoke, the words rolling through the room like thunder. "You have called; now speak and prove your worthiness or face my wrath."

Zaelith kept his voice steady. "Great one, I have been chosen to lead the incursion into the new world. But the System has altered the game. A champion of the humans was granted foreknowledge, and now we share that gift. I seek your counsel."

A long silence stretched between them, the weight of the god's gaze suffocating. Then, Xelaros spoke.

"A rare event," the god mused. "One that can be turned to our advantage. If handled correctly, this Culling will not be like the others. It will not be a mere raid. It will be a conquest."

Zaelith's breath slowed. A conquest.

"We could take permanent hold," Xelaros continued, his tone measured. "Divide the world among our forces. Establish dominion that lasts beyond the usual cycle of harvest and destruction."

A foothold. A chance to claim this world, not just strip it bare and move on. If they succeeded, it would reshape the dark elves' standing within the System forever.

"But there is a choice," Xelaros said, his voice deepening. "You may enter the new world ahead of our harvesters. Hunt down the Earth's champion before they can rise, before their knowledge becomes an advantage. Or you may wait. Gather your forces, use your knowledge to prepare them, then strike at the opportune moment."

Zaelith's fingers twitched. A test.

To wait meant to bring overwhelming strength, to ensure his people had every advantage when they struck. It was the tactical choice. But all of the races would have that same advantage, including the cursed dwarves, who had been such a bane to his people during the Culling and harvest.

But to go now... to kill the human champion before they could use their knowledge... that was the bolder move. It was dangerous. It was reckless, but it would genuinely grant an advantage. He would have an entire month on the new world to grow stronger and prepare the way.

It was his path.

"I will go alone," Zaelith said, his voice unwavering. "I will hunt the Earth's champion and secure our advantage before the others arrive."

The violet light of Xelaros' eyes flared, the weight of his approval settling over Zaelith like a shroud.

"Very well," the god said. "Then you must not fail."

Zaelith bowed his head deeper. "It will be done."

The god's form began to fade, the mist unraveling. The chamber shifted, reality itself seeming to realign.

And then, time froze.

The priests stood still, their chants cut off mid-syllable. The air stopped moving, the torches frozen in place. Only Zaelith and Xelaros remained aware.

The god's gaze bore into him, and when it spoke again, its voice was quieter but no less commanding.

"There is more, Zaelith," Xelaros said. "What I tell you now must remain secret."

Zaelith's heart pounded. He did not dare respond.

Xelaros spoke only a few sentences more. Their content enough to shake Zaelith to his core.

The god's final words echoed in his mind:

"Be aware of the places I have mentioned, and report back anything you find within. This is of equal importance to your mission of becoming a god and blocking the humans."

And then, in an instant, time resumed.

The chants picked up as if nothing had happened. The god's form faded entirely. The darkness withdrew.

Zaelith rose, expression unreadable, mind racing with the hint that there might be things outside the System's knowledge.

He turned, his decision made. He would inform his second in command. She would lead their forces while he hunted the human champion. He wasn't allowed to prepare them since he chose to go now, but he could at least inform her of her role in leading in his absence.

As he strode out of the temple, the weight of destiny settled on his shoulders.

The hunt had begun.

CHAPTER 23

TAKING STOCK AND MAKING PLANS

GETTING OFF MY ASS, I turned around and prepared to open the chest, but just to be safe, I hit it with my **Treasure Sense.**

When I activated **Treasure Sense**, the familiar pulse of energy spread through the room, highlighting everything of value in my vision. As expected, the treasure chest immediately lit up, but something about it felt... off. My instincts screamed at me to take a closer look. Sure enough, when the boss was a Lich, a trap was to be expected.

Focusing, I concentrated on the use of **Treasure Sense**, willing it to give me more specifics, honing in on the chest's aura. That's when I saw it—faint lines of magic woven into the air around the chest, barely visible to the naked eye. A trap. Not just any trap, either. It was layered with a particularly nasty enchantment. The kind designed to fry anyone foolish enough to open it without knowing what they were doing.

I muttered under my breath. "Couldn't have made this easy, could you, lich?"

The magic was a defensive ward, likely tied to some elemental damage. From the crackling energy it gave off, I guessed it was a lightning trap—enough to send volts through my System as a last 'fuck you.' At least the System wasn't pulling punches.

Looks like I had to be smart about this one. If I couldn't disarm it, I'd be in for a nasty shock. Literally.

Quickly activating **Scalebound Resilience** for the elemental resistance it provided and casting both of my **Shadow Ward** spells, I prepared to open it. I wasn't sure exactly how much resistance was provided, but between those spells and my new **Spell Resistance**, I should be rocking around 80% to 90% resistance for about a minute. Just before I did, I remembered my *Crown of the Eternal Sentinel*, which also gave another 10% magic resistance. If all these enchantments had visible effects, I'd be glowing like a Christmas tree!

Not having anything better to use, I flipped it open with my claws. I received a nasty little shock, but honestly, it wasn't any worse than touching an electric fence. Hurray for defenses! Anyone else who touched that chest would be on the ground twitching as their body spasmed in convulsions.

I flipped the bird at the spot where the Lich had died. "Suck it, necro-dude!"

Wasting no more time, I looked in the chest, perhaps a little too eager to see what I got for all my troubles. I mean, I always loved getting loot, but the dragon blood in my veins definitely upped the greed factor, and I wasn't going to lie to myself about it!

I was more than pleased. From the chest, I pulled:

Windwalker Greaves
Description: These sleek, silver-grey greaves shimmer with a faint, ethereal glow. The swirling designs etched into the

metal resemble gusts of wind, hinting at the greaves' ability to manipulate the air. Lightweight and flexible, they offer excellent mobility without sacrificing protection.

Stats:
+5% Agility
+5 Physical Defense

Special Ability:
Air Step: Allows the wearer to step on the air for up to 10 steps, essentially creating temporary footholds in the air. This can be used to navigate tricky terrain, evade attacks, or gain a height advantage in battle.
Cooldown: Once every 10 minutes.

But that wasn't all; where I had destroyed the Lich's phylactery, there was also the boss loot drop, one of the advantages of running dungeons solo. Twice the treasure!

I hadn't noticed before until my **Treasure Sense** detected it when I was looking for traps on the chest. After strapping on the new leg greaves over my boots, I hurried over to see what the small item was, and I wasn't disappointed.

Soul Shield Ring

Description: This dark, intricately carved ring is crafted from a mix of blackened bone and silver, with a faint, ethereal glow that seems to pulse from within. The centerpiece is a small, smoky gem that holds the captured essence of a powerful soul. Once worn by the Lich to tether its soul to the physical plane, the ring's energy still carries the mark of death and forbidden magic.

Stats:

+10% Magic Resistance
+5% Mana Regeneration

Special Ability:
Soul Shield: Once per day, the ring automatically activates a shield of spectral energy if a mental or soul-based attack is detected. Attack is partially reflected at caster doing 50% of the damage that would have been done had it landed.

Once again, I was thrilled that I had chosen to increase my Luck stat to the max. These items were insanely good! In my first life, I would have considered myself fortunate to receive a pair of greaves that just did a simple +5 to a stat. Having a percentage increase was nuts, not to mention that **Air Step** ability!

I went back to the chest, picked up the standard medium-grade healing and mana potions, and put them in storage along with my others. After that, I took a few minutes to try out the Air Step ability of the greaves. That would give me several advantages, not the least of which was allowing me to move in unexpected ways in combat.

While waiting for the cooldown on the greaves to practice with them more, I finally used the **Commune** skill to check in with Morgan and Viki.

It took a minute to connect, and I could immediately tell that Morgan was in combat from the panting and curses she was muttering, so I waited patiently for her to be able to talk.

After a couple minutes, she finally replied. *"Hey, sorry, we were just finishing a fight with a group of lesser orcs. What's up? We were going to come look for you later after this dungeon run. By the way, the couple we picked up from that group of religious nuts turned out to be pretty great. They are already Level 11. Another dungeon run, and they should be high enough to turn loose to spread the word about the System and the invaders."*

"Nice! Sounds like you guys are making solid progress! What about you and Viki? What Levels have you hit?"

"Viki caught up to me, and we're now both Level 21. We've run this dungeon four times already, and I think a couple more will destroy it. Should we keep going or leave it for others to train in?"

I was impressed. Being part of a four-person group and getting that many levels in a single day was nothing to sneeze at. If I was mathing correctly, that meant they were in a fairly strong low-grade dungeon, which made sense considering the area they were in was more populated and filled with a ton of retail businesses that had all become fuel for the Systemto build dungeons and mutate beasts.

Thinking about it for a couple of minutes, I replied, *"Go ahead and destroy it and collect the core. There will be more than enough dungeons in the metroplex for humanity to hope to make use of. Before the System is through converting everything, there will be so many monsters and beasts roaming the area that the survivors won't have any choice but to flee. The more we destroy now, the better. Only leave the dungeon if it has some good resources people can harvest or if there is a local group that needs it to level up, like the one in McKinney. I would be burning these medium dungeons down if it weren't for the threat of the champions."*

That brought me to the bad news...

"Speaking of which, one of them found me just before I entered this dungeon. The System gave them compasses that lead them directly to me, so I can expect to see them sooner rather than later, but I think that is a good thing. I'm hoping it will give me a slight advantage. They will be spending their time chasing me down while I'll be leveling. Oh, that reminds me. I got a new skill that lets me teleport anywhere I've already been within ten miles so long as it is in the shadows."

I could practically feel the shock over the link before Morgan replied, *"Seriously? That's amazing! You can jump to us at any time."*

Chuckling, I burst her bubble, *"I could, but I need to use this strategically. I also have a compass that the AI gave me in compensation for giving the champions their compasses. Mine lets me find dungeons of whatever type I set as the target. Meaning I can use it to find medium and high-level dungeons."*

"Dang... that's useful!"

"Yeah, I'm thinking I should head west down Spring Creek Parkway until I hit the area where the North Dallas Tollway meets Highway 121. That's a big area with a lot of stuff. There is sure to be at least a medium dungeon, if not a high-level one. With the champions coming for me, I only feel safe running a dungeon one time before moving on, so I think I'll run straight there and do whichever the highest level dungeon I can find is, and then use the teleport skill to jump back to this one afterward. That's got to throw them off."

I could hear Morgan relaying my comments to Viki before she asked, *"Weren't you heading south to get closer to downtown and the bigger dungeons? Doesn't this mess up your plan?"*

"Yeah, but I'm also hoping the bad guys will waste a bunch of time chasing me back and forth. After I jump back here, I can run south to the next area along Highway 75, where it meets the Bush Tollway. If they ran toward the last area I was to the west, they would have to turn around and backtrack a long enough distance to give me time to run another dungeon. If I can keep that up long enough without getting caught, I'll pull ahead in levels and gain a strong advantage over them."

Morgan sounded amused as she responded, *"Viki says she isn't happy with that plan since it means we won't be able to meet up with you."*

Thinking about that for a minute, I said, *"That's probably a good thing. With the champions hunting me, I don't want them finding you. You are both too strong now, and they would absolutely attack you to eliminate a potential threat to their people. However, if you head to the Spring Creek area, we might be able to meet up when I jump back here. You just need to be careful to stay inside low-level dungeons as much as possible. Don't camp outside. Wipe out the monsters until you reach the boss, and then camp for the night before entering the boss room. That will keep you safe."*

"Alright, we'll do that. After this run or the next of the dungeon, we'll need to find a new Herald candidate and start leveling them up. It should be easy to find someone around that area. Bob and Michelle, the young couple, will be heading south after this down toward the coast. They've got family down in Corpus Christi."

That sounded smart to me. Hopefully, they would be smart enough to circle around the outskirts of the city rather than go near downtown. *"Try to find someone who will go off east or west after this."* I stopped myself. *"Never mind, I don't need to tell you that."*

"Anyway, my cooldowns are almost up, so I'm going to head out of here and run as fast as I can to the west. With any luck, the champions will not be expecting that."

"Sounds good. Viki says to be safe."

"Y'all too!"

With that, I made sure I was ready for anything and headed for the dungeon's exit, hoping I wasn't about to get spawn-camped outside the entrance.

CHAPTER 24
JUKING AND RUNNING

WHETHER IT WAS luck or just timing, there weren't any champions waiting to ambush me outside the dungeon, so I ran like my ass was on fire!

Heading straight west on Spring Creek Pkwy would see me hitting the North Dallas Tollway just south of the big mall and the Dallas Cowboys practice stadium. That area had grown a lot in the last few years and was sure to have several dungeons.

With item boosts, I was sitting at an Agility score of 134, with a 20% movement speed boost as well, meaning I was running faster than a car would drive those streets. Even with just stats alone, I was at least ten times faster than an average human running, so with the boost, I was comfortably doing about 60 mph, and it felt like I was doing a fast jog.

If it weren't for obstacles in the way and needing to use my compass, I would have made it in about fifteen minutes. Thanks to needing to go around fallen trees, an unexpected sinkhole, and a couple of mutated beasts, it took just over half an hour. It was well after sundown at this point, so there weren't many people out and about. However, I did see several groups of survivors camping together in the streets around bonfires, obviously hoping the bright light and fire would ward off predators.

Every time I saw one of these groups, it was like a dagger to the heart, but I had a job to do, and I was being hunted. Stopping to try and help wouldn't be good for me or them.

Not surprisingly, the dungeon compass led me straight to the mall. Once upon a time, when it was brand new back in the late 90's, it had been a massive two-story mall and a big draw. Even in the 2020s, before the apocalypse, I had still occasionally gone there to see a movie with a date. I had fond memories of hanging out at the bookstore as well. Sadly, the books would all be gone, thanks to the fucking System. Almost more than the loss of human life, I hated the damned System for erasing our culture. Art, Literature, Movies, and even videos and memes on the internet, all gone. Even if I managed to hit the level cap and Ascend, I still wouldn't be able to bring back what had been lost.

I stopped in my tracks as an idea hit me. The AI should still have records— and after I Ascended, it said it would be allowed to communicate with me directly within the rules. Could I persuade it to restore some of our books and art?

Hmm... now that's a worthy goal! No way to know unless I get there, though.

It wasn't like I needed more motivation than the extinction of the human race and not personally dying, but still. I would love to have a good book to read once this is all over.

Putting aside those thoughts, I homed in on the dungeon portal and wasn't surprised to find it at the main entrance. However, the mall was no longer a conglomeration of shops. Even before the apocalypse, it had always made me think of shops built on top of a hill due to the way it had a raised parking lot in the front, but now it was more like a pyramid, partway under construction. The portal looked as if it led down into the earth to secret chambers beneath.

Thank goodness it wasn't another stronghold dungeon, but seemed to be a regular medium-grade one. However, considering its size, I didn't think it would be long before it upgraded to a high-grade dungeon.

Just out of curiosity, I reset the compass to high-grade, and it seemed to flicker between southwest toward DFW airport and south-by-southwest. That told me there were at least two high-grade dungeons in those directions.

That worried me.

I would have expected it to point straight south toward downtown Dallas. The fact that it didn't mean whatever was down there was worse. The convention had always been to call them low-grade, mid-grade, and high-grade dungeons, but the truth was there were more levels than that. Dungeon cores were graded by Lesser, Common, Greater, Grand, and Epic. Neither myself nor anyone I had ever known had claimed to enter anything above a Greater dungeon, aka a high-grade one. Being this early, I sure as hell hoped there weren't any Epic dungeons.

However, just to confirm, I turned the dial one more time, and it immediately pointed south and flickered to the southwest.

Damn, that meant the two downtown areas had already formed Grand Dungeons. Thankfully, nothing came up when I turned it one more time to the Epic setting.

I was almost sweating at the thought of what such a dungeon would be like. I didn't think I wanted to try one of those, even at level cap. That would suck!

I put my compass away and stopped delaying. It was time to see what this challenge would be.

As I crossed the threshold, the air thickened with an oppressive weight, dry as a desert wind but ancient—like time itself had congealed in this place. A sense of unease prickled at the back of my neck as if the very stones around me held grudges older than human memory. The low, flickering light cast long, shifting shadows that danced across the walls, amplifying the feeling that something here was watching, waiting. My heart rate picked up, and I felt a chill creep down my spine despite the warmth in the air.

The tunnel sloped downward, more expansive than any actual pyramid passage, easily ten feet high and just as wide, as though this place had been built to house something far larger, far more terrible, than what it seemed. Every step echoed off the stone, and the silence that followed was suffocating. As I descended deeper, the unmistakable scent of decay, mixed with dust, settled into my nostrils like a reminder that this was a place of the dead.

Alcoves lined the walls on either side of the passage, each one containing a figure, upright and still, encased in tattered bandages. Mummies. The old legends of curses and the dead that wouldn't stay dead drifted through my mind unbidden. Each one held a bronze weapon, frozen in time but somehow poised, like they could spring to life at any moment. I knew they would—this was their domain, after all. They would wake soon enough.

The pressure in the air shifted, like a subtle whisper in my mind, setting the mood. This was no ordinary dungeon. The whispers of the dead clawed at the edges of my thoughts, reminding me of every tale I'd ever heard about tombs like this. A feeling, like an instinct, washed over me, warning that the dead here would not rest easily. This was their realm, and they wanted to reclaim it, to drag the living down into their cold, silent world.

I took a breath, steadying myself. The deeper I went, the stronger that sensation grew—the sense that I was not just in a dungeon but in a forgotten grave of something far worse.

Growling, I shook off the System ambiance messaging that was beaming intrusively into my brain.

Damned System, I get it; this place is stronger than usual!

Honestly, though, while it wasn't necessarily more detailed or complex, what it had made me feel upon entering was far stronger than normal. It was warning me that this wouldn't be an easy dungeon. That caused me to suspect this thing was nearing the point of upgrading to a high-grade or Grand dungeon. Good thing I got here now rather than later. I wasn't sure I could handle a dungeon full of Level 50 to 60 monsters solo. Well, with my new Class and bloodline, I might be able to beat it, but it would be a significant challenge and one that might not be the wisest to face while also having to worry about the fate of the world.

Extending my claws, I moved forward, eager to find out what level these first enemies were.

The darkness of the dungeon engulfed me as I took a few steps forward, and I was immediately struck by an eerie sense of being watched. The alcoves to the side of the corridor each held their own horror, mummies wrapped in aged, tattered bandages. I knew better than to assume they'd just sit there. This was the System, and it never left anything purely for decoration.

Damn, the System was really laying it on thick with the messaging this time! I wish I could say I was getting used to it, having experienced it more in the last week than I had in my entire first life combined. However, it was beamed directly into my brain and nervous system, bypassing any possible defense. Still, I appreciated the warning despite being sick of having the System force me to feel and experience things for its own aesthetic purposes.

I edged closer, and as I expected, the closest pair shifted slightly, their glowing eyes locking onto me. They lurched out of their alcoves, their movements stiff at first but rapidly becoming more fluid as they shambled toward me.

I flexed my fists, my claws ready for action, feeling the comforting thrum of their magic. I had never faced mummies before, not even in my first life. I had tried to stay away from the undead back then, as I hadn't had magic of my own. Now, however, I felt confident I could take them despite the System really stressing that these were more formidable opponents. Still, I had a healthy respect for anything that had been animated by the System, undead or not.

I didn't have any more time for thought. The first mummy lunged forward, its desiccated hand reaching for me. Its speed caught me by surprise—much faster than its shuffling gait had suggested. I barely dodged, the fetid stench of decaying linen hitting me as its claws brushed past my shoulder. I spun to the side, slicing across its torso with my left-hand claw, the one that contained the magic of my Longknife of Shadows, leaving a trail of dark energy in its wake. It staggered back, the bandages smoldering from the magic-infused strike.

"Persistent bastard," I muttered. I guess I won't be one-shotting these guys.

The other mummy closed in, its glowing eyes narrowing. It opened its mouth, letting out a dry rasp, and suddenly, I felt a wave of cold wash over me. It wasn't just any chill; it was a numbing, supernatural cold that sank into my bones. I recognized it—a curse. My movements slowed, and I cursed under my breath as I felt my limbs becoming heavy.

No time to hesitate. I activated **Dispelling Burst**, the energy radiating out from me in a pulse. The oppressive cold shattered, and I moved again, lunging forward to meet the oncoming strike. My claws extended, and I swiped at the mummy's arm with my right-hand claw and triggered **Crippling Blow**, severing it at the elbow before it could reach me. Its glowing eyes intensified, but I didn't give it a chance to react further.

I twisted, driving my knee into its midsection, and followed up with a sharp upward slash from my left claw, severing the creature's head from its shoulders. It crumbled into a pile of dust and dried cloth at my feet.

Unfortunately, the first mummy had recovered by now, and it was angrier than before–the glow of its eye sockets somehow managed to express anger and rage. It raised both its hands, dark energy gathering in its palms. I recognized the buildup—some kind of necrotic blast, no doubt. I needed to end this now. With a roar, I activated **Dragon's Charge**, closing the distance in a split second. My shoulder crashed into its chest, the force of the impact driving it backward into the alcove it had emerged from.

The mummy tried to raise its arms, but I was already moving. My claws found their mark, plunging deep into its chest, somehow disrupting the energy that animated it, and the creature let out a final, wheezing breath before collapsing into dust.

I exhaled slowly, letting the tension ease out of my body. Not a bad warm-up, but I knew this was only the beginning. Whatever lay deeper in this place, it was going to be worse. Much worse.

To my amazement, once the remains of the two mummies turned to motes of light and were reclaimed by the System, there were two small piles of coins left behind.

Gold!

These were my first opponents in this new life to drop the much more energy-dense gold mana coins; eleven each. That meant they were Level 51, and no joke.

Taking a deep breath, I took a moment to process that. This dungeon really was on the higher end of its grade. Even in my first life as a Level 57 Knight, I had never faced monsters that strong, even with a full party.

I was torn. On the one hand, the instincts from my first life were telling me to get the hell out of this place and go find something more reasonable. On the other, my draconic blood was boiling at the idea of a real challenge. These mummies were the lowest-level critters in here, and they were at the same level as me and had multiple skills and abilities. The very first pair I faced caused me to use my **Dispelling Burst** to remove that status effect that slowed me by more than half. The skill only had a three-minute cooldown, but still. That wasn't a good sign.

The highest-level opponent I had faced so far in this new life was that Lich boss in that last dungeon, and this dungeon's base-level minions were sixteen levels higher.

I should be absolutely scared shitless, but honestly, I was more tempted than I was afraid. I had to forcibly control my instinct to roar out a challenge the way I had back in the first dungeon. Still, I wasn't a complete idiot and suppressed the urge.

Doing some quick math, I confirmed that if I managed to complete this dungeon, it would take me all the way to Level 60 and my next Class upgrade. That would surely give me an advantage over the other champions, right?

Another consideration was time. If I did run this dungeon, it would take a long time as I would likely have to heal up and rest frequently due to cooldowns on my skills, and that would give the champions a chance to catch up to me.

CHAPTER 25

PUNCHING ABOVE
YOUR WEIGHT CLASS

I SAT THERE LONGER than I should have, second-guessing myself, but in the end, I decided to just go for it. My thinking was that if the fights didn't seem to be going my way, then I would retreat and just leave. I didn't know what would come after the mummies, but these guys hadn't seemed too bad. If the dungeon followed the standard for a mid-grade, even if it was on the high end, then I could expect to face around seventy-five of these undead bastards. That alone would bring me all the way to Level 55, and I couldn't resist.

The passageway down into the guts of the pyramid gave me a bit of an advantage. It was 10' wide by 10' high, which wasn't really enough space for them to surround me. With my claws, I could reach out to either side and just about touch the walls. Meaning a mummy trying to get behind me was going to be in for a bad day.

Coming up on the next pair of mummy-infested alcoves, only about 30' further down the corridor, I paused to try and strategize. If I could come up with an attack plan that would get me a strong advantage, this would become much easier. The key to doing this efficiently would be to only rely on skills with short cooldowns. I'd love to pop **Iron Hide** to boost my armor by 50%, but it only lasted five minutes and had a twenty-minute cooldown. For now, I wanted to save that in case I had to face more than two of these at a time.

There were sconces about midway between each set of mummies; their flickering firelight did more to conceal the mummies than help me hide, unfortunately. Still, as I stood there, I started to chuckle, as an evil idea occurred to me.

I had a plan!

Creeping as close as I could without triggering them to attack, I prepared and cast **Arcane Singularity** right in the middle of the hallway, directly between the two niches in which the mummies were waiting.

The spell formed, a ball of darkness rotating in the center, drawing everything toward it, pulling the mummies from their hiding spots just in time to detonate, doing high damage and stunning them for two seconds. It was perfect.

I ran forward and got within range just as the stun was wearing off and triggered **Tempest Strike**, my claws lashing out to hit everything within 10' of me, hitting both of the rotting undead bastards. This attack also did high damage, and I could see that their health bars had dropped to less than 25% with just those two attacks, not to mention the 20% attack speed debuff they would have for a few seconds.

Unfortunately, they were undead, so pain and damage didn't affect their ability to respond. I quickly found myself the target of a pair of attacks. Both chose to open their mouths and breathe at me the cold death energy attack, leaving me with no choice but to leap and use the **Air Step** ability of my new greaves to sail right over the top of them. Thanks to the speed debuff from my previous attack they missed.

This also put me in the perfect position to land a hit with my claws, but their attack made me remember that I had a breath weapon of my own. With a bit of schadenfreude, I watched as my **Umbral Breath** engulfed them in a cone of elemental darkness that ate away at their being, reducing their health down to zero before it ended.

Shivering at the brutal efficiency of that combination of attacks, I couldn't help but be pleased, as well as amazed. I had just beaten two like-leveled undead enemies without taking a single hit. Better yet, all those skills would be off cooldown in three minutes or less, meaning I could repeat this without much delay. Considering that I had to wait one minute for the bodies to disappear and drop their coins anyway, the only downside to this tactic was that it would use a lot of mana. However, I now had the *Lich's Soul Shield* ring, which gave me 5% mana regen. With the need to wait at least three minutes between each fight, it should take me a long time to run out of mana, even as fast as I would use it.

The following eight fights went much the same. **Arcane Singularity**, **Tempest Strike**, dodge backward far enough that they grouped up to chase me and then finish up with **Umbral Breath**. That was twenty mummies dead and a whole lot of gold coins going into my storage. Only having to deal with a pair of them at once made it a good match-up for me, but I wasn't taking it lightly. They were the same level as me, so I never relaxed or let my guard down.

Of course, just as I started to breathe easier, that was when the System decided to change things up. The descending passageway came to an end at a "T" junction. To each side, the passageway continued a short distance before ending with an ornate stone door covered with faintly glowing hieroglyphs.

Frowning, I considered which way to go. This was shaping up to be an unusual dungeon already, but it was staying pretty 'on theme' with an Egyptian pyramid. There was even a wax-sealed rope curse on the doors. I didn't need my **Treasure Sense's Analyze** ability to know that sucker was a trap.

I quickly backtracked down the passage to the other pair of doors, only to find the same trap seal.

"Well, shit!"

I spent a couple minutes trying to think of ways to get rid of the trap without it blowing up in my face. Fortunately, I had a new spell for that. However, I first cast **Shadow Ward** and **Scalebound Resilience** just in case. The first would give me a chance to deflect status effects, and the second added some elemental resistance. I just wish I had a big ol' tower shield to hide behind as well.

Not wanting to waste any of my time from the defensive spells, I quickly stepped back and to the side as far as I could and stayed in range to cast **Dispelling Burst**.

There was a flash of reddish light followed by a flurry of angry sparks spewing out of the now-broken seal.

I was just about to pat myself on the back for not dying when the doors burst open, and I was charged by five mummies at once.

My asshole puckered so hard I could have made diamonds as I suffered a profound 'oh shit!' moment and began regretting my life choices.

Luckily, I had just cast two of my defensive spells, so I quickly added **Iron Hide** while backpedaling toward the tunnel junction.

That gave me a decent boost to defense; between the three of those, I had added around 70% to my armor, +elemental resist, 25% damage reduction, +deflect status effects, and increased evasion chance.

I was about to cast **Arcane Singularity** when they beat me to the punch. All five of the undead fucks opened their mouths in that 'too wide, creepy as hell' way and breathed their cold breath attack.

My evasion skill kicked in, allowing me to avoid one. Don't ask me how that works, considering they were all spewing their breath weapon into the same area of the passage where I was standing. Still, I could tell from the notifications that I had partially gotten lucky. My **Shadow Ward** deflected two more, but I got hit by the remaining two, bringing me instantly to a crawl. All my movements were 75% slower, the multiple hits adding to each other to reduce my speed more than it otherwise would have.

The pucker factor really ramped up. If even one more had landed that attack, I would be frozen in place, completely unable to defend myself.

My dragon blood was boiling within me at being restrained by their magic, and I roared in their faces as I cast **Arcane Singularity** to buy time.

The tiny blackhole-like ball of darkness drew the five mummies together into a clump for three seconds before exploding and sending them crashing into the walls and floor. Two lay prone, while three somehow managed to keep their feet under them, but even so, it had bought me five seconds to get off another attack. There was no way I wanted to be in melee range with those guys while having the 'slowed' status effect. That meant **Tempest Strike** was out, so I used my breath weapon instead.

As the waves of darkness spewed from my own mouth outward in a cone, it hit the three still standing as they were the closest. Their health bars plummeted to under 25%, but they weren't out of the fight yet, and I had no way to dispel the Cold debuff for another two and a half minutes while my spell was on cooldown!

I wanted to attack, but I couldn't risk it, so I cast **Stealth**, dodged the side wall of the passage, and flattened myself against it, hoping it would work.

It did. After a moment of watching the mummies flail around ineffectively, I breathed a sigh of relief—very quietly.

They looked around in confusion and stopped advancing. I knew it had been successful!

Without speaking, I activated **Shadow Walk** and moved past them. Even incorporeal while in the shadow realm, I was still at 75% reduced speed. Rather than try to run back up the tunnel, I moved to investigate the room they came from. Sticking my head into the doorway, I saw a chamber with two rows of sarcophaguses and another door on the end wall, but no other enemies that I could see. I exited the shadows but remained invisible.

Behind me, the mummies made breathy screeches, frustrated at my disappearance.

No matter. I quietly waited out the cooldowns on the attacks I had just used. Finally, the cold debuff disappeared after almost ten minutes.

I breathed a sigh of relief, warmth flooding back into my bones as the magical curse lifted.

Thankfully, they weren't very intelligent and were milling about searching for me by hearing as much as by sight.

Without the slowing effect, I cast **Arcane Singularity**, drawing them back together. Rather than waiting for the explosion, I immediately launched my breath attack. The three who had been damaged by both my previous spells dropped dead almost instantly.

Well, they were actually dead now.

The other two were hanging on by a thread as their bodies were sent flying again, one slamming into the ceiling and the other into the right-hand wall. This time, I happily jumped forward and used **Tempest Strike**, ending them efficiently with a final attack.

I was very grumpy as I collected the 25 gold mana coins and pocketed them.

That had been too close! I did not like the thought that I was one lucky dodge away from being dead.

Twenty-five mummies dead, and I had gotten another level and was two-thirds of the way to the next. That made me Level 52 to their Level 51, but honestly, it wasn't enough to make a difference, especially since I was outnumbered five to one in that last fight, and chances were the opposite room would be the same.

I needed a new battle plan to take on five of these guys at once. I didn't like the idea of getting that close to death in every fight. There was too much riding on my survival to risk it.

Looking from the trapped door on the other side of the junction back to the mummy room I had just hidden in, I contemplated which direction to go. I had another fifty of these bandaged-wrapped bastards to go, and I was almost positive there would be five more in the opposite room. However, I hadn't seen what was down the passage beyond the doorway at the back of the sarcophagus room.

Time to stare the unknown in the face!

I quickly searched the room, finding nothing, before passing through and entering the next tunnel. Like the original, it was 10'x10' square and continued downward before curving to the right. Very soon, I found alcoves containing more mummies. Just like before, there was one on each side of the passage.

Using the same tactics as before, I dispatched them efficiently enough–**Arcane Singularity**, **Tempest Strike**, and **Breath Weapon**. That helped build my confidence back up after that last big fight. Four more pairs appeared and died as I navigated the curving path. Pretty soon, I came to another trapped door, but by then, I was pretty sure I had circled back to the point where I would have met the original passageway if it had continued on straight instead of splitting in two.

Following a hunch, I jogged back around to the junction. If I were right, there would be a passage on the other side of the room ahead, and it would also curve around and meet back up down below.

Grumbling to myself, I was still in the same predicament. I was going to have to face five-on-one odds again. I had gained another level, but that didn't amount to much with those odds.

Knowing in advance what I would face, I had come up with a plan.

I quickly cast my defensive spells: **Scalebound Resilience**, **Shadow Ward,** and **Iron Hide**. This time, however, I didn't try to dispel the trap but stood well back and hit it with a **Shadow Bolt**, causing it to explode. Two seconds later, the doors slammed open, and five linen-wrapped, moldy undead shambled rapidly out. If they weren't so damned quick and dangerous, I might have laughed at them with how uncoordinated they seemed.

Instead, I was prepared. I cast **Arcane Singularity** for some blackhole goodness and watched as they were swept up in the pull of its gravity before exploding. However, instead of rushing forward to hit them with a **Tempest Strike**, I locked one down with **Umbral Chains**, doing a moderate DoT. By the time the shadowy tendrils burst up from below and wrapped around it, the others were recovering and starting to rush toward me again, minus about 40% of their health bars.

I continued to back away as they shambled forward, casting my most potent damage spell against the lead mummy.

Shadow Surge streaked across the intervening distance like a phantom rushing to eat its soul. However, there was no gentle kiss, but rather, the shadows slammed into the monster like a tenebrous wrecking ball. It hissed out a breath as it staggered back into another mummy, its health now below 25%.

One was now rooted, two were tangled up, but the other two continued relentlessly forward, trying to get in range for their breath attack.

Now it was time for a risk.

Dragon Charge! I rushed into melee range in an instant, putting the two tangled ones between me and the two that were still unaffected.

Before they could react, I put everything I had into a **Tempest Strike**, dealing heavy damage to all five.

That destroyed the one that was already heavily damaged and took the rooted one down to less than 30% hit points. The other three were now down to 35% or 40%. That skill also had the benefit of doing a 20% speed debuff, which was why I was willing to risk it.

I activated **Shadow Walk** and hurried past them into their room. With a quick glance, I was relieved to see that there weren't any other monsters inside.

There was no way I was going to stay in melee range long enough for them to get off an attack!

From forty feet away, I cast **Darkness** and then quietly moved to the side of the room, putting several sarcophaguses between me and the door.

The bastards weren't smart, but they weren't wholly unintelligent. They began feeling their way back into the room, but it took them enough time for my cooldowns to reset.

As they came through the door, the three free mummies flailed about, trying to find me. I cast **Arcane Singularity** again.

Boom!

The bodies went flying, landing in dirty, crumpled piles, never to move again. That just left the one still caught in my **Umbral Chains.** I ran back into the hallway and hacked it to pieces with my claws before the timer on the spell could run out.

Seeing the System notifications for the five kills, I relaxed but was still worried. That had worked, and I had taken out five strong opponents, but I had burned a lot of mana in the process. I took a few minutes to rest and drink a bottle of water. The one thing that made this possible was the fact that the mummies weren't fast. If they had, I would have been in deep trouble.

The dust in the air made me cough. That and seeing the desiccated mummies was making me thirsty.

Since I was catching my breath, I really looked around for a moment and let the System flood me with the 'feel' of the place.

The burial chamber was eerily silent, the air dry and filled with dust that clung to my lungs with every breath. The flickering light from my makeshift torch cast long shadows across the walls, dancing across faded murals that depicted scenes of rituals, sacrifices, and long-forgotten ceremonies. The walls were lined with carved symbols, the language of ancient times now etched deep into the stone like forgotten whispers of the past. In the center of the room, five sarcophaguses were arranged in a semicircle, each one slightly different but all sharing the same imposing presence.

The sarcophaguses themselves were impressive, with golden trim and elaborate hieroglyphs. Each lid bore a carved depiction of its occupant, faces worn smooth by the passage of time. The atmosphere was thick with age and an unshakable sense of dread. It felt as if the chamber itself was watching, waiting, the ancient stillness holding its breath. Dust swirled in the air, disturbed by my footsteps, and for a moment, it almost seemed as though the painted figures on the walls were moving, shifting in the dim light. I could feel it—something beyond just a room of old relics.

Something dangerous lay within, hidden beneath centuries of ritual and secrecy.

I chuckled. Not bad.

As annoying as I found those intrusive thoughts, sometimes you just had to appreciate the artistry. Even so, I still wondered if the AI, or whatever ran things, was pulling the dungeon themes from the cultures and histories of the conquered worlds. Leaving the devastated native populations to find their lost histories gone except for glimpses within the dungeons like now. Unfortunately, this was more of a caricature of what ancient Egypt was like than actual history, and that kinda pissed me off. Our descendants would see this sort of thing and think this was what it was really like.

Fucking System!

One of these days, I was going to have a very pointed discussion with the AI that fucked us over.

In the meantime, I stood up and placed the empty System-generated water bottle back in my inventory. As stupid as it was, that plastic bottle had a lot of value now, and I'd refill it when I found a clean water source.

Time to kill some more mummies!

CHAPTER 26
WHY DID IT HAVE TO BE BUGS?!?

THE ROOM where the two separate passageways met back up turned out to have ten mummies. It was the absolute worst battle of my life —not because I was beaten or even close to death, but because it was long and drawn out, and I was on edge the entire time. One slip-up and I knew I'd be utterly overwhelmed.

Much like before, I had to rely on guerrilla tactics—hit and run. But with ten opponents, there was no chance to plan things out properly. I was playing it by ear, hitting them with my big damage spells from a distance, then **Shadow Walking** away to let my cooldowns reset. It was exhausting, and for the first time, I really had to worry about running out of mana.

Once, in the middle of the battle, I used **Darkness** to cover the area, then got in close with my breath weapon, managing to hit six of those bandage-wrapped bastards at once.

They did manage to get me, though. One of their cold blasts caught me off guard, and the nearest mummy hit me with a life drain that dropped me down two levels. I was fortunate, though—I had been saving **Dispelling Burst** just in case something like that happened, so I was able to remove the Slow effect and get away before I could be surrounded. It also wasn't enough to drop me down below Level 50, so I didn't lose **Dispelling Burst**. At this point, it was a literal lifesaver.

In the end, it was a battle of attrition. One by one, the monsters dropped, and I managed the ten-to-one battle against foes at or near my level. Speaking of which, I was delighted when those two lost levels came back after the mummies' deaths.

The rest of the mummies went pretty much the same, although gradually, I was leveling as I slaughtered my way through the pyramid passages. By the time I reached the next section of the dungeon, I was Level 55, and just like that, my hard-won and very slight advantage in levels disappeared in an instant as I saw what I faced next.

It was pretty much my worst nightmare as a solo leveler.

Insects.

A fucking swarm of flesh-eating scarab beetles, just like in a horror movie!

They didn't come at me one at a time, but all at once, and there was nothing I could do about it other than fight. If I tried to run, I would have been a deadman. The one thing that gave me some small comfort was my **Shadow Recall** spell. If worse came to worse, I could duck into the shadows and then attempt to return to the dungeon entrance.

If I could get free of the swarm for long enough to cast the spell, that is!

The following two hours of my life were a nightmare....

The embalming room was huge, far grander than the cramped passages I'd just fought my way through. It looked almost ceremonial, with high ceilings and stone shelves lining the walls, each holding decaying remains of long-dead figures. Granite slabs dominated the center, covered with dusty, rusted tools for mummification—hooks, knives, some I didn't even recognize. Everything was draped in an unsettling silence, a dry, ancient stillness that made my skin crawl. Nothing moved, no enemies appeared. It almost felt like I was alone here.

Except I wasn't, and I knew it.

I crept, staying in Stealth—the non-magical kind, creeping toward one of the slabs. I needed a moment to get my bearings and figure out what the trap here was. There had to be one. It was too quiet, too empty. My instincts screamed that danger was close, but I couldn't see any danger.

I glanced at a ceremonial hook, picking it up for a better look—only to have it slip from my grasp and clatter to the floor with a sharp ring that echoed off the stone walls.

It was slick with blood, which was somehow magically still wet?

I chalked it up to System fuckery, but then I froze. A soft rustling sound reached my ears. My head snapped up, my eyes scanning the room. Nothing moved. Then, from the corner of my vision, I saw it—a beetle, fist-sized, crawling out of a hollow skull's eye socket.

One beetle. But the rustling sounds were all around me now, growing louder, too many for just one. I swallowed, my heart pounding. The beetle scuttled onto the floor, joined by another, and then another until the sound became an overwhelming hiss of insect movement.

Dozens.

They poured out of the corpses, flowing from the walls, the slabs, the dusty crannies where they'd been waiting. My eyes widened, and I knew—this was bad.

I had to move. Now.

The swarm rushed toward me, a seething carpet of chittering death. I didn't waste a second. I launched Arcane Singularity, feeling the pull of magic as it formed, sucking in beetles and crushing them together in a gravitational implosion. It took out a chunk of their health, but it was just a start. I spun and ran back toward the door, keeping my distance as I weaved between the granite slabs, trying to put as much space between me and those bugs as possible.

But I wasn't fast enough.

More poured in, too many for one spell to handle. I cast **Shadow Walk**, slipping into the shadow realm, becoming incorporeal. I had to buy time for my cooldowns—there was no other way.

In the shadow realm, I watched the beetles scuttle across the floor, searching. They couldn't see me, not here, but the second I came out of hiding, they'd be on me. I waited, counting the seconds, waiting for that cooldown to end. The moment it did, I stepped back into the physical world, as far from the beetles as I could.

I raised my hand, casting **Arcane Singularity** again. The spell detonated, pulling many members of the swarm together, crushing them, killing the already-wounded ones. But it wasn't enough. The rest turned, spotting me, and surged in my direction.

I didn't have time to think. I breathed deep, releasing **Umbral Breath**, dark energy spilling from my mouth, melting the first beetles that reached me. They burned in shadowy fire, collapsing into ash. But more were behind them. I turned, running full speed up the passageway, hearing the relentless scuttling of the swarm close behind.

I had to wait again—for both **Shadow Walk** and **Arcane Singularity**. This was going to be a long fight.

Time blurred into a cycle of casting, running, and hiding. Over and over, I used **Arcane Singularity, Umbral Breath**, whatever I could, to whittle down their numbers. Each time I reentered the physical realm, the beetles charged me, and I would retreat again, trying to stay out of reach. But they were fast, too fast. More than once, I felt their bites—sharp pain as they latched onto my skin, their necrotic poison seeping into my veins.

The first bite I ignored. The second, I cursed, feeling the poison start to work—slow, but there. By the third bite, I knew I was in trouble. The poison was cumulative, and the more they bit me, the faster it acted. I ducked back into the shadows, pulling out a low-grade healing potion. It restored my health, but it didn't touch the poison. I couldn't afford to get bitten again. Unfortunately, the three bitting me came with me into the shadows, and I had to physically crush them, ichor squirting out of their chitinous bodies.

Bugs are fucking gross!

No more close calls. I stayed out of range, letting my Shadow Walk cooldown reduce before creeping closer once again. I used spells from a distance after that, keeping my **Shadow Walk** ready to escape. I wasn't going to let these bugs be the end of me. Not here. Not like this.

The downside to this tactic was that they were no longer grouped up but spread out over the area where we had been fighting. I tried to minimize this issue by running back and forth when I ducked into the shadows, attacking from each side of the room rather than running further and further up the passageway.

It was more than an hour before the last of the beetles finally stopped moving. An hour of being hunted, of biting pain and poison, of dodging and running and fighting for my life. My breaths came hard, my body aching, poisoned but alive.

And I was finally alone.

Looking down, there were black veins slowly inching their way up my arms, leaving black dying flesh in their wake. This was no good. I had nothing to resolve this, no poison resistance, no antidote elixirs. Worse, I didn't want to call on Morgan in case something even worse came up later that required a summons. My other concern was pulling her out in the middle of a battle. That could cause Viki and her entire party to wipe if they were fighting a boss.

I opened and closed my fists a few times, and despite the gnarly look of my skin, I didn't seem to be losing any strength yet.

There was nothing for it but to move on. However, first I retraced my steps and found all of the piles of gold mana coins that had dropped as the damned flesh-eating beetles had died. That was one hell of a haul, there were 700 gold coins in total.

Better yet, I had received two more levels, bringing me up to 57 now.

That absolutely blew my mind. I was starting to lose track of time running all of these dungeons in such short succession, but only on the eighth day of the apocalypse. I had already reached the same level as I had after more than twenty years during my first life. Not only that, I was only three levels from my second Class upgrade! With luck, I might be able to reach it with the completion of this dungeon.

I took a look at my stats at Level 57 just to compare them with what they had been in my first life as a simple Knight Class.

Liam Bell: (Current)VSLiam Bell (Original)

Level:

Draconic Shadowblade - 57 / Knight - 57
Bloodline (Tier 2): Shadow Dragon / Human

Attributes:
Endurance: 127 / Endurance: 49
Strength: 127 / Strength: 48
Agility: 127 / Agility: 44
Mind: 127 / Mind: 30
Will: 127 / Will: 30
Magical Aptitude: 127 / Magical Aptitude: 0
Luck: 10 / Luck: 0

Health: 2540 / **Health:** 970
Mana: 2540 / **Mana:** 0

Damn, that really blew my mind. My physical stats were well over double what they had been! Mind and Will were quadruple what they were, and I had no MA or Luck at all in my first life. And look at the difference in health, more than one and a half times more HP. Is it any wonder why I had struggled just to survive?

As joyous as it was to bask in the goodness of these new stats, I couldn't help being more than a little pissed thinking of what this meant.

It was absolutely ridiculous what a difference a great class could make. Of course, I realized that I was now waaay out on the fringe of what was possible within the System and that the average 'good' class wouldn't come close to matching up with where I was now, but damn it, I couldn't help hating the AI and the System for screwing over the human race this way. If it hadn't deliberately and deceptively limited our choices, tens or even hundreds of millions of people would be a lot closer to where I am now than to what I had been in my first life. Hell, by the time I had been Level 57, most of the human race was dead. So even then, as pathetic as I was, I had been near the top the human race had to offer.

I fucking hate you for what you did, you bastard!

I hoped the emotionless piece of shit was listening to my thoughts right now. I also hated the creators of the AI that failed to have even the slightest shred of wisdom in letting it grow into the uncaring piece of shit it became. It wasn't like they had nearly a hundred years of warnings from Sci-fi authors on exactly what dystopian horror they would release on us.

With a sigh, I kept moving. I wanted nothing more than to lay down and take a nap or a short rest, but with the black veins slowly creeping up my arms, I couldn't afford to pause even for a few minutes. Maybe, if my Luck score was on my side, I'd get a magical item from the boss room that could cure me. At least, I could hope. If not, then I might have to risk summoning Morgan to heal me.

What came next was a nightmare made flesh.

Anubis Warriors. Seven feet tall, heavily muscled, and with the head of a jackal—these things looked every bit as intimidating as they were. Each one was armed with a massive khopesh, its curved blade glinting under the torchlight. Their eyes glowed faintly with an eerie red light, and I could feel the power rolling off them.

The first one came at me, swinging its khopesh in a brutal arc. I ducked under the swing, feeling the blade pass just inches from my head, and retaliated with a **Draconic Strike**. My claws raked across its side, but its thick armor absorbed most of the damage. It barely flinched, its glowing eyes locking onto me as it brought its weapon back around for another strike.

I gritted my teeth. This was going to be rough.

The fight was a blur of movement—the Anubis Warrior was relentless, each swing of its khopesh coming faster and harder than the last. I dodged and weaved, trying to find an opening, but its defenses were solid. I managed to land a few hits, but they were minor at best. Its vitality was off the charts—every wound I inflicted seemed to barely slow it down.

It wasn't just their strength and endurance that made them dangerous—they had skills, too. The first time I saw one use something like a Shield Bash, it caught me off guard, the force of the blow sending me stumbling back. The big bastard reached out his hand in a 'stop' position like a traffic cop telling a motorist to halt. Except instead of me stopping, a wave of force was released from his palm, slamming into me. I barely had time to recover before it was on me again, pressing the attack.

Each one seemed to have unique skills of its own– another used a skill to enhance its speed, its movements becoming a blur as it closed the distance between us in the blink of an eye. It was more than my **Dragon's Charge**; it was like fighting the Flash.

I had to be smart—use my spells and abilities to my advantage. I activated **Iron Hide**, feeling my skin harden, my defenses boosting just enough to withstand their attacks. I used **Draconic Fury**, my strength doubling as I launched a heavy strike at the nearest warrior. The blow connected, the force of it staggering the Anubis, but it wasn't enough to bring it down.

I cast **Shadow Ward**, the shadows wrapping around me, reducing the damage from their attacks. It gave me just enough breathing room to launch a counterattack, my claws slicing through the air, aiming for the weak spots in their armor. I used **Crippling Blow**, managing to land a solid hit on one of their legs, slowing it down. But even then, they kept coming, their endurance seemingly endless.

The second Anubis Warrior joined the fight, and I found myself dodging between the two of them, trying to keep from getting cornered. They were smart—coordinating their attacks, trying to pin me down. I used **Shadow Walk**, slipping into the shadows to reposition myself, coming out behind them to land a few quick strikes before they could react.

I couldn't afford to let up, couldn't afford to make a mistake. One wrong move, and they'd have me. I used everything I had—**Tempest Strike** to hit both of them at once, **Arcane Singularity** to pull them off balance, **Umbral Chains** to bind one while I focused on the other. Slowly, painfully, I wore them down, each hit chipping away at their vitality until, finally, they fell.

I stood there, gasping for breath, sweat pouring into my eyes, my body aching from the effort. My health was below 70%, my mana noticeably depleted, but I was still standing. And they weren't.

One by one, I faced them—sometimes alone, sometimes two at once. Each fight was a test of endurance, of skill. They were relentless, their strength and vitality making each battle a grueling ordeal. But I pushed through, relying on my spells, my abilities, my wits. I couldn't afford to stop, couldn't afford to rest. Not with the poison still coursing through my veins, not with the boss room waiting just ahead.

By the time I reached the massive doors that led to the final chamber, I was exhausted, my body battered, my mana low. But I was ready. It was time to end this.

The boss fight awaited. And I was going to take it down—no matter what it took.

CHAPTER 27

PHARAOH IDNOPEOUT, THE CURSED

I WOULD SERIOUSLY nope out of this fight if it weren't for one thing. The black veins on my arms were already up to my shoulders. I figured I had maybe an hour before they reached my heart and brain. I could always summon Morgan, but I didn't want to put Viki's life at risk, not knowing whether it was safe for them at the moment. I was also afraid that if I let Morgan summon me to them, they might get caught in a champion fight.

There were three things keeping me from it besides that. First, I was becoming convinced that this necrotic effect wasn't going to kill me. Well, it was. It just wasn't going to end me. Based on the fact that it wasn't really hampering me or causing my arms to stop working normally, I was pretty sure this was a curse rather than a poison, and it was trying to turn me into an undead. The problem was that I wouldn't become a fun kind; I wouldn't be a suave nightstalking vampire or even a gross but super powerful lich. Instead, considering what I had been fighting and where the beetles had been feeding, I seemed doomed to be a dusty, old, shriveled-up mummy of some kind. Aside from the 'ick' factor, I really didn't want that. It would probably result in a race change, taking away all my dragon powers and replacing them with shitty undead powers like that cold breath and life drain the previous mummies used. Those weren't bad, but compared to my claws, breath weapon, and living body?

"Hell, no!"

More importantly, I had two hopes to avoid that fate. If I could beat the boss, with my Luck score being maxed, I stood a pretty decent chance of getting a loot item that might remove the curse. However, that wasn't even the best option. After killing the Anubis warriors, I was Level 59, only one away from my Class upgrade. The boss alone wouldn't be enough experience, but the 20% bonus from soloing and completing the dungeon would.

The Class change would wipe out any negative effects and fully heal me up. Regular level-ups didn't have any benefits like that, but Class Upgrades were like a total reset, starting you off fresh with the new upgrade. With the bloodline changes, it basically rewrote my DNA.

There was only one problem. I had to kill the boss and at least five Anubis Warriors first!

The boss chamber was enormous, easily the largest room I'd seen in the pyramid. The air felt thick, almost charged with energy—like the entire dungeon had been leading to this one point, funneling all the power and magic to the pharaoh on his throne. The room was dimly lit by a series of braziers, the flickering flames casting dancing shadows against the ancient stone walls. Hieroglyphs covered every surface, glowing faintly with an otherworldly blue light pulsating like a heartbeat.

At the far end of the chamber, a raised dais held an ornate throne, and on it sat the Cursed Pharaoh. His mummified form was draped in tattered royal robes, his skeletal hands resting on the arms of the throne. A lapis lazuli and turquoise headdress, cracked and decaying, adorned his head, and in his eye sockets, a baleful green glow burned. The pharaoh's gaze seemed to pierce through me even from across the chamber, his presence radiating power and malice.

Six Anubis Warriors stood as silent guardians in the room—one at each corner and two more flanking the throne itself. Their massive frames were statuesque, each holding a formidable khopesh at the ready. They didn't move, but I could feel the tension in the room, the unspoken threat they represented. This was it—the final fight. They only waited for me to step fully into the room.

Jeez, and I thought the lich from the last dungeon was a reject from an Iron Maiden album cover.

This whole scene could have been an AI knockoff of one of those covers!

As I stood there, not yet crossing the threshold, I considered if this was something I really wanted to do. The Anubis Warriors were Level 57, and they outnumbered me six to one. However, the boss would be higher level than me, somewhere in the mid to upper 60's. I was confident in my abilities by now, but this...

This was a daunting challenge, something I wasn't sure I could beat. The only reason I was considering it was that the warriors were physical fighters and didn't have offensive spells of any kind. If they did, then I wouldn't have hesitated to nope right the fuck out of there. However, with only the pharaoh likely to use magic, I was sure I stood a chance if I was smart about this. The key would be to take the boss down quickly before it could cripple me with debuffs and attack spells.

I took a deep breath to steel myself and cast all of my defensive spells and buffs. I would need every bit of power and protection to survive this. I would also have to fight smart.

Ready, I stepped past the threshold, and two massive stone doors swung closed behind me. The pharaoh's glowing eye sockets turned to me. I could feel its eyes on me despite their lack of anything resembling normal eyeballs.

It started to monologue, so I started to cast my first spell. There was no way I would let this undead boss bastard get the momentum in this fight.

"Mortal, come and kneel before my throne, and you shall..."

I didn't let it continue, hitting it with **Umbral Chains** to buy me a few seconds to do some damage and kick this fight off on my terms.

The four Anubis Warriors spaced in the four corners of the room rushed toward me as soon as I attacked their boss. Still, it was a big room, I had time for two more actions before they reached me, and I was going to make the most of them.

Shadow Surge tore through the air and slammed into the pharaoh's bare chest, and I had the satisfaction of seeing its health bar drop to around 65%. Not as much as I would have liked, but it was a decent start.

If the enemy were my level or below, **Umbral Chains** would last five minutes, but it was higher. That meant it would break free in a matter of seconds. Worse, the Anubis Warriors closest to me were almost on me.

I cast **Shadow Walk** and ran to the throne through the shadow realm. The disturbing thing was that they somehow managed to follow me even though I was incorporeal. As I ran, I could see their heads turn, obviously seeing me.

"Oh, shit. That's not good!"

That scared the absolute crap out of me. Nothing corporeal was supposed to see me when I was in the shadows like this, but Anubis was the god of death, so maybe they were attuned to the shadow realm?

They were on my heels quickly, so I pulled another trick out of my bag of skills and used **Dragon's Charge**, instantly crossing the room and standing before the throne.

The jackal-headed bodyguards flanking the throne began to step forward to interpose themselves between me and the pharaoh, but it was too late; I had already arrived.

I burned my once-per-day ability of my *Spectral Longknife of Shadows* and boosted my first strike to automatically crit and ignore any defenses while initiating my strongest melee attack, **Heavy Draconic Strike**.

The results were incredibly satisfying; the boss' health plummeted to less than 30% with that one blow.

Enraged and activating some skill, its burning eyes flared, and it shrugged off my **Umbral Chains**. While its guards swung their bronze khopeshes at me.

I swallowed hard and took the hits, hoping I could survive them.

I had to finish this boss, or I would be screwed. I didn't know what its powers were, but I wasn't about to give it a chance to use them if I could help it.

They landed since I didn't dodge. However, between all my buffs and defenses, they only dropped my health by around 25%. That was still 650 health in two hits. However, I had the satisfaction of watching their health drop a bit. The damage reflection effects of my **Shadow Ward** spells bounced some of their own damage back at them, making them rock back.

I was preparing to finish off the boss and then run, but then it did the most annoying thing possible; it healed. It only came back up to around 50% of its full health, but still, that pissed me off. I had just taken two hits to try and end this bastard, and now I would have to do more.

Fuck it!

I still had a couple seconds before the other four jackal heads closed the distance.

Umbral Breath! Take that halitosis, you bastard!

The waves of elemental shadow erupted from my mouth, engulfing the three in front of me in a swath of darkness. Whatever the boss had done to heal itself had also covered it in a thin field of green energy, no doubt some kind of defense. Unlucky for it, my breath weapon bypassed traditional armor and had some ability to penetrate magical defenses as well.

It didn't do the same level of damage to the pharaoh as it did to the warriors, but it was enough. The fear effect of the darkness made the Anubis Warriors flinch back to avoid me, giving me full access to the boss for a few seconds, and that was all I'd need!

The undead pharaoh bellowed, "For daring to strike me, you shall be cursed!"

As last words go, those weren't bad, but they didn't stop me. I triggered my other strong melee skill, **Tempest Strike**, hitting all three before me for high damage and debuffing them with a 20% attack speed penalty for five seconds. Added to the fear effect of the breath weapon, they were no threat for the moment.

However, as my blade impacted the boss, I felt a terrible pain in my own chest as a wound opened up. The fucker had used a damage reflection skill!

Thankfully, enough damage went through that its health plummeted to nothing, and it sagged in its throne.

Something was off! That is, besides the fact that I was now down to below half health.

There was no notification for the boss's death!

"Son of a bitch!" I cursed.

Then I saw it. A golden feather amulet hanging from the dead pharaoh's neck. It was beginning to glow and get brighter by the second.

I didn't know if it was a second chance item or if the damned thing was going to do a retributive strike. Either way did not bode well for me.

Cursing that **Shadow Walk** was on cooldown, I picked the only option that I could. If it was going to blow up, there was nothing I could do about it, and there was no way to hide, but I could stop it from resurrecting him with full health!

"Luck, I need you now!" I yelled as I leaped forward in a desperate lunge toward the feather. Swiping with both claws, using **Crippling Blow** with one and **Searing Slash** with the other, I put everything I had into the strikes.

BOOM!

I came to a few seconds later, still half-stunned from being flung all the way across the chamber into one of the walls. I felt like shit, and a quick glance at my health told me why. I was down to less than 20% health. I had lost over 2000 out of my 2600 health!

My ears were ringing, but fortunately, I wasn't the only one in bad shape. The two Anubis Warriors standing next to the pharaoh had gone to meet their god. The remains of their bodies were scattered all over the room.

The other four were beginning to get to their feet and look around for me.

It was time to make a strategic advance to the rear, as my father used to say when things were going really bad.

Casting **Stealth**, I disappeared from their sight. I took out a medium-grade healing potion and downed it. Relief flooded me as my health bar slowly climbed back up to nearly full, and my wounds began closing. Unfortunately, the mummy's curse was still advancing, the black veins another three inches closer to my heart and head, now covering my shoulders, and bringing me that much nearer to an unwanted race change. Or maybe just death?

If I could kill these remaining four warriors, I could get out of this dungeon and teleport somewhere safe, away from where the champions might find me for a few hours, perhaps. Enough time to do my Class Upgrade and recover from it.

But first, I needed to finish this. Most of my spells and abilities were on cooldown, and I was at about half mana.

I was a bit worried after they had seen me moving through the shadows, but fortunately, the death-aligned warriors couldn't see me while I was magically stealthed. I quietly moved around the room to where the boss had turned to meat confetti. Sure enough, there was a loot drop. I might as well see what I got while waiting for my skills to cooldown.

Quickly using my **Treasure Sense**, I analyzed the small amulet on a golden chain to see its properties.

Amulet of the Cursed Pharaoh
Description: This amulet, made of dark gold and embedded with a glowing scarab-shaped emerald, pulses faintly with necrotic energy. Despite its ominous appearance, the amulet grants powerful benefits to its wearer.

Endurance +5%: Enhances the user's life force, making them more resilient against physical damage.

Necrotic Ward: Grants 15% resistance to necrotic or curse-based attacks and effects.

Special Ability: Once per day, the wearer can activate this ability to temporarily slow all enemies within a 50-foot radius. This marks the enemies with a glowing pillar of light visible only to the wearer of the amulet. Additionally, those marked will be unable to reenter Stealth for one hour. Their movements become sluggish, making them easier targets in battle.

Not hesitating, I swapped it out for the Berserker Amulet I had been wearing. I lost 10% damage reduction, but gaining a percentage multiplier to Vitality was worth it. Plus, it would be nice to pull enemies out of hiding if necessary. It was a solid upgrade.

By the time I had finished swapping my items, most of my timers had run out, and my skills and spells were available again.

Taking a quick look at my status showed that the Mummy's Curse was still in place, but I hoped that it would be slowed by the resistance to Curse-based attacks. Either way, I had to finish this fight before I could do anything about it.

Meanwhile, the Anubis Warriors were milling about in confusion, but they weren't close enough together to use my AoE attacks.

I had been thinking during this rest while I hid from them. Once I reappeared, that was it. Since they could see through **Shadow Walk,** there was no stopping. I would have a one-hour cooldown on Stealth, so it was time to go all out.

The four monsters all had about 25% of their health gone from the blast that destroyed the boss, so at least I wouldn't be starting from nothing. These guys were super tanky, so I would need to pile on the damage fast.

Resisting the urge to chuckle, I reached down and grabbed a broken chunk of stone from the boss's throne. I lobbed it toward the door, where it hit with a loud clatter in the quiet room.

Instantly, the jackal heads turned in unison like a pack of wild animals, honing in on the disturbance. They rushed to the door, suspecting that I must be trying to get out.

I snuck closer and hit them with the holy trinity!

Arcane Singularity was first; it pulled them together before exploding, doing a decent chunk of damage, but not nearly as much as it should have due to their ridiculous defenses. Their health bars dropped another 15% instead of the 30% it would usually do to an enemy.

Before they could recover, I hit them with **Umbral Breath**, not only doing another 15% of their health but also inflicting them with a fear debuff so that they didn't attack me for the next five seconds.

I finished up the chain of attacks with **Tempest Strike**, my last AoE. It also dropped their health bars another 20% and debuffed their attack speed for the next few seconds as well. They were down to 35% left on their HP, but that was still a lot.

Grinning, I triggered my last two trump cards, one that I hadn't been able to use this entire dungeon since the enemies had almost always been equal to my level, and the other I had been saving for a moment like this.

I bellowed out a roar of challenge, paralyzing them with **Draconic Fear**.

I was feeling my dragon blood boiling at the challenge of this fight, and I activated **Draconic Fury** as well, doubling my strength for the next 59 seconds.

Targeting the nearest warrior, I used **Heavy Draconic Strike**, slamming my claws into its throat and ripping its head from its shoulders.

One down.

I turned to the next and raised my left hand, casting Shadow Surge. Darkness crackled around my fingertips before coalescing into a concentrated blast of pure shadow energy. The spell shot forward like a bolt from a cannon, imbued with the doubled power of Draconic Fury.

The Anubis Warrior barely had time to react, its glowing eyes widening as the dark surge smashed into its chest. The impact was devastating—shadow energy punched through the hardened armor and burst out the other side, leaving a gaping, smoking hole right through its torso. The jackal-headed warrior staggered back, its khopesh slipping from its grasp, and collapsed to the ground in a heap, lifeless. The surge of power from **Draconic Fury** had turned the spell into an unstoppable force, and the warrior hadn't stood a chance.

Unfortunately, the fear had worn off, and the last two monsters advanced on me, one swinging at my side as it started to turn away from the one I had just destroyed.

I felt a burning pain in my side as its khopesh bit deeply into my ribs, cutting through my armor like it was paper.

The fury of my blood wouldn't put up with that, and I clawed at its throat with a swipe of my left hand, triggering **Crippling Blow**, my highest remaining damage attack. With the power of fury, it tore out the monster's throat in a spray of viscous black blood, sending it to meet its god.

One left.

It slashed at my other side, hitting my right arm and fracturing it badly enough that the bones were sticking out. It was a miracle that it didn't completely sever the arm.

A thought in the back of my head wondered why I wasn't a lot more disturbed by that, but the fury was in control right now!

With a roar of anger, I struck back with a **Searing Slash**, staggering it, and followed up with a **Draconic Strike**, watching its health plummet to nearly nothing. It swayed from side to side as it tried to muster the strength to make one final assault on me.

I wasn't having it. I raised my left fist and launched an empowered Shadow Bolt directly into its snout, blasting its head backward with the sound of a whip crack. It fell to the floor, its head cocked at an unnatural angle. It wasn't going to move again.

I won.

It was only then that I realized I hurt like hell, but it was over.

As soon as the bodies disappeared, I grabbed the mana coins and put them in my storage. I couldn't afford to wait another minute.

My **Treasure Sense** told me one of the Sarcophagi contained the treasure. Like the others, it was covered in beautiful hieroglyphs and inlaid with gold. There was no hinged lid. Instead, it was covered with a heavy granite top that would have required a lot of effort to move if not for my high Strength stat. Still, with one arm busted, I didn't find it easy, even with my 200+ Strength.

Thankfully, there were no traps this time. Within were two high-grade potions, healing and mana, but sadly, no potions to remove the curse. Not that I had ever seen such a thing, but this would have been good timing for a first.

However, potions were not what drew my eye. Beside them, there was an onyx Ankh symbol.

I wanted to dance for joy when I analyzed it:

Ankh of Vitality
Description: An onyx ankh, roughly the size of a person's palm, exuding an aura of protection and warmth. The ankh magically adheres to armor or any other solid item, either held or worn.

Effects: +10% Health Regeneration Rate.

Special Ability:
Once per day, the ankh can be activated to cleanse a single status effect on yourself or a target.
Provides +5% Endurance when worn.

I didn't know if it was my Luck or if the AI was fudging things to work in my favor, but either way, I would take it. That item was a literal lifesaver!

The black veins were crawling up to my neck now and almost reaching my heart. If I hadn't gotten this item, I would have had to risk Viki's life to summon the Priestess, and I would have felt absolutely terrible about that. If she got hurt, I'd spend the rest of my life cursed with guilt over it.

Wasting no time, I slapped it to the left breast of my chest and willed it to use the once-per-day ability.

A warm golden energy flooded through my body, washing away the necrotic curse. The magical black veins lifted off of my skin and dissolved into tiny golden motes of light and dispersed.

The health regeneration effect didn't suck, either. I could feel my wounds start to slowly close, but it was painful as hell. If I hadn't already taken a health potion just a few minutes ago, I would much rather have drunk another, as the healing was much faster and more comfortable.

To help things along, I reached over to my right arm and physically straightened it to pull the bones back into place. There were a few screams involved, but once the bones were lined back up, the regeneration ability had a much easier time knitting the bones back together, and I was in less pain.

It would still take a long time to put everything to right, and that was frustrating. I killed the boss and his minions and completed the dungeon, but something prevented the experience from being rewarded.

That meant no level-up and no Class upgrade until later. I wasn't going to risk going outside in my current condition. I could jump back to the Allen or Plano dungeons and rush inside to be relatively safe, but that **Shadow Recall** wouldn't be an instant spell, and I'd be completely vulnerable while casting.

Nope, better to wait it out and use another healing potion in half an hour when it was safe again. Besides, my best abilities were still on cooldown, so I wanted a rest anyway.

Not to mention that I was baffled by why I hadn't received the dungeon completion notification. I had cleared the dungeon and beaten the boss and its minions. What could possibly be left?

I took the high-grade potions from the Sarcophagus and stashed them in my storage ring with the rest. Then, I walked over and took a seat on what was left of the throne. The armrests and part of the back had been blown apart when the boss died, but the seat was still intact and relatively comfortable.

Slouching down in the chair and getting as comfortable as possible, I considered what I had accomplished. This dungeon had been on the verge of upgrading to a grand dungeon, aka a high-grade, as most people called it. Unlike all the dungeon runs since I first restarted in this life, this one had been a really deadly challenge with monsters at my own level through most of it. Hell, based on the five platinum mana coins the boss had dropped, it had been Level 65, a full six levels over my own.

I held one of the coins in my left hand and enjoyed the feel of its weight. I had never in my past life seen a platinum mana coin. I knew they existed based on prices in the System Shop, but this was my first!

Waking a bit later, I was surprised I had drifted off to sleep. Of course, I was also mostly healed now, so I wasn't too sad about the lost time. I was pretty sure I had only slept an hour or so. Thankfully, with my high stats, I didn't have that unpleasant disoriented feeling that a nap can give you upon waking. My cooldowns had also reset, and I was ready to go.

I was just getting up from the throne when I noticed something on my mini-map that I had never seen before. I had heard about it but never actually saw one in person.

The wall behind the throne was a slightly different shade than the surrounding walls as if the transparency setting for that section was lowered to 75% compared to the rest.

I had found my first-ever secret room! Maybe that was what was preventing me from getting the dungeon completion notification and the bonus XP.

Time to do some exploring!

CHAPTER 28

VIKI AND MORGAN GET A PLEASANT SURPRISE

VIKI

Viki crouched low, her sharp eyes scanning the overgrown field that used to be a parking lot as she followed Marsha and Dan toward the dungeon. Where the old movie theater and bowling alley loomed in the distance, their neon signs long since shattered and gone, the pavement cracked with weeds reclaiming the space. She hated that civilization had been wiped away, leaving only dungeons, monsters, and survivors stubborn enough to keep fighting.

Anger welled up in her as she remembered the happy times when her parents had taken her and her brother to that theater and played games afterward. She suppressed it, not wanting the loss to break her. Someday, she would remember all of that, but not now; she needed to get stronger and take the world back first.

In the meantime, if these two were going to be Heralds—if they were going to spread the truth about the System and what was really happening—they had to be strong enough to survive. Assuming they even wanted to be heralds, that is.

Marsha and Dan led the way, their hands clenched together. The nervous tension between them was thick enough to choke on. They had been devout believers, but now, faced with undeniable proof that the world wasn't what they thought, they were scrambling for something new to hold onto.

Morgan stepped up beside Viki, her expression as sharp as ever. "What do you think?" she asked quietly.

Viki tilted her head, watching the couple. "They haven't broken yet," she muttered. "That's a good start."

At the dungeon entrance, a swirling portal of dark green energy, housed within the doorway of a small castle-like structure, flickered, casting a faint glow over the cracked pavement. Viki turned to Marsha and Dan, crossing her arms. "Alright," Viki said, crossing her arms. "Before we head in, do you two actually wanna get stronger and help spread the truth about the System and what's really happening?"

The young couple looked at each other, sharing concerned looks, but then, without words, they came to a decision.

Dan straightened, his grip tightening on Marsha's hand. "We're ready. I'm tired of worrying and living in constant fear. I want to be able to protect Marsha from all the bad stuff that's out there," he said firmly.

Marsha hesitated, glancing at the dungeon's swirling entrance. "I want to help people. That Reverend Petty was a conman, and we bought into his lies because we were scared and didn't know what else to do. We're ready to learn."

Having said that, she got a nervous look on her face as she added, "But we still haven't picked our classes," she admitted. "The reverend told us the System was the work of the devil, so... we held off."

Morgan blinked in surprise, then her eyes lit up. "Wait... you mean you two are still Unclassed?"

They both nodded, and Viki felt a grin stretch across her face. That was perfect.

"Then we're about to fix that," she said. "Liam always told me that the best way to get strong is to pick a class that fits you but also helps you survive. And rare classes? Those are the best."

Marsha and Dan exchanged glances, uncertainty flickering between them.

Viki reached into her pouch, pulling out a hefty handful of mana coins, the small crystalline metal shimmering in the dim light. "Here," she said, handing them to Marsha and Dan. "Hold onto these while we run the dungeon. It'll help you get exposure to mana."

Dan stared at the coins like they might bite him, but Marsha took hers carefully. "What exactly are we doing?" she asked.

Morgan smiled. "You two are getting power-leveled," she said. "We'll do the hard work. You just make the kills. By the time we're done, you'll have enough mana exposure to get some really good class offers."

With that, they stepped into the dungeon.

The air inside was thick with the scent of damp earth and metal, the kind of musty, blood-tinged stench that told Viki this place had seen plenty of violence. The dungeon walls pulsed faintly, greenish veins of magic slithering through the stone like the place itself was alive.

Grimacing, Viki turned to the couple. "Do you feel that? Those feelings and thoughts that you got as soon as you saw the dungeon door? That, and how much worse it got once you came inside? How you felt all scared and intimidated and such?"

Dan looked thoughtful and nodded.

Marsha added, "Uh, yeah, why?"

Viki wanted to spit, this made her so mad. "Liam says those are the things the System wants you to feel and experience. He calls it ambe... uh, ambiance. Yeah, that's it. Anyway, that's all fake; it's put into your heads and isn't real. That's one of the things we want you to let people know about. How it tries to mess with us."

Their eyes were big with concern over something being able to get into their heads.

Morgan chuckled, "I'm guessing that being from a religious background, that must really sound like 'the devil's work,' huh?"

Marsha swallowed hard, "It sure does, but you say this is all just some computer thing that is running all this?"

They stood at the entrance for a good half-hour talking about what the System and AI were, how they had caused all this, and why.

Viki finally interrupted, "That's enough for now. We'll tell ya more as we go. I want to kill those orcs." She pointed off to the left of where they came in.

The orcs weren't far. Viki had seen them a couple times while they had been talking and, even now, could hear them grunting and shuffling deeper inside, their heavy footfalls echoing through the cavernous halls of the fake System-created castle.

"Stay behind us," Morgan instructed. "Let us handle the tough parts, but make sure you get the last hit. We're partied up, so the experience will be split evenly, but actually doing the killing will probably count toward what classes you get offered. At least, I think so based on how Viki got offered a bunch of archer classes after shooting orcs while she and Liam fought together."

Viki handed Dan a System-generated sword she had taken from the Orc arena in the big stronghold dungeon and a shortsword for Marsha.

The first orc rounded a corner, its beady red eyes locking onto them. It let out a guttural snarl, hefting a jagged cleaver as it charged.

Viki was faster.

She darted forward, her magic cleaver flashing in the dim light as she hacked into the orc's leg, severing tendons with a clean, practiced slice. The beast howled in pain, stumbling to a knee. "Dan! Now!" she shouted.

Dan's hands trembled as he raised the rusty sword she had given him. He hesitated for half a second before plunging it into the orc's chest. The System chimed in acknowledgment, the corpse dissolving into motes of green light a minute later.

"That's one," Morgan said approvingly. "Let's keep going."

The pattern repeated, Viki and Morgan systematically crippling the orcs while Marsha and Dan delivered the finishing blows. The more they fought, the steadier the couple became. Dan's swings grew more confident, Marsha's movements less hesitant. By the time they reached the boss room, they were breathing hard but still standing.

The orc chieftain loomed over them, twice the size of the others, its armor pieced together from scavenged scrap metal. A massive, rusted axe hung from its grip, its jagged edge already stained with old blood.

Viki cracked her knuckles. "Alright, final test," she said. "Morgan and I will kill its minions really fast, then soften the boss up. You two finish it."

She moved in first, her **Eclipse Barrage** severely wounding three of the elite Orc warriors. Almost on top of her shot, Morgan launched her own AOE, **Shadowflame Burst.** The three Viki had just wounded died, and the other two were severely injured. A couple more arrows took them out.

Then, it was time for the Chieftain. Viki rushed forward, ducking under its initial swing, her cleaver flashing as she sliced deep into its calf. Morgan followed, shadows swirling around her as she sent a blast of dark energy into the beast's chest, staggering it back.

"Now!" Viki barked.

Marsha and Dan rushed forward. Dan struck first, his blade biting into the orc's stomach. Marsha, hands trembling, lifted her shortsword and drove it into the creature's throat.

The System rang out with their victory. The chieftain collapsed, its body eventually vanishing into motes of green light, leaving behind a small pile of mana coins.

They had done it.

Marsha

Marsha's heart pounded as the notification flickered in her vision. A soft glow surrounded her, the System acknowledging her growth. She forced herself to breathe, to push down the swirl of emotions threatening to overtake her.

She hadn't wanted this. Not at first. The System was supposed to be evil, a trap, a lie. But her mother had prayed for healing that never came, and now, standing here, alive, stronger, she couldn't deny the truth staring her in the face.

The System wasn't a god. It wasn't divine. But it was real.

A menu appeared before her, listing her choices. Four basic options. Fighter. Mage. Two types of Crafter.

She swallowed hard, fingers hovering in hesitation. Viki's reminder echoed in her mind; she needed to think: "Options."

The list expanded instantly.

She gasped. Dozens—no, hundreds—of choices scrolled before her, a flood of potential paths, each more overwhelming than the last. Her hands trembled as she scrolled, looking for something... something special. Something rare.

There were no asterisk marks '*,' indicating limited classes available, but after sorting, she did find rare classes.

And then she saw it. Something that called to her.

Draconic Acolyte.

Her breath caught in her throat. It wasn't just a healing class—it was a rare one infused with draconic magic. A class that would let her heal, truly heal, without needing the blessing of some distant, uncaring god.

She flinched at that thought. Even now, months after her mother died, it felt like she would be struck down by lightning for thinking about God that way.

Her heart clenched as she thought of her mother, of the prayers that had gone unanswered.

This decision wasn't about faith. This was power. Maybe God was real but just silent and uncaring, or maybe there was nothing but the System. Either way, she knew what she had to do!

She pressed accept.

A warm rush of mana surged through her, settling into her bones. She exhaled sharply, feeling something click into place. She wasn't just surviving anymore.

She was fighting back.

Morgan turned to her, eyes bright. "Well?"

Marsha smiled, the first real, unburdened smile in what felt like years. "Draconic Acolyte."

Morgan grinned. "Ooh, that sounds cool. What does it do?"

She went on to explain the Class. It wasn't a bloodline like Viki and Liam had, but just Dragon 'themed,' with powers based on Draconic ones. The only real downside was that she didn't get the ability to bond with dragons the way Morgan had, so there would be no long-distance communications or summoning. She did get a Title for being power-leveled, but it wasn't as good as Viki's when they compared them. Still, it did provide a small boost to all of her stats, and that was not something she would turn down if it meant being able to heal people that the System hurt.

Dan

Marsha had finished, and Dan made sure she was okay. Then he took a steadying breath as he opened his status page, his fingers twitching slightly. The System's interface glowed before his eyes, the familiar prompt waiting for him:

Choose Your Class.

He still wasn't entirely sure how he felt about all this. Everything he'd believed in had been turned on its head in just a few short days. But one thing was clear—the world had changed, and if he wanted to protect Marsha, if he wanted to survive, he had to change with it.

Four basic options appeared first—**Fighter, Mage, Blacksmith, and Enchanter.** He frowned. They weren't bad choices, but they weren't enough. Viki had said the rare ones were stronger. He wasn't about to waste this chance.

"Options," he muttered, and immediately, the list expanded. As Marsha had described, the sheer number of choices now available was staggering. There were melee-focused classes, magic-heavy ones, hybrids that blended the two. Some sounded more advanced, but he kept scrolling, looking for something rare—something that fit him.

He stopped the instant he saw the word 'draconic'.

Draconic Warblade.

His breath caught as he read the description. A class that seamlessly blended physical prowess with draconic-infused magic, empowering each strike with elemental force. A warrior who could cut through enemies with enchanted blades, unleash bursts of magic mid-combat, and adapt to both close-quarters and ranged encounters.

It wasn't a bloodline class, but it didn't matter. This was exactly what he needed. He could fight up close, reinforce his strikes with magic, and still have ranged options when things got rough.

He pressed **Accept.**

A surge of mana rushed through his body, hot and electrifying like fire threading through his veins. His muscles tensed, then relaxed as the energy settled, a strange new sense of power thrumming beneath his skin. He clenched his fists, feeling the difference immediately. Strength. Speed. Magic humming just beneath the surface, waiting to be wielded.

He exhaled, a small grin tugging at his lips as he turned to face the girls.

"I got my class," he said, rolling his shoulders as he adjusted to the new sensation. "Draconic Warblade."

Morgan's eyebrows shot up. "Nice. Hybrid Class?"

Dan nodded. "Yeah. Melee and magic combined. I can reinforce my attacks with draconic energy and use mid-range spells, too."

Viki smirked, clearly pleased. "Not bad! Means you won't just be swinging a sword like a dummy."

Dan chuckled, shaking his head. He already felt lighter, stronger—like his body finally had the right tools to fight back. This was it. The first real step toward making sure neither he nor Marsha ever had to feel powerless again.

Viki

The next few hours passed in a blur of steel, fire, and mana. Viki and Morgan pushed Marsha and Dan relentlessly, dragging them through wave after wave of orcs, their once-uncertain movements sharpening into something resembling real skill.

"Faster, Dan!" Viki barked, darting between two hulking orcs. "If you're gonna use magic, don't just stand there charging it up like some idiot! Move! Weave it into your attacks!"

Dan gritted his teeth, shifting his stance as another orc lunged. Instead of raising his blade for a simple block, he twisted, letting the attack slide past before channeling his new abilities. A shimmering arc of draconic energy flared along his blade as he slashed upward, carving a glowing line into the orc's chest. The creature staggered, its flesh seared from the inside out before it collapsed.

Viki gave a sharp nod. "Better."

Nearby, Morgan knelt beside Marsha, watching as she healed a deep gash on Dan's arm. "Don't just dump mana into it," Morgan instructed. "Control it. Healing isn't just about patching wounds—it's about efficiency. If you burn out mid-fight, we're screwed."

Marsha's jaw tightened in concentration, her hands glowing faintly as the wound sealed up faster, the energy more precise. "I think I've got it," she murmured, looking up at Morgan.

Morgan smirked. "Then prove it in the next fight."

Between fights, when they stopped to catch their breath, Viki and Morgan filled in the gaps in the couple's knowledge about the System.

"So the dungeons aren't natural?" Dan asked, wiping sweat from his forehead.

Viki scoffed. "Natural? Hell no. The System's making them constantly. Think about it—monsters don't breed, they don't have families, and every dungeon resets. It's like... I dunno, a game on repeat, except the people who play it die for real."

Morgan nodded. "And it's not just dungeons. The AI is a bastard. It hands out classes, but it hides the best ones behind hoops you wouldn't even know to jump through unless someone told you. That's why rare classes matter. That's why magic matters."

Marsha glanced at her hands, flexing her fingers as a small wisp of golden-draconic energy curled around her fingertips. "So we have to use the System's own tools against it?"

Viki grinned. "Exactly."

They ran the dungeon again. And again. And again. Each time, Marsha and Dan grew sharper, faster, and stronger, leveling up. Dan's swordplay became fluid, his draconic magic weaving seamlessly between strikes, while Marsha kept the team alive, her healing more precise, more controlled.

By the time they hit Level 11, they weren't just keeping up—they were holding their own. By the time they hit 13, Viki and Morgan were sure they could survive on their own.

At the end of another grueling run, as they looted the orc chieftain's corpse, Morgan exhaled sharply, checking her status. "Level 23," she said, glancing at Viki.

Viki grinned, bouncing on her toes, still riding the high of the fight. "Same." She turned to the couple, who were still catching their breath. "You guys are getting better, but don't think this is enough. You're still just getting started. Now that we've trained you, you need to grow stronger on your own."

Morgan added, "And spread the word!"

Dan wiped the blood off his blade, giving her a tired but determined look. "I think we need sleep, but then we will head out in the morning. Our families, what's left of them, are down in Houston. We'll head that way."

Viki's smirk widened. Liam was going to be so proud of them. She couldn't wait to tell him!

CHAPTER 29

SECRETS NEVER MEANT TO BE SEEN

LIAM

The boss fight had been grueling, and despite my regeneration, my body still ached from every hit I had taken. Still, I couldn't pass up the chance to see a hidden area. Maybe, just maybe, it was a secret stash, something the Pharaoh was protecting that could help me out. I needed every advantage I could get!

I approached the back of the throne and laid my hand on the stone wall behind it. Nothing seemed unusual at first, but there was definitely something behind it—the mini-map didn't lie. I gathered my strength, channeling my power into a **Heavy Draconic Strike**. The impact sent shockwaves through the chamber, and the stone cracked, dust cascading as the wall gave way. I pressed on, prying apart the crumbling remains until there was a gap large enough to slip through.

Inside, the hidden space was unlike anything I had ever seen. It was a chaotic jumble of different environments, mashed together as if someone had taken pieces of various worlds and dropped them into a single chamber. To my left, the stone walls were carved like those of an ancient monastery, with scrolls stacked haphazardly in niches, their edges crumbling with age. The air smelled dry, the faint scent of old parchment hanging in the air.

Next to the monastery-like section, the environment abruptly shifted into what looked like a lizardman's swampy hut. The ground became damp, and a murky scent filled the air, like stagnant water and decaying vegetation. The walls here were made of wooden planks, covered in moss and lichen, giving the impression of a swamp that had swallowed an entire dwelling. Bundles of dried herbs hung from the ceiling, swaying slightly in an unseen breeze, and a crude stone basin sat in the corner, filled with a thick, dark liquid. It was a sharp contrast to the monastery's austerity, an environment more primal and untamed as if drawn from the deep recesses of an ancient marshland.

Moving further, I found myself in yet another environment, one that appeared to be an ancient temple, complete with intricately carved stone pillars and faded murals depicting scenes of long-forgotten rituals. The air here was thick with the scent of incense as if the space itself was imbued with the memory of countless offerings. Vines, unnaturally green and vibrant, wrapped around the pillars, and patches of moss had overtaken the ground, giving the area a sense of solemnity and age, as though this piece of history had been frozen in time. Stone steps led up to an altar, where a few weathered artifacts lay scattered, hinting at the temple's original purpose—perhaps a place of worship or ancient study. It seemed almost out of place amidst the disjointed environments, but there was an inexplicable energy that radiated from the altar, something that seemed oddly at home within the chaotic chamber.

I grumbled, uttering curses under my breath. With each new area, the System tried to implant the atmosphere into my thoughts as usual, except they were perhaps less pushy than I was used to. This whole place was strange as if the System itself had dreamed these things into existence.

Could something like the System even do such a mundane thing as dream? I shook that thought off as I continued to explore the surreal hidden chamber.

The fourth area looked as if it had once been part of a highborn estate, but one that had been abandoned for centuries. Grand arches led into a hall filled with broken furniture—cracked marble tables, shattered vases, and curtains torn beyond recognition. The room was dim, the light filtering through fractured stained-glass windows that depicted noble scenes of ancient figures not quite human, now faded and lost to time. Intricate carvings decorated the walls, but they were marred by deep claw marks as if some great beast had rampaged through the area. The grandeur that this part of the chamber once held was almost drowned by the decay, yet there was a strange juxtaposition between luxury and ruin—a beauty in the brokenness that spoke of stories long forgotten. Dust motes danced in the beams of fractured light, adding an ethereal quality to the abandoned estate, and the distant echoes of what may have once been music seemed to haunt the stillness.

There were more areas, a place that looked like it belonged to a smithy or a forge. Rusted weapons and tools were scattered across stone tables, and a large anvil stood in the center, worn and damaged from long use. The walls were blackened with soot, and the smell of burnt metal lingered in the air.

The next was perhaps the most unsettling. It resembled a cavern, with jagged rocks protruding from the ground and ceiling, giving the impression of being deep underground. Pools of dark, stagnant water were scattered around, and the walls were damp to the touch. Strange symbols were carved into the stone, glowing faintly with an eerie green light.

This entire chamber was a bizarre puzzle, a jumble of mismatched environments that somehow coexisted within the same space. It was as if different parts of history and culture from a dozen worlds had been torn from their origins and thrown together, each section telling its own story, yet none of them fit together. I could feel the magic in the air—strong, disorienting, and ancient. The energy seemed to pulse through the walls as if the very chamber was alive, breathing with the remnants of these past worlds.

Another thing I noticed was that each of these areas had a different feel to them that gave me a sense of age, which varied from one to the next. It was like walking through an Ikea, but instead of room vignettes filled with generic Swedish furniture, it was bits of a dozen worlds all dropped together in a single massive chamber.

I continued to explore, intrigued and confused until my eyes caught something peculiar on one of the walls. It was in the more futuristic section of the strange chamber. The thing that really hurt my brain was that this next one ironically felt the oldest by far. Unlike the others, this part of the chamber looked almost sci-fi in its sleek, metallic simplicity. Smooth walls, dimly lit panels, and a sense of cold detachment filled the area. It was like how I imagined being in a starship might feel.

How could this most futuristic place seem the most ancient?

I peered closer at the runic script etched into the metal walls— symbols that looked different from any I'd seen before, almost as if they were a language of pure magic. But what truly caught my attention was a pictogram in the center of the runes—an image of a humanoid figure with a halo, giving the impression of ascending to the skies. It was haunting, powerful, and strangely familiar. It felt like I should know this, but I couldn't say that I had ever seen it before.

Frowning, I was torn between leaving immediately to teleport to one of the other dungeons in order to upgrade my Class and staying to study those odd runes. There was something about this place that called to me, something that felt important, even if I didn't understand why.

Of course, that was when the AI spoke.

> *Liam. You seem to have entered a restricted area. I am unable to see you and read your thoughts. Please exit the area and return to the dungeon. There could be unforeseen complications that could result from straying beyond the designated dungeon zone. If you can hear me, please return immediately!*

Oh, shit. This is never good!, is what I thought upon hearing Earth's not-so-benevolent overlord. Then, what the AI said registered.

How could it not see me or sense my thoughts? That shouldn't be possible....

It, or the System, created this dungeon; how could it not know of the hidden section?

My mind started racing, and my heart began beating a mile a minute. I was outside its zone of influence, and it didn't know what was in here. That meant this wasn't some hidden treasure chamber but more like a hidden area left in the code by the game developers. Not a perfect analogy, but maybe it was accurate. Or perhaps the System wasn't being as open with Earth's AI as the bastard thought it was. Maybe it was getting screwed just as much as the people of Earth?

I pretty quickly dismissed that, as I couldn't see any purpose to this out-of-bounds area that would make the System prevent the AI from knowing about it. More likely, it really was similar to remnant code left in a game that players weren't expected to be able to access.

My eyes drifted back to that pictogram of a being that appeared to be ascending. Could this perhaps have some connection to the Ascension quest line?

Regardless of the reason for its existence, I wanted to learn more about those runes and symbols. I really wished I had an upgraded memory that would allow me to perfectly recall anything I saw. However, I didn't. Next best thing would be to copy this down somehow. Unfortunately, pens and paper ceased to exist when the damned AI kicked off the apocalypse.

Then I remembered something. In that first section, there was an entire wall filled with scrolls. It might not be Grade A paper from Earth, but whatever it was made from seemed to have lasted for ages.

I didn't know how long I had, and even without the AI urging me to return, I was still on a clock, so I rushed back to the first section and picked through the scrolls until I found one that was nearly blank. I also shoved them all into my inventory to check out later.

Who knows, maybe they might contain something useful.

Okay, paper, or at least something close to it acquired. Actually, from the feel of the thing, I was guessing these were somehow made from animal hides. I knew Earth had those in the past as well, but couldn't remember what those were called.

Codesus... no, that wasn't right. Parchment maybe? *Whatever, I don't have time to worry about trivia!*

That was when I realized I didn't have any way to write on the scroll. For a second, I considered cutting myself and using my own blood but dismissed the thought. Blood might dry, but it wouldn't last; it would flake off and probably be illegible. I racked my brains for a moment, then remembered the soot in the forge area. I knew just how to do it.

It was a little trick I learned in my first life from other survivors. I scraped off a good amount of soot from the forge into an empty water bottle, added enough water to mix it into a dark liquid, then took out one of my spice tins and put in some gum arabic as a binder agent and to give it the right consistency. I then pulled out a cotton swab to use as a makeshift pen. It was crude, but it would work.

Hurrying back to the sci-fi section of the zone, I quickly laid out the scroll and began to copy what was on the walls. I was appalled with how bad of a copy job I did, but to be fair, I was sprawled out on the floor and writing with homemade ink and a cotton swab.

On the other hand, I made corrections where necessary, and after only a few minutes, I was satisfied that I had all the runes correct and legible enough.

Liam! I must insist! If you can hear me, return immediately to the dungeon zone. Straying outside the intended area could have dire consequences.

I impatiently hurried the drying of the scroll by waving it in the air, thankful that the ancient thing wasn't so brittle that it would tear or fall apart. Whoever those ancient monks had been knew how to make good parchment.

Finally, I rolled it up and tied it closed with the silk ribbon attached to its edge with a wax seal, then shoved it into my inventory. After that, I ran back to the entrance, unsure what those 'consequences' might be or if the AI was just using that as an excuse because it lost track of me.

The second I appeared, the AI spoke in my mind, and I could feel a sense of relief from the damned machine. Bastard!

You must not do that again; I have reviewed the System records. It is known that some residual artifacts can crop into the dungeon designs from time to time. The records are redacted, but there is a note accompanying the records stating that if a being who enters the anomaly becomes erratic in their behavior afterward, then it may become necessary to expose them to more intense challenges to resolve the situation. When the System says 'resolve'...

I finished the AI's sentence, "It means 'kill the person.' Yeah, I get it."

That is not all. It also says to notify the System of the anomaly if erratic behavior occurs, regardless of resolution.

"What's this about? How is it possible that you couldn't see me when I entered the hidden area? How can there even be areas that you are unaware of and do not control? Didn't you make the area? Also, I am not acting erratically, so no need to phone home."

I cannot say more. Continued contact with you beyond recalling you to the dungeon area and ascertaining that you were not negatively affected is all that is allowed. To continue would mean allowing the other AIs to contact their own champions. This would not be acceptable. The last piece of this protocol is to immediately recycle the dungeon to eliminate the anomaly. You will be teleported to the exit.

I kept my mouth shut, but inside, I was cursing out the bullshit AI for this whole situation. I knew it could read my mind, but these thoughts were nothing new or anomalous. It didn't care. It had slaughtered most of humanity, after all, and only sent me back because its own resources were being negatively affected by our downfall.

There was a tiny little spiteful part of me that just wanted to flip the fucker the bird and let it die in obscurity, a victim of its own ruthless efficiency. Except that would also mean humanity's extinction, and I couldn't allow that.

Then, I found myself fading out and reappearing outside the dungeon entrance.

I wasn't ready.

I hadn't healed fully, I was over 2000 Health, and the wounds had repaired, but I still felt like shit. The only upside was that most of my cooldowns had reset; only my hour-long ones hadn't. Those were my trump cards, and I hated being outside and exposed without them.

Time to get the hell out of dodge!

Quickly glancing around, I dropped into a defensive stance while I began to cast the **Shadow Recall** spell to teleport back to Allen. I could duck safely into the medium dungeon there and heal up once I was inside.

Just then, the pyramid behind me started to collapse, and I was flooded with notifications. Unfortunately, I couldn't check them nor finish my spell as I had to run at full speed down the ramp to get away from the dungeon entrance. Even the ramp was starting to crack and break apart.

I felt like Indiana Jones fleeing a temple after stealing an artifact, except I wasn't a movie star, and these weren't props on a soundstage. These were real, massive multi-ton blocks of stone falling apart under my feet and rolling toward me from behind as the pyramid disintegrated.

"This is bullshit!" I yelled to the sky as my legs pumped, and I ran like my ass was on fire.

Finally, as I got clear of what used to be the mall's parking lot, I breathed a sigh of relief. I just needed three minutes to cast that teleport spell, and I'd be safe. Then, I could upgrade my Class. I was sooo looking forward to that!

I began to cast the teleport spell again when a fly buzzed my ear. I turned a fraction as I swatted at it, then felt an intense pain in my back. It was excruciating, one of the worst things I had ever felt. I could only thank my maxed-out Luck that it hadn't severed my spine or pierced my heart. If it weren't for my Luck, and I hadn't begun to turn at that moment to swat the insect...

CHAPTER 30

DAMNED ASSASSIN!

I COULD FEEL the blade lodge dangerously close to my heart. Worse, it wasn't being removed. I was balanced on a knife edge with death a tiny fraction of an inch away from my heart.

A hissing chuckle sounded by my ear. "I'm amazed that you survived my initial strike. What an unexpected circumstance."

I tried to ask who he was, but almost choked on the air bubbling up my windpipe from the blood beginning to fill that lung. It was everything I could do just to hold still and not cause the dagger to nick my heart and end me. A wave of guilt washed over me. If I died, the human race wouldn't be far behind.

Despite the dark laugh of my assailant, he held his blade rock steady and seemed greatly amused as he spoke all too close to my left ear. So close that I could feel his hot breath.

I would have shuddered at the creep factor if not for my life being on the balance.

He went on, "Needless to say, do not move, and do not attempt to cast any magic. If I sense you casting, all I need do is turn my blade a hair's breadth, and you will be dead. Nod very carefully if you understand."

I bowed my head a fraction in response.

The pain was excruciating, but the adrenaline of the situation was allowing me to think past the agony. I had to get out of this!

This was like one of those nightmares where you are running full out, but no matter how fast you go, the monster is right behind you. That's how my thoughts felt. They were racing, but at the same time, it felt like they were trying to run through molasses; any second could be my last.

I ran through every ability I had as fast as my mind could process thoughts, discarding them one after another. Dragon's Charge would get me off the knife and to a short distance away almost instantly. That could give me enough distance to cast Stealth or Shadow Walk. Except that this was a Champion. I didn't know which one yet, but he had to have stats near or even better than mine. Even if I could activate the skill without him sensing it, he could kill me in the same instant I moved. I'd reappear fifty yards away, but I'd fall on my face dead the instant I appeared.

I briefly wondered if my regeneration ability from the amulet would bring me back to life, but no. He was sure to loot my corpse before it could do enough to repair me and regain consciousness. Besides, I doubted he would be stupid enough not to check my corpse and make sure I was dead. Only idiots in movies did that.

What about Shadow Walk? I would become incorporeal, but as fast as the spell was, it wasn't instant. Worse, with his blade lodged next to my heart, he might be pulled into the shadows with me. Plus, I didn't know if he was bluffing about being able to sense me casting a spell, but I couldn't afford to test it.

My thoughts were interrupted by his following words. "I suppose I should introduce myself. You have the honor of being killed by Zaelith Duskshade, Chosen of Xelaros, and after your death, I will become the next god in the Dark Elven pantheon!"

The asshole practically radiated smugness. I couldn't even see his dumb face, and I knew from his tone and words that he had a sneery shit-eating grin on it.

Then what he said registered. Dark Elf. They were among the worst of all the invaders. Unlike most who were primarily interested in securing land and resources, the dark elves delighted in cruelty and sadism. They captured humans and enslaved them not just for labor but to torture and degrade.

And with that realization, I understood why I wasn't dead yet. He was getting off on the cruelty of this situation. He had me completely at his mercy, of which he had none.

He laughed again at my silence. "You know the future. You know we carved out a large area around your state of Colorado. While I love your mountains and the home we carved below them, it is a shame we did not arrive somewhere more populated. After a few years, we ran out of slaves. With your death, our future will be secure, and I will lead my people to your West Coast. How does it feel to know that you have doomed your human species? Instead of a few dozen thousands of slaves, we will have millions."

I was trying to ignore his rambling and taunting, but thinking of a way out was difficult. There was guilt in my guts mixing with the internal bleeding and feeling almost as sharp as the blade touching my heart.

To give myself time to think and give him a reason to keep monologing, I carefully forced out the words, "The dwarves will stop you. They know the future, too... and they... didn't send their champion to kill me. They are preparing for you...."

It was a bluff. I had no idea if the Dwarf Champion had come after me or not, but I did know the rumors that their people had clashed in many bloody battles throughout the Rocky Mountains in my first life. It was a good bet that they would be thinking about the dark elves. Humanity hadn't been any threat to them, after all.

The dark elf hissed in anger at my statement but didn't kill me immediately. I tried to tune out his rant about how he would return to his people after my death and prepare the way. They would leave the heartland and occupy the mountains to the west instead and hit the dwarves from an unexpected angle and at a time of their choice. Blah, blah... we are the superior race, blah, blah, dwarves don't stand a chance...

I was ignoring him, the pain, and guilt alike.

I was focused on how I could escape without triggering his reflexes. I had to assume he could do as he said and detect me casting spells, but what about artifacts, skills, or abilities? I ran through my items in my head, but none had any effects that could help with this situation. Many could help after I got away, but none could help me get loose in the first place.

Skills? Same. Iron Hide didn't do a lot of good with the knife already in my back! Neither would any of my attack skills. I'd be dead before I could form my claws!

What about abilities? Some of those were promising. Draconic Fear might paralyze him if he were below my level, which he might well be. How much leveling could he have done and still run down to Dallas from Colorado? I could try that as a last resort, but I had a feeling I'd be dead before I could escape, even if I followed it up instantly with Draconic Charge to get free. The shout needed to activate the skill was vigorous; I'd probably kill myself on his knife, with no need for him to even act.

I thought about analyzing him with Treasure Sense to test whether he noticed ability use but realized I was already using a passive one. My mini-map still displayed its heads-up display in my vision, and the bastard was right there, a big red x with a circle around it. Unfortunately, he was behind me, so I couldn't see his Level or health and mana bars.

Feeling hopeless, I morbidly thought of using Commune to let Morgan and Viki know I was about to die.

I blinked, sudden hope surging in my heart.

That didn't fall under the heading of Skills, Spells, or Abilities. It was a Special Ability, granted not as a Class skill of mine but of Morgan's. I just happen to have use of it as a function of her Class and the bond. It didn't require mana usage at all from me; it was pure System fuckery, as far as I could tell.

If that worked... what about her other Class Ability?

Zaelith, the Dark Elf dipshit, was still snarkily droning on about how the human race was doomed because of me, and all those I loved and cared about would die now that I would no longer be there to protect them. Blah, blah, let me rub lemon juice and salt in your wounds, blah blah, blah...

If I survived, this guy was dead!

I initiated the Commune, and without any delay, just in case he did sense something, I shouted through the mental link, *"DYING! SUMMON ME, NOW!"*

The link connected, and I was not dead yet. Did the dark elf not detect it, or was he just taking his time since my action wasn't doing anything to attack or flee?

The sketchy part of this plan was that I had never been summoned before and didn't know how quickly it happened. Nor did I know if there were visuals or tell-tale signs of something happening. If he noticed, I would die before I even disappeared.

He noticed.

Yelling for me to stop, he gripped my left shoulder with his free hand hard enough to break my collarbone. He wasn't going to let me go, certainly not alive.

In the instant before I felt absolute pain spike in my chest, I activated my amulet, triggering its once-per-day ability, and marked the assassin. If I survived, I was going to come back and end him!

Unfortunately, for the second time in my existence, I experienced what it was like to die.

***

Morgan

Morgan and Viki had just said goodbye to Sam and Jonathan, the young couple they had rescued from the crazy religious group. They had turned out to be great. A little timid perhaps and uncertain when it came to attacking, but they weren't cowards. Once they had been taught how to do it and had gotten a couple levels, they began to step up and pull their weight.

Finally, after a full day of leveling them and running dungeons over and over, they reached Level 13, which was enough to release them to go out and spread the word about AI and the System. They had headed south, and Morgan was sure they would do fine. They had each other and weren't alone.

Morgan stretched her neck and frowned. It was late in the evening now, on the eighth day of the apocalypse, and Viki had just made them a meal of canned corn and beans. It wasn't great; in fact, it was one of the worst meals she'd ever had, but it was filling, and there was no telling how long these cans would last before the System broke them down and reclaimed them. At least the food inside had been organic and contained no added preservatives. Otherwise, she dreaded to think what it might be like.

"Morgan, do you think we should head toward Spring Creek next or try that other low-level dungeon?" Viki asked distractedly.

"Spring Creek. That's where Liam said he would go next after his current dungeon. I imagine he ought to be done in the next couple hours."

"Can we call him?" Viki was suddenly intense, eager to do so.

Morgan shook her head, "No, he said he would Commune with us later once he was done. If we find a dungeon to run down by Spring Creek in the morning, we should be able to meet up with him after he finishes the one he told us about earlier. I'm sure he'll duck in there and clear out everything up to the boss room, then camp for a few hours. Same thing we're doing now."

The not-quite teenager frowned, not liking that answer. "I don't like this. Being separated sucks. He needs us."

Morgan was about to reply when Liam's voice was suddenly in her head, yelling!

"DYING! SUMMON ME, NOW!"

Her adrenaline instantly spiked, almost sending her into a panic, but the urgency of his message was enough to short-circuit any hesitation or fumbling.

Viki's eyes got big seeing Morgan's instant change of demeanor.

Tapping into her Class ability to summon those bonded to her, Morgan pushed the ability, shoving as much power into it as she could, hoping it would cut seconds off the process.

Whether it did or not, the glow formed, circling motes of light spinning crazily, almost frantically, in the spot next to their campfire.

Liam faded into existence, but something was wrong. The magic almost seemed to stutter, as if her bond was slipping, on the edge of dissolving.

Viki screamed, "LIAM!!!" She dove for him, but Morgan shoved her aside. "Stop, I have to heal him!"

The girl looked horrified by the sight of her friend with blood staining his lips and chin, looking pale and lifeless.

Morgan rushed to his side and placed her hands on his head and chest, triggering her healing abilities, starting with **Analyze**.

What it told her made ice pierce her spine. Liam was dead. He had minor injuries that weren't fully healed, a shattered colla bone, but the thing that froze her in place, wiping all thoughts from her mind– his heart had been sliced in two. He had died instantly.

In a frozen moment, dozens of thoughts flitted through her mind while her body was in shock at the discovery. The human race was doomed. Viki would be crushed. Her own hope was shattered; Liam had been an anchor in these insane times.

But at the same time, a determination filled her. Maybe it was related to her Class and the Dragon blood her two bonded friends provided, but a fierceness welled up in her.

NO!

I've got magic!

Even before the magic came along, science could bring people back from the dead if they had only been gone a few minutes. Besides, her bond had not yet disintegrated. That had to mean it was possible!

Remembering her bracers that Liam had given her, she triggered their once-per-day ability, increasing her spell effectiveness by 50%, then triggered her staff's ability as well, restoring 25% of the total HP of all party members over 10 seconds.

When they were in effect, she flooded Liam's body with her mana and cycled through all her healing spells. **Regeneration! Cleansing Ray! Purifying Touch!, Draconic Vitality!**

His body was practically radiating magic as she cast **Analyze** again to see what her efforts had done.

The wounds closed almost instantly with the massively boosted power of her magic. His heart knit itself back together, and his HP bar refilled to more than half in seconds. Not waiting for her cooldowns to finish, she pulled a mid-grade healing potion from her storage and poured it down his throat, spilling almost as much as made it into him.

Even that wasn't enough, so when her timer had counted down, she hit him again with each of those spells one more time. **Draconic Vitality** finally refilled his hit points to the max, and he gasped in a breath but then began coughing up blood that had filled his lungs.

Morgan had to hold Viki to keep the girl from rushing to his side and potentially undoing some of her hard work.

It was almost five minutes before he regained consciousness.

CHAPTER 31

ROUND TWO!

LIAM'S PERSPECTIVE:

I HAVE no idea how long I was dead.

I unexpectedly opened my eyes, my thoughts scrambled, knowing something was very wrong.

"It's okay! It's okay! I healed your wounds, and you're alive!" Morgan seemed nearly manic as she said those words. She seemed to be shaking with the aftermath of a massive adrenaline rush.

Viki, on the other hand, was crying as she yelled, "You died! How dare you die on me!"

She broke free of Morgan's arms and hit me in the chest with her small fists, and I saw stars as the intense pain in my heart almost sent me right back into the grave.

Morgan was pulling Viki away and wrapping her arms around the girl's shoulders again, "It's alright, he's alive now! Don't hurt him. He's not fully recovered yet!"

My young friend was sobbing as she tore loose and threw herself on me, wrapping her strong arms around my waist and crying into my chest. "Don't ever die like that on me again! Not you too... not you too!"

I reached down and patted her hair and back. "I'll be fine. Don't worry. I'll make it to the immortal levels yet, just you wait and see." It was all coming back to me now. The high-grade dungeon, the secret room, and the Dark Elf Champion waiting to assassinate me outside.

Looking back at Morgan, I asked urgently, "How long?"

She shrugged, "I don't know, things were pretty crazy there for a few minutes. Not long, though, ten, maybe fifteen minutes, max? You remained unconscious for several minutes after I patched you up."

Gently pushing Viki away, I tried to sit up. "I've got to go back! I marked him, and I've only got forty-five minutes, at most, before it fades. This is my best shot at taking him out. He thinks I'm dead."

I could see Morgan about to object, but Viki beat her to it. "NO! You just died!!!"

"Kiddo, I have to. He's an assassin. I'll never have another chance to find him while he's unable to stealth. If I don't do it now, I'll never know if he's sneaking up behind me. Every waking moment will be filled with terror it will be my last. I'll be jumping at every shadow and every sound."

"Then we're coming with you! You need us!" My young friend was pulling her bow from her inventory and practically stamping her feet in determination.

"I have to unsummon myself to reappear back where I left. It's the best chance I've got. I'm hoping he still thinks I've died and hasn't left the area. Either way, I marked him with an artifact, and there should be a glowing column of light shining into the sky above his head for the next forty-five minutes."

I checked myself and found that all my gear was still in place. I formed my claws, ready to go. I wished I could wait and level up and get my new Class upgrade. I'm sure it would make a big difference in the fight, but I was on a timer, and the upgrade could eat up what time I had left. I'd have to risk it.

Morgan spoke before I could disappear. "We can't teleport with you, but we are going to find you. Where did the fight happen?"

Pausing for just a moment, I considered. I really didn't want them to risk it. I would not be able to live with myself if they got killed trying to protect me. On the other hand, I knew them too well. They would not give up.

"Fine, follow Viki's homing thing, and it will point right to me. I was out front of the mall in Frisco. It turned into a massive pyramid, but the System destroyed it after I beat the dungeon, and now it is a big pile of rubble. I'll be right at the base of where the ramp once stood. You can't miss it."

One thing was bothering me, though. If the bastard had realized I came back to life, he would be running here at top speed, so I added. "If he isn't there when I arrive, I will head back in this direction and meet you in the middle. Be prepared to run into him before you get there. Maybe not even halfway, so stay on your guard and look for that spotlight shining into the air. It's night, so it should be easily visible."

Morgan nodded decisively, "Got it! If we see the light, we'll set an ambush. We won't attack unless you are right behind, though."

"Good. Do that. If you get there and I'm in the middle of a fight, then jump in and hit him, but keep your distance. If time runs out and he's able to stealth again, then get the hell out of there. Don't worry, I will too. His stealth is so good his icon didn't appear on my mini-map until his knife was already hugging my heart."

Granted, I was distracted from dodging massive boulders as the dungeon collapsed and then trying to cast the Shadow Recall spell, but still, I hadn't detected even a hint of danger until it was too late.

"Be safe!"

I cast Stealth and got into a fighting stance, ready for blood.

Morgan triggered the summon ability, and I was returned to the very spot where I had died.

I knew there would be a bit of a light show as I returned, but I was invisible. Even so, I moved as quickly as I could while remaining silent, just in case my killer was waiting.

What I found was the dark elf celebrating. I had gotten lucky, and his back was to the place where I had appeared. I slowly approached to an appropriate distance and listened in. He was singing a happy tune and drinking wine. It quickly became apparent that he was confident he had destroyed my heart, and the compass had shown that it no longer pointed to me, convincing him I was, in fact, dead. He did grumble every now and then about losing my body and the items I must have had on me. He was also mad about the beacon over his head and occasionally looked around to make sure no one was coming to investigate.

"Gods damned light better disappear soon. If it is a permanent effect, I will find the scum's corpse and desecrate it!"

Still, even the annoyances couldn't completely darken his mood.

"So what shall I do next? I suppose I ought to go and increase my level before my minions arrive. If I can reach Ascension before the beginning of the Culling, that would raise my status immensely back home. Even Xelaros could not find fault with my achievements!"

He began to laugh uproariously for a long moment before smugly remarking to himself, "Perhaps I could even designate a zone of conquest over the mountains and deny the dwarves their foothold! Wouldn't that be glorious?"

I had heard enough. On the one hand, it would be nice to wait for Morgan and Viki as backup, but I didn't want to chance being discovered or putting them in danger. No matter how nice it would be to make this three-against-one, it wasn't worth the risk.

Gauging the distance, I figured I was in as good a position as possible, and I was behind the assassin. I was sorely tempted to use **Shadow Walk** to get right up behind the bastard and do unto him what he did to me, but he might have some kind of spidey sense or Luck, and I didn't want to risk it. While listening to his happy ramblings, I formulated my own plan.

Here goes nothing!

Umbral Chains! Tenebrous bonds surged out of the ground and wrapped the assassin's arms and legs, rooting him in place, doing moderate damage, and applying a DOT that would continue to eat away at his health until he escaped.

Zaelith Duskshade (Rooted, DOT)

Health: 85%... 84%...

His health bar dropped around 15% and continued to slowly tick down.

Twisting his body to try and see his attacker, he exclaimed, "But how?! I killed you! You were dead, I know it!"

His moment of shock gave me time to cast my next spell, **Shadow Surge,** my most powerful attack magic. Dark shadows burst forth and slammed into his chest, rocking him back despite the bonds holding him in place.

Zaelith Duskshade (Rooted, DOT)

Health: 55%

Arcane Singularity! The darkness condensed into a ball before the assassin, drawing him toward it along with all the debris in the area doing minor damage from the shrapnel alone, and then the explosion, again slamming the champion against his bonds.

Zaelith Duskshade (Stunned, Rooted, DOT)

Health: 30%

I used **Dragon Charge** to close the remaining distance and position myself behind him. Using both claws at once, I slammed them into his back, aiming for his heart. My left-hand talons had armor-piercing properties since they were assigned to my *Longknife of Shadows*, and the right-hand talons had the massive 35% crit chance and +25% damage from the *ogre's Warhammer*.

The dark ivory of the wickedly sharp claws plunged into his back using a **Heavy Draconic Strike** with the left hand and **Crippling Blow** with the other.

It was way more than what was required. My left claws plunged in without even noticing his armor, doing high damage. At the same time the right-hand claws pulverized his spine, also doing high damage and scoring a crit and 25% boosted damage.

Zaelith Duskshade (Dead)

Health: 0%

His health bar instantly plunged right through the red zone and hit zero before I could even see it change. Removing my claws was a bit disturbing. I had done sheer carnage to his back and internal organs. He wouldn't be coming back to life even if he had a healer on call!

"That's how you do it, and make sure it stays done!"

I felt like kicking his corpse, but I was honestly kinda grossed out by the mess I had made.

"Yuck, this is going to make looting gross."

Not wanting to take any risks now that I had killed another champion, I quickly looked around and checked my mini-map for red dots.

Nothing.

Of course, Zaelith Dipshit hadn't shown up on the mini-map either. Deciding discretion was the better part of valor, I sent his entire body into my storage ring. I would loot him later and make sure his corpse was fed to a dungeon like I had with the ogre. That would keep any mutated beasts from gaining a sudden level spike from consuming him.

After that, I ran. I headed back toward where I had left the girls but kept a slow pace so that they could meet me somewhere in the middle.

They were waiting for me on top of the overpass where Highway 121 crossed over Alma Blvd. The expressions on their faces said they weren't happy that I hadn't waited for them.

"It's done. I had no issues at all with killing him. He was busy celebrating my death and didn't even know what hit him until it was too late."

Their faces softened, but Viki rushed over and hugged me around the waist. "Good. Next time, don't die!"

I felt bad about that for a whole lot of reasons, but I knew the girl had already been through some serious trauma with the death of her family, and now she had almost lost me. Morgan and I were all she had left. I'd be upset, too, if I were her.

"Don't worry, I don't plan to. I'm not going to say the other champions will be less dangerous because I don't know who is after me, but I will say none of the others should be as likely to sneak up and assassinate me as that guy was. The dark elves were some of the absolute worst, most evil invaders; now they've lost their champion."

Speaking of which, I had gotten a notification about that.

System Notification

Champion Defeated!
Your quest **Defeat Five Champions** has been updated.
Progress: 2/5 Champions defeated.
Continue striving to eliminate all threats, or your second chance may end here.

No surprise there. I had a ton of other notifications that I had been ignoring since completing the dungeon, but I wanted to get somewhere safe before going through them.

I pulled out my dungeon compass and tuned it for a low-grade dungeon, and unsurprisingly, the needle pointed to the north, and it was very close. There were a bunch of apartment complexes and businesses at this intersection, and in fact, my apartment had been only a few blocks from here before things went to hell.

It only took five minutes to find it. Right in the middle of a group of buildings on the Northeast corner of the intersection, there was a green space that had once been a little spot for diners and shoppers to relax. Now, it had a sinister red stone arch that twisted in a way that the eye had a hard time following. It stood in the middle of what had once been a lawn. The buildings had been converted to small stone hills, leaving this arch in the depression in their center.

We stepped through the twisted red arch, and the world shifted in a heartbeat. *The weird stone arch disappeared, replaced by a wide forest clearing bathed in green light. Tall, ancient oaks ringed the area, their leaves forming a thick canopy overhead that let only fragmented rays of sunlight filter through. The ground was soft moss, springy beneath our feet, and vines curled around fallen logs, each one dotted with bright blue mushrooms that glowed faintly. A gentle breeze rustled the undergrowth, but it carried no warmth—only a subtle wariness that made my skin crawl.*

In the distance, I caught a flicker of movement—low-slung shapes darting between the roots and shrubs. Monster foxes, I realized, their crimson fur blending almost too well with the dappled forest floor. They moved with a predatory grace, tails swishing as they watched us from behind the trees. A musty, animal scent hung in the air, mixed with the damp earth and decaying leaves, and I felt the weight of the dungeon's magic press down, reminding me this wasn't some tranquil forest preserve. This was a place designed by the System, teeming with creatures that wanted us gone.

Ignoring the System's intrusive thoughts, I looked at my two companions, "Let's group up and demolish this place real quick; then I can level up. I hit my Class Upgrade point but haven't had a chance to do it yet."

"That's awesome!" Viki exclaimed, and even Morgan, normally a bit more reserved than our younger friend, gave me a big beaming smile and congratulations. The girls were super excited for me and promised to clear the dungeon quickly.

CHAPTER 32

CLASS UPGRADE AT LONG LAST!

Forty-five minutes later, we were already done. There had been various forms of fox monsters roaming the forest of this dungeon, but the only challenging thing was chasing them down since they were able to roam the entire area. Of course, we left the boss room so that the dungeon wouldn't boot us out. It was a low-level dungeon, so I only earned a little over 15,000 experience, not including the boss, which we'd leave for the morning once we had rested. I didn't even bother picking up the mana coins but left them all for the girls.

We set up camp outside the boss room, I brought out my fancy tent, and the girls "oooh'd and aaaah'd" over it.

Feeling safe, I settled into my comfy chair and finally took a look at my notifications:

System Notification

Dungeon Cleared: Pyramid of the Cursed Pharaoh

XP Reward Calculation:

Title: "Dungeon Conqueror" — +10% XP
Title: "Solitary Sovereign of the Depths" — +10% XP
Total Bonus: +20% XP

You have emerged victorious from the Pyramid of the Cursed Pharaoh! Your titles grant an additional 20% experience for conquering the dungeon and going it alone.

That one was followed by the one I had been eagerly awaiting:

System Notification

Level 60 Achieved!
You have reached a new milestone. Your second Class Upgrade is now available.

Choose wisely—this upgrade will define your next evolution in power and abilities.

Beyond that, the bonus xp for the dungeon had actually been enough to boost me to Level 61. Nice!

I also hadn't had a chance to really check out my Level 55 skill and spell, so I pulled up my Status and then checked them out.

Hmm... those weren't bad, but they were both utility abilities rather than combat-related ones. Still very useful, though.

Level 55:
Skill: Shadow Tag
Description: Mark up to three targets (ally or enemy) with a small, invisible "shadow sigil" that syncs to the mini-map. Marked enemies appear as distinct icons at all times, making them trackable even if they leave the immediate line of sight.

Shows vital signs (e.g., health percentages) and status conditions.
Duration and Cooldown:
Duration: 1 hour, or until canceled.
Cooldown: 10 minutes per mark.

Spell: Arcane Cipher
Description: Grants the ability to interpret or bypass magical runes, glyphs, and wards for ten minutes, revealing hidden messages or disabling lesser enchantments.
Cooldown: 30 minutes.

And that was it. That's what I looked like before my Class upgrade. I shared that Status with the girls and the descriptions of my skills. They seemed duly impressed. The big reveal was yet to come, though. I couldn't wait to see how things would change after this Class upgrade.

"Still, I'd be lying if I said I wasn't nervous. My last upgrade was pretty momentous, beyond my expectations, and it changed so much about how I fight and face the world. What if this one is disappointing compared to the last, or what if it changes significantly again but screws me up?"

Morgan patted me on the shoulder. "Don't stress over it. Everything you've gotten so far has been great, even the things you didn't expect. Could you have survived and then stalked that assassin and wrecked him so easily as a Black Dragon?"

That was true and a comforting thought. It had been a tough adjustment learning to fight without the acid-based abilities I had grown used to, but the shadow-themed stuff was pretty great now that I had learned how to use it.

"Thanks. I guess I'm putting it off. Time to take the plunge!"

Viki puffed out her chest. "We'll guard you while you do it. Don't worry!"

That made me grin. I was so focused on my gains I hadn't had a chance to see their statuses yet. Something I would definitely correct after I got this upgrade out of the way!

I lay down on the floor in case things got messy or painful, which seemed likely. "Okay, here I go...."

Available Class Upgrades - Level 60

Shadowblade Duelist – A master of blending swordplay and shadows, striking with speed and precision while weaving in deceptive illusions.

Umbral Assassin – A silent executioner who moves unseen, striking from the darkness with lethal precision and shadow-infused weapons.

Nightstalker Adept – A rogue who thrives in the unseen, utilizing heightened stealth, evasion, and ambush tactics with deadly efficiency.

Ebon Fang Marauder – A brutal melee specialist who harnesses the power of darkness to enhance their physical strikes and durability in combat.

Phantom Warlock – A spellcaster who binds their soul to the shadows, allowing them to phase through attacks and wield dark arcane forces.

Veilborn Sorcerer – A magic-user who draws power from the plane of shadows, bending illusions, teleportation, and shadow constructs to their will.

Abyssal Reaver – A relentless warrior who feeds off the life force of their enemies, using darkness to strengthen their body and blade.

Dreadbound Knight – A heavily armored melee fighter who radiates an aura of fear and wields cursed weapons that sap the will of their foes.

Specterblade Hunter – A hybrid rogue-warrior who binds spectral energy to their weapons, delivering devastating attacks that drain stamina and disrupt enemy defenses.

Abyssal Dragon: Nightfall Reaper *(Bloodline Class Upgrade – Exclusive)* – An apex predator of the dark, channeling abyssal power to instill fear, drain life, and unleash devastating shadow-based attacks, all while exuding an aura of dread that weakens those around them.

Holy crap, those all sounded awesome. There were some that sounded more awesome than others, however. Some I could outright reject because they just didn't sound like what I was after. The ones that seemed to abandon either the melee aspects or the magic aspects weren't of interest. Sorcerer, Knight, and Warlock were right out. Same with the Hunter and Duelist, those sounded cool, but not what I was going for.

I wanted to see more on #2, 7, and 10.

Checking out #2 first, I was impressed.

Umbral Assassin
A master of silent execution, the Umbral Assassin blends stealth, agility, and shadow magic to eliminate enemies with ruthless efficiency. This Class enhances all forms of stealth, granting nearly undetectable movement in darkness and the

ability to step between shadows at will. Lethal precision strikes bypass enemy defenses, and critical hits from the dark deal increased damage. Specializes in assassination, poisons, and debilitating curses that cripple foes before they even know they are under attack.

Perks: Shadowmeld, Assassination Techniques, Lethal Precision, Shadowstep

Core Abilities: Umbral Execution, Cloak of Night, Shadow Venom

That sounded powerful, and I could attest to just how devastating a good assassin could be since I had just died to one a couple hours ago. Still, I hesitated on that one. Not every situation could be handled by hiding and striking from stealth. Sometimes you had to go toe to toe with a group of tanks like those Anubis Warriors or the damned constructs of that Dwarven Runesmith. What would happen then if you put all your eggs into the stealth basket?

#7 also looked promising, so I expanded the details on that one as well. It occurred to me that I was getting more info on these classes at Level 60, and I wondered if that was just something the System did as you grew more powerful or if it had to do with my upgraded Treasure Sense ability to analyze things.

Shadow Reaver

A relentless predator on the battlefield, the Shadow Reaver thrives in chaos, using a combination of abyssal magic and brute force to carve through enemies. With every strike, they siphon the life force of their foes, healing their own wounds and growing stronger. Shadow Reavers are terrifying to face in battle, as they do not falter, feeding off the destruction they bring. They can manifest shadowy claws, corrupt enemy attacks, and radiate an aura of dread that weakens all who stand against them.

Perks: Life Drain, Shadow Fortitude, Shadow-Fueled Strikes

Core Abilities: Reaver's Hunger, Dread Aura, Shadow Rend

That sounded absolutely badass! The idea of life steal would really ramp up my survivability against formidable foes. Not to mention that Aura sounded incredibly effective against groups. This one was a top contender! There was just one more I needed to look at before I made my decision, and I had a good feeling about the last one.

Abyssal Dragon: Nightfall Reaper *(Bloodline Upgrade - Exclusive)*

The Nightfall Reaper is the harbinger of darkness, an apex predator born from the fusion of abyssal magic and dragon blood. As a dragon of the abyss, you gain access to devastating abilities that drain life, instill terror, and manipulate shadows at a level beyond mortal comprehension. Your physical form evolves further, gaining hardened abyssal scales, extended claws wreathed in black energy, and the ability to harness raw abyssal power. Fear radiates from your very presence, sapping the will of those who dare to oppose you.

Perks: Abyssal Regeneration, Aura of Fear, Abyssal Scales

Core Abilities:
Reaper's Presence: Enemies within a certain radius suffer increased fear, reducing their combat effectiveness.
Abyssal Soulflame: Upgraded claws that not only burn but drain vitality and suppress healing, feeding the Abyssal

Dragon a portion of the lost vitality to restore either health points or mana.

Night's End: A devastating ultimate attack that channels the full force of abyssal energy, crushing enemies under a collapsing field of darkness.

In some ways, it sounded a lot like Shadow Reaver but even more potent due to the bloodline upgrade. I presumed this would take me up to Tier 3 on my bloodline. Basically all the goodness of the Reaper class, plus a stronger bloodline.

No-brainer! I didn't even bother reading the warning message about the bloodline change. I had been through this rodeo before.

I selected Nightfall Reaper and the bloodline upgrade.

Then my world erupted in blinding agony, just as bad as last time, but perhaps not quite as bad as the first race change. Like the previous ones, it felt like it lasted for an eternity, and I had no doubt I was screaming my lungs out, but all my senses were consumed and overwhelmed by the pain of every cell in my body being fundamentally altered at the DNA level.

Laying there panting when it was finally over, I didn't move. I lacked the energy to do anything but bask in the bliss of not having every single bit of me feeling like it was on fire, dragon fire at that.

Viki was holding my hand, and Morgan was bathing my forehead with a cool towel. She said apologetically, "I would heal you, but you are perfectly healthy despite what you just went through, and I wouldn't want to mess anything up."

I croaked out, "That's okay. I appreciate you both. I'm going to pass out for a bit, and I'll look at my stats when I wake up. You guys get some sleep, too.

There was a little snark in Viki's voice as she quipped, "Maybe we can sleep now that you've stopped screaming!"

I could tell she was forcing the humor. It couldn't be easy to watch someone you cared about go through that kind of pain.

With that, I drifted blissfully to sleep.

Thanks to my high stats, I needed very little sleep, but that had been an exception. I slept a solid four hours, and when I woke, I felt like a million bucks.

The girls were still fast asleep, so now was a good time to review my gains.

CHAPTER 33

TIER 3 BLOODLINE ROCKS!

I OPENED my Status and was amazed at the changes.

At first, I was very confused; even with the massive +30 to all stats from the bloodline upgrade, my stats seemed too high, but then I remembered the Title for being the first to hit Level 60 and Tier 7. That also came with an additional +5 to all stats, and then there were my six auto-assigned stats per level and another +5 free stats that I quickly assigned. The results were mind-boggling. My stats were now fully more than three times what they had been in my first life.

Liam Bell:
Nightfall Reaper - Level 61
Bloodline (Tier 3): Abyssal Dragon

Experience: 59900/110640

Attributes:
Endurance: 164

Strength: 163
Agility: 163
Mind: 163
Will: 163
Magical Aptitude: 163
Luck: 10

Health: 3270/3270
Mana: 3260/3260

Abilities:
Active: Aura of Fear, Abyssal Breath, Claws
Passive: Dark Vision, Abyssal Scales, Treasure Sense, Regeneration

Active Skills:
Draconic Strike
Draconic Fury
Searing Slash
Dragon's Charge
Tempest Strike
Heavy Draconic Strike
Stealth (Advanced)
Crippling Blow
Iron Hide
Shadow Tag

Passive Skills:
Claw Mastery
Abyssal Soulflame

Spells:
Shadow Bolt

Darkness
Shadow Ward
Arcane Singularity
Shadow Walk
Umbral Chains
Shadow Surge
Ward of Shadows
Shadow Recall
Arcane Cipher
Night's End

Unlike the shift from Black Dragon to Shadow Dragon, this time, there wasn't too much of a change. Abyssal Dragons were still more or less based on shadows; they just seemed to be more powerful in general.

That said, there were some differences. My Draconic Fear had been replaced with Aura of Fear, which was a Passive rather than an active skill.

Aura of Fear
Your presence radiates an oppressive aura of dread, instilling terror in all who stand against you. Enemies within a 20' radius suffer a 50% movement reduction, with an additional 10% per 5 levels of difference between you and your foes.

That meant enemies 25 levels below me would be completely paralyzed if I approached within twenty feet of them. That was insanely good. I could power-level people like crazy. Just walk into a dungeon with a group of noobs and get close to the bad guys, and they could slaughter the monsters with complete impunity. Shame I didn't have time to raise up new heralds myself. Unfortunately, my time was much better spent worrying about my own leveling. Still, going through medium-grade dungeons just got a whole lot easier. As long as they were my level or below, they would be half as fast as before.

A quick glance at **Abyssal Scales** showed that it was just an upgraded version of my previous Scales draconic passive. It would be like the difference between wearing chainmail armor vs leather. Always nice to have a little more passive defense!

Like the scales, my breath weapon also upgraded to the Abyssal version. Not much to say about that one other than it should be more powerful. I would have to try it out soon and fry some baddies.

Then there was **Regeneration**, my completely new Level 60 Bloodline passive ability. It provided a straight restoration of 10 HP per second of health. Added to the amulet, I wouldn't have to worry much about health potions as long as I didn't need the healing immediately.

That brought me to my Level 60 skill, Abyssal Soulflame, and it was worth the Class upgrade all by itself!

Skill: Abyssal Soulflame (Passive)
All of your attacks—whether from weapons, claws, teeth, or unarmed strikes—are wreathed in Abyssal Soulflames, a dark, searing fire that burns beyond the physical. Any successful hit applies *Abyssal Burn*, dealing continuous damage until the target dies or the effect is purged. Additionally, each strike siphons 10% of the damage dealt, restoring both Health and Mana. Enemies afflicted by Abyssal Burn experience an unnatural dread, their will faltering in the presence of the abyss.

Holy crap! I just got a whole magnitude more dangerous than I was before!

Finally, last but not least was my Level 60 spell:

Spell: Night's End
Unleash the abyss itself in a devastating area-of-effect attack, engulfing all enemies within a 30-foot radius in crushing darkness. *Night's End* deals extreme damage, consuming light and hope alike while forcing all affected targets to their knees, rendering them prone for 1 second per 5 levels of difference.
Cooldown: 5 minutes.

Damn! I didn't even know damage ratings on skills or spells could go above '*high*'. Not only that, it was an AOE, but it also rendered enemies prone! Enemies would have a hard time attacking if they couldn't stand up.

The one thing that worried me about how awesome these things were was that it meant that my opponents would also be getting stronger as well. Once I found a dungeon with Level 60 critters, they would be twice ranked up as well, and even with these extreme boosts to my abilities, they would still be a challenge.

I just hoped this would give me an advantage over the remaining Champions!

I stepped out of the tent and spent a couple of hours testing out my new abilities and getting used to my increased attributes. I was faster and stronger than ever, and it took some effort to integrate the changes into my muscle memory and stop tripping over my own feet as I moved faster than expected or swung with more power and completely cleaved through a tree as if it were cardboard.

That wasn't the only issue that took getting used to. As I leveled up, I noticed that the dragon blood in my veins had been getting stronger. That was especially true when I upgraded to Tier 2. Still, I had been able to adapt to the change reasonably well since Shadow Dragons tended more toward stealth and debuffing rather than the more physically focused Black Dragons, who used acid to destroy opponents in direct confrontations. In other words, I had slowly become used to the Black Dragon bloodline, and the Shadow Dragon blood had only a slight increase in power and aggressiveness. It wasn't much more difficult to control the instinct that came with the bloodline.

Abyssal Dragon, on the other hand, was a very noticeable step. It was similar to the Shadow Dragon, which was certainly related, but they were on a whole different level in power, and I was feeling it. There was still a desire for the shadows and attacks from stealth, but the bloodline felt far more aggressive. It was like there was a palpable desire to destroy and devour anything that came within my domain.

In other words, Shadows were relatively passive and wanted to be hidden. Not so with the abyss; it was just waiting for the opportunity to devour everything. I was going to have to be careful, or this bloodline would drastically influence my behavior.

I was still coming to terms with that when Viki came out of the tent and told me Morgan was up and preparing breakfast.

It turned out to be MREs that I had found in that first dungeon at the missile silo. She discovered them on the shelves in the tent and opened them up for us. Not exactly the celebratory meal I might have liked, but I couldn't complain. It was better than a lot of the supplies I had in my storage, and at least it was filling. Millions of people were going hungry already as edible food began to run out or go bad without refrigeration.

Over breakfast, I shared my new Status with the girls and watched as their eyebrows tried to climb up their foreheads.

"I can't believe you are a higher Tier than me now!" Viki huffed. "At least I'm not that far from my own Class upgrade!"

I chuckled and teased her, "Speaking of... you haven't shown me your Status yet!"

She beamed with pride as she shared her Status.

Victoria Blue, aka Viki:
Draconic Sniper - Level 24
Bloodline (Tier 2): Night Dragon

Experience: 24126/38880

Attributes:
Endurance: 41
Strength: 41
Agility: 44
Mind: 41
Will: 41
Magical Aptitude: 44
Luck: 3

Health: 820/820
Mana: 850/850

Abilities:
Active: Shadow Veil, Shadow Step, Treasure Sense
Passive: Dark Vision

Active Skills:
Arrow: Night
Arrow: Shadow Bind
Eclipse Barrage

Piercing Shadows
Dark Burst

Passive Skills:
None

Active Spells:
Whispering Bolt
Gloom Shroud
Midnight's Grasp
Stealth
Hawkeye

"Daaang! I can't believe you've hit Level 24 that fast! And that is even with power-leveling others!"

Viki's grin was from ear to ear as she metaphorically preened at my compliment.

"We've been killing the monsters almost non-stop! I don't want you to get so far ahead that we can't catch up. Also, we need to be able to help against the Champions!"

Morgan's grin was more subdued, and she had that proud older sister vibe as she put one arm around Viki's shoulder. "We know we can't go toe-to-toe with the Champions, but we really can help, and you don't have to worry about us getting in the way or being used against you. We are not so far behind now that we would be completely overwhelmed if we ran into one of them."

My gut response was to tell them to stay well away from danger, but I knew that would not only be ignored, but it might also negatively affect their mental states. They would feel like I didn't trust their strength, and that could lead to all kinds of bad things. They would run face-first into danger regardless, and they'd do it with a chip on their shoulder, feeling like they had something to prove. At least, I was 99% sure that is how Viki would take it. Morgan was a mature woman; she could probably handle it, but it might make her doubt herself.

After a long moment, I said, "You're right. I want you both to be safe because if anything happened to you, it would destroy me. But you are both strong and talented, and you've proven you can handle danger. Just keep in mind, if we do run into the other Champions, they aren't dungeon monsters. They might be somewhere around my level, maybe even lower, if I'm lucky. Still, they are the best of the best of their worlds, and they've got more than twenty years of experience with their classes and skills. They will be far more dangerous than anything you've faced. Just keep that in mind and fight accordingly."

Even Viki nodded solemnly, seeming to take the warning seriously, and that's all I could ask for.

I reached over and hugged her shoulder along with Morgan. "I know you've got my back."

Her smile could light the room.

Morgan cleared her throat and jumped in. "I guess I should show you my stats as well. Viki and I are tied now on Levels. Mine's less exciting since I don't have a bloodline. I've been putting all my stat gains in Mind and Magical Aptitude for more mana. It's worked out pretty well so far."

Morgan Pickering (Current)
Dragon Priestess - Level 24
Bloodlines: Shadow Dragon / Night Dragon

Experience - 14397/38880

Attributes:
Endurance: 15
Strength: 15
Agility: 15
Mind: 55
Will: 20
Magical Aptitude: 54
Luck: 3

Health: 300/300
Mana: 1290/1290

Abilities:
Active: Commune, Summon, Umbral Cloak (Pact)
Passive: Dark Vision (Pact)

Spells:
Blessing of the Dragon's Grace
Draconic Vitality
Shadow Bolt
Purifying Touch
Cleansing Ray
Shadowflame Burst
Regeneration
Dark Aegis
Dragon's Grace
Shadow Step

That Shadow Step looked interesting, so I asked about it.

"Oh, yeah, that is pretty cool. I can teleport through shadows anywhere within 100 yards, even during combat. Only has a 30-second cooldown, too, so I can use it pretty frequently to either get out of trouble or get to someone that's injured and needs healing."

"Nice!" I was impressed. That would be a super useful spell to have.

My thoughts were already racing forward to what would come next. "Okay, so I'll let the two of you kill the boss without me so I don't cut into your experience. It won't be enough to move the needle for me but you guys are pretty close to your next level. Run it one more time without me, and you'll boost yourselves past Level 25 and be a good chunk of the way to 26."

Viki practically growled. "That means you are going to go outside without us and possibly face Champions. Not happening!"

I chuckled. "No, I'll wait for you to kill the boss, and we'll all exit together. That said, we need to be ready for a big fight if one of them is out there. When we do, I'll go first with you guys a step behind me, and we will scatter and find cover."

Ten minutes later, we were outside, and miracle of miracles, we were alone. With as much time as we had spent inside, I was a little surprised none of the other Champions were waiting on us like spawn-campers.

After seeing that we were safe, I had time to appreciate the scene. The cool morning air hit like a welcome shock after the dungeon's stifling depths. The sky was a pale, washed-out blue streaked with the first hints of sunrise, and the world outside felt eerily still—like it was holding its breath. Dew clung to the overgrown grass around the dungeon entrance, and the distant sound of birds waking filled the silence left by the absence of monsters. For a brief moment, everything felt normal, like the world hadn't ended. It almost seemed hopeful.

The girls were about to reach Level 25, and then they would find another herald to power-level. I had a thought about that.

"Before I go, I wanted to make a suggestion for your next herald."

That got their attention.

Viki started literally bouncing in her excitement, "Oooh, first, we have to tell you about Dan and Marsha! They hadn't yet selected their classes! They were able to get magic classes!"

I blinked in surprise, "Holy Schnikeys! Seriously? What did they get?"

Morgan grinned, "Marsha got a dragon-themed healing class, based on me being her teacher apparently; Draconic Acolyte.

Jumping back in, Viki added, "Dan got Draconic Warblade, a hybrid melee and magic class, kinda like your first one."

Her young face fell at the end, "Neither were bloodline classes like we got though, they were just rare dragon-themed ones. Still, it's very cool!"

"That's awesome! They will really be set up for success with that combination of classes together. Sounds like they have all the bases covered for an entire group despite it just being the two of them. Great job, you two!"

I pulled Viki into a shoulder hug, and gave Morgan a big grin. I was proud of my girls!

Morgan grinned for a second then became serious. "Back to the topic of finding new heralds, are you sure you wouldn't rather us level up as quickly as possible to back you up when the next Champion appears? We could always train heralds to spread the word after the bad guys are dealt with."

I thought about that for a second, then shook my head. As much sense as that made, I couldn't stand the thought of them dying because of me. I'd rather face the Champions alone. Besides, with my Shadow Recall spell, I would need to jump all over the place. My plan to get the Champions running around chasing me while I continued to level was a good one, but that wouldn't work with others. I explained as much, then added, "Besides, the heralds are even more important."

Gesturing toward the northwest, I said, "Try to find someone from the military next. I want someone to go to Colorado and rally the troops there. There are a lot of Air Force personnel around the Colorado Springs area due to the base there. Cheyenne Mountain probably became a Stargate-themed dungeon, knowing the AI. Still, the dark elves are going to appear between there and Denver in three weeks, and they are going to be without their Champion. If humans can get organized and fight back, it could save tens of thousands of lives. Dark elves were the absolute worst of all the invaders, enslaving and torturing pretty much all of the survivors in the state. The dwarves are going to pop up somewhere in the Rockies as well, and if an alliance could be formed with them, we might be able to make that entire part of the country safe from invaders."

It was a long speech, but I could tell they were listening intently. "They will still have to deal with beasts and dungeons, but compared to the dark elves, that is nothing."

Morgan was nodding in agreement. "Yeah, that makes sense. I wish we had told Shane to head that way. From now on, we ought to tell all the heralds about the invaders as well. What can you share on that?"

It was a good idea, one I wish I had thought of myself. Sadly, I didn't know a whole lot myself. Travel hadn't been a big thing in my previous life. Most of what I knew was second and third-hand rumors.

"I only know what I've seen or heard about. The ogres take over Florida. There were a lot of lives lost, but honestly, most of that was just how hard it was to survive the environment after the apocalypse; the ogres were just the last nail in the coffin for Floridians. Dark elves hunt humans all around the Colorado area, enslaving them and working them to death. The high orcs appear in Arkansas, or Orkansas as we called it in my last life. They weren't too bad; they didn't care about killing us so much as driving us from 'their lands.' They had a strong sense of honor but loved to fight; anyone who challenged them died."

I rubbed my chin as I thought about the others.

"I fought a lot of lizardfolk in southern Louisiana; they spread all along the Gulf Coast. The rest of what I'm going to tell you is at least second or third-hand information, but is probably accurate. Goblins swarmed all around the Chicago, Milwaukee, Detroit area. There was talk of Frost Giants in Canada and Alaska. And if it can be believed there were demons in Las Vegas, but take that with a grain of salt. I mean, Sin City and *demons*? That could just be people talking out of their ass, but who knows? I never saw one myself and never met anyone who did with their own eyes."

"Oh yeah, gargoyles, harpies, and the undead along the East Coast. Unfortunately, I have no idea what was out on the West Coast and the Northwest since no one survived going through the Rocky Mountains, thanks to the dark elves. Last but not least, there was some kind of beastkin in Mexico and Central America, but not the fluffy bunny-girl kind from Anime and Isekai stories, more the jaguar-men type that like the taste of human meat."

Viki looked grim as she asked, "What about the rest of the world?"

Shaking my head, "They are out of luck unless I can make it to Ascension and get some kind of control over the System on Earth. In my last life, no one ever crossed the oceans. Sea monsters gobbled up any small boats that we could make without modern technology. If anyone ever made it across, I never heard about it."

Morgan made some very unladylike comments about what the System could do with itself, and I smiled sadly, fully understanding her feelings. The System would have a lot to answer for if I could ever gain enough power to challenge it.

Still, I had some thoughts about that. If the System was willing to kill people who entered the 'secret rooms' in dungeons, the places that glitched, then those were places I wanted to learn more about!

"From now on, I will be checking every dungeon I enter for more of those strange hidden locations. With the way the AI reacted, I get the distinct feeling the System doesn't have a clue what is inside, or if it does then it is scared of us finding them, and anything that scares that galactic group of tin cans, is something I want! Hell, maybe something in them will be useful in the fight to take our world back!"

The story is heating up for Liam, Viki, Morgan, and the human race!

The adventure will continue as Liam races against humanity's greatest enemies to reach the level cap and beyond all while trying to uncover the secrets that the System wants to keep buried. Only then can he gain a measure of control over the System and begin to undo the damage brought about by the apocalypse.

Sign up for a free short story and receive the newsletter to stay current on what's happening with Greymantle and the other worlds of J David Baxter's imagination.

Support me on Ream to get early access to works in progress and exclusive content not available elsewhere. (It's like Patreon for authors).

AUTHOR'S NOTE

Please leave a review here! Help other fantasy readers and tell them why you enjoyed this book.

I would love it if you would tell your friends so they can join us on Liam's epic adventure to save humanity from a genocidal AI and a horde of murderous orcs, goblins, ogres, and more. If you do leave feedback for AI Apocalypse: Restart where you purchased the book, Goodreads, or your blog—I'd love to read it. Don't hesitate to email me the link at info@jdavidbaxter.com.

ALSO BY J DAVID BAXTER

LITRPG GROUPS

The LitRPG genre is a friendly and welcoming community. To learn more about books in the genre and connect with other fans and authors, check out these groups:

https://www.facebook.com/groups/litrpgs

https://www.facebook.com/groups/LitRPGGroup

https://www.facebook.com/groups/LitRPG.books

https://www.facebook.com/groups/LitRPGReleases

ABOUT THE AUTHOR

David's journey through his career has been anything but conventional. Transitioning from the exhilarating world of Renaissance Festival Jousting, where he braved falls from horses, to orchestrating teams and projects at Fortune 500 companies, he's held diverse roles. Armed with a degree in English and teaching certifications in English, History, and Professional Pedagogy, he's ventured into the realms of education and literature. Notably, he lent his expertise as an editor to the recent Stargate Roleplaying Game core book by Wyvern Games. Additionally, as the co-founder of Silver Paw Publishing, he's committed to empowering aspiring authors on their self-publishing journey. David embodies versatility and a passion for storytelling, leaving an indelible mark on every path he treads.